LUCHA OF THE FORGOTTEN SPRING

ALSO BY TEHLOR KAY MEJIA

Lucha of the Night Forest

We Set the Dark on Fire

We Unleash the Merciless Storm

Miss Meteor

LUCHA OF THE FORGOTTEN SPRING

Tehlor Kay Mejia

MAKE ME A WORLD
NEW YORK

MAKE ME A WORLD is an imprint dedicated to exploring the vast possibilities of contemporary childhood. We strive to imagine a universe in which no young person is invisible, in which no kid's story is erased, in which no glass ceiling presses down on the dreams of a child. Then we publish books for that world, where kids ask hard questions and we struggle with them together, where dreams stretch from eons ago into the future and we do our best to provide road maps to where these young folks want to be. We make books where the children of today can see themselves and each other. When presented with fences, with borders, with limits, with all the kinds of chains that hobble imaginations and hearts, we proudly say—no.

Published in the United States by Make Me a World, an imprint of Random House Children's Books, a division of Penguin Random House LLC, New York.

Make Me a World and the colophon are registered trademarks of Penguin Random House LLC.

Visit us on the Web! GetUnderlined.com

Educators and librarians, for a variety of teaching tools, visit us at RHTeachersLibrarians.com

Library of Congress Cataloging-in-Publication Data is available upon request.
ISBN 978-0-593-37840-3 (trade) — ISBN 978-0-593-37842-7 (ebook)

The text of this book is set in 12.1-point Adobe Jenson Pro.

Editor: Lois Evans
Cover Designer: Carol Ly
Interior Designer: Jinna Shin
Production Editor: Alison Kolani
Managing Editor: Jake Eldred
Production Manager: Tim Terhune

Printed in the United States of America
10 9 8 7 6 5 4 3 2 1
First Edition

LUCHA OF THE FORGOTTEN SPRING

1

The city of Robado was a night place, so its emptiness beneath the stars was twice as eerie as any normal sleeping city's might have been.

Overhead, a crescent moon provided little illumination. The stars themselves felt distant. Lucha Moya, after days of traveling on foot through unforgiving terrain, had been prepared to stick to the shadows. To avoid detection. Pick her moment . . .

But there was no one here to hide from.

She wandered down the center of the north road. The torches that had once burned with oily animal grease stood cold and dark along the roadside. The subtle colors of the night were easy enough to read after a solitary trek through much darker places.

Still, the hair on the back of Lucha's neck prickled. A warning.

Behind her stood the forest she'd only just emerged from. The Bosque de la Noche. Most Robadans avoided even looking at it—afraid monsters from their folktales would snatch their souls for gazing too long. It had been the subject of Lucha's endless fascinations as a child. Though back then she'd never dared to go deep enough into the trees for the city to be lost to her.

Now she'd traveled farther into the forest than anyone in Robado could ever have dreamed. She'd communed with it, summoned its power. Visited its goddess's sanctuary. Defeated the feral, captive god intent on its destruction.

Lucha felt she'd learned the forest's rhythm, its language, but on this trip back to the town she'd never expected to come back to, that rhythm had been disrupted. Plants were overgrown, or else scarce in places where they should have been plentiful. The whispers had changed.

And now this. Robado, empty.

In Lucha's dreams she'd arrived to clear the city of innocents, then set the place on fire. Stood in the shadow of the trees to watch it burn.

But she couldn't burn it now. Not even as empty as it seemed. She couldn't do anything until she knew the people would be safe—otherwise she'd be no better than *him*.

During her long trek through the changing forest, Lucha had tried to keep thoughts of Salvador at bay. The sneering son of Elegido's revered forest goddess. The slender, pale young man who'd wormed his way into her consciousness. He'd convinced her their goals were aligned, only to betray her.

She'd fought him just a few weeks ago. A battle where she almost lost something infinitely more precious than her life. She could sometimes still feel the decay as it threatened to swallow them both. On those nights, she woke with a scream lodged in her throat, believing she stood there still, on the precipice between creation and destruction, watching the mushrooms devour every bit of him that was left.

In the present, an unseasonably chilly gust rattled the branches. Sent two dried leaves skittering after each other down the road.

You're here, and he's gone, Lucha reminded herself. *And you still have work to do.*

But how to begin when she didn't even recognize the city she'd returned to save?

Lucha had come from the west, headed for the normally quiet stretch between the north ward compound and the marketplace. The last time she'd been here, she'd been imprisoned for months. Starved and beaten. Presumed dead by anyone who might have cared enough to look for her.

That had been before she left Robado's prison, Encadenar, in what one might consider spectacular fashion. She'd taken her sister—Los Ricos' property at the time—and using power gifted to her by the goddess Almudena, enhanced by the dark presence of her monstrous son, Lucha had killed several guards, destroyed high-security doors, and generally left behind a tale worth telling.

The question was, had the stories made a hero of Lucha? Or a monster?

Lucha startled at a skittering noise behind her. With instincts born of years as a cazadora—hunting monstrous creatures to put food on the table for her family—she pulled her bone knife from the place where it had hung on her hip since she was thirteen years old. So armed, she whirled around to face the threat.

But there was nothing there.

A hunched shadow, perhaps? Disappearing into the trees? She was sure she'd seen something. Forgetting her purpose for a moment, Lucha ran to the place where it had disappeared, casting around for any evidence that someone had been following her.

Had they heard she was coming? Cleared the city to confuse her? Were they surrounding her as she stood here wondering? Lucha's heart pounded hard against her ribs. It wouldn't be the first time she'd been surrounded by enemies, but last time she hadn't been alone . . .

The thought of Paz fierce beside her, bowstring taut, stung worse than the nettle scratches along her arms. Lucha shoved the memory aside, irritated with herself for even thinking of the girl she'd left behind. She had more important things to worry about. And if there was no one following her, it was time to stop chasing shadows and get back to the task at hand.

Lucha continued down the north road toward home—or what had been home until a few months ago. If the south ward was empty too . . . She could barely imagine it.

The bulk of Robado's population lived crowded into a few dilapidated buildings up against the serpentine curve of the cursed salt river. The units were small, damp, and lightless. Nothing but holding cells to shelter the city's workforce between shifts in massive warehouses.

Warehouses built to refine and process Robado's only export.

Lucha didn't want to think of Olvida now. Not after being away from it so blissfully long. But it was impossible not to remember here. Impossible not to think of her mother, lost in the drug's potent forgetting as she held a splintered chair leg to her daughter's throat.

Impossible not to remember Lis, wasted away to nearly nothing, a ladder of scars climbing her arm . . .

Lucha's entire life had been spent in the mud pit Olvida created. Subject to the whims of the cruel men who profited off its existence. Life in Robado was lived beneath their heavy boots. Dangerous, joyless, and usually short. That was how they kept the population hooked on the forgetting drug. Kept them chasing an oblivion that would never last.

What Lucha hadn't known, as she watched the drug poison her family and neighbors, was that it had been created by design. A perverted version of a plant meant to help people commune with the gods. She had carried a grudge against Olvida and the kings since she first became aware of how things worked here, but after Salvador, she was more determined than ever to achieve the goal that had originally driven her from the city and into the fathomless wood it bordered.

To destroy Olvida.

Destroy the kings.

Free Robado and all the people suffering here.

The south ward greenhouses loomed into view ahead of her. Dark silhouettes against the slightly lighter sky. No illumination came from the ventilation shafts. No sound of movement from within. Most workers would be off their shifts by now, gathering in the streets.

The quiet was unnatural. Terrifying. In her whole sixteen years of life, Lucha had never heard the greenhouse machinery go silent.

Sure, by now, that this wasn't some elaborate ruse to lure her out of the woods, Lucha walked in disbelief down the path to the housing units. A path she'd walked so many times before that her feet followed it by rote.

This left her eyes free to scan the dark, empty windows. The doors open to the elements. The silence. Crushing here, too. Robado had never been a light place, or a joyful one, but there had been life here. Families. Children. Now there was nothing.

Lucha meant to leave the moment she realized there was no one here. Make her way to the north ward, see what she could discover. But her steps carried her onward instead. To the doorway of the last place she'd called home.

Whatever she hoped to find there, she should have known better. From the moment her boots stepped across the threshold, she knew it was all wrong. Someone else had been living here, even before this mysterious mass exodus. There was nothing left of the Moya family.

No bright quilt on her mother's bed. No flowers arranged in a jar on the table. No cinnamon stick above the stove, waiting to be shaved into corn porridge.

Instead, there were bodies. Hundreds and hundreds of them. Covered respectfully, but piled and abandoned.

Lucha ran back to the doorway, her stomach heaving.

Lis is safe, she told herself. *She's at the sanctuary with Río. With Paz.* She drew the image of her sister around her like that quilt. Bright-eyed, green-robed, glowing with purpose as Lucha had left her. She was, at this moment, being educated in the healing and fighting arts of the acolytes of Almudena. She was safe.

Safe.

And their mother?

She had made her choice long before this place gained new occupants. Lucha had never been able to change her mind, even in the end. Lucha had made her peace with it. This was no time to unearth a hope that had nearly killed her.

As she headed north once more, Lucha's every nerve jangled in her body.

Robado had been a dangerous and awful place for its whole sordid history. Its inhabitants were used to exploitation, addiction, cruelty, and worse. But the bodies in the housing units . . . it made no sense. What could have killed so many of them this quickly? And why hadn't Los Ricos done anything to stop it?

When she reached the marketplace, the reality of the situation settled over her, more real than anything. The entire place—which had served mostly as a hub for buying, selling, and trading Olvida locally—was trashed.

The slanting wooden stalls had all been tipped over or

smashed. The wares behind them—a front, mostly, for the drug stored beneath their counters or in the pockets of their proprietors—were spread across the plaza.

This destruction wasn't recent, Lucha realized as she walked through in stunned disbelief. Food had gone rotten, attracting flies. Puddles of various liquids had dried to stains on the stone. Candle jars, wooden carvings, dishes and artwork and cloth were all strewn about as if by some angry animal. Then there were the wrappings of Olvida bricks, piled like fallen leaves, empty as if they'd been licked clean.

Olvida gone. So many Robadans dead. Lucha struggled to put the pieces together in her mind. Where were the rest of them? Where were the soldados? Why wasn't anyone doing anything?

And what could Lucha do?

Her musing was cut short by the sound of shouting voices up ahead.

Lucha's heart leapt into her throat. She oriented herself on the road, the marketplace behind her, the mushroom grove that announced the north ward just ahead. The grove was a special place to Lucha. The first evidence she'd seen of the forest's sentience. The destruction it could cause when its life force was threatened.

It was from there that the unmistakable sounds of protest emanated.

Lucha knew these woods better than anyone. She took to them now, skirting the main road, looking and listening. She'd been caught on this road often enough to have learned to avoid those who walked it—even if they were strange sentinels now.

The first people she saw were not soldados, but they moved like guards on patrol, eyes scanning the tree line and the road ahead. They passed right over Lucha, concealed in the leaves, which gave her a chance to observe them.

Their clothes were tattered and torn, filthy. Immediately Lucha recalled the Lost House, where she'd gone to find her mother during the worst of her disappearances. But these men didn't seem to be lost in forgetting. They were upright, faces alert if not particularly bright. But what would have caused these men to give up their forgetting?

Lucha crept past them, making her way closer to the gate, where she was now sure the sounds of protest came from. What other strange things had happened here in her absence?

She got her next shock in the mushroom grove, where a few hundred people—most in an even more desperate state than the two men she had seen on the road—were camped in deteriorating conditions. Most were dirty, gaunt, their eyes haunted as they chased children listlessly or wrung out clothes in a bucket.

From this distance, they all looked vaguely familiar, but none stood out. Although it wasn't as if Robado were a place where you knew your neighbors, so that was hardly a surprise. All she knew for a fact was that there weren't nearly enough of them.

Still hidden by dense forest, Lucha moved soundlessly, a

pit forming in her stomach long before she reached what appeared to be a field infirmary. There were so many people here, at least a hundred on cots, blankets, some on bare ground. They moaned, shouted, thrashed, or lay troublingly still. No one seemed to be attending to them.

This behavior was familiar to Lucha. Too familiar. She remembered the long journey through the forest with Lis. The way her sister had suffered as she detoxed from the massive doses of Olvida given to her by Alán and his cronies.

So these people were detoxing too. But so many of them? All at once? There was only one explanation for that, and that was that the Olvida was gone. But how? The kings would never have let it happen.

As she watched the infirm from the trees, Lucha thought again of Paz. The skill of her healing hands. The power of her sanctuary's medicine. Lucha longed to ease the suffering here—it was what she had come to do, in a roundabout way—but she hadn't the skills or the tools, much less any understanding of what was happening here. It was time to find someone who did.

The north gate came into view next, and here were the protestors. The sight of the gate closed, unguarded, and the people rattling it from the outside struck Lucha more than anything had so far. If Los Ricos had abandoned their gate, something was badly wrong.

The north ward fence—a metal, spiked monstrosity that had horrified generations of Robadans—was close enough that Lucha could see what was impaled on its spikes.

Los Ricos had a long-standing tradition of leaving a body part or two on display when someone was foolish enough to attempt to scale their protective barrier, but this was unlike anything Lucha had ever seen. There were so many new additions they looked like misshapen birds gathering.

Every single spike seemed to display a piece of a human body. Flies buzzed ceaselessly around the silhouettes.

A few hundred more Robadans gathered here, shouting at the locked gate, hitting the metal of the fence with sticks and makeshift weapons so it rattled all along the north side. Around them were threadbare shelters and more livestock than she expected to see, a sort of crude battle camp. It looked lived in. These people had been here for some time.

Yet still there was no sign of the soldados. Any evidence at all of Los Ricos' rule. For all Lucha's life there had been no authority, no government in Robado but the kings. Yet someone had clearly done their best to organize what was left of the citizens here. If she wanted to do what she'd come to do, Lucha would have to find out who they were.

After that, depending on their agenda, she'd have to make a choice. To work with them, or to destroy them. Either way, she wasn't leaving here before every last brick of Olvida was gone and the bodies of Los Ricos were cold in the ground.

With that conviction burning in her heart, Lucha climbed the tallest, sturdiest tree with a view of the camp and settled in to wait for her moment.

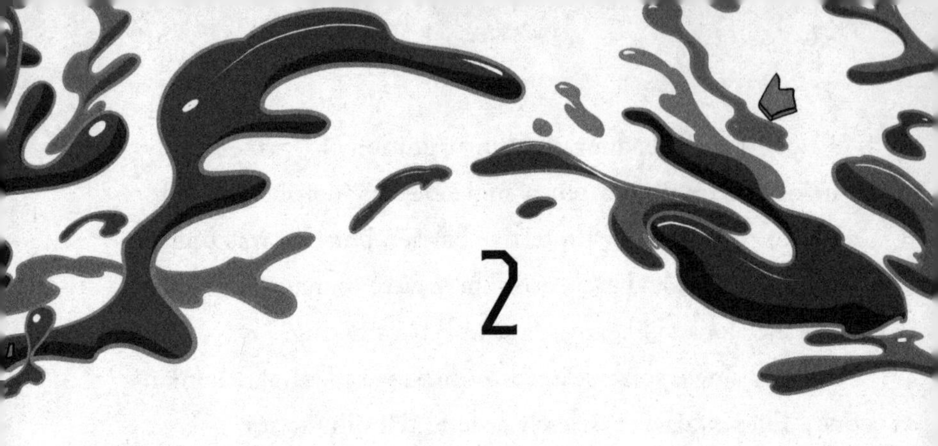

2

Lucha watched and listened to the goings-on in the camp as she'd once watched rabbit tracks or creek currents. In the forest or among people, power followed certain patterns.

It didn't take long to find a promising tent. A few people walked in and out of it purposefully, with the swagger of new leadership. Others who approached it looked hesitant, a little cowed.

The whispers that passed below her tree offered the name: the Syndicate. A group of survivors who had collected the rest here for some purpose. But survivors of what? And what was their agenda?

There was fear, Lucha could almost smell it on the air. Trauma. Something awful had happened, and the folks who had survived were barely holding on. The people who carried themselves with authority appeared young, as disheveled as the rest.

Mostly, the action in the camp was focused on the barrier. Lucha was able to surmise that there were resources inside. It was like Los Ricos to abandon their people after some disaster, to hoard what they had. The people left out here certainly didn't have much on the best of days, but now they looked desperate. In all the hours she watched them, Lucha rarely saw them eat.

So they wanted to get through the fence, she thought. It was possible their goals were aligned with hers. Lucha didn't care much about whatever Los Ricos were hoarding inside, but she would have to accomplish the same goal if she was going to kill them. Perhaps a mutual desire to tear down this fence was enough for a temporary alliance with the Syndicate, whoever they were.

As she watched, she felt they were not brutal. There was no beating, no shouting, no fear of them among the people who approached their door. Most shocking of all, there was respect. And leaders who could earn respect in a place like this had to be worth a look at least.

Satisfied by the information she'd gleaned, Lucha settled in and waited for nightfall. As she'd suspected, the Syndicate gathered inside their tent alone when darkness fell. The rest of the camp went to their makeshift bedding. Cries still emanated from the field infirmary, echoing eerily through the trees.

Lucha's feet touched the ground when the moon, a conveniently dim sliver, reached its apex in the sky. She clung to the shadows, stealing through the sleeping camp, avoiding the fence where a few still shouted and rattled at the bars.

There were two entrances to the tent. Lucha chose the one

that faced the trees so her silhouette wouldn't be cast in candle-light, giving her away. She could no longer call on the power of the forest—she'd lost that right when she defeated Salvador—but the darkness was an old, reliable friend. She slid in without ruffling the fabric. Silent as if she were a shadow herself.

The members of the Syndicate were gathered around a table at the far end. Adjusting to the light, Lucha saw them first as silhouettes. A tall, slim one at the head, leaning over the table. A bulkier one standing back with arms crossed over their chest. Two more, bent close together at the other end.

"It'll never work," said one of the two at the end. "We've tried a hundred times. And if we don't get through soon, every-one will starve."

"Or riot," offered the slim one. "No Olvida for weeks. People and animals dying every day. They were happy enough to let us take charge, but leaders always get blamed when things aren't going well."

The bulkier one grunted in agreement.

"If the damn thing wasn't reinforced, we could just knock it down," said the other shadow Lucha couldn't quite make out. "But it's not like we have much physical power."

A dispirited silence followed. This was when Lucha stepped forward. "Perhaps I can help with that."

The reaction was immediate. Four weapons drawn. Two bodies came toward her while two hung back to flank them. Not a bad strategy, Lucha thought appraisingly. She ought to have held her hands up, but she didn't. She wasn't surrendering.

"Who the hell are you?" One of the silhouettes from the

end of the table was closest to her now. A young man. He looked familiar. One of the degenerates who had hung around with Lis, maybe. Or someone who looked like him.

"Haven't you heard the stories?" Lucha asked in her most sinister voice. "Daughter of the Forest, Bride of the Dark Prince, Summoner of Sombralados."

She watched as the lies Alán had spread about her registered on the faces of her audience.

"Lucha Moya?" said the slender shadow. The one who'd predicted riots. "I thought you were supposed to be dead."

"I was," Lucha said, stepping forward. "Dead, I mean. But there's no peace for the wicked, haven't you heard that one?"

The boy who'd first spoken to her stepped closer still. He was the only one who didn't seem intimidated by her words. "I heard those were all lies," he said, sneering at her. "That you were just some scared girl who ran into the woods and got eaten by a bear."

"Care to find out?" Lucha asked. She held her hands up as she once had when she was summoning her power. She'd never admit that her chest ached with missing it. "There are strange folks in the forest, you know. They had plenty to teach me."

It was only a stroke of luck that the wind kicked up then, extinguishing one of their candles, creating a strange shadow on Lucha's face. But it did the job. The boy backed off.

"What do you want with us?" asked the smallest of the figures, a young woman who looked just like the young man. She reminded Lucha of Lis. Perhaps that was why Lucha answered almost honestly.

"I'm here to kill Los Ricos," Lucha said simply. "I think we may have similar enough goals to help each other."

They were all so young, Lucha thought, a bit of the ageless divine still lingering in her memories. A war led by children. But hadn't she been a child herself when she took on El Sediento? Wasn't she a child still in many ways?

"Why should we trust you?" The slender one again. A girl halfway to boy, with short hair, tattoos crawling up her arm and along the bare side of her head.

"You shouldn't," Lucha said bluntly. "But you should use me. I know the forest better than anyone here. I can get you inside the gate. I can help you get whatever you're trying to take back from those thieves."

"And in return?" The slender one stepped closer. There was pain in her features. A ladder of scars up her arm. But something sparked in her eyes, flint and stone. The boy thought he was the leader, Lucha realized. And maybe he was, for now. But this girl was the strongest among them.

"In return, you help execute the plan that will get us inside. You allow me to take up residence in your camp until then. And you tell me what happened here."

They all exchanged glances. Lucha could tell right away that the boy and the girl who looked like him were skeptical. That the slender girl with the tattoos was in favor, and that the burly one with the beard would do what she decided.

"I know you're at the end of your rope," Lucha said as they communicated silently with one another. Weighing her fate in the balance. "I know your people respect you, but you're losing them to starvation and withdrawal. If you don't do something soon, they'll lose faith in you."

She saw the truth of this on every expression. Finally, the boy—the de facto leader, though he obviously wasn't suited for it—nodded. "We'll listen to your plan," he said. "And we'll tell you what we know. But one whiff of betrayal from you and I'll kill you myself."

It was almost adorable, Lucha thought, how much he believed this. "If I betray you, you're welcome to try," she replied. "Plenty of people have. It never seems to stick."

There was a moment of tension when Lucha thought the boy might leap forward and attack her. That she'd be forced to slit his throat. But the tattooed girl stepped forward, dispelling it by sticking out her hand.

"Cruz Miranda," she said as Lucha shook it. "Any enemy of Los Ricos is a friend of mine."

The burly young man stepped into the candlelight next; his hair was long—nearly elbow length—and he had a dark beard, ferociously bushy. His leather vest strained over his muscles, and a short sword hung at his side, clearly well taken care of. "Armando," he grunted, and his handshake was gentle.

The other two still stood close; in the light it was clearer than ever that they were related. They had the same piercing, intelligent eyes. Fathomless black pupils.

"Maria," the woman said finally, though she didn't offer her hand. "And this is my brother, Miguel."

Lucha nodded at them both. "Now," she said, "what the hell is going on out there?"

"It isn't anything some gossiping, sour-faced vieja outside wouldn't tell you for free," Miguel said, his own face as sour as those of the gossips he invoked.

"I'd like to hear it from you," Lucha replied easily. "Hence the bargain."

Armando pulled some crates from the edge of the tent. Cruz sat on one and gestured for Lucha to take the one opposite.

"We'd never trust you if things weren't dire," said Miguel, the only one still standing. "You should know we'd accept help from anyone. It's not because I believe you're some forest witch, or that you want to help us."

"I never asked you to trust me," Lucha replied. "In fact, I told you explicitly not to. Our goals are temporarily aligned, that's all. Once we're through the gate and Los Ricos are dead, we go our separate ways."

This didn't seem to please Miguel, although Lucha wondered if anything did, but he sat down at least, folding his arms, gesturing to Maria. "Tell her."

"It started with the Pensa plants dying," Maria began.

"*All* of them?" Lucha asked.

Cruz nodded in answer.

"When?" Lucha asked hoarsely. But she thought she already knew the answer.

"It was about three weeks ago now," Maria replied, confirming it.

Three weeks ago, Lucha had fought Salvador—Olvida's creator, god of destruction and chaos. Three weeks ago, he'd been erased from this world forever.

The Syndicate, who didn't seem to know this story yet, continued their own, Maria still speaking in that haunted tone. "Greenhouse workers showed up for their shifts to find every leaf wilted and browned. They were terrified of what the kings would do, so they tried to hide it. Tried to process the plants anyway. By lunchtime they were all crisp and dry. Useless."

Lucha could scarcely imagine what it had been like. The chain of production grinding to a violent halt. The workers terrified. The soldados realizing what was at stake.

"The kings were furious. They blamed the workers." Lucha noted the disdain in Maria's voice when she spoke of them. The angry expressions blooming on the faces of the others. "They rounded up every greenhouse employee. Accused them of sabotage. The smarter ones fled before then. They already knew what was coming . . ." She trailed off, her expression pained.

Miguel put an arm around her, consoling. He picked up the story where she had left off.

"They started the questioning that evening," he said, his own voice thick with pain. Lucha wondered who they'd lost, these beautiful and suspicious siblings with their haunted eyes. "It went through the night and into the next day. No one was allowed to go home. And of course, no one knew what was happening. Why all the plants had died and no new ones were sprouting or growing. They just kept saying they didn't know until the soldados started hurting them. After that, they mostly screamed."

Lucha could see it all too well. The terrified workers being tortured for answers they didn't have. She wanted to tell Miguel to stop. But she couldn't turn away. She had to understand. Her anger was the friction that sharpened her blade.

"All the while they had teams of soldados and their loyal followers, foraging in the woods. Anything to stop the bleeding. The foragers must have been scared too, because they didn't come back until the following night. Empty-handed. The plants in the forest were just as dead as the ones here.

"The kings killed the foragers to a man. Didn't want word getting out."

Nausea writhed like a pit of snakes in Lucha's belly. *Killed them all.* She thought of the bodies in the housing units. She had known the kings were monsters. Capable of anything. Still, she had imagined a disaster. A disease. Poison in the drugs or the food. Even she was shocked sick by this. Mass murder, and no one to hold them accountable.

"They stopped the interrogations then," Cruz chimed in. She laughed—a wry, humorless bark. "Not because they'd grown a conscience, of course. But with the wild Pensa dead, they knew they'd get no answers. Didn't want to waste the manpower on torture. They let everyone go, but without Pensa there was no processing. No packing. No distributing."

"No jobs at all," Lucha said, hearing her own hollow voice.

"They cut off all payment," Cruz confirmed. "Workers had already been away from their families for nearly two days during the questioning. Most of us were jonesing and hungry, some with mouths to feed. Before we could demand pay, our so-called *leaders* locked themselves in that compound. Every last one of them. Armed guards patrolled the gate from the inside and killed anyone who got too close."

"They left you out here to starve?" Lucha asked, revolted. But in the midst of all this, her anger, always kindling, built to a blaze she could warm herself by.

Lucha might have lost her gift in the fight against Salvador, but anger had been the first power she'd ever wielded. She kept it close now. She had a feeling she'd need it before long.

"The first week there was looting," Armando said, his voice gravelly and rough. "Violence. Plenty of soldados defected when they realized there'd be no more drugs. No more girls. No more of that Los Ricos lifestyle. Not enough of them, though. The kings were still protected. Out in the streets prices went crazy. Food was bad, with the ration counters all closed, but Olvida was worse. Anyone holding jacked their prices through the roof. But the money just made them targets."

Lucha had spent every moment of her life *hating* the men who sold Olvida in the marketplace. The ones who lingered on street corners, whispering, jackets bulging with contraband. How many of them had been responsible for her mother's disappearances, after all?

Because of this, Lucha's first thought when Armando mentioned them being targets was one of vindication.

But she had been gone from Robado long enough to get some perspective on those kinds of choices. None of those dealers had forced Lydia to take Olvida. To leave her daughters to fend for themselves. Like her, they'd been victims of their circumstances.

Lucha didn't have to mourn them, but she could pity them for the way they'd lived.

The way they'd died.

"After about a week," Armando continued, "the last of the street vendors ran out. There were no more drugs to buy at any price. The detox made people sick, violent, terrible. Plenty of them died." His voice choked up here, and Lucha thought of her own mother, and wondered who had been lost to him. "On the tenth day, the river flooded the housing units. Hundreds of people died. Anyone who hadn't already made the crossing was stuck here. Nowhere was safe."

"And the kings stayed in there?" Lucha asked, already knowing the answer. "While people were starving and killing one another and being flooded out of their homes?"

"Haven't seen a single one of them since the last day of interrogations," Cruz replied. "That's why we need to get inside. They have Olvida in there. Food and water and supplies. You saw most of the folks who tried on the fence as you came in, I'm guessing. So we obviously need a different approach."

The reality Cruz painted was somehow far worse than anything Lucha had imagined as she'd walked through the deserted city. And the smug bastards who'd created this system hiding away from the consequences of it all. Hoarding the last of the resources as people starved and drowned and killed one another . . .

In the eyes of the desperate group before her, Lucha found

something so familiar it nearly took her breath away. The rebellious fire, the anger toward the men who had kept them down—coupled with the feeling that the fight was too big. That even this anger and all the power that could be stolen from them wouldn't be enough to save everyone.

The Syndicate had the respect and loyalty of the people camped outside. They'd gathered everyone together, done their best to feed and heal them. They'd earned the trust of the Robadans in a way Lucha—always set apart from the rest by her disdain for the drug they depended on—never could have.

But the people standing before Lucha were also tired. They were beginning to despair. They needed perspective, and a strategy. Understanding of what it took to fight against what was killing you and win. Lucha knew she could provide that.

That perhaps, together, they truly could do what needed to be done.

"So," Cruz said, breaking Lucha's reverie. "Now you know our story. It's our turn to ask some questions."

Lucha inclined her head, mind still half planning the victory she imagined.

"Did you really escape from Encadenar using dark magic?" Miguel asked, eyes narrowed in suspicion.

Lucha paused. The fear and awe that her exploits might engender here could be useful, but it wasn't like she could demonstrate her power. It would be a tricky line to walk.

"I made a bargain with the wrong monster," she said at last. "What I got was the power to kill those horrible bastards. To escape. To get my sister free. But what I gave up was much more precious."

Miguel nodded, but his eyes remained narrowed. "They say you killed Alán Marquez yourself. Choked him with a vine. Is that true?"

"It was mushrooms," Lucha said, seeing it like it was happening in front of her all over again. "I just grew them. They ate through his heart on their own."

A low whistle from Armando. Lucha felt the pleasure she'd seen on the faces of her captors then. It felt good to impress these people. These leaders.

"Can you still do the thing with the mushrooms?" Maria asked. "I can think of a few people I might like to dispose of that way."

Careful, Lucha reminded herself. "While I was gone, I learned a little something about the cost of power like that," she said. "I like to use my other skills now, if I can."

"And what skills might those be?" Cruz asked.

Lucha smirked. "If you agree to work with me, I'll show you all of them. In fact, I'll do you one better. We'll have Los Ricos in the ground before the week is over and the city will be yours."

Cruz's eyebrows shot up. Lucha watched one last silent conversation transpire. She thought she was starting to understand.

"It's a hell of an offer if you can deliver," Cruz said when they had finished conferring. "But there's one condition. We're after the Olvida they're hiding in there. All of it. We're willing to cut you in, but we need your word you won't try to take it for yourself."

Cruz's scars seemed to stand out in sharper relief than they had a moment ago. Armando's were covered with tattoos, but the ridges were still visible in the low light of the tent. They wore them like badges of honor.

"I don't even want the Olvida," Lucha said. "You can keep my share."

She had thought this would please them, but the silence that followed her words grew thorns.

"If you don't want any Olvida," said Armando, getting to his feet, "then what's in it for you?"

"Does it matter?" Lucha retorted, knowing her defensiveness was a confession. That she needed to get herself under control.

"Of course it matters," said Miguel, leaning forward, examining Lucha again. "Would you trust someone whose agenda you didn't know?"

It was a fair question, and one Lucha couldn't answer. Not truthfully, at least not in its entirety. So she stuck as close to the truth as she could.

"My mother most likely overdosed on Olvida. Before I left Robado, Alán Marquez swore to forcibly evict my sister and me from our unit. Let her indenture herself at Pecado to keep us housed. They threw me in prison when I tried to save her. Pumped her full of drugs she didn't want. They destroyed my family."

None of the people assembled replied. They didn't move. But Lucha could feel something shifting in the room. They knew her story. They had probably lived similar ones themselves long before the disaster that had happened here in recent weeks. Alán's lies had given her the ability to intimidate them into listening, but now she saw something different in their eyes. Solidarity. Understanding. Lucha felt the strength of it help her through what came next.

"I got out. I made it far away. I was offered a new life, a family, peace. A chance to leave this all behind." For a moment, the memory was close enough to touch. To taste. The garden in front of her pilgrim's hut. Paz saying she'd wait as long as it took . . .

Lucha shook herself. The past scattered like drops of water off her skin.

"But I couldn't be at peace knowing what the kings were still getting away with. You want to know what's in it for me? I'll tell you. The chains this place hooks into your chest don't let go, no matter how far away you run. As long as the kings are still breathing, I'll never be free of them."

It was Cruz who nodded first. The others quickly followed suit.

Miguel stepped forward. "Let's take these bastards down," he said, extending his hand.

Lucha took it, and an alliance was born.

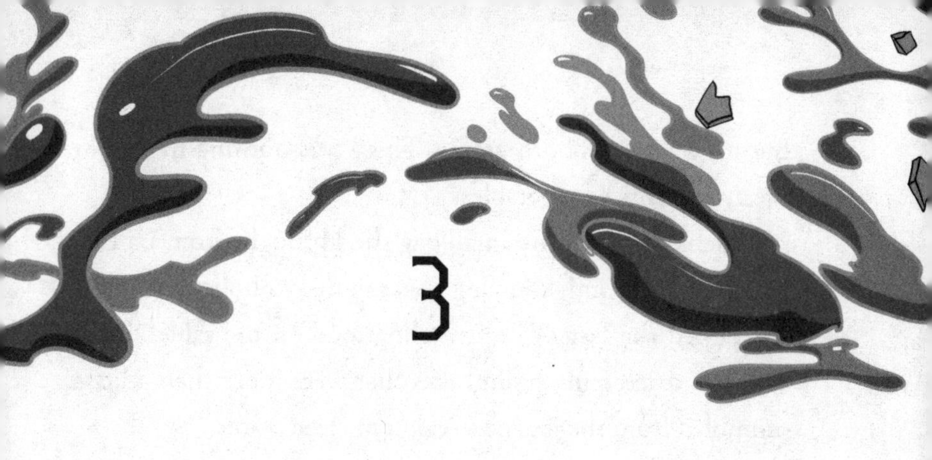

3

The next day, Miguel led Lucha around the camp. People watched, whispered. Lucha heard many of the tales Alán had told of her circulating, but no one was brave enough to approach her directly.

Clearly they had heard the stories. All that remained to be seen was which ones they had believed.

With Miguel leading, Lucha, Armando, Cruz, and Maria moved through the squalor, familiarizing Lucha with the lay-out of the camp. Miguel pointed out the infirmary area and the sleeping quarters, which seemed to be mostly bedrolls in the mud.

"This is where we distribute rations," he finished, gesturing to a decidedly unsanitary table a few yards from the tree line. At least they'd managed to keep it out of view of the body parts on the fence, Lucha thought grimly.

"When we have them," Maria added bitterly.

There was little here at the moment, Lucha could see that plainly enough. She recognized the bags of corn porridge that had so often been the only thing in her home cupboard—empty but for a few stubborn grains. There was nothing fresh. No meat, no fruits or vegetables.

Lucha dug into the small bag she'd brought from La Catedral de Asilo and, knowing it was more symbolic than helpful, placed the last of her traveling food on the table. Some strips of dried fruit, grain cakes that were more than a little crumbled from the journey. A skin of clean water.

"It's not much," she said, turning back around. "We'll need to find a way to get more. That's the first order of business."

Miguel's eyes flashed. "The *first* order of business is to get through that gate," he said. "There's food in there. Clean water. Olvida."

Lucha had seen most stages of Olvida withdrawal in her life, and most of the different types, too. These four were all past the physical withdrawal that could kill you, but it was clear the psychological effects still had a hold on Miguel, at least.

"You think getting through the gate will be the end of it?" she asked him, refusing to back down. "Because it won't. The second you breach it, there'll be war with the soldados inside, and they're better provisioned than you."

As if to illustrate her point, Robadans had begun to wander toward the table with their hungry, haunted expressions. The presence of food drew them out of their stupor.

"They won't last five minutes like this," Lucha said, stepping out of earshot as the downtrodden folks began passing around the meager supplies. "A real meal will remind them they're people and not animals in a cage."

Miguel's expression grew stormier. The rest of them watched as if this were an interesting game of sport. "Don't you think we would have fed them if we could? There's nothing here. Those greedy bastards are keeping all the food inside the wall."

Lucha, who had been expecting this, turned toward the trees. "You're all starving twenty feet from a feast," she said. "There's plenty of food to be foraged in the forest, you just have to know where to look."

Her opponent was seething now, and Lucha didn't mind. "There's nothing in there but poisoned berries and curses," he spat. "You won't get any of my people in there. Not for anything."

"Not to survive the night?" Lucha asked, looking pointedly at a group of children fighting over a single fruit strip. "I beg to differ."

Miguel looked to his sister, Cruz, Armando, expecting their support. But they were all gazing curiously at Lucha. It was so easy to forget after just a few weeks that the forest was completely foreign to everyone in Robado.

They'd been taught to fear it so Los Ricos could control the resources, and they had sown their terror well. "None of us know what's safe and what isn't in there," Cruz said, stepping forward. "We didn't want to risk it. But if you know . . ."

"I do," Lucha said. The thought of Paz surfaced again, burning like a hot iron. "When I left, I had to travel through the forest for hundreds of miles. I learned a few things." *Berries passed between fumbling fingertips. A rabbit roasting on an open flame as gazes met, dropped, met again.*

"Let's go, then," Cruz said, paying no attention to Miguel's indignant huff. "You're right. If we can feed them, we might have a fighting chance."

Armando joined Cruz without hesitation.

"This was a mistake," Miguel said, turning on his heel and storming off.

With an appraising glance at Lucha, his sister followed.

Lucha turned to Cruz and Armando, deciding not to comment on the departures. They would come around when there was a meal in front of them, or they wouldn't. If Lucha had to choose among the four of them, she would have picked the two still standing here, by a landslide.

"What do we do?" Cruz asked, her leonine eyes wide and curious.

"If you can, round up a few people with sharp eyes who won't mind trying something a little unorthodox," Lucha said. "The more pairs of hands we have in there, the better."

Not many were willing. Even Armando looked highly skeptical as Lucha stood in front of the ragtag group at the forest's edge.

"We don't go into the forest," said one round-faced woman when Lucha had explained the plan. As if it were a law of nature.

"Yeah," said a boy no older than Lis. "Plus, everyone knows if you eat food from the forest, you'll be stuck in there forever. Like a maze you never get to the end of."

Lucha had lived in Robado long enough to know that words alone wouldn't make a dent in these superstitions. Instead, she stalked into the trees herself. Still in view of the crowd, she pulled deep violet berries off a flowering bush and brought them back to the forest's edge.

Several people—including the round-faced woman—gasped when she popped them into her mouth. They tasted tart, not quite as ripe as the ones she'd found deeper in—but still completely edible.

"See?" she asked when she'd swallowed them. "No harm done."

The Robadans continued to mutter. Cruz had the audacity to smirk from behind them.

"Listen," Lucha said, losing her patience. "I've spent the better part of the last month in that forest. I traveled with an acolyte of the goddess who was trained in the art of foraging. She kept us alive, and I learned from her. If you take the plants I show you and no others, you'll be perfectly safe. But if you refuse to eat from the forest, you'll die of starvation before we get a chance to take back this city from the kings. It's your choice. I suggest you make it quickly."

There was a long silence. Lucha waited.

It was the boy who stepped forward first. "I'll go in," he said.

After that, the rest couldn't resist. Who wanted to be shown up by a child?

Lucha led the way. She showed them the berries, the safe greens, the white tubers that Paz had once cooked to such perfection. The boy, Junio, was a quick study. He gathered twice as much as the others with his nimble fingers.

After a few hours had passed, the suspicious grumbling

from the others had become excited chatter. Between them, they had enough for a full meal for everyone at camp. Not a large or elegant one, but Lucha supposed it would hardly matter to the starving rebels.

The best part came at the end, when they were heading back to camp with their bounty. Junio stopped cold, holding up a hand for quiet. Ahead in the clearing was a pair of fat brown hares.

Giving Junio a nod of gratitude, Lucha waved the rest of the group back, then approached slowly on the balls of her feet, a knife in each hand.

So many emotions overtook her as she got into position that she almost couldn't hold her weapons steady. She remembered the hare the goddess Almudena had offered them near the end of their journey to Asilo, its meat laced with Pensa. The visions that followed. Paz coming out of hers desperate and searching for Lucha . . .

To quiet her thoughts, Lucha threw the knives one after the other, with the hushed crowd behind her, watching.

When they collected the kill, each one had a dagger right through the eye. A quick death, Lucha told herself, giving silent thanks to the forest for sustaining them. Gods knew they would need whatever support they could get if they were going to get this done.

Back at camp, dusk was settling. Lucha and her group got a heroes' welcome when their bounty had been examined. A fire was lit, the rabbits skinned and cut up, the foraged vegetables and greens diced with hunting knives.

Within half an hour, there was a large pot of soup bubbling over the fire. Even the smell was enough to rouse the downtrodden group—it attracted most of them before long. Junio took it upon himself to guard the pot, brandishing a stubby little knife at anyone who got too close.

Lucha stirred in silent contemplation. Part of her was still back in the clearing where she'd seen the hares. With the memories of Paz they had brought with them. She wasn't shaken from her thoughts until the Syndicate arrived at the fire—even Miguel, whose scowl had lightened if not entirely disappeared.

"Not bad," Cruz said, approaching the pot, inhaling the steam now spiraling into the twilight.

"Not so fast," Miguel said, joining her. "We can praise her when it doesn't poison everyone."

"I hope you're ready to grovel," Lucha said, sticking her recently cleaned knife into the pot and licking it. The soup was delicious. The hearty weight of the tubers and hare cut with the zest of the herby forest greens.

Miguel's eyes flashed with jealousy.

Lucha, holding his gaze, clanged the spoon against the pot. Folks began to gather. Armando took his place beside Junio to maintain order as bowls, cups, and various other dishes were filled with fragrant soup.

There were superstitious mutterings here and there about eating food from beyond the tree line, but they were quickly swallowed in sounds of slurping, groaning, and compliments to the foragers.

Lucha herself ate a full bowl, watching as the hot meal

transformed the people in front of her. The pot was soon empty, but they stayed. Talking. Helping with cleanup. They thanked the Syndicate members and the foragers profusely—some even shyly approached Lucha to offer nods or smiles.

The atmosphere quickly became celebratory. Lucha watched Miguel make his rounds, whispering to a few of the stronger-looking men, leaving them more fired up than he found them. Cruz, on the other hand, was good for a joke, a compliment, help with a weapon or a piece of armor. Armando shadowed her at a distance, clearly vigilant for any threats to her safety.

Maria stayed close to the fire. She spoke to the worried mothers, passed out the last of the berries to the children underfoot. It was Maria who Lucha approached when it was time. She was the most accessible of the bunch by a mile.

"They seem happier," Lucha said softly as a little boy ran away giggling from Maria's outstretched, tickling fingers.

"You did a good thing today," Maria replied, straightening up. "The superstitions felt so real. It's been generations since anyone even ventured into the trees. Maybe people just needed to see it wasn't all poisonous."

"The knowledge was hard-won," Lucha admitted, thinking of Paz again. How difficult it must have been for her to stick to medicine, to keep her cover by pretending she didn't love the woods. "But I'm happy to share."

Lucha paused, surveying the Robadans along with Maria. "There's more work to be done," she said after a time. "We need to tend to the wounded, make sure the children are cared for."

Maria nodded. "I've been saying that for days, but Miguel

thinks getting through the fence is all that matters. That everything else can be decided after the fact."

Across the fire, Miguel clapped his hand on a tall, broad-shouldered man's back, saying something inaudible. It was clear to Lucha he was rallying the fighting folks, using the momentum Lucha had created with a plan he objected to.

Sneaky, she thought, but smart.

"Hopefully he sees the value of caring for your people now," Lucha said mildly. "We can't win a fight with starving, dying fighters."

"He's not bad," Maria said after a long pause. "Just single-minded sometimes."

"Well then, it's a good thing he's not doing this alone."

Later, when the night had aged and the stars were visible up ahead, Lucha stood back from the rest, watching. From this vantage point she could see it in their faces. Joy. Camaraderie. The last two sentiments you'd ever expect to find in Robado.

After a lifetime longing for the kind of atmosphere that surrounded her now, Lucha found herself moved. Hopeful. She thought of the future for the first time since before she could remember. Imagined Robado without the kings, whole. The kind of place where folks fed and cared for one another. Worked together.

"This is all temporary, you know," came a voice from behind her.

Miguel stood close. Lucha hadn't heard him coming.

"Plenty more soup ingredients in the forest," she replied lightly.

"You know what I mean." Miguel looked out, tracking Lucha's gaze to the firelit, smiling faces of the Robadans.

Lucha didn't answer, holding her gaze. Miguel didn't seem like the type of person who would be deterred from giving his opinion because no one asked for it.

"You've been gone awhile, Lucha Moya," he said after a beat. "But don't forget where you are. There's only one reason we're all united now, eating and laughing around a fire instead of stabbing one another full of holes. And when we get it out of that compound . . ."

Lucha waited, heart sinking, though she kept her features neutral.

"This will all just be a memory."

Miguel walked off without waiting for a response, but his words settled heavy and cold in Lucha's chest, extinguishing the kindling warmth that had been there moments before. He was right, of course, little as she liked to admit it. The Robadans were united now in their pursuit of the drug behind the fence, and getting their hands on it would ruin all of this.

Only, Lucha didn't intend for any Olvida to come out of the compound. She had destroyed Salvador, and his drug was within her reach. She couldn't let anything derail her from that purpose.

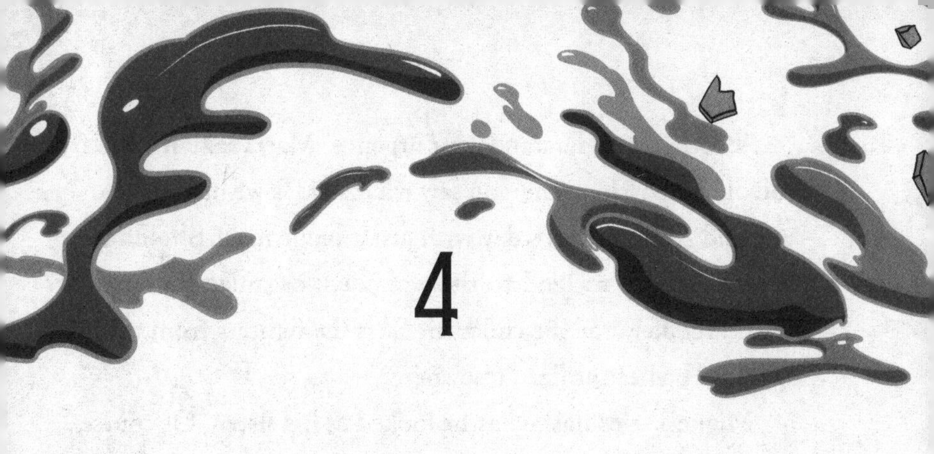

4

Lucha settled that night in a hammock behind the Syndicate tent alongside the rest of them.

She expected to be up for hours considering Miguel's words, her plans for the coming days. Deciding how long she could ally herself with people intent on their own destruction, and when would be the most advantageous moment to break away . . .

Instead, she fell asleep immediately. She didn't remember her dreams but awoke just in time to swallow Paz's name as it rose to her lips.

Miguel and Maria were just rousing, Cruz and Armando fast asleep, when Lucha slid out of her hammock.

"Today's the day," Miguel was already saying, his own feet hitting the ground still in their heavy boots. "One more meal and then we launch ourselves at that gate with all the power we can muster."

Lucha instinctively disagreed. Plenty more needed to be done before they'd be any match for the soldados in the compound. But she waited to voice her concerns, and she was rewarded for it almost instantly.

"Brother, I understand your urgency," Maria said in a voice full of compassion. "But you saw what strides we made in morale and strength yesterday with just a single meal. Should we not take today to tend to the wounded, organize the camp, find caretakers for the children? Sort the fighters from those who can be best utilized elsewhere?"

Miguel's eyes flashed as he looked at his sister. "Of course we can," he said in a smooth, dangerous voice. "In fact, why don't we give up our goals entirely? We could build permanent houses here, beneath the body parts rotting on the fence. Get nice and comfortable."

"It's not all or nothing, you know," Maria said mildly. "We have a better chance of winning if we're stronger, that's all."

Now Lucha offered her support, feeling a swell of pride for Maria. "Most of these people have had one meal in a week," she said. "Many of them are suffering through untreated wounds and illnesses. They're hungry and disorganized and worried for their children. If we address those concerns first, we'll have fighters focused on the task at hand."

Miguel didn't even turn to face her. "You don't know what you're talking about," he snarled. "You just got here. We're the ones who have been here for weeks, doing our best to care for these people."

"I don't deny it," Lucha said. "But I do think you're missing the forest for the trees. None of your passion is worth anything if every one of us is slaughtered by the soldados inside. Your sister is right."

Maria looked gratified; Miguel, murderous. His hand twitched toward the long, thin sword that hung at his side. But before he could escalate the conflict, Cruz's boots hit the ground, followed by Armando's.

"Hate to be the voice of reason, but I agree with the ladies," Cruz said, yawning and stretching. She seemed entirely unconcerned at the storm that overtook Miguel's features, and Lucha respected her for it.

"They need food," Armando said simply. "And forcing them to fight in this state makes us no better than the kings."

"You heard the man," Cruz said, settling it.

Maria, livelier than Lucha had seen her since they met, started passing out assignments then. And Miguel, though clearly upset at being outvoted, seemed to understand that he couldn't compete with such an overwhelming majority.

Lucha—who was to take the foragers out again today—wasn't fully sold on the idea of Miguel's role as general and weapons master. She understood why his aggressive nature had appealed to a group of lost, struggling survivors. But Miguel wasn't cut out to be a leader. That much was obvious.

Lucha's foraging group was much more enthusiastic than the day before. Having survived a trip into the forest *and* not been poisoned by the food they gathered there had done wonders for their confidence.

Junio took the lead, remembering the correct plants without any help from Lucha. He also had a keen sense for the presence of animals, and Lucha managed to snag three more rabbits and a young deer with her daggers—though the buck he spotted, the real prize, spooked before Lucha could aim properly.

"Where are your parents?" Lucha asked as he dutifully brought the third rabbit back, removing Lucha's dagger from its throat.

"Dead." He pretended nonchalance, but his lip quivered. "Mama never came home from work on interrogation day, and Papa . . . the flood . . ."

"I'm sorry," Lucha said, stringing the hare onto her belt. "Mine are dead too. You stick with me, okay?"

Junio, fully recovered from his lip-trembling moment, stuck out his tongue at her. "If you can catch me." He darted off into the forest.

Lucha laughed. Two of the superstitious women carried an overflowing basket between them. She could hear them chattering about grinding down the tubers, making a paste for flatbread. Planning for a future beyond the next few days.

As they walked back, she wondered how many of them would survive the week. And if they did, how many would stay if Lucha managed to dispose of Los Ricos' Olvida stash?

You came here to do a job, she told herself severely. *It's better not to get attached.* But Junio darted between the trees ahead, smiling at her, and the women planned another outing to find tubers to experiment with, and Lucha couldn't help it. Her heart ached.

When they arrived back at camp, Lucha couldn't believe the difference. In the hours that had passed, Maria had managed to erect a lean-to for the sick and wounded. The children were gathered near the fire, minded by some lanky older kids. One of these she recognized as a friend of Lis's. She'd last seen her smoking under a light near the housing units.

Units that were now filled with corpses. They'd have to address that soon if they didn't want disease spreading through the camp.

Still, progress had been made. The ground was clear of refuse. The cooking fire was kindling, the clean pot awaiting the forest's bounty, but there were other fires lit now too. For warmth and for gathering. There was a purposeful energy about the place that Lucha could hardly equate with the dismal, foul-smelling place she'd been dragged into just yesterday.

She looked for Maria to congratulate her but found her happily and busily directing some sturdy-looking Robadans making a shelter. She smiled, though, and Lucha returned it.

Lucha's eyes scanned the crowd for Miguel next. He was harder to find, but eventually she spotted him huddled over a distant fire with some of the bigger men from yesterday. They leaned in close together, discussing something at a low volume.

The back of Lucha's neck prickled at the sight. She had tried to keep an open mind, and to remind herself she was only allied with these people for the moment. But she didn't trust Miguel.

Cruz approached, gesturing out at the camp as she squatted down. "Not bad, huh?" she asked.

"Not at all," Lucha agreed. "The foragers are so good after two days, I think I've become irrelevant."

"Well, someone had to teach them the ropes," Cruz said kindly. "And convince them their firstborns wouldn't become demons if they crossed the tree line."

Lucha allowed the compliment with a nod. Her eyes were drawn again to Miguel. His secret conference around the fire.

"It was good of you to back up Maria this morning too," Cruz went on, seemingly oblivious to Lucha's preoccupation. "Sometimes I think she's the best of us, but she's the least vicious, so she gets flattened from time to time."

Another nod. Lucha enjoyed Cruz's easy manner, but she still didn't know how much sense it made to confide in her. "Having a . . . spirited sibling can make being heard a bit of a struggle," she said finally.

"Sounds like you can relate."

Lucha thought of Lis with a pang. She was safe, of course. Ensconced at Almudena's sanctuary learning to be an acolyte of the goddess. As often as they had clashed in their youth, Lucha missed her fiercely. Only an understanding of how much danger Lis would be in here kept Lucha from wishing they were together.

"Sometimes you just need someone to listen," she said after

a long, contemplative silence. "Remind you your ideas are worth something."

Never mentioning that the first person to listen to Lucha had been a trapped god bent on earthly destruction . . .

"Miguel's not much for listening, or giving a fuck, but he's good at that last bit," Cruz said.

Lucha snuck a glance at her face, which wore an expression too complex to be easily read. There was distrust there, Lucha could tell. But there was also a grudging admiration.

"You have to understand, we've spent these past weeks thinking we were dead meat every day. Miguel gave us something to hope for."

"Getting the Olvida back," Lucha clarified without thinking.

"Hell yeah, getting the Olvida back," Cruz said, her smirk becoming a full smile. "But also sticking it to the people who did this to us, like you said. For some of us, the idea of killing the bastards inside that gate is the only thing keeping us going. So getting fed and healthy makes sense, but there's no building anything while they're still hiding in there, watching us. Miguel knows that."

Lucha nodded again. "I'll keep it in mind."

The smell of food began to drift through the camp, and Cruz took her leave. Lucha stood for a while, thinking of what she'd said. Of Miguel, and his plans, and his warning last night.

They would need to get through the gate soon. Cruz was right about that. But Lucha found herself dreading it. She had never felt at home in Robado, nor at the sanctuary with the acolytes. But here, in the past couple of days, she'd felt herself connect. Imagine a future for the first time.

A future that would never exist.

When Miguel insisted on a meeting—a war council, he called it—the next day, Lucha could find no reason to disagree. The foragers were off on their own, the camp was running as smoothly as it was going to, and a couple of days of meals had the fighters in decent form.

There was no reason to delay, so they didn't. They spent the day huddled up in the Syndicate tent, planning, and before long a decent way forward had begun to take shape. Miguel wanted to rely on brute strength, not considering who or what might be lost. Maria, emboldened by her success in the camp, wanted a more stealth entry that might preserve as many lives as possible.

Cruz, backed always by Armando, proposed something in between that even Lucha couldn't find fault with. Or at least, couldn't find any way to drastically improve.

They deferred to her knowledge of the compound's layout and the strength of the soldados inside, and she felt useful sketching maps and warning of pitfalls they might not recognize. But on the whole, the plan was simple enough to work. If they didn't meet with any surprises inside.

Besides Lucha's own agenda, of course, which would be the biggest surprise of all.

By the end of the next day, they would be ready.

Miguel had taken to spending most of his time around the fire with the other men who were in fighting shape. He insisted he needed to know them inside and out to get the job done, but Lucha still felt suspicious of his motives. Unfortunately, there was no one to voice these suspicions to. Not when Miguel still held the loyalty of the majority of the Robadans.

It didn't matter much, Lucha told herself. Once the Olvida was destroyed, it wouldn't matter if they agreed. And if Miguel got in her way . . . well, he was no god. Just a man with all the critical weaknesses his humanity implied. Lucha had tangled with worse.

But when she'd done most of her tangling, she'd had the help of Almudena's gift. Now she was only a girl with knives again. She would have to tread carefully.

She allowed herself just a moment to feel the emptiness in her chest. The ache. Then it was back to the task at hand.

Word began to spread throughout the camp that tomorrow was the day. Maria discussed plans for moving the children and the infirm to a safe place in the forest. She'd stay there to guard them in case the fighting spilled beyond the gate.

Miguel, of course, was smoking around the fire with his little knot of comrades. They'd be going through the main gate with a battering ram crafted by Armando, hopefully drawing the bulk of Los Ricos' remaining forces away from the compound.

That was where Lucha and Cruz came in. As the deadliest from long range, they'd be sneaking up the outer fence to the little dock at the back of Pecado. The one Lucha had hoped to escape through with Lis what felt like a lifetime ago.

The existence of the dock had been a surprise to the Syndicate. It was the linchpin of the entire plan. Cruz and Lucha would sneak in through the back door and, with the bulk of the soldados engaged in combat at the gate, would take out the kings.

It was risky beyond belief. There was a good chance they'd all die. But things were only getting worse, so they'd go in the morning. By the end, someone would rule Robado unopposed.

If they lost, Lucha thought as she and Cruz checked the necessary supplies, she'd be dead, and none of these alliances would matter. But if they won, she'd be the enemy of every olvidado counting on their next fix. And by her estimation, that was almost everyone here.

"Pago for your thoughts?" Cruz asked.

Lucha shook her head. "Just going over the plan."

"And . . . ?"

She sighed, relenting. It seemed Cruz had that effect on people. "I was thinking about after we win. What the city will look like. Who will stay."

Cruz's smile widened. "For the first couple of days," she said dreamily, "I won't even know there *is* a city."

A now-familiar pang burrowed in Lucha's chest. Of all the Syndicate, she respected Cruz the most. It was hard to imagine her lost to the forgetting that had stolen so much from Lucha. Hard not to feel the grief of what would be lost if the Syndicate succeeded.

"What will you do when it runs out?" Lucha asked, knowing it was a gamble. Unable to keep herself from taking it. "The Pensa plants aren't growing, right? So once whatever stash they have in there is fought over and used up . . . what then?"

Cruz waved a hand, seemingly unconcerned. "When we get inside, we'll figure out how to get them growing again," she said vaguely. Undaunted, apparently, by the fact that Los Ricos, with all the tools at their disposal, hadn't managed it yet.

It sounded like one of Lydia's plans. Long on expectation and short on details. Ambitions propelling her no further than her next dose. Lucha understood the desperation that drove plans like these, empathized with the people who made them, even, after everything she'd been through. But she found that her hard-won enlightenment about her mother, about olvidados in general, put her under new pressure here.

"Why do you care, anyway?" Cruz asked. Her tone was light, but her eyes narrowed slightly. "I thought you were just here to smash some Ricos skulls."

"I am," Lucha said, shrugging. "I just . . . I grew up here too, you know. Seeing it like this, people working together, planning, building. It seems like a shame to give it all up for something that can't last."

"Yeah, well, I guess that's our problem, isn't it?"

"I guess it is."

Lucha watched Cruz walk away from her, left with the feeling that she'd said too much and not nearly enough at the same time.

5

When dawn arrived, the atmosphere was tense with expectation.

All the children, as well as the sick and wounded, had been moved to a place beyond the trees—Lucha was proud of her foraging señoras for dispelling the superstitions of the mothers.

Armando hauled the massive battering ram into view. Miguel's expression was feverish as he called out to the fighters, gathering them before him. Little as Lucha trusted the sharp-faced young man, there was no doubt he was the one they wanted to hear from now. The one who could rouse them into a prebattle frenzy and give them the best chance.

"You've worked hard the past few days," he began softly, making everyone lean in and quiet down to hear him. "And so have we."

Miguel gestured to the battering ram. To the well-organized camp, and the flushed faces of the well-fed warriors before him.

"Today, we're going through that gate." This statement was louder, and the cheers that met it nearly deafened them.

Lucha stood at the front of the crowd with the other Syndicate members, trying to put everything out of her head but the coming conflict. Life or death.

"When we get inside, every one of you is gonna cause utter chaos. Show those so-called *kings* exactly what you think of the way they've been treating us."

Pandemonium, pure and simple, greeted this. Cruz waved enthusiastically and motioned for Lucha to do the same. The crowd surged forward, swallowing the Syndicate and bearing them aloft as Miguel cried:

"To war!"

Cruz took Lucha's arm, leading her into the trees as the forces wheeled the battering ram toward the gate.

Lucha's heartbeat was steady, and so were her hands. She always felt best in these moments, when life and death were on the line and there was no time to think. When only instinct could guide her, and her thoughts only got in the way.

All was silent as they stole up to the fence, overgrown with vines and trees without soldados to keep them at bay. It was a good sign, Lucha thought. It meant Los Ricos didn't have enough men to keep up appearances.

The silence broke soon after, and in dramatic fashion. They heard the first collision of the battering ram so loudly that it seemed impossible Los Ricos had not.

Cruz raised her eyebrows at Lucha from up ahead. Phase one was in motion.

Into the trees, Lucha released grief for the community they'd formed here over the past few days. For the hopeful future Robado might have had. Perhaps some of them had felt it too, and would remember it. Separate from their longing for the drug inside. Follow this new purpose toward something that would sustain.

But healing Robado was not Lucha's purpose. Destroying Olvida was.

"Hear that?" Cruz asked. Another resounding crash echoed through the trees. Shook the fence even where they stood.

"I think the whole compound heard that," Lucha said.

"Let's hope so," Cruz replied, and led them on.

The distance between the two of them and the dock at Pecado shrank, and as it did, the tension mounted. Lucha had expected they'd meet at least a few guards, but they were quite alone as they hacked through the overgrowth.

If they were lucky, the majority of Los Ricos' protection had been sent to deal with the commotion at the gate. Their absence was a sign of the plan's success. But when had a Robadan ever had luck on their side?

Lucha continued on, not voicing her suspicions. Trying not to jump at the sounds of underbrush rustling behind them. She couldn't let Cruz think her a coward.

But as they got closer, the real reason for the lack of guards was suddenly too obvious to ignore.

"Fuck," Cruz swore from a few steps ahead. "The river."

Lucha saw it only seconds after she spoke. The dock and the back gate were gone, as if they'd never existed. The salt river—capricious at the best of times, downright destructive at the worst—was high today. Too high.

The dock was underwater, as was most of the path Lucha had hoped to take to the back entrance. A swift current made its way past, and on it, Lucha thought she felt their momentum drifting away to the east.

"We can't get through," Cruz said, almost disbelieving.

The sounds of battle carried up from camp. People were fighting down there. Dying, perhaps. All to give Cruz and Lucha a chance to get to the kings. They couldn't throw that away.

Not when they were this close.

Darting everywhere for a solution, Lucha's eyes finally snagged on something with potential. It was a window—high and small—through which she was reasonably sure she'd once summoned lye-smelling white vines to strangle two of Los Ricos' guards.

If they could reach it . . .

They had to reach it. They would never get another chance.

"We can get in," Lucha said. "But we might get cut to ribbons in the process."

Cruz followed Lucha's gaze up the wall of Pecado until they were both staring at the window together. The razor wire at the top of the fence.

They could hear nothing through the thick steel of the walls. They had no idea what they'd be facing inside. And only one of them could go through at a time.

"I'll go," Cruz said, stepping forward. The look of longing

Lucha had seen briefly on her face the night before was more pronounced than ever now. She was so close to what she wanted. What everyone at the camp wanted.

And that was exactly why Lucha couldn't let her inside first.

"I'm shorter," Lucha said. "It'll be easier for me to squeeze in."

"You'd be surprised what tight spaces I've gotten myself into."

"I'm sure," Lucha said, her thoughts spinning wildly. She had known a reckoning of their separate agendas was coming, but she hadn't counted on things breaking down so soon. Before they'd even dispatched the kings. Even gained the inside of the building.

Cruz's eyes, usually squinted in a sardonic expression, narrowed.

Lucha wasn't sure if she had imagined her hand twitching toward her weapon.

But before things could deteriorate further, a crashing in the bushes had them wheeling around on instinct. Standing side by side as a figure made its way to the water's edge.

"What are you doing here?" Cruz barked, recognizing the man. She lowered her long knife, but Lucha kept hers where it was.

"You thought I was gonna let you get to the Olvida first?" the man asked in a rasping voice. Lucha thought she might recognize him from camp, but there were so many faces, and it had only been a few days . . .

"Diego, don't do this," Cruz said in a low voice. "We're in

this together. Whatever I find in there comes to you all first. We split it up. That's the agreement we made."

"Save it," Diego spat. "There's no *us*, Cruz, you know that as well as anyone. Don't think I forgot where you came from. How many people you ripped off."

"That was before," Cruz said, but her tone had changed. "Now we have something good. Let's not fuck it up. Come on. We'll go in together. You can keep us honest, how about that?"

But Lucha knew better than to think Diego would be swayed by reason. She had seen his expression on her mother's face too many times. Experienced what happened after. It didn't matter how long Diego had gone without a dose of Olvida—he would do whatever it took to get it.

He proved her right a moment later, lunging at the fence. Climbing it despite the razor wire, knife in hand.

Cruz looked genuinely betrayed, and for a moment Lucha felt for her. Then she remembered she was planning to betray Cruz in the same way. She hadn't expected it to feel complicated, destroying the drug that had destroyed her family. A creation of Salvador's that had caused nothing but ruin. But it did.

"Don't make me kill you, Diego," Cruz said. "I thought—"

"You thought wrong," Diego said. And he pulled a wire cutter from his belt, snapping the razor-sharp barbs down the middle and smashing the window.

Cruz's eyes were back on Lucha now, a challenge in them. Her expression asked if Lucha would truly fight her for the honor after what she'd seen. If this alliance, like the one between Diego and the rest of them, was destined for the chopping block.

"Go," Lucha said, telling herself it hardly mattered now. "I'm right behind you."

Cruz didn't hesitate. But just before she went through the window, she glanced back at Lucha, now waiting below her.

"See you on the other side, Lucha," she said, and then she was gone.

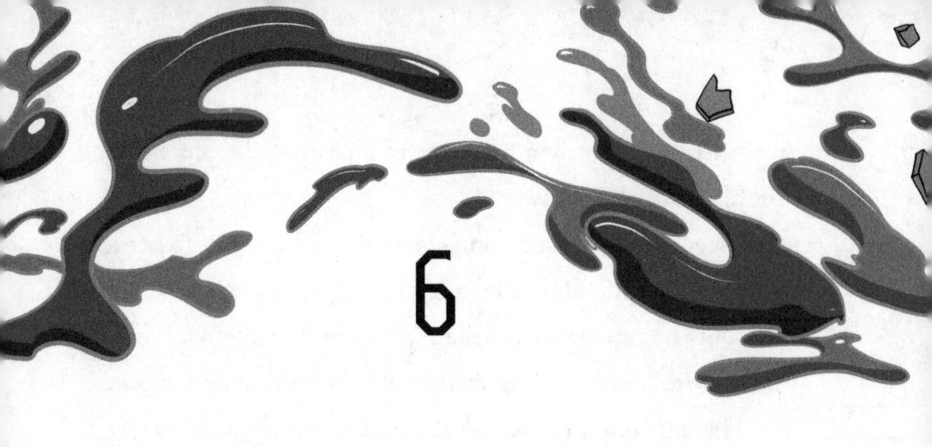

6

Lucha readied herself to climb, but just before she pulled herself up, she heard another rustling in the bushes. She whirled around. Expecting the worst—more defectors here for the Olvida, and Cruz on her own inside.

But there was nothing there.

"Show yourself!" Lucha called.

No one did.

Lucha, shaken, pulled her eyes away from the place where she'd heard the sound, wondering if she'd imagined it. It wasn't like her to be so jumpy. But as she climbed, the back of her neck prickled like there was someone watching. Even as she grasped the top of the fence.

Even as she caught her first glimpse of Pecado's crimson interior.

Launching herself through the window, Lucha freed both her knives on the way down. In her right hand, the bone blade that had been to hell and back with her. In her left, the silver blade with the goddess's blossom on the top. A gift from Paz.

The few seconds she'd taken to get inside had clearly been

eventful. Lucha took a moment to survey the scene, holding her blades at the ready.

Diego was the first person she saw, just a few feet to her left. A soldado's knife was at his throat. His eyes were wide, terrified, but the craving was in them too. The craving that had told him to break with his best chance of survival and go it alone.

The only question, Lucha thought as she swiveled her head slowly, was why the soldado hadn't already killed him.

She got her answer almost immediately. Cruz was a few feet to Lucha's right. She'd obviously been faster than Diego, because she was in the position of power here, her own knife at the throat of the soldado who'd unwisely attempted to attack her.

Before Lucha could even meet Cruz's eyes, or take in the rest of the scene, there was a man on her as well. At least a head taller than Lucha and heavily armored. He moved quickly despite his impediments, and for a moment Lucha thought it would be a real fight.

Then he saw her face.

The scarred and grizzled man—who had clearly fought many battles for Los Ricos in his career—blanched as he recognized her. Had he been in the room when she summoned Salvador in the tongue of the grave? Lucha wondered. If he had, all the better for her.

She did not need vines or demons or mushrooms to subdue him this time. His shock slowed his approach, leaving Lucha just enough room to act.

She hit him in the throat with the butt of her bone knife,

kicked him in the ribs when he fell, and placed her boot on his neck before turning to face the men who had not kept enough guards behind to defend them.

Los Ricos were rarely seen in public—they preferred to give the illusion that they lived a charmed life. Traveling the world with their money and their drugs and their girls. As a child, Lucha herself had only glimpsed them once or twice.

She remembered strong, black-bearded men with ruddy faces and cunning eyes marching through the streets as part of a parade.

But there was no way these were the same men she had seen just a few years ago. The ones now sitting in front of her were *old*. Paper-skinned and wrinkled. Their cheeks and eyes were sunken, and something vital seemed missing from their expressions. Like they were closer to the next world than this one.

Lucha thought of the Pensa plant. Shriveling and dying after Salvador's defeat. Was it connected somehow to the kings' rapid decline?

"Your Majesties," Lucha said mockingly. "We meet at last."

Their faces registered no emotion as they looked at her impassively, like men with nothing left to fear.

Scanning the room, Lucha realized with a thrill of triumph that she and the Syndicate had calculated correctly. The kings had sent everyone to the gate. They'd underestimated the citizens of Robado for the last time.

Lucha could see it then, in the eyes of Los Ricos. In the eyes of the soldados who found themselves outmatched in the last seat of their masters' power. Certainty. Holed up in this compound, these men had always assumed Olvida would keep the Robadans at heel. That their power would never falter.

But nothing in this world was certain. Lucha and the Robadans both knew that. Nothing save death, and death had come for them all today.

Lucha looked to Cruz, finding the other girl's eyes already on her. When Lucha nodded once, a sharp, ruthless gesture, Cruz did not misunderstand.

The third to last of Los Ricos' protectors slumped to the ground a mere second later, his throat open, his blood pooling at the feet of those assembled. Long seconds elapsed, and still no one spoke. No one moved. The soldado holding Diego cast frantically around for some instruction, but the men in charge seemed unwilling to give it, and he was only a soldier. He wouldn't act alone.

"We've come to right the wrongs you've perpetrated on this city," Lucha said, pleased to find her voice clear and strong. "For too long you've oppressed us, kept us sick and dependent on your money and your drugs. You call yourselves rulers of this city, but you abandoned the people when they needed you most. We no longer recognize you as *kings*." She spat at their feet. "We're here to negotiate your surrender of the city."

The man in the middle, his beard gone straggly and white, his eyes rheumy and red in their sunken sockets, made a sound then. At first, Lucha thought he was coughing, but then she realized it was laughter.

"Stupid girl," he said in a rasping, weak voice. "You can't take this city from us. It is ours by right. Given to us by the god of destruction himself. *Try* to take it. See what curse befalls you."

Cruz, Diego, and even the soldados looked utterly perplexed by these senile ramblings. But for Lucha, so much was finally falling into place.

Lucha felt more than triumph ballooning in her chest. This was joy. This was *glee.* She'd come here to destroy the men who had inherited Salvador's Olvida empire. She'd never dreamed she'd be allowed the honor of destroying the men who first allowed Salvador's temptation to claim them.

The men *responsible,* as much as Salvador himself, for all the destruction and death and addiction that had plagued Robado. That had spread around the world.

"So you understand," said the king on the left. "You understand that a mere mortal will never defeat us."

Lucha laughed, an irreverent bark that echoed through the room. "I've already done worse than defeat you," she said. "I defeated *him.*"

"Impossible," the man on the right spat. "A god cannot be defeated."

"Think again," Lucha said, increasing the pressure on the windpipe of the soldado at her feet as he began to choke and wheeze. "I was possessed by El Sediento, didn't you hear the stories? I wielded his power right in this room, killing your men. Consuming them in fungus and dying vines. I broke out of your prison and let the roots swallow the guards who chased me."

"Lies! Blasphemy!"

"And then," Lucha went on, like poison was being purged from her drop by drop, "when he betrayed me, I released him from his amber prison beneath the earth and I made sure he could never destroy anything ever again."

"Kill her!" shrieked the man in the middle. As if there were anyone left to do his bidding. To alleviate some of the horrible pressure building inside her, Lucha stepped down hard on the neck of the man lying before her. Snapping it. His spine bent at a horrible angle.

No one else dared approach her.

"Didn't you wonder what was happening to you?" Lucha asked, stepping toward them now that the man she'd guarded was dead.

She was guessing now, but she felt the rightness of it in her chest, saw it on their faces as they huddled together, pushing themselves away from her.

"Didn't you wonder why faces that hadn't aged in hundreds of years were suddenly sagging? Vitality fading away?"

"You're more wrong than you know," said the man in the middle, the spokesperson for the rest. "He's returned, girl, and now we will be gods!"

"In a few minutes," Lucha said, slowly and deliberately, "you'll be nothing. Do you understand me? I joined forces with him because he promised your destruction and *killed* him when he did not deliver it. You really think I'm going to let you live after that?"

Lucha was conscious as she spoke that Cruz knew none of

these things about her. It didn't matter. Lucha had hated these men and their drug every day of her sixteen years.

There was no choice to be made.

"Your god has failed you," Lucha said, stepping closer still. "The Olvida is gone. Your health is fading. Now you have a choice."

"You're wrong!" screamed the middle king hysterically. Spittle flew from his mouth. "He will never die! He is Death itself!"

He was so certain, Lucha half expected to see Salvador sweep through the doors of Pecado, alive and well. He, of course, did not. And so, the kings finally learned how it felt to scream for an ousted god and get no answer. There would be no rescue, no return of Salvador from his arboreal grave.

The same lesson Lucha had learned in this very room not so long ago.

"As I said," Lucha continued, "you have one choice left to make. The same choice you offered the starving, sick, desperate people of your city when you locked them out of this compound and condemned them to death."

"We will never obey you," rasped the king. "We will delight in watching him tear your flesh from your bones and consume it."

"You can die now," Lucha pressed on, a terrible stillness in her voice, "at the hands of those you've condemned. Or take your chances in the crossing."

Lucha had seen the river from the top of the fence. It was higher than she'd ever known it to be. There would be no crossing, not for men as old and weak as these. There would be only drowning.

"EL SEDIENTO!" screamed the man in the middle. "COME TO US NOW! SMITE THIS—!"

Cruz's knife was buried in his chest before he could finish. Before Lucha even saw her move. His blood dripped white from the place she had plunged it in, just like his god's had done at Lucha's hand.

When she was sure he would not rise again, Lucha looked at Cruz. She only shrugged, smirking. "You gave him a choice," she said. "It's more than I would have done."

"And the rest of you?" Lucha asked, brandishing her knife at the other two kings. At the last soldado, still clutching Diego like a lifeline.

"I'll kill him!" The soldado was young, Lucha realized. Too young to die for this. "I'll kill him if you get anywhere near me."

Lucha and Cruz exchanged a glance.

"Kill him," Cruz suggested. "He's a traitor anyway."

At this, the soldado entirely lost his head. He let go of Diego and bolted for the back door. The very same door Lucha had planned to open for anyone who chose the river crossing.

As the boy wrenched rusted metal against metal, the water—higher than the door itself—crashed in like a wave, knocking him off his feet. Knife out, Cruz followed him.

Without a word, the boy leapt into the water, swimming valiantly for three, four seconds. The current took him after that.

Once again, Lucha was surprised by the remorse she felt. She had always seen things in terms of right and wrong. In terms of choices, and what they told the world about who you were. What was a choice in a place like Robado? The same one she had offered the boy. Between dying one way and another.

The two remaining kings hadn't moved from their places. Perhaps they were too feeble to power their ancient bodies now, or perhaps they'd been shocked into silence by the downfall of a man they'd known five hundred years.

"Please," said the man on the left, as if he'd heard Lucha's thoughts. "Please, girl. Have mercy. After everything I've done . . . I can't face it . . . I was never supposed to face it . . ."

He threw himself onto the ground, his knees now wet with the milky blood of his compatriot. He cringed at Lucha's feet, his gnarled and twisted fingers reaching for her boots, his head downcast in a posture of utter supplication.

Lucha stepped away from him, revolted. "Mercy?" she asked. "You ask for mercy now? When I spent most of my childhood with an empty belly, waiting for my mother to return from a forgetting of your design? When my father *died* in a warehouse you wouldn't evacuate during a fire? Mercy." She laughed. "I don't think so."

"Girl, I beg you . . . I promise you . . ." He looked up at her now from the ground. But Lucha could barely see his expression.

"Knife or crossing?" she asked, ice in her tone. Perhaps she had felt for the boy, but there was nothing for this monster. All she could see was the blood on his hands.

"Girl, I beg you . . . I promise you . . . ," he mumbled again.

Cruz stepped up, kicking him in the ribs. He sprawled

into the white blood, which was now curdling to a sickly yellow. "She asked you a question," Cruz said calmly, kneeling beside him. "Crossing or knife?"

Desperation was clear in every line of the man's face as he looked pleadingly from Cruz to Lucha, then back to Cruz. When he found no sympathy, all the fight seemed to go out of him. His body went slack, his face losing its elasticity as he slumped to the ground.

"The crossing," he rasped, utterly defeated. "I'll let my god decide."

"Your god is dead," Lucha said.

He made no reply.

Lucha walked beside Cruz as she dragged him to the door by the scruff of his neck as if he were a disobedient dog. Outside, the water raged. Lucha waited a moment as he stood on hands and knees at the doorway. The water continued to spread across the floor, washing the blood away.

"*I'm sorry,*" Lucha thought she heard the man whisper, and then she pushed him through the door and into the water. He was lost in seconds. His god had not come.

And only one enemy remained.

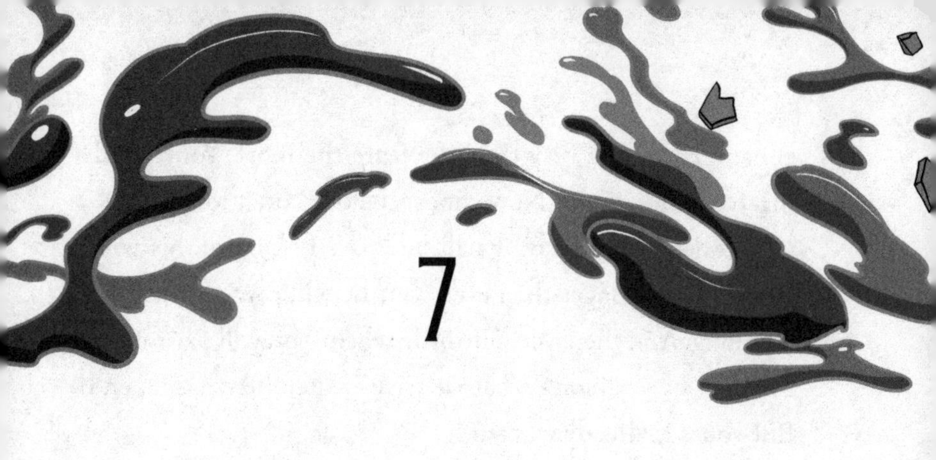

7

Lucha and Cruz expected to find the final king where they'd left him. But he stood directly behind them, gaze eerily on the place where the second had just disappeared.

Lucha started at his closeness, but recovered quickly.

"The crossing for you as well?" she asked with disdain. "Your god didn't seem to have much pity for your brother."

"You're wrong, you know," the man said. His voice was clearer than the other two's had been. His hair and beard were slate gray instead of brittle white. Of the three, he'd held on to the most of his humanity.

"I don't care what you think of my conclusions," Lucha said. "Crossing or knife?"

This last king, the only one with any regal bearing left, looked down on Lucha with his ancient eyes. "The Dark Prince will never die. He has taken a new form. He walks among us, even now."

"You lie," Lucha said as viciously as she could. She stepped forward. Unafraid. "I watched him die. Watched him be consumed by the very thing he fears the most. Your words mean nothing to me. Now choose, before I do it for you."

"When I die today, it will be a relief," he said, his voice clearer and stronger than ever. "But he will come for you before long. And then, you silly little whelp, you will pay for this moment of rebellion. What we have created here has no end. But yours is already written."

Before Lucha could reply, before Cruz could silence this arrogant monster, he stepped under his own power into the river. He didn't even bother to swim. He was lost much quicker than the others, and then the room was empty. The battle won.

Lucha strained for her moment of catharsis, but it didn't come. Not immediately, anyway.

These are the men who ruined your family, she reminded herself. *Who tortured generations of Robadans, condemned them to poverty and squalor, all for their own greed.*

Still, the relief did not come. Nor did any fizzing in her veins. Even the satisfied exhaustion of a victory hard-won evaded her.

Perhaps when you'd killed a god, she told herself, drowning three shriveled old men was bound to feel anticlimactic.

"It's over," Cruz said. But her tone reflected Lucha's unsettled feeling. "I can't believe it's over."

Lucha knew it was time to sever her connection to the Syndicate. To get to the Olvida first, wherever it was stashed, and send it to meet the same end as its creator.

But she found she couldn't. She had grown up alone, and

lived alone. Killed alone and died alone. It had only been a few days, but the feeling of belonging, of being needed, of working toward something with people who understood, was more precious than she could have imagined.

Just a moment, Lucha told herself. *Just a moment to mourn it, and then . . .*

The barred door into the compound flew open with the force of an explosion. Lucha and Cruz reached for their weapons once more, in unison, and a flood of bodies poured into the room.

It took a while for Lucha to recognize them as allies who'd fought their way up from the gate. Armando was in the front, rushing for Cruz. He was bleeding from a gash in his forehead but didn't look too much the worse for wear as he grabbed her in a bone-crushing embrace.

Miguel was behind him, borne by the arms of his fellow fighters, mud-covered and bloody but screaming in victory. "The city is ours!" he roared as more Robadans crowded through the door.

In minutes, La Casa del Pecado was filled with bodies. With roars and screams. Lucha tried not to count the dead. To discern how many they'd lost. Robado was theirs, and for a moment she let that reality, and nothing else, sustain her.

The looting began immediately, of course. What was valuable was piled onto a wagon outside. No one wanted to remain in this place. The place where so many of their own had been tortured and used and discarded.

Lucha sat back and watched. It wouldn't do to appear eager to find the Olvida when everyone with eyes was searching for it too. She would wait. She would plan. With luck, she would destroy it with no one the wiser.

If Diego's betrayal had taught her anything, it was that trust was thin. Good faith was not a given. And there were so many of them—if it disappeared, who would blame Lucha? The one person who had expressed no interest in forgetting?

As if summoned by Lucha's thoughts, the crowd parted a little then. Armando, with Cruz beside him, dragged Diego to Miguel near the door. The frantic looting stalled for a moment as Cruz spoke.

"He followed us," she said. "Said he wanted to take the Olvida for himself."

Miguel didn't ask Diego if she was telling the truth. He just drew his sword.

"But . . . Miguel . . . ," Diego spluttered against Armando's iron grip. "I was only . . . you s—"

His head hit the floor before he could manage another word. Taken clean off by Miguel's viciously sharp blade.

"Let that be a lesson to the rest of you," Miguel said, looking down at Diego's body with disgust. "Anyone who tries to cheat or steal will meet the same end."

Coincidence or not, his gaze met Lucha's across the crowd. Though she had condemned Diego to a traitor's death herself, Lucha found herself wondering what he might have said had his head stayed attached just a few more seconds.

Diego's blood pooled quickly on the floor, mingling with

the water coming in through the river door until it bloomed like a rose.

And Lucha, turning away for the moment, vowed not to underestimate Miguel.

The sacking of Pecado became a celebration the likes of which had never been seen in Robado. Maria arrived with those who had been unable to fight, kissing her brother on both cheeks and congratulating Cruz with an affection that nearly made Lucha blush—and brought Paz painfully to mind.

Los Ricos had delicacies beyond imagination stored here. Food and clean water, fermented drink from the lands across the river. There was clothing for all seasons in rich fabrics. In one of the cabinets lining the walls, they found gold bars. These things were worth more than Lucha could fathom . . . useless, now, to the men who had so coveted them.

The food and drink were consumed, anything immediately useful piled on the wagon outside. But still the Olvida remained elusive. And the longer it did, the more the tension in the room began to thicken. To sharpen. To take aim between fragile allies.

A cache of weapons was discovered, and while most were taken out to the wagon, a few remained in the hands of the broad-shouldered men Miguel had so often been in conference with. He stayed out of the action—far be it from a leader of the Syndicate to look so desperate—but their eyes returned to him frequently.

Tapestries were torn from the walls, furniture ripped apart

with knives and filthy hands. Axes and hammers were swung at walls until the celebration was more riot than jubilee. It was only a matter of time, Lucha thought, watching Miguel watching his men.

A hope bloomed in her then, so sudden it was almost painful. That the kings had used all the Olvida. That there was nothing here to find. Nothing to rend the connections they'd so tenuously built over the past days . . .

The sound of splintering wood tore Lucha from her fantasy. In the center of the room, three of Miguel's fighters had taken to smashing a massive cherry-red table—clearly harvested from some ancient tree.

How many hundreds of years had Los Ricos stood over that table? Lucha wondered as they landed blow after blow. How many plans had they made for the death and oppression and suffering of their people?

It took far longer than she would have expected for them to do any meaningful damage to it. A corner chipped here, a long gouge left in the lacquered wood there. But at last, with most of the compound watching, a mighty blow from an axe split the thing down the middle.

From a hidden compartment inside it, individually wrapped bricks of Olvida spilled onto the floor. The water now soaking the carpets didn't damage them, packaged as they were in airtight wrapping of the kings' invention. There was enough here to satisfy every person at the camp for months . . .

Or a single person for years.

Everyone in the room froze, still as a statue, for a half second. Maybe less.

And then they charged.

The celebration, the camaraderie, even the tension were gone as the frenzy swept through the room. People who had fought side by side only an hour ago now tore at one another's clothing, hair, and flesh in an attempt to reach the stash first.

Lucha's plan had never been to seize the Olvida first, so she stood some distance back, watching. Revulsion and pity overtook her. She tried not to think of her mother. Instead, she thought of Salvador. His sneering face. His plot to destroy the thing his goddess mother loved best.

Most of all, she thought of her promise to end that plot once and for all. No matter which bridges she had to burn to do it.

Once the initial shock wore off, Lucha's eyes sought the Syndicate members. She found Cruz first, standing at the edge of the fray. Her eyes were fixed hungrily on the Olvida over the writhing mass of bodies, but she didn't join them. Lucha found herself relieved, though she wasn't quite sure why.

Miguel sat on a plush sofa, watching with what appeared to be little urgency. He had taken a jacket from among Los Ricos' things. Red velvet. He looked handsome but sinister, or was that only Lucha's imagination?

A renewed ferocity seemed to come from the pit beneath the broken table. The crowd parted just long enough for Lucha to see a man she didn't recognize standing above the rest, holding a brick aloft. He seemed poised to tear into it then and there, but before he could, Miguel got to his feet at last.

"Stop," he commanded, his voice ringing through the metal building. Echoing strangely. "Vicente. Put it down."

The man, Vicente, was clearly torn between obeying Miguel and finally reaching the blissful forgetting he'd been chasing for weeks. He didn't immediately drop the brick.

"Well, I asked nicely," Miguel said sardonically. And with a quickness and grace of movement Lucha had rarely seen, he pulled a hidden knife from his coat and flicked it toward Vicente.

A moment later, the knife had buried itself in Vicente's chest. He fell to the ground, dead. The brick of Olvida slipped from his hands into the pool of river water and blood.

No one dared to reach for it.

"Now, as I recall," Miguel said, his sword drawn, the promise of more daggers beneath his coat, "we had a deal when it came to Los Ricos' stash. Does anyone remember what it was?"

No one spoke at first. Maria—the lone Syndicate member to attempt to stop the frantic Olvida grab—looked at her brother like she'd never seen him before. Cruz and Armando, eyes torn from the pile of bricks in front of them, seemed wrong-footed as well.

"We would *share*," Miguel clarified. He said the word with a sneer. "That's what you all wanted, right?" He looked to his sister. To Cruz. Finally, to Lucha. "You wanted a community where we all held hands and distributed our resources equally, right?"

Still no one answered. The room was silent save for the inexorable river outside, spilling water in through the doorway. It was inevitable, Lucha thought clinically, before one of them decided the risk of a knife through the heart was worth it. And Miguel couldn't fight them all. Not alone.

"Well, I think we've all seen the folly of *that* idea, haven't we?" he asked, stepping forward over prone Robadans, his boots making small splashes in the rising water. He reached down and picked up a brick of Olvida.

It was then that Lucha noticed his face. There was no longing when he looked at the drug. Not like there was on the faces of everyone else in this room. Whatever Miguel wanted the Olvida for, it wasn't to forget. And that made him even more dangerous.

"A little help here?" Miguel asked, his tone almost bored.

From the shadows of Pecado, at least twenty men stepped forward. Lucha recognized them immediately as the broad-shouldered bunch he'd been huddled around the fire with every night. So this was what they'd been plotting.

"My friends and I are going to gather all this up," he explained cheerfully, "and put it somewhere safe. After that, we'll decide how to divvy it up. Anyone have a better idea? I'm sure Vicente down there could use some company."

As he stood with his men—each armed with a fearsome-looking weapon—there was no thought of resisting. All they could do was watch helplessly as Miguel's men did exactly as he'd promised.

Lucha, for her part, was almost relieved. Before, the path ahead had been shrouded. Now it was clear as day. Her goal in coming here had not changed, and if she had to go through Miguel to accomplish it—so much the better.

8

The Olvida was piled in the center of camp—a temptation and a reminder. It was patrolled at all times by Miguel or his men.

He tried to pretend nothing had changed. He invited the other Syndicate members to weigh in on the food, the infirm, the structures. What to do with the bodies. But the Olvida was his sole domain, and it was on this that everyone fixated.

Most, of course, wanted a dose. But even those who didn't recognized the power wielded by whoever controlled it.

Paranoia had taken the place of exhaustion. The trust was gone, along with the camaraderie. Every glance was tense and suspicious. Every meal was eaten in silence—and only eaten at all because Maria had encouraged the foragers to keep up their work.

Not all of them had. But the two señoras and Junio from Lucha's original group went dutifully every morning. *For the children,* she'd heard the ladies whispering, and her heart had nearly broken.

Even Lucha, who had come here for the express purpose

of destroying this awful stuff, was amazed by how quickly its presence corrupted everything around it. This fact only strengthened her resolve. The kings were dead, but her job wasn't finished.

It had been three days of nonstop rain. Everything was mud and misery.

Lucha waited, staying apart from the action, not sure whether she could trust Maria or Cruz enough to ally herself with them—but not sure she could avoid it, either. She looked for signs of resistance to Miguel when she could afford to be seen looking.

The Olvida was a wild card. Maria seemed to ignore it entirely; she focused only on keeping the children fed, the wounded cared for, the camp in order despite the relentless rain. She scarcely approached her brother at all, but Lucha couldn't tell if that was to quell her own desire for the drug, or because she disagreed with his methods.

Cruz was more inscrutable. She and Armando hadn't broken their attachment; he still followed her like a knight protecting his queen. But Cruz hadn't approached the Olvida or Miguel, and Lucha had seen her whispering with Armando more than once.

If there was an alliance to be made, Lucha thought, they both had their pros and cons.

Maria might still be too attached to her brother.

And Cruz might still be too attached to Olvida.

But in the end, the only ally Lucha needed was the cursed salt river. It had been three days of nonstop rain. Treating wounds was almost impossible. The children were half feral. Miguel still hadn't kept his promise to share the drugs.

Last night, someone had finally broken. Rushed the guards with a weapon.

His body was buried a few yards into the trees. At least the wet soil made for easy digging. The river was swelling so quickly that Lucha imagined the bodies in the housing units washing away on the same flood that had killed so many of them.

The Olvida was rationed at Miguel's discretion. He claimed he only wanted to make sure things were fair, to make sure they didn't run out before they could discover the process by which more could be made.

It was this task that consumed his days, and those of his men. Unrest built like pressure beneath the earth, destined to explode sooner or later. There was no denying that Miguel's favored men "earned" their Olvida faster than anyone else in the camp—and even then he doled it out in doses so small that what it mostly did was make people restive.

Lucha could see his game. The moment it ran out, he would have nothing to hold over their heads. This benevolent dealer bit would only last so long. The tension was so thick Lucha felt as though she were choking on it half the time.

But watching them so closely, she found something that gave her hope: There were people, far more than she would have expected, that chose not to return to the cycle. That guarded their newfound freedom from it and refused Olvida.

They fell quickly from Miguel's graces, as he had no reliable means to control them, and Lucha took heart.

Her plan built slowly over the first few days. She thought she'd whisper in the ears of the guards. Get them to revolt. Take the Olvida in the chaos. It would take time, she knew, but without allies, she had few options.

Lucha was sleeping fitfully on the fifth night when she was awoken by screams, and she knew before she opened her eyes that this was it. The only chance she'd get. Whatever the distraction was, she had to use it.

It didn't take long to discover the source. She was ankle-deep in it before she'd fully shaken off her dreams. The river was flooding. The rain was still pissing down. And this was Lucha's moment.

In the camp, there was chaos. Lucha's eyes, much as she resented them for delaying her purpose, went first to the wounded. The children. The foragers. Maria had them well in hand, to her immense relief. Everyone—despite the proximity of the Olvida—was making for the trees. The dry ground up the hill.

It made sense, she supposed. Most of them had lost loved ones in the last flood. It had only been a few weeks. The water was a greater enemy than Miguel and his men. Than even the superstitions that had kept them out of the forest all these years.

They did not want to drown, and Lucha was pleased that their instinct for self-preservation was stronger than their desire for the drug.

Cruz must have been helping Maria, and Armando with her, because Lucha didn't see them anywhere. Which left only one member of the Syndicate in the camp. Lucha made her way toward where she knew he would be, her hair trailing wet behind her, her knives at the ready.

All over, people scrambled for their meager possessions as wave after wave of water came from the river. The salt seeping into the soil that already could grow nothing. The mud so deep and thick it was more likely to break an ankle than not.

And in the center, Miguel, still in the red velvet jacket, though it was soddened from the rain. His men—half of them slack-jawed from Olvida—trying desperately to round up the drugs. But the water was rising too fast, and there weren't enough of them.

Lucha slunk to the tree line, trusting the sheets of rain to disguise her. They had already lost an open brick to the water. As she watched, one of the men was taken out by a surge of salt water, swept away. There were only five of them. Four and Miguel. Everyone else was headed for the trees.

In her hands, Lucha examined her knives. The bone and the silver. The past and the future. Hopefully, she wouldn't have to use them, but even if she did . . . this was the only chance she was going to get.

The first man to see her started as he tried to shove Olvida bricks into his shirt. He lunged for his weapon as she made to tackle him into the water.

"Don't," she pleaded with him. "It's not worth it. Just leave it and run."

He hesitated, just for a moment; then his fingers tightened on the weapon and he jumped for her. Lucha's knife was faster. She twisted around his body, went for the back of the knee to slow him. He dropped the bricks, his eyes wide with fear.

"Run," she said. "Please."

This time, he did. As he hobbled through the water, relief took Lucha by surprise. She had once thought of all olvidados as the enemy, but she knew these people. She had built community with them, shared food and hope with them. Fought alongside them. She wouldn't kill more of them than necessary to save her life and achieve her purpose.

The next two men she encountered were already dead. One had drowned. The other's blood bloomed on the water. Lucha wondered if he'd tried to use this distraction for his own purposes. If Miguel had killed him for it.

She would find out soon, she thought grimly. Miguel was just ahead in the knee-high water, still struggling to secure the drug. His expression was murderous, furious, but there was no fear in it.

The last of his lackeys looked down at the rising water. At the bodies of his dead friends. He ran as Lucha approached, and she let him. Hopefully, he would join the others. Survive the night.

And still Miguel didn't turn to look at her. Didn't even seem to realize. He had been suspicious of her, but he had never considered her a true threat. He would pay for that, Lucha thought, as those before him had.

"Where is everyone?" Miguel cried, still focused entirely

on the Olvida threatening to float away. Scrambling to hold it all. "You idiots, get over here and help me with this! Don't you know what will happen if we lose it?"

Another wave came from the river. That punishing salt water that had taken so much from Robado. From Lucha. She weathered it, but what little Olvida he had managed to secure was scattered again, sinking or floating. Its waterproof wrapping holding . . . for now.

"They're gone," Lucha said, approaching him with the rain streaming down her face. "It's just you and me now." At last, he turned to face her.

"Good," he snapped. "Help me gather all this. I'll cut you in, give you drugs, supplies, whatever you want." He sounded sure that she would accept, but he didn't turn his back on her again.

"I told you, I don't want your drugs," Lucha said, stepping closer, the water sloshing at her knees. "I don't want the power you bought with them."

"Then what do you want?" Miguel asked, an edge of desperation in his voice now. "Whatever it is, it's yours. Just help me."

"There's only one thing I want," Lucha said. She felt removed from her body, as if watching the scene from above. Stalking through the rain. The swollen river on her side for once. Miguel, who had not even drawn his weapon—his hands too busy reaching for Olvida.

Lucha took her knife and stabbed it into the closest brick, tearing it open, letting the powder inside merge, harmless now, with the water rising to their thighs.

"What are you doing?" Miguel screamed. He lunged at

her, but the water made him slow. She kicked him square in the chest and sent him splashing into the salt.

Lucha cut open another brick.

Miguel staggered to his feet and made for her again. This time she stepped forward, grabbing him by the hair, turning him so her knife was at his throat.

"I'll kill you!" he shouted, out of his mind with anger and panic.

Lucha would have laughed if it hadn't all been so sad. It seemed more likely, of course, that she would kill him. And she thought about it for a long moment. But it wasn't her place to pass this ultimate judgment on Miguel or his men. She only had one job here, and he couldn't stop her from doing it.

"The way I see it, you have two choices," she growled in his ear. "The time of Olvida is over. The time of men lording over us, using our desires as weapons, is over. Stay here, help us build something that will last, or leave us be."

"And if I choose neither?" Miguel growled.

Lucha sliced into his neck then, just deep enough to make her point, and kicked him into the water. Away from the place where Maria had taken the Robadans. Toward La Casa del Perdido and the barren land east of it.

He turned to face her, bleeding, wide-eyed. Choking on salt water.

"It's up to you," Lucha said, holding her knife ready to throw. She could almost see where his heart was beating beneath his sopping shirt. "Stay or go. Choose now."

"You're making a big mistake," Miguel called over the

rushing water. The punishing rain. "Without the drug, they'll never follow you. They'll never respect you. It's the only thing they want." And then he turned and ran.

Lucha watched him go, waves coming more frequently now from the river. Some of the Olvida bags had opened on their own. Some had sunk. The camp was entirely deserted, and soon there would be no way to get back without risking the current.

She took a brick in her hands, holding it as the water rose. It was more Olvida than she'd ever been close to. Lydia, for all her faults, had at least kept the drug itself out of the house—and this was more than she could have afforded in a lifetime.

Lucha dug her fingernails into the thin, waxed wrapping until it tore. The wind kicked up, the rain slashing sideways at her face. There was a dreamlike quality to the way the particles trickled out. Mixing immediately with the rain. Lucha watched clinically, still feeling raised above the scene.

Fewer than ten bricks of Olvida were left intact. It seemed impossible that her quest to destroy the last remnant of Salvador in this world could be wrapped up so neatly . . .

But that wouldn't stop her from trying.

The rain, impossible as it seemed, came down harder than ever as Lucha tore the brick in her hands apart. Nine more, including the ones she could just see beneath the water.

If she hurried, she could do it without drowning. And then she would be free.

When she heard the voice behind her, Lucha's first thought was that she should have known it couldn't be so easy. She would have ignored it, come what might, if she hadn't felt the point of a knife at the back of her neck.

"I said *what are you doing?*" Cruz repeated.

Over the sound of the rain, Lucha hadn't heard her come closer. Now it was Lucha who had a choice to make, options to weigh. She could continue to slash the Olvida bricks open, knowing it was possible Cruz would kill her—or she could turn the knife on Cruz instead. Fight. Potentially lose.

"You should be in the woods with the others," Lucha said. "The water's rising."

The point of the knife dug in deeper. "Give me the Olvida," Cruz said through clenched teeth.

"I can't do that."

"You don't even want it," Cruz said, her voice halfway between frustrated and persuasive. "I know an olvidado when I see one, and you've never taken a dose in your life. So what is it? The power? You want to take over for the kings? Make us all bow down like Miguel?"

Reason left Lucha at the thought. She turned, surprising even herself, and shoved Cruz, hard, sending her sprawling into the now-waist-deep water. The Olvida brick she'd been holding was still in her hand.

"Don't," Lucha said, chest heaving as Cruz resurfaced. "Don't ever accuse me of that. I'm trying to *free* all of you, not hold your chains."

Instead of replying, Cruz tackled her. She was shockingly fast, even in the water. Lucha didn't have time to brace herself. The salt water swallowed her, and if Cruz had held her under, she would have drowned. But she didn't. She went for the brick instead.

Lucha broke the surface of the water, gasping, hair streaming down her back.

Cruz was standing in front of her, holding the brick. She looked at it like it was a key to a better world. But she didn't know the truth.

"You heard us at Pecado, right?" Lucha called. "The kings and me. Talking about their god."

"Nothing you say to me is going to matter," Cruz said to the brick as the waves continued to pour in. Filling the camp. Destroying what they'd built.

"You call him El Sediento," Lucha said. "But his name was Salvador. And he's the one who created Olvida. He made it for the sole purpose of destroying this world."

"I don't care, Lucha!" Cruz said over the rain. "I don't care who made it, or why. It's my reason for living. It's the only thing that keeps it all at bay. I want it so much that you can't beat me, do you understand that? Because I'd rather die than give it up."

"You can't beat me," Lucha said, holding her hands up in surrender. "Because I already won."

This got Cruz's attention. She tore her eyes from the brick at last. "What are you talking about?"

"I came back here to destroy this drug once and for all, Cruz. I destroyed its creator. Why do you think all the Pensa plants died? I promised myself I'd see an end to it before I even began to think about what my life would look like after."

Cruz looked gobsmacked by this revelation. "You . . . ," she managed. "It was because of you?"

"Because I killed the most evil being that has ever called this world home," Lucha confirmed. "And I'd do it again in a second."

"Then you used all of us," Cruz said, her shock making way for more anger. "Took advantage of our hospitality and stabbed us all in the back."

"Maybe that's true. But now the kings are dead and gone," Lucha continued. "And the five-hundred-year-old knowledge of how to make Olvida is gone with them."

"The plants will come back," Cruz snarled. "We'll figure out a way to make it again—we're already working on it."

Lucha faced her, dripping wet, conviction building in her. She was almost glad she wouldn't have to leave without someone understanding what she'd done here. That there would be one witness.

"I came here to cut these bricks open and dump them in the river," she said. Holding nothing back. "I lied to you all to do that, yes. It's been my goal since before I even knew it. I let El Sediento *possess* me, I threatened the fate of the entire world for this. No matter what alliance we've struck these past few days, that comes first."

"So one of us dies, then," Cruz said. "That's the only way."

"No," Lucha said. "It's not. Because if I walk away right now, I'm only leaving you to do the job for me."

"What the hell are you talking about?" Cruz said, wiping the blood from her nose on her sodden sleeve. "If you think you're going to use some forest witchery to trick me into—"

"No," Lucha said again, impatient. "I won't have to. You won't dump the drugs, I know that. I'm not stupid either. But you will use them, won't you? Pass them around to whoever's left after the flood?"

"It's the right thing to do."

"And then what?" Lucha said. "Trust that everything won't devolve into a bloodbath the second it's in play? Didn't you see what happened with Miguel?"

Cruz was quiet.

"But maybe you're different, Cruz, maybe you pass it all out equally. Do what the kings could never do. Keep folks from getting sick or going too far."

"Why not?" Cruz asked, indignant.

"Why not indeed," Lucha said. "But then you start using. You and a lot of other people. And there's no way to replenish the stash, of course. Not with the warehouses flooded and the plant dead. Not with the kings gone and El Sediento feeding the roots of the tree I left him in."

"Get to the point," Cruz growled.

"Every dose that goes into an arm, or a leg, or a neck, or a face, is one less dose of Olvida in the world, Cruz. Within a matter of months, it will be like you dumped it all in the river yourself."

Another silence. Longer this time.

"But instead of a group of clear-minded folks with a common goal, the rest of the Robadans will be worse off than ever. No one will forage, or farm, or clean, or tend to the sick. Everyone will grow increasingly desperate until they all start killing one another over the dust that's left. Mass withdrawals will return worse than ever, and there'll be no one to care."

Lucha pushed her soaking-wet hair out of her face, making sure Cruz could see her eyes.

"And then, one day, maybe a month from now, maybe a year, depending on how hard you work to control it, the last dose will go in the last wound, Cruz. Olvida *will* be gone for good." Lucha turned around, aware that she was opening herself up for attack.

Cruz did not take advantage of her vulnerability. Not yet.

"So take it," Lucha said, gesturing to the brick in Cruz's hands. The two still visible in the water. "They're all up the hill—Maria, the survivors. Bring it to them, get them all sick. Get sick yourself. Ruin everything you fought to build here. Like I said, I won before we even started."

"So why even try to dump it?" Cruz shouted, the water at her chest now. "Why not just let us use it all up?"

"Because I care!" Lucha shouted back, realizing it as the words met the space between them. "Because I lived here my whole life and watched my mom die and my sister get close and everyone who had a fighting chance waste away. Because I've looked into the lifeless eyes of the reason that drug exists, and before we took the compound, I saw hope of a world beyond it for the first time."

There was something raw and vulnerable in Cruz's eyes as she waited for what came next.

"I saw a community," Lucha said. "The thing I've wanted for longer than I ever wanted to destroy these bastards, or that drug. And if you take these bricks up that hill, it'll be gone in one night. By the time you sober up again—if you live that long—I'll be gone, and this will be over. So if that's what you want, then go. I won't risk my life stopping you."

For a moment, Lucha thought she had gambled and lost.

Every muscle in Cruz's body seemed to strain toward the drug she craved. Her expression said that had she not been free of forgetting for this long—for even one day less—she might have gone. Taken the bricks. Left Lucha in this rising water with her regrets.

But she didn't.

Her eyes met Lucha's, that vulnerable, naked emotion in them again. "It was all true, then?" she asked, as if the words were being torn from her throat. "What you said to Los Ricos? The death of El Sediento?"

Lucha knew this was a time to move carefully. That any misstep could send Cruz over the knife's edge she was balanced so carefully on.

"It's true," she said. "When I escaped from Encadenar, when I fled Robado, I followed *his* instructions to reach the place where he was buried by Almudena. I fought him there with power she granted me. He's gone and the plants are gone with him."

Cruz looked as if she was ready to protest. But there was a hopelessness eclipsing her desperation.

"And you're certain it won't return?" she asked, her voice hollow. The rain seemed to slow to make sure she was heard. "It won't grow again. Not here or anywhere else."

Lucha wasn't. How could someone be sure about something like that?

"Los Ricos were chosen by El Sediento when he was still a god," she said carefully. "Olvida was created five hundred years ago. They've been here all that time. Making it. Distributing it. Spreading his destruction and discord around the world exactly as he intended." Lucha took a deep, shaky breath. Remembering. "I know him, Cruz, maybe better than anyone. He would have left them with every contingency to ensure production didn't stop. If they couldn't bring it back in all that time . . ."

Cruz was silent. Her face said she was trying to integrate the possibility that the escape she'd been chasing her whole life was closed off to her forever.

Lucha let the silence stretch, remembering her mother. The way she'd chosen forgetting again and again. The way her sojourns in that other world had taken her away from everything she loved. Everyone who counted on her.

Olvida lied by nature. With every promise. With every seductive whisper. But that didn't make the hope it offered any less powerful. The hope that you could transcend what you'd been born to suffer. That you could control the life you were given, instead of letting the world make you small.

Perhaps for the first time, feeling her way into Cruz's conflict as the water rose in these ruined woods, Lucha understood what her mother had been chasing. Why it had been so important. Why she had never been able to stop—no matter what was waiting for her in the world where she belonged.

"I understand," Lucha said to Cruz, emotion in her throat.

"I know what it's like to want something so much there's nothing you won't do to get it. No one you won't betray. I know what it's like to want to lose yourself in something that makes you feel powerful. And free."

"You *don't* know," Cruz snarled. "You've never taken a dose in your life. You don't know what it feels like to need it this badly."

For a moment, Lucha felt as if she were back in her cell in Encadenar. Surrounded by metal walls. Buried so deep beneath the earth that no one could hear her screaming her throat raw.

She remembered Salvador appearing to her then, his face gently illuminated. As if he were a tunnel through the metal and the earth. A way out. She remembered his power flaring to life and, later, Almudena's filling her veins like liquid gold.

Even now, she could feel the ache in her chest where it had once been. That limitless power. That eternal connection.

"You don't have to believe me," Lucha said, unsure if the rain would wash her words away. "But I promise you, I do."

The rain was the only sound for a long moment. Cruz appeared frozen, letting it wash over her as she stared down at the choice in front of her.

"I don't know how to live without it," she whispered. Lucha thought she saw tears gathering in her eyes. "I don't know how to accept the world as it is without the chance to break free. To escape. How does *anyone* live through it?"

"You don't live through it," Lucha said, feeling her own remembered hopelessness ebb. "You work to make it better."

Cruz scoffed. "It's not that simple."

"It isn't," Lucha conceded. "But I imagine there's a year's worth of doses here, tops—even if you keep it all for yourself. So it's this or going through it all again as soon as it's gone. The withdrawal. The hopelessness. All of it."

Cruz's face was carved from stone, impenetrable.

"It's your choice, Cruz."

And Lucha turned, sloshing through the water toward the hill where the remaining Robadans had gathered. She didn't look back, because it didn't matter. What she had told Cruz was right. The end of Olvida had arrived. What Cruz chose to do about it was up to her.

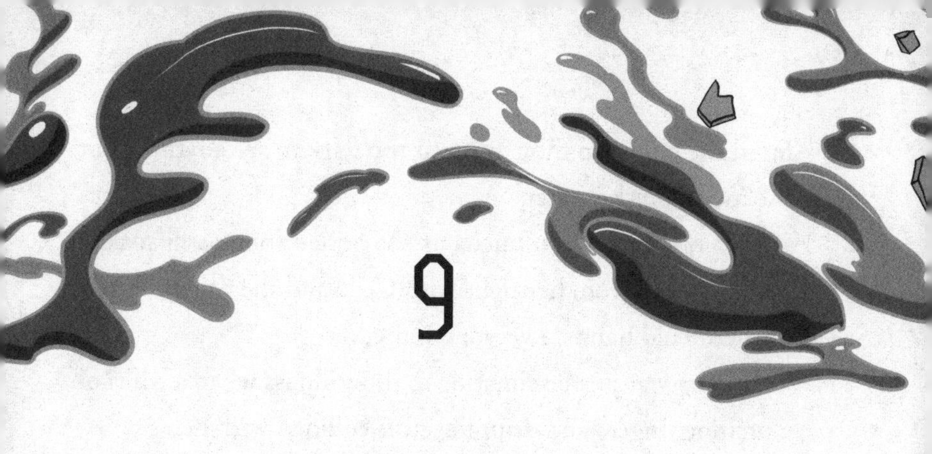

9

Lucha had walked a mile into the woods before she realized she didn't know where she was going. Her thoughts were filled with Paz, the luxury of thinking of her no longer foreign now that her goal had been achieved.

She could feel Paz's bright heart as if a tether attached her to it. Tugging from the other side of the fathomless forest. Waiting for her to return. Lucha had promised herself so many times that she would, as soon as this was done.

Only, things weren't so simple. Lucha hadn't planned on the attachment she felt to the remaining villagers. To Robado itself. Half her mind still lingered in the drowning city. With Cruz and the brick and the forked road in front of her.

Lucha didn't tell her feet to turn, but they did. It felt like dragging herself into wakefulness from a very sweet dream. One she knew could never keep her. She made her way to the gathering of Robadans atop the forest hill, looking down into the city.

The atmosphere among the survivors was utter shock. No one slept but the children. The adults stood together. They faced the city even though it was too dark to see anything but the moon on the water.

No one reacted to Lucha as she joined them, still soaked and bloodied from her fight with Cruz and the others. A few of them held hands. Everyone waited.

Lucha was just acclimating to the stillness when a whirl of clutching fingers and dripping curls collided with her.

"Where is he?" asked a voice, half sobbing. "Where is my brother? Is he alive?"

Maria, Lucha realized after a particularly emphatic shake of the young woman's head revealed her desperate face.

"Someone said you were with him. Where is he?"

Lucha felt like she'd lived four lifetimes today. She forced herself back into the memory of her conflict with Miguel reluctantly.

"When I saw him, he was alive," she said in as calming a tone as she could muster. "His men weren't so lucky. I gave him a choice—to stay and help us rebuild, or to leave us. You can probably guess which one he chose."

"No." Maria ran to the closest point on the hill to peer over it, as if she hoped Miguel would climb up any minute. That he'd changed his mind. Lucha had spent enough time herself waiting for someone who was lost; she knew not to intrude.

In here, the trees protected them from the worst of the rain. She didn't take her eyes off the place where she knew Robado was. The place where she'd left Cruz with their destiny in her hands.

The night passed. The rain subsided, clouds clearing to

show the moon at its highest point. Few of them slept. The Robadans watched their city for signs of life. Lucha watched for signs of Cruz. The Olvida. The fate of this place, as well as her own.

No one was gratified until predawn had begun to brighten the sky. Lucha heard it first. Footsteps through the trees. Her hands were on her knives before the silhouette made itself visible, and by then it was too late anyway. Maria was flying past Lucha, and before long she was half dragging a bedraggled Cruz into the small crowd.

Lucha kept her distance, looking for the signs she'd seen in her mother so many times. A haziness in her eyes, an indistinctness to her words. New wounds to join her ladder of scars. She found none of these. Cruz's face was wan, pinched with exhaustion, dark circles ringing her eyes. She looked as though she'd been through hell—but perhaps not through forgetting.

Hating the hope that swelled in her chest, Lucha stepped forward with the rest, pressing toward this one tired girl like cold hands reaching for a fire.

A few of them whispered names of loved ones lost in the flood. A good many more of them spoke the name of their drug. Their solace.

"It's gone," she heard Cruz say in a hoarse voice to Maria. "All the Olvida is gone."

Cruz met Lucha's eyes over the heads of the others, briefly, then looked away again.

"Miguel is gone, and I tried to salvage it, but the water

was too high, and the bricks were breaking open, and . . ." She trailed off, looking so miserable Lucha thought they'd have to believe her. "And there's no more. We searched all night. There's nothing left."

Everyone was exhausted, but the news spread quickly anyway. In whispers first, then in panic. Lucha, tired as she was, became instantly vigilant. Anger would follow the panic, at least for some, and they would need to be ready.

There were twenty-five people on the hill, she estimated, not including the children. Cruz and Maria were allies, at least for now, but the three of them could still be easily overwhelmed if the Robadans misplaced their grief.

"What do you mean, Miguel is gone?" called a man near the back of the group. He drew a staff with a rusted saw blade at its end. "I'm sure he has the Olvida. He'll know what to do."

Lucha's temper flared, and she stood taller, turning to look at him. "Miguel is *gone*," she said. "He knew where to find you. If he'd really wanted to, he would have. We need to move forward without him."

The man was easily a head taller than Lucha. His eyes were small and narrowed in an angular face. It was an expression that said he intended to find an outlet for this anger, and soon. Lucha doubted the speech she'd given Cruz in the water would work on him.

"I'll give you the same choice I gave him," Lucha said, trying to sound braver than she felt. "You can accept that the Olvida is gone, stay and help us rebuild, or you can seek your fortunes elsewhere."

The man stepped forward. The crowd parted for him. In two long strides, he was face to face with Lucha.

"There is no Robado without Olvida, you stupid girl," he said, and he spat at her feet. "The city's purpose *is* Olvida. It's our trade. It's our escape. It's our life. Without that, you have nothing, and I'm not gonna stay and watch it fall apart."

Maria and Cruz drew weapons then, stepping up beside Lucha. A few joined the man, looking ill disposed to listen to a lecture on unity. The majority stood listless, lost, staring between the two groups as if they didn't understand.

"There's nothing left to fight over!" Cruz shouted. "So stop this. You looked to the Syndicate to guide you before, so listen to us now. Fighting won't bring the Olvida back. All we can do now is look forward. Maybe it's true that there wasn't any Robado without Olvida, but that doesn't mean there can't be."

"Think of the children," Maria said in her soothing voice. "The wounded. The people this city has failed at every turn. We owe them something better than a bloodbath. I don't know if my brother is dead or if he left of his own free will, but it doesn't matter. We're the ones left."

The man spat again. It splattered the toes of Maria's boots. "I won't stay here singing campfire songs with a bunch of useless women," he said. "I'm going to find Miguel. He promised us Olvida, he wouldn't let us down." He turned to the rest of the crowd. "And if any of you have any sense, you'll join me."

He stared menacingly down at the three of them. Lucha knew that the loss of a strong, able-bodied fighter wasn't a small one, considering what was ahead of them. But what could she say? If he stayed, he'd only continue looking for something to rebel against.

When no one spoke, he scoffed again, stalking off into the trees.

The real blow came when almost all the rest of the fighter types followed him. Lucha didn't know them personally, had only known them to be folks who favored Miguel's style of leadership, but panic set in nonetheless. Even with the few people left, they would need hunters. Fighters. Defenders. They would need strong backs to build shelters and to move them when the water came.

With Miguel and his followers long gone, a dismal silence settled among the remaining crowd. Lucha herself had planned to leave. To make for the sanctuary, regroup. Decide what her life would look like now that her job was done.

Only, she didn't feel any longer that her job was done. Miguel had fled the city rather than help them. Anyone with a lick of survival instinct would run. Lucha knew that. She had accomplished what she'd come to. She had killed the kings and destroyed the last of Salvador's poison.

Did she owe Robado more?

Looking around at them, she found it didn't matter if she owed them more. She didn't want to leave them like this. She didn't want to leave . . .

"Thank you," Lucha said to all of them. "Thank you for staying. I know this isn't what we were hoping for, but remember that Olvida was part of Los Ricos' Robado. We needed it to hide from the horrible reality of living under their rule.

Now that they're gone, the city is ours. We can make whatever we want out of it."

For a long moment, there was quiet. Everyone was still miserable and wet. But there was hope, Lucha realized, on a few of their upturned faces.

Not all of them. But enough.

"There were a few folks waiting out the rain on a hill east of here," Cruz said, a bit more strength in her hollow voice now. "Armando is down in the city with them, seeing what can be saved. I say we do our best to scrounge up a meal, and we help them out. Who's with me?"

It wasn't a rousing response, but there were nods. Handshakes. People woke their children and gathered what remained of their belongings. A tugging at Lucha's shirt revealed Junio, dirt smeared across his face.

"I can get the food," he said. "I know what to look for."

Lucha's heart broke a little when she noticed he was missing a front tooth. He should have been allowed to be a child—but here he was, more of a man at six than Miguel, who had left them all to drown.

Before Lucha could overcome her emotions to answer, the two older women who had gone foraging with them the first day approached.

"We'll take him," one of them said. "We know what to look for too."

Everyone was wrong about what made a hero, Lucha thought as the three of them made their way into the dripping trees. She had fought the forces of destruction with divine power. She felt the ghost of it every day, aching in her chest. And still she felt she had never been so heroic as these two women, overcoming their exhaustion to make a meal.

The water had receded by the time they reached the city, but the mud was more treacherous than even the currents had been.

Armando and a few Robadans from the other hill were hard at work laying scraps of wood in paths around the muck, clearing out an area for a fire, constructing lean-tos for shelter. No one spoke much, but everyone took up a task.

Lucha was doing her best to salvage the loot from the compound when Cruz approached.

"I want to talk to you," she said. She still looked miserable, but her eyes were clear. Lucha wondered what it had cost her to tear open that last brick. Where she had found the will.

Lucha straightened up, depositing a mud-caked sword on the makeshift sledge she'd been pulling through the mud. She gave Cruz her full attention.

"I did what you asked, but that doesn't mean I trust you. You lied to us. You betrayed us. That doesn't just go away."

Lucha nodded. "I understand. But for what it's worth, I appreciate what you did out there. I know it couldn't have been easy."

"We're not talking about that," Cruz said, pushing her short hair off her face, revealing tattoos winding their way up her neck. "Listen, I've spent my whole life here. I have nowhere else to go. I decided to stay. Rebuild. But these people . . . they're looking up to us. To you. So if you have some secret agenda, or you're gonna flit back off to wherever you went before, it would be better to do it now, before anyone starts to rely on you."

The expression on Cruz's face was angry, of course, but there was something vulnerable in it too. Something that made Lucha feel she owed her this honesty. Or as much of it as she could offer, anyway.

"I never meant to stay," she confessed. "I thought I'd come in and do some noble thing. Free the place where I was trapped for so long so I could find some closure and then go on to whatever was next."

Cruz furrowed her brow. "You hear yourself, right?" she asked. "Talking about us like we're animals you're saving from cages or something? We're people, Lucha, like you. We didn't need you to save us from the ability to make choices for ourselves."

Lucha felt the impact of these words mingle with the realizations she'd made since she came here. When she didn't kill Miguel or his men. When she gave Cruz the freedom to do what she would with the Olvida.

"You're right," she said. "I've had to make all the decisions for my whole life. Just to survive. It's been my job to try to save people from themselves . . . But thinking about everyone like that . . . it's not fair. I'm sorry."

Cruz's posture softened a little; her expression relaxed. "I get it," she said. "We all have shit we learned to do to survive that doesn't work anymore. But if you want to be here, be here *with* us, not for us. Be here because we all want the same thing."

Cruz was gone before Lucha could respond, leaving her in the mud, thoroughly humbled. The world wasn't always a fight between good and evil, she thought. She'd have to release the part of her that believed it was. But could she stay? Could she do what Cruz asked and be a part of this for the long term? What about Lis?

What about Paz?

The other girl flooded Lucha's thoughts then, so real it was like she was actually there. The shape of her body, the scent of her hair, the way her eyes lit up when she smiled.

Lucha's heart ached to return to her, but Paz wasn't a destination. She was part of a whole. To return to her meant to return to Asilo. To Lis. To the acolytes who would never see her as the person she felt like now, digging in the mud half a mile from where she was born.

Her eyes strayed to the trees, the forest where she and Paz had discovered each other, and lingered there.

Lucha didn't feel that now was the time to make permanent decisions, but she knew in that moment that she couldn't go back. That her heart was telling her to stay here. To discover who she could be if she was part of something—not some shining example of good, held above everyone else, but really part of something.

Her determination shredded her impulse to go where things were easy. Where she was sure she would be cared for and loved. Regretful tears hit the mud at her feet, where nothing would ever grow. But she stayed.

The foragers came back as the afternoon sun was drying

the topmost layer of mud to a crust. Lucha, stomach growling loudly, looked up hopefully before her heart sank.

There was one basket between them, and it was only half full.

Junio ran ahead of the señoras, a crease on his smooth child's forehead.

"The tubers are all gone!" he cried when he reached Lucha, holding up one of the desiccated plants for her perusal. The vivid green leaves had gone pale as death, wrinkled and listless. The tuber itself was shriveled, tough and inedible.

With all the rain that had fallen, it made no sense.

"And there were no rabbits, either!" Junio was saying now. "All we found were berries and greens."

Lucha, her heart sinking like a stone, reached out to ruffle his hair. "Then we'll have a salad," she said. "And tomorrow I'll go with you. See if we can find anything useful."

Junio appeared heartened by this. He ran back to the señoras with a spring in his step. Lucha, on the other hand, held the dead tuber in her hand and turned her gaze back to the trees, now swaying ominously beneath gathering clouds.

She had a feeling they hadn't seen an end to their problems yet.

10

The following weeks did little but prove Lucha's suspicions right. The tubers did not revive, and within a few days it was as if they'd never grown there at all.

Thankfully, the rabbits returned, but they learned to avoid the forest around the city as their numbers dropped, forcing hunters to range farther and farther into the woods to bring home enough. Food was a constant struggle, especially with only five able-bodied Robadans who weren't needed elsewhere and dozens of mouths to feed.

Lucha went with the hunting party most days, and she was disturbed by what she saw in the more distant groves—though she kept her fears to herself for now. The landscape of the forest was changing, and fast. She barely recognized anything anymore. The plants she had so relied on during her last trek were different, or gone, and new invasive species were taking over in their place.

Today, Lucha had come upon a grove that looked burned, or eaten through by some corrosive liquid. She'd sent the others back. Morale was the only thing suffering worse than their food stores. They couldn't take more bad news, and there was no doubt that was what this signaled.

"Anything?" Cruz asked when Lucha returned from the woods alone, a paltry three rabbits on her belt.

Lucha shook her head. "Not enough."

Cruz sighed, falling into step beside her. They had reached a grudging truce in the weeks since the flood. With most of the camp hungry and in low spirits, they had precious few people to share the burden of leadership with. Lucha still didn't trust Cruz, not entirely, and she was sure the feeling was mutual. But they carried on.

"Maria?" Lucha asked as they made their way through knots of people huddled around fires, hanging clothes on makeshift lines.

Cruz shook her head. "She hasn't left her tent in days. Losing Miguel . . . on top of everything else that's happened to her, I don't know if she'll recover."

A sigh made its way past Lucha's lips. Losing Maria had been a blow. She'd been instrumental the first few days, finding space for the children and the wounded amid the muddy wreckage, making the meager food they foraged stretch.

After all this, she collapsed. She didn't eat or sleep in the two days after the flood, it turned out. Sheer mania had carried her through the first forty-eight hours, but once she'd slept for a day straight, she'd woken up different. As if the reality of what had befallen her, befallen all of them, had sunk in while she was still.

"We'll take her some food," Lucha said, trying to push aside the hopelessness. "See if we can get her to talk."

"Something happened out there, didn't it?" Cruz asked when they reached Lucha's tent.

Lucha stopped, examining the tent as she considered her answer. It was made of the fine crimson fabric that had draped Pecado—now sun-bleached and crusted with mud. She liked the reminder that they'd accomplished *something* since she'd arrived here.

Cruz was still waiting for a reply. Lucha thought of the grove. Its unnatural appearance, but also the feeling that had emanated from it. Something twisted and strange, *wrong*. She didn't want to tell Cruz. She was always waiting for that tense thread within her to snap; when it did, Lucha knew, she'd be entirely alone here.

But this fear too was too much to bear alone.

"Out in the woods . . . I had to go pretty deep to find anything," Lucha said finally. "I saw a grove that looked . . . I mean, it was destroyed, but I don't know by what. It looked like it had been burned, but not by fire. Eaten through by something."

"Just what we need." Cruz dropped to her haunches, the closest she ever got to relaxing. "How close was it?"

"Miles," Lucha said, sitting cross-legged in front of her tent.

"Well, we'll keep an eye on it, but for now we have problems closer to home."

Lucha didn't want to know, but she didn't have a choice. "Tell me."

"The river's rising. We might have to move the tents closest to the road."

"Again?" Lucha's heart sank. "We just got the Sanchezes settled after the last time."

Cruz nodded. "That's not all."

This time, her silence was query enough.

"We lost three more. Armando heard folks talking—they're going to find Miguel, the fools."

Lucha felt her temper rising at the mention of his name, and she didn't attempt to corral it. The day's frustrations had stretched her patience to its breaking point. "Why?" she asked. "He doesn't have Olvida, he doesn't give a damn about any of them, he might not even be *alive*."

Nodding again, Cruz looked more pensive than angry, which made Lucha feel like a petulant child. "They've spent their whole lives chasing something," she said when Lucha was quiet. "I think the hope that there's something better is easier to face than the reality here."

"It's not so bad, is it?" Lucha asked. "Not worse than when the kings were in charge and everyone was in chains?"

Another thoughtful pause. "Not so bad for us, maybe," she said finally. "But most of these people were living what they thought was a real life before the plants died. They worked, they ate. They had shelter and Olvida. And now . . ."

"Now they live in a mud pit and they're always hungry," Lucha finished for her. "But that's not *our* fault! Los Ricos abandoned them to the floods and starvation!"

"Yeah," Cruz said, scrubbing a hand over her face. "And they hated them. But now we're in charge, and nothing is any better. Can you blame them for hating us, too?"

Lucha didn't answer, but she found she couldn't blame them. Not really. She had railed against every authority figure that had been put in front of her since the moment she understood the concept. Why should they be any different?

"At least tell me the cows are good," she said after a long minute. An attempt to lighten the mood.

It worked, at least for a moment. Cruz's face broke into a reluctant smirk. "The cows are good," she said, and Lucha smiled too.

Many of the animals Los Ricos had kept in lightless warehouses and butchered with abandon had died in the flood that took the housing units, and the few that had survived had mostly starved. In the end there'd been just two cows left, and a handful of scrawny river ducks.

Armando had surprised Lucha by taking a shine to the creatures, and had spent most of his free time trying to bring them back to health.

Unlike almost everything else they'd tried these past weeks, it was working.

The cows were putting on weight. One of them, to everyone's surprise, had been pregnant, and just two days ago the calf was born—a velvety little animal with sweet eyes that was probably the sole reason the rest of the Robadans hadn't abandoned them for the woods.

"I know you're not gonna want to hear this . . . ," Cruz began, rocking on the balls of her feet, not meeting Lucha's eyes.

"We can't," Lucha replied flatly. "I already told you."

"If we stay here, we're all gonna die, Lucha. That church of yours might be our only hope."

Lucha had immediately regretted telling Cruz about Asilo. It had been intended as a moment of vulnerability, a sharing of knowledge about her past to create some trust. She'd kept the details vague, not mentioning her divine status among the acolytes. Or Paz. Even so, Cruz had been pushing the issue ever since.

"There's no way we'll all make it there alive," Lucha said for at least the twentieth time. "It's weeks of travel, and with the forest as it is . . . it's not an option, okay? I mean it."

Cruz looked rebellious, and a familiar uneasiness fell between them. Obviously, Lucha's objections were based in truth. It would be nearly impossible for all of them to cross the forest, and even if they did, by some miracle, there was no guarantee they would be welcome.

But of course, that wasn't the whole story.

Lucha had done her best not to think of Paz since she'd made the decision to stay. In the daytime, it was easier—with so much to manage, there was little time for anything else. But at night, Lucha couldn't escape the memories of her, the guilt that came with each day she didn't return . . .

The worst part was, she didn't want to return. Through this work in Robado—the anonymous and thankless work of digging and hunting and bandaging and so much more—Lucha had found more meaning and purpose than a lifetime as Asilo's mascot could have brought her.

She couldn't picture herself in a green robe, posing for her portrait in a window, listening to the hushed and reverent tones that would follow her.

But neither could she picture Paz here, separated from her sisters, her life's purpose . . .

"This conversation isn't over," Cruz said, cutting into Lucha's futile musings. "And don't think I don't know you're hiding something about that place."

When she walked away, Lucha didn't stop her. Even though it meant being alone with her unsolvable puzzle.

The sanctuary didn't intrude on Lucha's thoughts again for another week, but when it did, it returned with all the force of a dammed river breaking through its wall.

Lucha was bent over the table where the foragers prepped dinner, looking at a collection of bones she didn't recognize. Across from her, the señoras looked terrified. One of them clutched some talisman to her chest, and the other kept muttering words that sounded like a spell. Or a plea.

"Where did you find them?" Lucha asked at last. They were like nothing she'd ever seen. At one point they'd belonged to a medium-sized animal, but she could be certain of nothing else.

Lucha had seen a good many bones in her day—some lifeless, some animated into massive creatures. Some human. She'd seen them after decay and rot and burning and flooding. Bones endured. Lucha knew this. It was why she'd wielded a bone dagger most of her life.

The ones in front of her hadn't disintegrated, or charred,

or worn away with time. These bones had come into contact with something sinister. They were warped and twisted, as if they'd grown around some grotesque, unnatural organ. The surface of them was blistered, too, corroded in a way so violent it made Lucha want to cringe.

"A few miles from here," the shorter señora said to Lucha. They'd refused to give Lucha their names all this time—some superstition, she would have wagered, based on the stories they'd heard about her and El Sediento and the forest's magic.

Lucha could have found out from someone else, but she respected their wishes. A name was a powerful thing.

"We were chasing a fox," said the taller one, still clutching her talisman. "For stew. We came across a terrible place. Burned or blighted . . . unnatural." Her eyes flicked to Lucha's suspiciously as she said so. "This was there, in the blackened grass. I thought you'd want to see."

"You did well to bring it to me," Lucha assured her, headache already building behind her eyes. "We'll see what we can do."

The señoras both nodded, backing away.

"Wait," Lucha called when they'd turned. "Did you get the fox?"

Their silence was all the answer she needed.

Alone again, Lucha wanted to smash her fist against the table. To cry, or curse the sky. The berries and greens were gone now too. Withered by some force she couldn't see. The rabbits had vanished. Overhunted or else wisely fled to less dangerous pastures.

Everyone was hungry, and no rain had fallen since the

flood. The heat—unseasonable for spring—was getting unbearable.

And as if that weren't enough, Lucha thought bitterly, this skeleton had been found only a few miles away. Much nearer than the damaged grove she had found the week before, which meant that whatever it was, it was getting closer to the city.

Maria had yet to leave her tent. Cruz was as exhausted as Lucha and had no more answers than she did. Another five Robadans had left the city in search of Miguel.

Lucha was at the end of her rope.

But when Junio walked up a moment later, she hitched on a smile—the same one she'd smiled for Lis a thousand times when things were dire and there was no way out.

"Hey there," Lucha said, hiding the strange bones as best she could. "You need something?"

"There's . . . a lady," Junio said uncertainly. "She came out of the forest. She asked for you."

Everything in Lucha went ice-cold.

"Out of the forest?" she asked, trying to maintain her cheerfulness with considerable effort. "What does she look like?"

Junio shrugged. "A lady?"

"Where is she now?" Lucha heard her own words as if they were coming from underwater. Of course, she knew several *ladies* who might emerge from the forest knowing her name. But most of them she would not have been glad to see.

Her mind strayed to Paz. Had she come to remind Lucha that she was waiting? Sensed that Lucha's heart was being pulled in another direction? Or was it Lis?

No, Lucha thought, Lis would have announced herself. Charged right in.

"Armando and Cruz have her by the big fire pit," Junio said, animated by the deviation from the usual drudgery. "They said to bring you right away."

"Of course," Lucha said. "Let's not keep them waiting."

She felt utterly numb as she picked her way through camp, avoiding the eyes of anyone who might ask something impossible of her. Her mind raced with possibilities, none of them good.

The walk seemed to take hours. Still, Lucha was not ready when they reached the pit.

Armando's broad back faced her, blocking the identity of the visitor. Lucha could hear Cruz speaking quickly, asking questions . . .

"I'm back!" crowed Junio, eager for the praise he was sure to receive from Armando—who had taken the boy under his wing.

"What's going on?" Lucha asked with all the authority she could muster through the panic now pounding in her ears. "I was told someone had come to see me."

Lucha hadn't realized how much she was expecting—perhaps *hoping*—to see Paz until Armando turned to reveal the second-to-last person Lucha would have wanted to see standing in the mud of Robado's north road.

Obispo Río, head priestess of the Asilo sanctuary, stood there like it was her own office in the Catedral. She seemed unimpressed by the Syndicate members guarding her, undisturbed by the mud on her deep green robe. She looked as Lucha remembered her looking—as if she had one foot in this world and the rest of her walked with Almudena in some other.

Lucha, having met the goddess herself during a vision, knew this was not the case. That the goddess disapproved, in fact, of the way mortals like Río had twisted her teachings to create the bureaucracy that now characterized the church.

All that aside, Lucha thought, what was the priestess doing *here?*

She felt the person she had been trying to be all these weeks wavering as this piece of her past stepped forward. The tough-as-nails savior of Robado, doing her best to take care of the people the kings had abandoned . . .

Cruz pushed past, approaching Lucha with an accusatory look on her face. "She says you have unfinished business," she said in an undertone.

Lucha still hadn't figured out how to answer when Río spotted her at last, joining the group like it was nothing out of the ordinary.

"Miss Moya," Río said. Her voice was crisp and businesslike. No roughness in it, nor warmth. "We meet again."

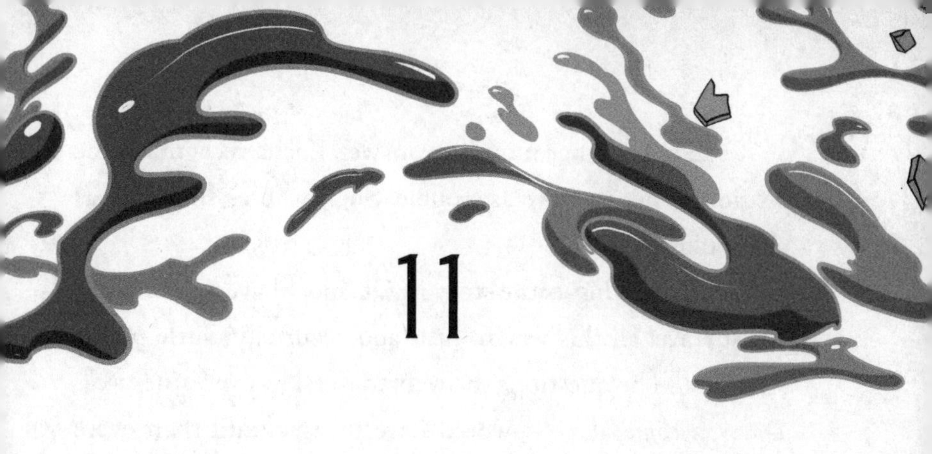

11

"Obispo Río," Lucha said. Her voice was mild. *Good*, she thought. The panic was only on the inside, then. "You've made quite a journey."

"You don't know the half of it." Río breezed past Cruz without an introduction.

"I assume this friend of yours isn't a threat to our security?" Cruz asked through gritted teeth.

"No more than I once was to hers," Lucha said. It would all come out, she supposed. All the things she'd avoided when she told Cruz about her time in the forest. Lucha's role in the mythology of the goddess. The position she'd been offered at the sanctuary and the reasons she'd turned it down. Paz . . .

Cruz, oblivious to all this history, stepped forward. "Cruz Miranda, and this is Armando Perez. What can we do for you?"

"It's a pleasure," Río said, though she sounded as if it was anything but. "And as to what you can do for me . . ." She paused, looking around at the state of the camp. The bedraggled Robadans. "Can I infer from the general untidiness that there's been a regime change?"

Cruz opened her mouth to answer. Lucha recognized the tension in her posture as trouble. She cut in as smoothly as she could.

"As fascinating as the story is, Obispo, I have a feeling you didn't travel all this way to hear about our city's little power struggles." The questions she wanted to ask—*Is my sister well? Did you come alone?*—would have to wait until there were fewer people Lucha would have to explain them to.

Cruz knew about the sanctuary in theory, but if these starving, miserable people all found out that Lucha had had allies and a place to travel to all this time, they wouldn't wait to hear the reasons it wouldn't have worked.

"That's true," Río replied without shame. "I have something to discuss with you. Is there somewhere private we can talk?"

Her eyes lingered on Armando and Cruz as she said this last part. Río looked at them—not as a person might size up another, but as a guest takes the measure of their host's house pet. Lucha's defenses flared. She remembered the feeling of those eyes on her when she'd first arrived in the sanctuary.

How dare Río, with all her power and privilege, judge the people who had risked their lives to save this city?

But she couldn't say these things aloud. Not until she found out what Río was here for, what she knew. If there was any chance the priestess could help the Robadans, Lucha would have to swallow her pride.

Unclenching her fists, Lucha turned to Cruz. "Would you

mind checking on Maria? I'll find out what she wants and join you as soon as I can."

"If she's from where I think she's from . . . ," Cruz muttered.

"I promise I'll do everything I can," Lucha said. "We can discuss it once I know what she wants."

Cruz looked at Lucha for a long moment, like she was reading something behind her gaze. Finally, she dropped her eyes. "I'm trusting you," she said to Lucha's boots.

"First time for everything," Lucha said. An attempt to lighten the mood.

Cruz was gone before Lucha could tell if she'd smiled or not.

"Please," she said to Río when Armando had left as well. "Come this way."

The abandoned Syndicate tent was the only semiprivate place in the camp. They had been so busy these past weeks trying to keep everyone fed, they'd had little time (or materials) for more than the lean-tos that dotted the landscape. Plus, the flood had created such an unstable surface for building that it was almost impossible to do more without running the risk that anything they erected would fall on the head of the person unlucky enough to sleep inside.

"I suppose all this has something to do with the task you came here to accomplish," Río said as she scanned the wreckage down the length of her nose. "The one that was more important than—"

"Is my sister safe?" Lucha asked, whirling around the moment the tent flap fell closed. "Is she with you?"

"Lis remains at the sanctuary. She is safe, as far as I know."

Río paused. "Well, as safe as any of us are." She surveyed the tent with distaste. A musty smell permeated it, of poorly dried belongings in a humid space.

Lucha sat on a crate, trying not to think of the first time she'd come in here. Río chose to stand rather than take the other. Lucha didn't insist.

"If Lis is safe, what could possibly have brought you all this way?"

"Something more important than the safety of one girl," Río said ominously.

Lucha didn't take the bait. "There's nothing more important than Lis's safety. I thought I made that clear when I left her in your care."

"Point taken. I've come all this way, to your charming . . . *city*, because I need your help. The *world* needs your help."

Lucha barely fought the urge to scoff. "I've heard that one before," she said. "I told you, I'm out of the savior business."

Río, of course, ignored her. She continued, as if reading from a prepared statement:

"Ever since you left the sanctuary, the balance of the forest has been shifting. Rapidly. Every day brings a new disaster within the Bosque. Fires. Floods. Droughts. Storms. Plants die out while others grow unchecked. The symbiotic relationships that make up the forest's ecosystem are failing."

The urge to scoff was long gone. Lucha leaned forward on her crate, recognizing the problems that had been circling Robado like hungry dogs.

"Why?" she asked. "Why is it happening? And why are

you here instead of at the sanctuary trying to stop it? You know my power is gone."

The look that flashed across Río's face was pitying. "Of course, we've been tracking the situation using all the knowledge and instrumentation at our disposal. The forest has thrown its tantrums in the past. It's never been anything we couldn't rebalance or ride out. But this is something different. Something almost entirely without historical precedent."

"So find a solution," Lucha said, frustrated by Río's wordiness. "Río, the people here can't withstand many more disasters. Every day there's something new. I thought it was the curse of the Scar, but if you're saying there's a *reason* for all this . . . you have to find it. You have to stop it."

"You think I haven't been trying?" Río snapped. A rare display of emotion. "The issue isn't that we don't know the reason. The issue is that the reason is bigger than all of us. An unstoppable force we can't hope to stand against."

Lucha hated the way these words resonated. She'd worried about this exact thing as she helplessly watched the city flood, then heat up to unbearable temperatures. Watched the food sources die out one by one. The rabbits flee. The strange skeleton. Whatever was happening was too big to be stopped.

"Tell me what you know," Lucha commanded, as if she had the right. "Everything you know."

Río massaged her temples for a moment. Lucha resented her for looking tired. With all her power and wealth, safe behind her walls, what did she know of exhaustion?

But then she began to speak, and Lucha couldn't help but be swept up in the tale.

"Ancient stories say that when Almudena landed in this world, she brought order to chaos. Created a world of balance. And from that balance and order, human life was born and allowed to thrive.

"You know what happened next. She created a son. A god as different from her as it was possible to be. A punishment from the celestial plane for her arrogance, intent on the destruction of all she held dear."

Lucha knew this part as well as the lines on her palm, of course. Salvador had been part of her. Entwined inextricably with her fate until she ended his life and returned him to the forest he so wanted to destroy.

"When he died, when the gift given to you by Almudena extinguished itself, it represented the end of divine power in Elegido," Río explained, shadows beneath her eyes. "It was a consequence no one thought to consider, given the nature of the conflict. No human living remembers a time when there was not a guardian in our world. But without divine order, chaos has crept in . . ."

Lucha sat in silence for a long moment, trying to understand. "Please tell me you're not saying that by killing Salvador to save humanity, I doomed . . . humanity."

Río did not respond.

"You're not serious," Lucha said. Anger flared to life in her chest, a welcome distraction. "You can't possibly have come here to tell me off for saving the world. Aren't you people *currently* making one of those stained-glass windows with my defeat of Salvador on it? Didn't you ask me to stay at the sanctuary as a *mascot* because I killed him?"

Lucha got to her feet now, pacing restlessly.

"Have you forgotten that your goddess came to me in a vision and granted me her power *to get rid of him?* If you have a fate problem, Obispo, it's not mine. If things didn't work out to your satisfaction, you'll have to take it up with your goddess."

"You stupid girl," Río snapped. "Why do you think I've come to this rotten place?"

Lucha barked a humorless laugh. "If you're looking for a god, you came to the worst place imaginable. The gods abandoned Robado a long time ago, Obispo."

"I'm not looking for a god," Río said impatiently. "Not here, anyway. I'm looking for a way to communicate with one."

For a moment, Lucha was stumped. Then she remembered all at once.

"The Pensa plant," she said. "Yours are gone too."

"And along with it, our ability to communicate with her," Río confirmed. "To divine her will. To carry out her instructions. We are alone, Miss Moya, and without her guidance we will die."

"What do you mean, we'll die?" Lucha asked.

"I mean that we will all *die,*" Río said ruthlessly, getting to her feet as well, standing mere inches from Lucha. "Every one of the people and creatures that inhabit the forest. The forest itself. And without access to the clean water and air it provides, eventually the rest of the world will follow. I *have* to speak with Almudena. And you are going to help me, or this little mud puddle you're trying so hard to save from extinction will be the first to go."

It all came back to Pensa. Of course it did. Lucha had been so determined to rid the world of Olvida that she'd momentarily forgotten the plant's original purpose. A gift from the goddess to commune with her in times of need.

"You didn't even know I was here, did you?" Lucha asked as realization dawned. "You came looking for Pensa. After you ignored this city for decades. Left it in the hands of his minions. You came looking for a fix."

"Don't be childish," Río said. "I came looking for the tool I need to save the world. And yes, when I asked to speak to the city's leaders and heard your name, I was surprised. But don't you see that it's her will for us to work together once more?"

Lucha tasted metal, her vision washed over with red.

"You would have worked with *them,*" she said. "You people in your shining sanctuary could have saved us from this anytime you wanted to. But you left us alone. And you would have worked with our oppressors without giving it a second thought . . ."

"To save the world, Miss Moya. And every creature in it—including yourself."

"Well, you're too late, anyway," Lucha said, feeling a vindictive thrill as she said it. "We killed the kings. Every last Pensa plant is dead. The Olvida they were hoarding was destroyed in the flood. Robado is free, and we can't help you. Sorry you wasted a trip."

Lucha pushed her way out of the tent. Río didn't stop her. But there was one thing Lucha had learned about the head of Asilo: she didn't give up on what she wanted without a fight.

12

Lucha stormed blindly through the camp, not thinking about where she would go, not caring. Rage pounded in her ears. She wanted to go back into that tent and punch Río in the face. She wanted to run into the forest and never look back.

She hadn't made it halfway across the city before she heard it. Commotion. With everyone hungry and hopeless, it had been a long time since she'd heard clamoring.

"What happened?" Lucha asked the first person she reached. A man named Al who sometimes helped with the hunting.

"It's coming from Armando's place," Al said, his eyes round with worry. "They told us not to come close."

Lucha swore. If something had happened to Armando or Cruz . . .

"Stay here, will you?" she asked Al. "Make sure no one comes any closer."

He nodded and Lucha took off, running toward Armando's

shelter near the tree line. She could see it in the distance. His little lean-to and the larger one for the cows.

She hadn't even reached it when the smell hit her. She covered her mouth and nose with her shirt before she gagged.

It wasn't the lye smell of a sombralado's grove. Nor the filth of the starving and wounded from the north gate camp before the kings had been killed. This was the smell of years of putrid decay. Sulfur and shit and rot.

"What the hell?" she asked no one, choking on her words as she made her way closer. Every one of her instincts told her to flee, but she couldn't. She heard Río's words echoing in her mind. Floods. Fires. Disasters.

We will all die.

Lucha pushed onward, her shirt still over her face, not remotely equal to the stench now permeating the place. There were voices up ahead. Shouting. Her eyes were watering so much she didn't see the obstacle in her path until it was almost too late.

"Watch out!"

A man's voice from up ahead. Closer than the others. Lucha stopped instinctively, looking down at an innocuous puddle of some kind, steaming in the afternoon air.

At first, it looked like an ordinary puddle. She only would have clocked it as strange because there hadn't been rain for weeks. But as she approached it, she could see something *moving* inside it.

No, she realized, horror dawning along with the awareness.

It was the liquid itself, shifting and re-forming as if it was sentient. Reacting to her closeness.

Ahead, there was more of the strange stuff. A red so deep it was almost black. *Blood?* Lucha thought, her stomach turning. But no. This was stranger even than that. Viscous and thick and bubbling. Moving in such an unnerving way it made the hair on her arms stand up.

"Don't touch it!" came the voice from up ahead. The man was running toward her, deftly dodging all the liquid on the ground—Armando, she realized when he was close enough.

"What's going on?" she asked.

"Come and see," he grunted. "Just—"

"Don't touch it," Lucha said, carefully stepping around the stuff. "I got it."

Armando didn't explain further, just kept an eagle eye on their steps as they made their way closer to his shelter. Cruz was already there, facing something Lucha couldn't see.

As they ran, Lucha tripped over a stick, sending it clattering across the road into one of the puddles. She knew she shouldn't, some instinct told her to look away, but she couldn't. She watched instead as the substance inside bubbled up, climbing the stick. Consuming it.

Digesting it.

Shaken, Lucha let the fabric around her mouth drop. Her stomach turned again. She sensed some horrible vertigo drawing her closer to this substance until she felt a bracing hand on her shoulder. Armando wasn't much of a talker, but the look in his eyes held compassion for Lucha. Horror of his own.

"We should keep moving."

Lucha nodded, trying to stop her knees from shaking.

They followed Cruz's shouts, but soon a more horrible sound broke through. It was the keening of a wounded animal. Desperate. Enraged.

Lucha thought of the cows, and her stomach sank into her boots. She dreaded what they'd find when they reached the shelter, but there was no time to waste.

"Cruz!" Lucha called when she was close enough. "What's happening?"

But Cruz didn't look over. Her eyes were fixed on the sight in front of her, a mixture of pity and revulsion twisting her features.

Lucha reached her side in seconds, turning her gaze to whatever had Cruz's attention. It was a creature, pawing at the ground, braying that horrible sound over and over. A dying sound.

She understood now why no one had answered when she'd asked what was happening. How could you possibly explain this?

Up against the shelter wall was the little calf that had so raised the Robadans' morale a few weeks ago. Half her face was still deep brown, covered in soft hair, a dark eye looking mournfully up. But on the other side was something too horrible to understand.

The calf's face had been eaten away by the red, bubbling blight spread in puddles across the field. But instead of leaving nothing behind, it had multiplied into the empty space, creating a grotesque, fungal effect that was still growing. Still devouring the calf even as they watched.

Lucha thought of the warped skeleton she'd seen this morning. The señoras with their talismans and prayers. The calf brayed again, a sound a normal animal could never have made. Its one visible eye rolled back in its head. The bloodred growth on its right side seemed to pulsate, to spread.

"Watch out!" Cruz called, dodging, pulling Lucha with her as the thing unexpectedly charged.

It did not run with a calf's clumsy gate. Some demonic power seemed to seize it, to propel it forward at unnatural speed. If Lucha had not fought all manner of terrifying creatures since childhood, she would have screamed.

But she didn't blame Armando when he did, dodging just in time.

"Don't let it touch you, whatever you do!" Lucha shouted, probably unnecessarily. She thought of the strange substance that had devoured the branch. Tried not to picture Armando with this blight covering his face, lurching toward them with unnatural power and speed.

Cruz was light on her feet, dancing out of range. Lucha drew her knives, trying to gauge how best to get close to the beast without letting the substance that coated it touch her.

Armando had fallen to his knees, clearly broken by the sight of this creature he'd nurtured so carefully and what it had become. Lucha wondered if he'd been running away when he found her. She couldn't blame him for that, either.

"Armando, you need to get clear of it!" Lucha called from

her position between him and the creature. "Whatever it is, it's not your calf anymore."

The man did not move. His shoulders began to shake with sobs.

Lucha hesitated, not sure whether to go for the calf or Armando first, and as she did, the calf threw itself forward again. Lucha barely dodged it in time. This time it made for Cruz, who was brandishing a spear with a serrated blade on the end.

"Careful!" Lucha called, making her way toward Armando as quickly as she could. "Try to hold it off while I get him out of here!"

Cruz grunted in answer, and Lucha turned her attention to Armando, still frozen in place, his eyes glazed with tears.

"You have to go," Lucha said, trying to haul him up, though he was nearly twice her size. "Armando, we can't lose you, we can take it from here, please."

But he would not move, and she could not move him.

"A little help here!" Cruz shouted, and Lucha swore.

"We're just gonna have to keep it away from him," she called, brandishing her knives and joining the fight. Hoping to corral the creature away from its master. She knew what she had to do, as much as she dreaded it. But she had spoken truly. They could not lose Armando. Not after everything else they had already lost.

"Easier said than done," Cruz said, sweat dripping from her brow as the calf readied itself to charge, crouched low to the ground.

"Okay, see if you can keep it a spear's length from you. I have an idea." It wasn't a great one, but they were quickly running out of options. And if this thing got loose . . . made for the city . . .

"What are you thinking?" Cruz asked.

Before she could answer, the calf shot forward again. Gooseflesh erupted all down Lucha's arms at the strange way its leg joints bent as it ran.

Cruz held out her spear, bravely holding her ground and stopping the calf in its tracks. The animal screamed a hair-raising scream, attempting to find a way through as Cruz stabbed forward with the blade.

"Just like that!" Lucha said. "Try not to let it move! I'm almost there!"

Lucha circled around, aiming carefully but as quickly as possible. The last thing she wanted was to startle the beast and trigger another unpredictable charge.

In her hands, Lucha weighed both knives as she positioned herself. The bone knife, and the silver one that had been a gift from Paz after the battle they fought together. She would have to throw one of them and hope it hit its mark. Even if the blight devoured the weapon as it had the branch.

To lose her history, the bone knife that had brought her mostly unscathed through so many awful circumstances, seemed unthinkable. But *this* knife, the silver knife, was the last thing she had of Paz. The reminder she'd hoped to carry with her until . . .

"What's the plan here, Lucha?" Cruz demanded, strained with the effort of engaging with the creature.

"I've got it," Lucha said. But did she? She was lined up

perfectly now, she could take the shot. Bone or silver. Which part of her was she willing to sacrifice?

Before she could decide, a whizzing sound caught her attention. She turned her head to see nothing but Cruz. Her answer came when the calf let out one final, demonic low and fell dead on the ground.

Lucha looked back, utterly bewildered, to find Maria standing just behind her. Her eyes were puffy and red, her hair tangled and skin pale from weeks without sunlight.

Dazed, Lucha looked at Cruz, whose expression mirrored her own. They both watched as Maria knelt down, whispered something to Armando, then led him off in the direction of the city.

Once they were gone, Lucha looked back at the poor creature. She found that even her surprise over Maria's return couldn't distract her from the emotions welling up. She turned away, making for the trees nearby, needing some air. Some distance.

This calf had been the sole symbol of hope in a city rapidly falling apart. Losing it felt like more than a blow. It felt like a candle snuffing out in the wind.

"You okay?"

Cruz's voice startled Lucha, who'd thought she was alone. She looked up at the other girl, surprised to find her face free of its usual suspicion.

"It just feels like we're losing everything. I know this calf wasn't going to save the city, but for her to die like this. For Armando to lose her. It's starting to feel unbearable."

Kneeling beside Lucha, Cruz sighed. "Armando lost his daughter, you know. In the first flood. I think this calf was sort of the place he was putting all that energy."

This new grief crashed hard over the rest of it. A bottomless pit of misery. And now Lucha had Río's devastating prediction to contend with as well. The end of the forest. Of the world. And no one knew how to stop it.

"I have to do something," Lucha said, standing up abruptly. "I'll see you back at camp."

Cruz didn't answer, but Lucha felt her gaze until she was well into the forest. She crashed through the trees without caring what she disturbed. This hopeless feeling, it had taken everything over. There was no Pensa; even Asilo was helpless in the face of this mounting threat.

But Lucha had been a vessel for Almudena's power. Almudena, who had abandoned her people to the whims of her terrible son. Who had tapped Lucha to fight her battle when she couldn't.

Reaching an area of the forest that seemed far enough from Robado, Lucha threw herself to her knees. She pressed her palms against the earth. She closed her eyes.

"Almudena," she said aloud. "I don't know if you can hear me, but you have to fix this. You can't let the entire world suffer for your mistakes. People count on you. People *believe* in you. I know you're heartbroken that you can't come back here, but give me the power to fix this. Or give it to someone. Please."

Lucha finished speaking and waited. She reached for the place where her power had once been, remembering the way it had burned in Asilo when she was within the protective walls of the sanctuary. Her heart had been a scarred battleground for a war between gods, but there was no evidence of it now.

"You owe me!" Lucha called, louder now, a flurry of birds too small to eat taking flight from the nearby brush. "You led me to slaughter and you owe me. This is the repayment I'm asking for."

She screwed her eyes shut tight, reaching deeper than before, willing the liquid light to well up. To fill her veins. To connect her to the beating heart at the center of the earth as it had once . . .

But no matter how long she stayed there, she remained a girl on her knees in the mud.

No one answered. No power returned to her. And Lucha let gravity pull her forward onto the ground, where she cried until there was nothing left.

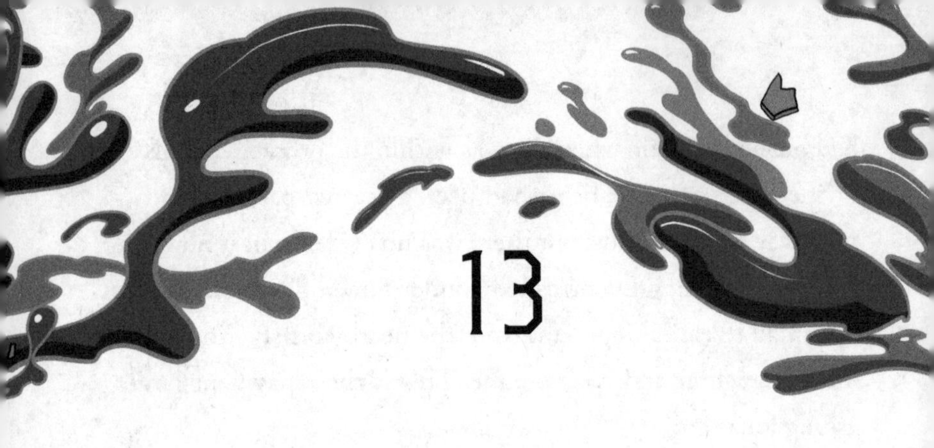

13

On the walk back to camp, Lucha felt she was seeing everything through a new lens. She had known things were bad. That the food was dying. That the forest's balance wasn't as it had been.

But with Río's warning ringing in her ears, the memory of the calf, it felt less like scrambling for an answer and more like grieving something that had not yet come to an end.

If Río and all the power of the sanctuary couldn't stop it . . .

If Lucha couldn't access the power that could rebalance things . . .

From this perspective, it looked a lot like the future Salvador had promised her if she didn't join him. A future where the world careened into nothing but bone and ash. Was this his doing, somehow? Had Lucha been naïve to think a god could be defeated?

Her skin prickled now as she walked through the trees. As if he were watching her from somewhere. From everywhere. Putting obstacle after obstacle in her path.

"He's not here," she said aloud to steady herself. "He's gone. The Pensa plants prove it. The changing of the forest proves it."

But the fact that she had to say it at all felt like a weakness. And still there was the feeling of eyes on her. Slimy across her skin. Creating a pit in her stomach.

Closer to town, Lucha could hear raised voices. She put aside her endless, circular riddles and tried to access the person she'd been these past weeks. Someone who could be steady in times of disaster. Someone who was worthy of the trust people placed in her.

She picked up the pace. Soon enough, a crowd came into view. She didn't dare hope they were gathering to face this new conflict head-on.

"*Everyone calm down!*" Cruz's voice rose above the rest. Lucha could see her now, standing atop a crate, her head just above those of the people gathered before her.

She looked smaller without Armando beside her for protection. But no less fierce. Lucha took in the scene as she approached. A mob of angry Robadans muttering, pressing closer to Cruz. Some of them were armed.

Cruz had come a long way since their fight in the water. The people were angry, but they looked to her as a leader. Only, right now a leader was a dangerous thing to be.

"If you'll just let me explain," Cruz said as Lucha made her way through the crowd to the front to join her. "Passing stories around isn't going to keep us any safer."

"Julissa said the cow turned into a monster!" one woman cried.

"Six legs, and ten eyes!"

"They say it's a demon! That it killed Armando!"

"Armando is fine," Cruz said, clearly exasperated. "He's grieving the death of his pet, but he certainly hasn't been killed by a demon. We all need to remain calm."

"Calm?" called one of the few men who hadn't gone off after Miguel. "How can we stay calm when there's no food? When we're running out of water! When there's no Olvida, and we're living in the dirt!"

"I know things have been hard," Cruz said, and Lucha was impressed with her for remaining firm. For not giving in to the desperation she must feel. "But building something new is never easy."

"We're not building anything. We're dying. Everyone knows it. And if there are monsters in the city now . . ."

"There are no monsters," Cruz said, holding out a hand. "The cow got sick. It was behaving strangely. But it's gone now, and we'll get back to the plan, all right? Building something the kings would never let us have. That's why you all stayed, isn't it? Because we wanted something more than we had under their rule?"

Lucha had reached the front. She stood a little way to the left of Cruz, so as not to steal her thunder. She thought the last bit had gone over well until the shorter señora from Lucha's foraging group stepped forward. That was when she knew they were doomed.

I should have hidden the skeleton, she thought. The arrival of Río had sent it all out of her head. But the señora had retrieved it from the table, and she held it aloft now.

"It's not only the cow," she said in a trembling voice. "This blight is spreading. The city will be full of demons before long, and who will protect us then?"

Lucha stepped up beside Cruz as horror and outrage spread through the gathering. Hearing stories about a demon cow was one thing. Robado had always been full of strange and terrible tales. But this was more than a story. This was proof.

"We can't stay here!" came a cry. "We have to leave, to find Miguel!"

"Miguel is gone!" Lucha shouted, at her wits' end. "Miguel is a coward who abandoned you all when the Olvida ran out. We're the ones who stayed, and we can keep you safe. We can."

"You can't even feed us!" Another wave of mutters spread, gathering in strength. "You promised us a community, food, shelter. A better life than we had under the kings. But we're barely hanging on."

"And if you go out there, you'll die," Lucha said frankly. "The forest is imbalanced, the food is dying, the weather is unpredictable. As bad as it seems here, it's ten times worse out there, and a hundred times worse alone."

This statement, however true, did not seem to affect the fervor with which most of their people were plotting their escape from Robado. Lucha didn't know what else to say. Miguel was likely dead, and if he wasn't, there was no way they were going to find him in a fathomless wood full of blight and creatures and lacking in reliable sustenance.

But if they didn't believe that, what could she do?

"We have to stop them," Cruz said in a low voice. "You know what will happen to them out there."

"How?" Lucha asked, spreading her hands. It just figured that the Robadans would finally discover their collective bargaining power when someone who cared was in charge. Only further proof that it had been Olvida keeping everything together. Olvida keeping everyone docile. And now . . .

"I say we leave tonight!" called the man from earlier. "The city isn't safe!"

There were far fewer dissenters than Lucha had hoped. Junio stayed loyally near Cruz and Lucha, with a few others. Maria and Armando were nowhere to be seen. The five or so others who seemed torn were the weakest, sickliest among the crowd. The ones who believed, rightly, that they wouldn't survive in the forest.

Possibilities for what to say coursed through Lucha, each more futile than the last. This was it, she thought clinically. The end of their big experiment. The end of Robado . . .

"My good people," came a voice from the other side of the crowd. "If I might speak with you all for a moment."

It only took a second to spot Río's green robes through the agitated masses. She had a calming, authoritative presence that immediately dampened the flames of disquiet. Lucha felt a pang of inadequacy as the Robadans turned their backs to her in unison, facing Río, waiting.

"You may not know me, but I am Obispo Río, the high priestess of the goddess Almudena."

The whispers that came from the people now were more wondering than restive. To most of them, Lucha knew, the goddess was only another story. One less believable than the monster stories in a place like this.

"I have come because I know the cause of the chaos that is disturbing your community. I have come because I need help to repair it. But I promise you, before we accomplish that goal, nowhere you run will be safe from its effects."

"But . . . what can *we* do?" asked the señora, still holding the warped skeleton.

"That can all be discussed at a later time," Río said with a wave that disguised a significant glance at Lucha. "For now, what I need from you is a promise that you will remain here, where it is safe. That you will listen to the good counsel of your leaders." This time, she gestured to Cruz and Lucha on the other side, and every head turned to take them in. "That you will stay safe until such time as we can restore your community to its rightful abundance."

Lucha's temper flared at this intrusion. The assumption that she needed Río's help to keep her people in order. But there was no doubt it had been effective. The people who had seemed ready to flee into the trees moments ago were nodding their agreement to the very request Cruz and Lucha had made of them minutes before.

"Good," Río said. "Now let's see what we can do about freshening up this place. I have some clean water and a little food from my travels. Let me share them with you, and we'll see if we can't turn things around."

She spoke to them like they were children, not equals, Lucha thought. But they didn't seem to mind the condescension. In fact, everyone here seemed much relieved to have a task, and the illusion of an adult making the decisions.

Within minutes the place was transformed. The Robadans bustled busily around, cleaning up, repairing their shelters, approaching Río for a piece of dried fruit and a smile and walking away fortified.

"Nice friend you have," Cruz said, watching the transformation with the same mixture of reluctance and awe that Lucha had just been feeling. "Why is she helping us?"

"She has an agenda," Lucha said, not taking her eyes off Río. "If she's helping us, it's because she wants something in return."

It was another hour before Río acknowledged Lucha's existence again. Lucha had taken advantage of the momentary motivation and compliance of the Robadans to make her rounds. Help with repairs. Make assurances to those still looking afraid.

She should have been pleased at the way they deferred to her, offered her their respect. But she couldn't help thinking that the only reason for it was Río's speech. Río telling them to follow her. Making a mascot of Lucha for her own gain, just as she'd tried to do back at Asilo.

Still, the Robadans were safe. For now. Talk of fleeing into the forest had ceased. She supposed she'd have to be grateful for that much at least.

And so, when Río caught her eye and moved away from camp, Lucha followed. If only to find out what that display of solidarity was going to cost her.

Río made her way toward the fence around the compound. No one had stepped outside it since the battle, and already the forest had begun to overtake it.

It had happened quickly. Lucha wondered how much of their lives the soldados must have spent hacking back new growth to keep it clear all these years. A violence against the forest, and in the end it hadn't gone unpunished. At least Lucha could feel good about that.

The fence was wound through with green. The tough vines—some nearly as big around as Lucha's wrist—coiled like snakes. Some gripped the fence so tightly they'd begun to warp the metal.

On top, the body parts left during the siege waited their turn to be reclaimed. Lucha thought of the mushrooms she'd once wielded. Their love of decay. It would be a feast for them when the time came.

Río didn't slow, and Lucha didn't chase. She kept a safe distance until the woman chose to turn and face her. As Lucha walked, she wondered once more what Asilo's relationship with the kings had been. They must have been aware of one another, after hundreds of years of existence. How many of the activities in Robado had Río herself condoned?

She hadn't been afraid to come here seeking aid, had she?

Aside from the foliage seizing the fence, there were saplings growing from the ground. Some were waist-high even after only a few weeks. Soon enough, this place would be indistinguishable from the surrounding forest. A brief blip of history, forgotten by all who had not lived it.

Lucha found the thought strangely comforting until she remembered the reason she was here, following this woman through a ruin.

How much history did they have left to live?

"You certainly showed Los Ricos the cost of aligning with a god of destruction," Río said, slowing down as Pecado came into view.

"Five hundred years too late," Lucha replied bitterly, joining her. "Listen, Río, I appreciate what you did back there, but you have to understand I have nothing left to give you. Whatever your agenda is, I can't help. I spent the last of my power. This is all I have now."

She gestured around her to the destruction of the compound. Río's expression did not change.

"You still don't understand your significance," she said after a long moment. "You didn't when you left the sanctuary, but I thought it might have sunk in after the fact."

Lucha shuffled her feet uncomfortably. Not only had the idea of her *significance* not sunk in in the aftermath of her fight with Salvador, but she'd been actively avoiding thinking about it since. Her significance was the reason she didn't know how to trust Paz. The reason she couldn't stay at Asilo, even though it was the kind of home she'd always wanted.

Significance without power made you a mascot, and that was the last thing Lucha had ever wanted to be.

"What does my significance matter?" she asked when Río continued to stare at her. "I can't save anyone. Not without the gift."

Río made an impatient sound in the back of her throat. "Haven't you been paying attention? We don't need power, Lucha. We need guidance. The kind we once received from chewing the Pensa plant."

"Well, I already told you I don't have any Pensa," Lucha snapped. "So I ask you again, what do you want from me?"

Infuriatingly, Río continued as if Lucha hadn't asked. "Divination is a shoddy business, you know," she said. "Not all of us can drop right into a conversation with Almudena and then carry out her instructions as stated. Often, it's a single leaf falling into a pond. An arrow flying through the sky. Ten saplings cut off halfway up their trunks. Nonsense, in short, that we do our best to find meaning in."

"I understand how divination works," Lucha said through gritted teeth.

Still Río didn't stop to acknowledge her words. "Lucha," she said instead. "You are the only *living* being who has wielded divine power. If we cannot commune using Pensa, you are the best chance we have of discovering Almudena's intentions. Her will. Do you understand *now* why I didn't leave when I found out there was no Pensa here?"

Río's expression as she turned it on Lucha this time was blazing. Pleading.

"I need you to come back to the sanctuary with me," she said.

"No," Lucha replied automatically.

"With our resources and our knowledge, combined with your experience, we will be giving humanity the best chance it could have. When you return to this city, if that is your will, it can be with the knowledge that generations may grow up safely here. Isn't that what you want?"

"You went out there and promised the Robadans you would help them!" Lucha said, incensed again. "You said we would figure this out and save everyone. But really you just want to haul me back with you so we can keep the world safe for your acolytes and damn everyone else, right?"

"If you don't come back with me, they *will* all die, and you will only die among them. Is *that* what you want?"

"It doesn't matter what I want!" Lucha shouted, glad they were far enough away that no one at camp could hear her. "It doesn't matter what *you* want! I don't have anything to offer you! Here, or at the sanctuary. I got *on my knees* in the woods today and *begged* her for some shred of knowledge, some minuscule spark of power that might help me save them, and guess what, Obispo? No one answered."

Río looked appropriately taken aback by this confession, but she didn't back down.

"In Asilo, we could lead you through the divine trances. We would have the resources to teach you how to access your inner divinity. There are many things we could try. But wasting away here in the mud, you are just as useless as you fear you are."

The trouble was, Lucha did want to help. More than anything, she wanted to find the secret that would correct what was happening. That would save the forest she loved and the people who trusted her.

But she knew what would happen if Río got her back within Asilo's walls. Robado would cease to exist for her, no matter what Río had said to the people at camp. No matter what she'd promised Lucha.

It was then that a plan started to sprout in the back of Lucha's mind. A way to get the relentless obispo off her back and possibly provide aid for the Robadans she was so helpless to feed or shelter . . .

"You really believe that your acolytes could uncover some secret truth of Almudena's will lingering in my mind?"

"I *do,*" Río said emphatically, seeming emboldened by Lucha's concession. "I truly do."

"Good," Lucha said, brushing off her hands. "Then they can do it here."

"Excuse me?"

"I'll let you pick my brain, try to bring forth Almudena's will or reawaken my powers or whatever else you want to do. But I won't leave Robado. If I'm *that* important to this process, you can bring your acolytes and all their food and supplies and information to me. And if not, you can go back on your own. It's your choice."

Río's face was utterly blank. She offered no endearing platitude. No smooth transition.

"That's the deal," Lucha said. "That way, if this all fails, as I strongly believe it will, Robado will have some support while we try. And if we succeed, you can't forget the little mud pit at the edge of the world. Robado will heal first."

"You're asking me to drag my people and our priceless scrolls and divine instruments two weeks through a rioting forest for you?" Río asked, a brow arched.

"No," Lucha said, turning to leave. "You're asking me for help. I'm just stating my terms. Take them or leave them."

And with that, she walked alone back to camp, feeling less useless than she had in weeks.

14

It was getting dark as Lucha made her way out of the compound. Río hadn't followed—she was probably rooting around for Pensa in the wreckage of Pecado, Lucha thought. A last-ditch effort to circumvent her need for Lucha's co-operation.

A lot of good it would do her. If there had been any Pensa or Olvida to be found, it would have been discovered by now.

Off to the left, Lucha noticed a flickering light, breaking through her thoughts and putting her on her guard. It was coming from a building, and she crept closer, hands on her knives until she realized what it was.

Alán Marquez's office had not been spared the wrath of the river. It leaned precariously to one side on its foundation, its warped and rusting metal doors no longer closing properly. The light was gone now, but Lucha felt sure it had come from inside.

She moved closer still, knives drawn now, aware of how alone she was in this moment. How exhausted after her fight with the calf and the scene in town.

"Who's there?" she called, her skin prickling. "I'll warn you, I'm armed."

Nothing. Lucha waited, unmoving, tensed, until she started to believe it had been a trick of the light.

The steps up to the door were wood, rotted through. All was quiet. Lucha's instincts told her she would be better off staying away. If there was anyone there, and they followed, at least she'd have allies if a fight came.

Still, she hesitated, picturing the boy who had once used this office. The boy who had once been her neighbor and friend. The slimy bootlicker he'd become. Starving Lis and pumping her full of Olvida, imprisoning Lucha for months—all to claim a piece of the forest's power for himself.

She felt the old hatred burning in her veins, tried to calm herself with a vision of him in the end. Trapped in the cell he'd intended for Lucha. Mushrooms eating him alive.

"Good riddance," Lucha said, and spat on the ground in front of the listing building.

This was her city now, and all the men who had tried to keep her captive here were dead. If there was another one inside this room, Lucha thought, he'd join the list before long.

With that comforting thought, she made her way through the gate, vowing to torch the office and all its contents as soon as it dried out enough to burn.

Back at camp, a welcome chill had arrived with the dusk. There was a fire burning in the distance. Most of the Robadans were in their shelters, or finishing up tasks set to them by Río. Tomorrow, they'd have to figure out how to survive on what they had, but tonight Lucha followed raucous laughter and the sound of spitting flames to the Syndicate tent.

Cruz, Armando, and Maria were gathered around the fire there, passing around a glass bottle that glinted in the firelight. Armando's eyes still looked haunted, and Maria's cheeks gaunt, but they were smiling. Together.

"Is this seat taken?" Lucha asked, feeling suddenly eager for company. For conversation. She needed to prove to herself that Río's arriving hadn't changed anything. That she still belonged here, in Robado.

Armando waved her over to an unoccupied crate across from Cruz. Maria passed her the bottle, which she drank from without asking what it was. It burned on the way down, and by the time it settled in her stomach, she felt a little braver.

For a while, she only stared into the flames, listening as the others spoke about times she had not been present for. Stories plucked like seeds from the lifeless mud. *This is worth saving,* she thought. *We are worth saving.*

When long minutes and many stories had passed, she felt their attention shift to her, and knew what it meant.

"So," Cruz said, reaching out for the bottle herself. "Of what use can we be to Her Highness?"

Lucha grimaced. "Let's talk about something else."

"Great," Maria said, deadpan. "Should we try my dead coward brother, or the fact that there's no food? How about the horror of a calf that almost killed us all today? Plethora of uplifting options here."

"You know something, don't you?" Cruz asked. The bottle was empty. The easy camaraderie was gone. "About what she said earlier? The destruction that's coming for all of us."

There was no point in lying, Lucha thought as she looked around at their flame-kissed faces. They would know everything soon enough, anyway.

"It's a lot," Lucha said, trying to organize her thoughts. "The reasons are mostly mythological, but they're no less real for that. I'll have to ask that you trust I'm telling you the truth, no matter how outlandish it sounds."

Armando, who had spoken least since Lucha had sat down, leaned forward. "Today I watched a calf I raised from birth bend its knees backward and run like a spider," he said. "Whatever is happening here is far from normal."

Lucha nodded. She opened the latch on the box where she kept her memories of the sanctuary. Of Almudena and Salvador. Of what it had felt like to wield divine power, what it had felt like to transform. To die . . .

"The simple version is that what's happening here is happening all over the forest," she began. "The food sources are dying, there are freak storms, and floods and fires. The ecosystem that keeps the forest alive is out of balance, and if we can't restore that balance, the forest will die."

She took a deep breath. It was easier to speak to the fire than to the faces of the people here, so she did. Leaving nothing out.

"The complicated answer is that the imbalance was caused by the destruction of the last immortal being in Elegido. A few weeks before I came here, I fought El Sediento, the goddess's only son. He was a god of chaos and destruction, bent on the decimation of the world his mother loved, and I wielded her power to end his life. He's the one who created Olvida, gave his power to the kings. The curse of the Scar is his."

She chanced a look now at their faces, which were wide-eyed and tight-lipped. She tried to remember hearing all this for the first time. What it had felt like. What she had believed.

"At the sanctuary where Río came from, there are acolytes who have studied and served the goddess for five hundred years. They're well provisioned and knowledgeable about the myth that shaped the forest. They grow Pensa in its pure form to commune with her, seek her guidance and her wisdom. But their plants are all dead too. They can't communicate with her anymore."

Maria spoke up then, lifting her chin from her hands. "The Pensa is gone," she said forcefully. "The Olvida is gone. We can't help her."

Lucha nodded. "You're right. It's gone. I told her that, and I hoped she'd leave, but she has . . . contingency plans. Involving me. At the sanctuary they have libraries full of history, mythology. It's the place where the last of the goddess's magic is stored. Because I've wielded her power, spoken with her on the plane of the gods, Río thinks I can be of help to them. That if she brings me back to the temple, they can find some way to use me to discover the goddess's will."

There was not an immediate reaction to this—at least not a dramatic one. But Lucha saw the truth in the hardening of their expressions. The settling of this new weight on their shoulders.

"So she only wants you," Cruz said. "And damn the rest of us regular people. Got it."

"Good luck out there," Maria said bitterly. "Send us a smoke signal if the world is gonna end."

"This Syndicate just gets smaller and smaller, doesn't it?" Armando asked the flames. "I'm not even sure we can *call* it a syndicate anymore."

"I told her no," Lucha said quietly, and immediately the atmosphere changed.

"You what?" Cruz asked.

"I told her no," Lucha repeated. "I told her I wouldn't go and leave Robado to fall apart. I told her I'd made a commitment to stay. To rebuild. And I plan to honor it."

"You're really cracked, aren't you?" Maria asked, almost admiringly. "You're gonna let the forest keep dying and the whole world go down the drain with it just so you don't break a promise to a bunch of mud brats?"

Lucha shook her head. "I told her I'd help her, but not if Robado was going to be forgotten. I said this is my home, and if she wants my help, she can bring her acolytes and all their fancy supplies and books here, support us while they try to find an answer. I told her it was either that or the world could burn—I wasn't leaving. So I guess that means you're all stuck with me."

For the looks on their faces, Lucha would have gone toe to toe with Río a dozen more times. The grudging respect and appreciation breaking through those bitter exteriors. The way it made Lucha feel—like taking that stand had been for something.

"Well, damn," Cruz said, reaching below her crate for another bottle. Pulling the cork out with her teeth. "I guess I'm gonna have to stop vaguely suspecting you of betraying us now, huh?"

Lucha laughed. It felt good. "I don't know if she'll agree. Maybe the acolytes of Asilo would rather let the world collapse than spend one minute in the mud with us. But I'm not going anywhere." She got to her feet, wanting to make some more formal pronouncement but not quite sure what to say.

"I'm really sorry I abandoned you all," Maria said before Lucha could speak, getting to her own feet. "Life before the Syndicate was . . . bleak, but without Miguel I didn't know how to do anything. Everything I knew about myself was in reference to him. To lose him felt like losing myself. But I'm . . . I'm here too. I want to be of use."

"There are two more cows," Armando said, standing to join them. "I'll keep them safe. I'll do my best to hunt. To build. To protect us."

Cruz stood last. "I'll be honest, before this, all I did well was sling Olvida and lie. But if you lot can become upstanding leaders and citizens, I'll do my best to find some way to contribute."

Lucha couldn't help it, she beamed at them.

"To Robado," Lucha said, her voice husky with emotion.

"To staying free," said Maria.

"To protecting everyone who's left," said Armando.

"To Lucha," Cruz said after a long pause. "For giving us a fighting chance."

They passed the bottle then, sealing the alliance that felt so much more real now than it had before.

Nothing was any more certain than it had been yesterday. Maybe Río was already gone, and the reinforcements weren't coming, and the blight would spread and the food would die and the place would flood or burn or both.

There was no way of knowing what would happen. But they were free, and they were together, and that was a start.

Lucha woke the next day in her old hammock behind the Syndicate tent with a headache. It took her a moment to notice Río standing over her, and when she did, she yelped, upending the whole contraption and landing painfully on the ground.

"Good morning, Miss Moya," Río said, looking down without offering Lucha a hand up. "I trust you slept well."

The rest of the hammocks were empty. Lucha vaguely remembered stumbling into hers a few hours before dawn. It was her first time drinking anything so strong, and she was regretting it as she got to her feet, stomach unsettled, the dull ache in her head now spreading to her neck.

She didn't know where the obispo had slept, but regardless, she looked as put-together as she had back at the sanctuary, with her impressive private quarters and a staff of acolytes to bathe and robe her.

"I slept fine," Lucha said, rubbing her hip where she'd landed in the dirt. She had no delusions of being put-together herself. "I assume you've made your decision."

Río regarded Lucha imperiously. She always appeared to be looking down from some lofty height, even when you were eye to eye with her.

"We'll need to build some platforms to raise the shelters above the mud when it rains. And there *must* be more than these crude lean-tos. My acolytes will require privacy for their studies."

"So, you're saying yes?" Lucha asked, trying not to wince at the headache.

Río, of course, ignored her question, barreling ahead with her growing list of demands. "I will instruct my people to bring such food and provisions as the sanctuary stores can spare to aid in the survival of the Robadans"—she said the word with marked distaste—"but let me be clear, Miss Moya. The support of your little band of misfits is entirely contingent upon your enthusiastic participation in our studies. There is much I have yet to tell you about our theories, and the answers we most need. Should you break your agreement with us, it's your people who will suffer. Is that understood?"

"Entirely," Lucha promised, though the back of her neck

prickled at the idea of agreeing to something she didn't know the details of. The last time she'd done that . . . well, she'd gotten more than she bargained for.

But this wasn't about her, or even Lis. This was about the survival of her city, the home she'd reclaimed when she refused to turn tail for the sanctuary. This was about stopping the chaos sweeping through their forest so that they might live to see what their fight for freedom had earned them.

"I'll send my missive, then," Río said, businesslike. "In two weeks' time we'll need to be ready to begin."

She was already walking away when the reality of their agreement settled on Lucha at last. Her already woozy head spun with all the implications.

"Obispo?" she called.

Río paused.

"How many acolytes are you sending for?" It wasn't the question she really wanted to ask, but she couldn't figure out how to ask *that* without giving away too much.

"I'll send for fifty," Río said, nonchalant. "That should be enough to keep the place in working order and make the inquiries we need to make."

Fifty, Lucha thought. That was fifty chances that one of them would be Paz.

"Will you send for anyone in particular?" Lucha managed, not willing to circle closer to the heart of the matter.

"My guard, of course," Río replied. "A few of those best versed in the histories and myths. The rest will be volunteers or acolytes from the outermost tier in need of completing a service mission."

Still too vague. The next few weeks would be torture.

"Thank you," Lucha said. "We'll do our best to get the place in shape."

It turned out Río and the promise of ambassadors from the goddess's sanctuary were invaluable in that regard. *This is what has been missing,* Lucha thought as the camp transformed from one day to the next.

A purpose.

Before, they had worked together in the hopes of reaching Pecado, serving justice to the kings. Living through each day to face the misery of the next had made a poor substitute. But the common goal of preparing for the acolytes unified them once more.

The Syndicate's energy was also renewed now that each day wasn't a fight against the growing resentment of the Robadans. Río's decision to relocate her acolytes, to make Robado the base camp for the fight against mythic forces, was seen as a savvy leadership decision on Lucha's part, which overcame the last of the *forest witch* suspicion they'd regarded her with since her arrival.

She took charge of the food and clean water initiative, bolstered by Río's expanded knowledge of edible plants. The meals were still meager, not nearly enough to sustain them long-term. But there were two of them a day, and the promise of supplies arriving soon.

One day, as she was chopping a skinny rabbit for stew, the taller señora came up timidly with an apronful of greens.

"Thank you, Señora," Lucha said, taking them from her to wash.

"Marisol," the woman whispered, pointing to herself.

"Hi, Marisol," Lucha said, understanding what a gift she had been entrusted with. This wasn't just an old woman's name. It was a declaration that she no longer thought Lucha was a monster.

Armando oversaw the building of platforms. Now that the mud had dried, they could anchor the supports deep enough to withstand the rain and the swelling of the river. They used the undamaged wood pulp from the roofs of the housing units, hauling it up the road on sleds with anything else they could salvage.

Within the first week, Armando was smiling again. His little crew adored him. Lucha doubted the sadness of losing his calf the way he had would ever disappear, but she was grateful they hadn't lost him.

Maria, thankfully, took charge of the clinic. Río worked most closely with her. She had brought a satchel of medicinals from the sanctuary, and she taught Maria to make them herself from what plants they could still forage in the Bosque. Maria would fit right in with the acolytes when they arrived.

But it was Cruz who was the biggest surprise. Her skills for *slinging Olvida and lying* translated incredibly well to leadership, as it turned out. She did a little of everything—not expertly, but the skill she employed was better than digging or foraging or patching up wounds. She moved from one group to another. She told stories. She laughed and joked. Encouraged and bolstered.

When blight was discovered in the middle of the north road one day, it was Cruz who found out it could be neutralized by salt water. Cruz who made sure no animals—or worse, villagers—were infected as the calf had been.

From reluctant refugees to a disjointed work crew, Cruz made them a community. Soon she was the person they all came to with their complaints, their triumphs—the person they asked when they were in need.

She was a leader, Lucha thought one day, watching her joke with a father while bending down to tie his little girl's shoelace. And no one seemed more surprised than Cruz.

15

The night before the acolytes were slated to arrive, Lucha couldn't sleep. She paced the camp like a caged animal, feeling as though her bones were vibrating inside the prison of her flesh.

She had not been able to bring herself to approach Río again about who was arriving. The obispo had even come to *her* a few days before to let her know that Lis had elected to stay behind in the sanctuary and focus on her training.

Lucha's selfish disappointment had warred with her relief that Lis would remain safe. She understood why her sister would choose not to return to the site of so many unhappy memories; it was hardly a surprise.

It had been the perfect time, in the moments after, to ask about Paz. The words beat against her throat like hummingbird wings until she swallowed them, unspoken.

And now here she was, on the eve of seeing her city—her life—change forever, with no idea what to expect.

From the trees up ahead, a rustling sound made Lucha tense, reach for her knives. Most of the Robadans were too superstitious to wander far after nightfall, but just as Lucha was about to shift into fighting stance, Cruz appeared on the road, her hair a little ruffled, her eyes wide with surprise.

"What are you doing out here?" Cruz asked, wiping futilely at some dirt smeared across her cheek.

"Can't sleep," Lucha said, remembering the promise the Syndicate had made to one another. Doing her best not to let her innate suspicion take over. "What about you?"

A scene entered Lucha's mind unbidden. One where Cruz had buried the brick of Olvida she'd been given the night of the flood and was now sneaking out to take small doses from it without the others seeing. Lucha tried, surreptitiously, to check Cruz's pupils. Her general demeanor.

All she saw was sheepishness.

Cruz rubbed the back of her neck. "Honestly, I just went out to climb a tree, see if I could spot them. But no such luck. I've . . . never met anyone from outside Robado before—if you don't count the grumpy priestess. I'm kind of excited?"

She spread her hands helplessly in front of her, and Lucha's suspicious fantasy collapsed under the weight of her guilt.

"I figured no one would be awake to see how eager I was," Cruz finished, thankfully unaware of Lucha's thoughts. "Don't tell anyone."

"I wouldn't dare," Lucha said. "It's good you're excited. I am too." She wondered, as they fell into step along the road to camp, if that was the truth.

"Yeah, but you've been *out* there before," Cruz said, looking enviously at Lucha. "You've seen places. Met all kinds of people. Sometimes I wish I'd done that, you know? Just walked into the forest and never looked back."

"Well, if it makes you feel better, it was less *walking* and more *fleeing for my life* when I did it."

"Honestly, sounds even cooler."

Lucha smiled, letting the conversation stall there. They walked in companionable silence, but Lucha could feel Cruz's eyes on her, feel the question she was working herself up to ask.

"So, you usually sleep like the dead," Cruz said finally. "What gives?"

For a moment, Lucha thought she'd lie. Say she was worried about the food stores or integrating the acolytes with the Robadans or any other number of legitimate concerns. And perhaps it was the lateness of the hour, or the fact that she had no one else to talk to about it, but she told the truth instead.

"The time I spent at the sanctuary wasn't the easiest for me," she began. "The obispo was basically keeping me locked up because she thought I was a threat to humanity, but after I defeated Salvador against her wishes, she kind of changed her tune."

Lucha took a deep breath, reliving those days in the clinic on the brink between life and death.

"I burned out all the power I'd been given to destroy him. There was nothing left. But the acolytes wanted me to stay anyway, as a kind of mascot. Proof of the miracles their goddess could work. Just sit there in fancy robes and *inspire* everyone."

Cruz stopped walking, so Lucha did too. They stood together on the north road, facing the trees.

"I don't blame you for running," Cruz said after a long moment. "That doesn't sound like any life I'd want to live."

It was stupid, Lucha thought, how much she'd needed to hear this. That she hadn't made a mistake by leaving. Everyone had thought so at Asilo, though they'd been too polite to voice their concern for her sanity. Río, Lis, even Paz.

Especially Paz.

Lucha remembered it again like she was sitting there now. The war she'd waged in her head—to stay or to go.

"There was a girl there too," Lucha found herself saying. She needed someone to know, in case Paz returned. In case she didn't. "We had something, I think. But she was sworn to the goddess. And I never knew if she saw me for who I really was or just what I represented."

Cruz whistled, long and low. "Sounds tricky. How'd you leave things?"

"I just left," Lucha said, shrugging as if it hadn't been the hardest thing she'd ever done. "I wasn't finished with what I'd sworn to do, and she said she'd wait for me. But I couldn't promise her anything without knowing for sure who she saw when she looked at me. So I didn't."

"Is she coming tomorrow?"

Lucha strained her eyes, as if she could see them from here. The acolytes. Paz among them, or not among them. But all she saw was the dark trunks of trees silhouetted by hazy moonlight.

"I don't know."

Cruz barked a laugh that echoed into the forest. "Lucha!

Who knew you were such a hotbed of interpersonal drama. I thought you were just this stoic girl who was good at stabbing things."

"I'm also that," Lucha admitted with a grudging smile.

"So, do you hope she's coming? Or not coming?"

"*That* is what I'm out here trying to figure out," Lucha replied. "But since it isn't working, I guess I'll go to bed and let fate decide."

"Good luck with that," Cruz said, laughing again and shaking her head.

They walked the rest of the way back to camp in a warm silence. Before they separated for the night, Lucha called out Cruz's name, and Cruz turned.

"Have you ever had someone like that? Someone you were drawn to but didn't know if you could trust?"

Cruz didn't laugh this time. For a moment, her eyes were very far away, like she was looking deep into the past, or into some feeling she didn't have a name for.

"Yeah," she said finally, her voice rough. "It never gets any easier."

Lucha slept so little that she didn't even feel tired when Junio ran into camp shouting. The exhaustion would hit later, she knew, but for now it was only that false energy that would make it all the more painful when it did.

"I saw them!" Junio said, shaking Lucha awake in her hammock. "People in robes! Lots and lots of people!"

"That's good," Lucha said, getting to her feet, rubbing the glorified nap from her eyes. "We'd better get ready."

The camp was in the best shape possible—which might not have been saying much, but Lucha was proud. There were platforms for all the sleeping quarters now, including in the infirmary, and extras for the acolytes. Río had been specific about their lodgings, of course. Five smaller separate areas for the priestesses, and a larger bunk situation for the younger ones on their missions.

If Paz was coming, Lucha thought, one of the small ones would be for her. She took care to keep them all a good distance from her own sleeping area just in case.

Despite the early hour, the camp was a flurry of activity. Cruz was at the center of it all, naturally, barking orders in that good-natured but authoritative way that came so naturally to her.

They had all eaten sparingly the night before to prepare a welcome meal for the acolytes. There hadn't been blight closer than a mile out for over a week. There was nothing left to do . . .

And Lucha was crawling out of her skin.

Sounds through the trees. Footsteps, horses' hooves. Singing. The acolytes were famous for their chants and hymns, Lucha remembered. Could she hear Paz's voice among the others, or was she hallucinating?

For the first time—and it seemed a terrible oversight now—Lucha realized there were more than two options when it came to Paz. Lucha had spent these weeks expecting a yes or no. Paz would arrive and expect something of Lucha, or she wouldn't come at all.

But there was another option. One where Paz arrived having moved on entirely from what had happened between them.

Lucha had been picturing Paz all this time waiting right where she'd been left. A forlorn girl in a green robe that settled over every ample curve, her long black hair curling nearly to her waist. Tears in her eyes that sparkled . . .

But just as much time had passed for Paz as it had for Lucha. What if she'd found it easy to slip back into her old life? What if Lucha's absence had made it easier to move on?

Lucha tried to picture Paz walking arm in arm with another acolyte. Surrounded by friends. Exchanging looks or even kisses with someone new—or perhaps even someone from her past. Someone who had known her far longer than Lucha had.

How would she feel about it? Lucha wondered when her imagination failed to kindle any emotion besides embarrassment. Was there any way to prepare for that sort of thing before it was staring you in the face?

"You all right there, killer?" Cruz asked, sidling up to Lucha. "You look a little pale."

"I'm fine," Lucha said, though her high, tight voice betrayed her.

"If you say so," Cruz replied, then walked to the front of the crowd, throwing a smirk over her shoulder and making Lucha deeply regret her candor the night before.

"I see them!" called Junio, as close to the tree line as the señoras would let him get. "I see the horses!"

Lucha's stomach churned. She felt light-headed. She knew this was what she had wanted, what was best for Robado, but she still wished fervently in this moment that she'd never suggested it.

Junio was right—the horses came into view first, glossy and massive through the trees, backlit by the sun, which had not been up for long.

Their riders had all dismounted. Draped in green robes against the morning chill, they approached slowly. Almost ceremonially.

Hurry up and get it over with, Lucha thought, clenching her fists to keep her hands from shaking. As far as she knew, Almudena didn't have any particular rules about walking at a normal speed.

Río—wearing her green cloak and robe as well—stepped forward at the same pace to greet them as Lucha fantasized about running ahead, pushing their hoods back one by one until she found Paz or reached the end of the line.

"Welcome, my sisters," Río said, extending her arms as the group cleared the tree line.

She removed her hood.

The acolytes removed theirs.

It only took a moment to spot her, of course. Lucha's eyes were drawn like moths to a flickering lamp. The answer to the question she'd been so afraid to ask these past weeks, and with it a thousand more questions, like sprouts just pushing through the soil.

Río made some flowery speech Lucha couldn't hear over the pounding in her ears. She couldn't take her eyes off Paz, who so far hadn't looked her way. Hadn't looked away from her obispo's face at all.

Lucha didn't tune back in until a sharp tug at her jacket alerted her to the silence. Plenty of people were looking at her now, though Paz still wasn't one of them.

It was Cruz pulling on her arm. "She just called up the leaders of the city," she hissed. "Let's go."

Lucha stumbled forward as though she were sleepwalking. Halving the distance to Paz. Then halving it again until she was standing right in front of Paz and the other acolytes in green.

"—the brave liberators of the city of Robado," Río was saying now, gesturing to the four members of the Syndicate.

Cruz hadn't let go of Lucha's jacket, like she was trying to prevent her from bolting into the trees—which wasn't an altogether unnecessary precaution, Lucha was forced to admit. Río introduced Maria, Armando, and Cruz before turning to Lucha with an irritating air of saving the best for last.

"And of course, you all remember Lucha Moya, defeater of Almudena's son, conduit for the goddess's power and infinite wisdom. Even in her weakened state, she traveled here straight from the sanctuary's infirmary to finish the job she'd begun. Eradicating the long-reigning Ricos of Robado and restoring freedom to her people."

Lucha's face was burning. The neck of her jacket felt

horribly tight. The acolytes were dropping to their knees, one by one, and the Robadans followed suit once it became clear what was happening.

"Please, don't," Lucha said weakly, holding out a hand as her mind calculated escape routes, only to toss them all out.

Paz was the last to kneel. As she did, her eyes met Lucha's for the first time, and a spark ignited between them—as if Lucha had needed more heat.

At her side, Cruz offered an exaggerated smirk before dropping to her knees.

"Please," Lucha said again. "There's no need for all this. I did what needed to be done, and I didn't do any of it alone. We're all in this together now, and there's a lot at stake, so I don't think being dishonest about any one person's contribution serves us."

The Robadans stood almost immediately, looking relieved. Paz and some of the higher-ranking acolytes followed suit. In their white robes, the lowest-ranking of Almudena's disciples looked to Río, still kneeling.

With an impatient gesture, she brought them to their feet.

"Thank you," Lucha said before Río could double down on her earlier false praises. "I know you're all used to one way of life at the sanctuary, but things are different here. We work together using the skills we have. While you're here, that will be the way it works. No one is better than anyone else."

Río looked affronted by this. But when Lucha found Paz again, a hint of a smile was just visible at the corner of her mouth.

"If that's all the pomp and ceremony for now," Lucha said with a pointed look at Río, "there's work to be done. Maria will show you to your quarters, and after that Armando will help you discover how you can be most useful. Cruz and I will be finding places for provisions and supplies, so please leave those here on the center platform."

If Río was going to falsely inflate Lucha's significance, she'd make her regret it, Lucha thought with grim satisfaction as the acolytes rushed to follow her orders.

"And I suppose I'll be cleaning up after the horses," the obispo said under her breath as she walked by.

"Wherever you think your skills will be best utilized, Obispo," Lucha said.

Paz, now approaching with careful steps, let her smile widen behind Río's back. Lucha's previous nervousness had transformed into something unwieldy. Twin desires to run away as quickly as possible and to kiss this girl until there was no air left in her lungs.

Río stalked off. Cruz was already gathering provisions near their cook fire, and Lucha knew she should be helping, but time had made its plans clear by standing utterly still as Paz approached.

"You still know how to get under her skin," Paz said, as if it had been minutes and not months since they'd last spoken. "No one else does it quite like you do."

"If that's my legacy, I can't say I'm disappointed." Lucha's throat was dry; her voice caught a little on her would-be casual words. Paz stood a polite distance away, but Lucha felt they were putting on a show for all the camp to see.

"Hi, Paz," she said, letting herself meet the other girl's deep brown eyes. Paz's skin glowed against the green of the robe, which could not hide the joyful arcs of her body. Her hair cascaded in curls over her shoulders, glinting with the early-morning light.

"Hi, Lucha," she said. "I like what you've done with the place."

"Not alone," Lucha said quickly. "And there's still work to be done."

"But they're free," Paz said, a note of wonder in her voice. "In more ways than one. That's something to be proud of."

"Thank you," Lucha said, feeling her face heat up again.

"When you said you were leaving, I never guessed this was what you meant."

Lucha felt something in her lock up at the mention of her leaving. Paz seemed to realize what she'd said, too, because she immediately raised a hand.

"I didn't mean to . . . I mean, this wasn't how I wanted to . . ." She trailed off. Lucha was almost amused to see her flustered; she was usually so collected. Centered.

"It's okay," Lucha said, even though she wasn't sure it was. "We obviously have a lot to talk about. I just have to get over and help with the provisions." She gestured to Cruz—who was doing a fine job on her own—by way of explanation.

"Of course," Paz said, backing away. "I have things to do too. I just wanted to say hi."

"Hi," Lucha said again, trying not to think about how pretty Paz was when she blushed.

"Hi," Paz said, the color deepening along with her smile.

Lucha walked away, her feelings a hopeless jumble. Why was it so hard to remember, when they were face to face, the very real reasons they weren't together? She would have to figure it out soon if she wanted to survive what was coming next.

"Nice of you to join us, *savior of the goddess, liberator of all the swine in Robado's mud pit*." Cruz bowed deeply as Lucha approached.

"Stop it," Lucha muttered. "Give me something heavy to carry."

"Are you sure we should *sully the blessed hands of the chosen champion* with *manual labor*?" Cruz asked, still bent in half with her arm at an odd angle.

Lucha pushed her. Cruz wobbled alarmingly before surfacing mid-cackle. Grudgingly, Lucha laughed too.

"I can see why you didn't want to go back there," Cruz said when she'd recovered. "They're a *lot*." She chucked a massive bag of grain at Lucha without warning, trusting she would catch it.

As she did, Lucha saw Paz still lingering nearby, casting her gaze to the group at the fire. A few folks were beckoning her over, possibly recognizing Paz from her time posing as a Robadan. Working in the night greenhouse and patching up olvidados as part of her mission.

When Lucha caught her eye, Paz turned quickly and hurried away. But for a long time after, Lucha wondered what she'd seen in her gaze. What conclusions she had drawn from it.

16

It took the better part of the day to get tents set up, rations stored, horses fed and watered. Armando approached the last task with an enthusiasm that brought a smile to Lucha's face. Cruz was in top form, traveling from group to group, making sure everyone had what they needed and was contributing where they were best suited.

Lucha, for her part, did whatever task was in front of her to the best of her ability while keeping an eye on the commingling. For the most part, the acolytes were gracious and the Robadans were awed—by the robes and the horses and the provisions in their clean cloth sacks and the books and scrolls, which needed a whole cart to themselves.

Lucha tried to remember how she'd felt when she first arrived at Asilo, but it was so muddied by the rest. The pain of her separation from Salvador. The worry for her sister. The fact that she'd technically been a captive at the time . . .

Paz stuck with Maria's group. Distributing medicine in the open-air infirmary and getting supplies set up for the care of the sick and wounded. Lucha only looked when she was certain Paz was otherwise occupied.

Lucha thought of the girl she'd met in Robado a lifetime ago. Hiding her tattoo and her true identity. Sneaking around administering healing to olvidados in the dead of night. Risking her life to reach them in the Lost House, the dilapidated and dangerous building just outside the city where olvidados went when they had nowhere else to go. Where Lucha's own mother had gone when it was too late to save her.

She tried not to think of the night she'd been one of Paz's patients, under cover of darkness in the night greenhouse. How it had felt to be stitched by her hands. The promises of more their tangled heartbeats had made each other, with no idea of what was to come.

"Funny, I didn't see *tortured yearning* on the official list of integration day activities," Cruz said, startling Lucha out of her memories. "But she's a looker, I'll give you that much. I remember when she worked in the night greenhouse. She used to sing. It was nice."

It was such an absurd oversimplification of Paz's beauty, her talents and voice, the pull she had on Lucha. She didn't even know how to respond. She glanced back instead at where Cruz had just been helping to erect a canvas pantry tent.

"It's leaning a little to the left," she said. "You might want to focus on that."

Cruz snapped to attention with a faux-serious expression and made a half bow. "At once, Your Saviorship." Then walked off laughing again.

Between Cruz's teasing and Paz's continued presence, it was a long day for Lucha. But as the sun began to sink, the camp looked better than she'd ever seen it.

The warm cream color of the acolytes' tents glowed from within. The paths were raked and swept. A cheerful fire kindled in the cooking area, and Cruz was supervising a larger one for a gathering near the center of camp.

Lucha stayed to the outskirts as people began to drop their tasks and move toward the fire. There was something here, she thought. Something so close to what she'd hoped for for this place. And yes, she wished she could have done it without the resources of the sanctuary, but did it really matter how they'd gotten here?

"All right, everyone!" Cruz called once the fire was roaring. "Work is done for the day, and you've all been amazing."

Everyone turned, including Lucha. The chatter quieted down. Even the acolytes seemed engaged.

"Look around at this place," Cruz said, shaking her hair out of her face, lit by the dancing flames. "After the flood, when we'd lost everything, I never dreamed it could look like this. Be like this. But it happened because of all of you."

Appreciative murmurs went around the crowd, and Lucha

found she wasn't immune to the glow of this reflection. They had done it. They had overcome so much.

"Now, we know there's a lot happening in the world. Things that threaten the forest, that threaten us. But we're not sitting by waiting for that to happen to us. In our new partnership with the acolytes of the Asilo sanctuary, we'll be working hard to keep this place safe for all of us."

Around the fire, folks began to look at one another. Acolytes and Robadans. Robadans and their neighbors and friends.

"Okay, I'm not sure about y'all, but I haven't had a real meal in about a month, so let's enjoy ourselves tonight, huh?"

A cheer went up at this, and Lucha cheered too. Cruz was a thorn in her side, had been since the day they met, but in this moment Lucha was proud of how far she'd come. Of what a leader she was to everyone here.

Needing no further prompting, everyone moved toward the cooking area, where Marisol and Junio stood with a few acolytes, readying the feast. Lucha was hungry, of course—they'd been subsisting on berries and greens and spare bites of rabbit for weeks. But she hung back once more, wanting to make sure everyone ate before she took her portion.

The food the acolytes had brought was all from their preserved stores, and it tasted incredible. Flatbread made from tuber flour; grilled vegetables with citrus marinade; meat, salted and cured. The greens and berries that had made such a miserable main course served as a perfect salad, and Lucha felt herself relaxing into fullness and warmth, letting the feeling spread through her.

Around her, the members of the Syndicate and the higher-ranking acolytes ate their meals with similar gusto. Overhead, stars began to wink into view. Lucha, dazed and euphoric and exhausted, let the conversation drift over and past her until she heard her name.

"Tomorrow Lucha and I can get some folks together to build extra shelter for the horses," Cruz was saying, clearly in response to a question from someone.

She was about to chime in with her agreement when Río responded instead.

"Actually, Miss Moya will be with us tomorrow," she said, gesturing to herself and a few of the acolytes around her—Paz included. "We need to get started."

Lucha bristled before she remembered the terms of their agreement. The reason proud, fastidious Río had sent for her precious robed devotees and all their priceless literature to be carted to Robado through the underbrush.

The reason the Robadans were all talking among themselves with full bellies and expressions of hope in their eyes.

"I'm at your service," she said sardonically, with a little seated bow.

Cruz looked at her then, something like disappointment on her face. Lucha felt it too. The end of something. She had been a member of the Syndicate, a Robadan survivor. Until now, when her past had arrived on white horses to make her something she had never wanted to be again.

"I'm really looking forward to getting started," said Paz, who'd been quiet. She leaned into the firelight, catching Lucha's eye. "There are some amazing meditation techniques we were able to find in these old scrolls. Rituals that used to use Pensa but can be adapted to—"

Lucha leaned forward, cutting her off as her discomfort built. "I'd rather we talk about it tomorrow, if you don't mind."

Paz looked immediately cowed, hurt flashing momentarily in her eyes before that cool calm of hers settled once more. "Of course," she said. Her eyes went distant, staring into the flames.

Lucha felt guilty. She hadn't meant to embarrass Paz.

"Smooth," Cruz muttered as she stood and stepped over Lucha's legs.

"Leave it alone," Lucha said under her breath. But of course, Cruz never would.

"I'm gonna head to bed," Cruz said with a yawn and a stretch. "See you all in the morning. Or not, if you're busy with your top-secret stuff, I suppose. You can trust that the horses will be well cared for."

"Thank you," Paz said softly.

Río rose next, and the other acolytes with her. "Bright and early tomorrow, Miss Moya." Her expression said she knew exactly how much Lucha was dreading it.

Lucha smiled, determined not to give her the satisfaction. "Rest well, Obispo."

"And you."

They were gone in a susurration of hushed good nights.

Lucha realized too late that their departure left her and Paz alone at the fire.

She hadn't been avoiding this moment because she didn't want to be alone with Paz, she recognized the moment they were. She'd avoided it because she wanted it too much, and she didn't know what that meant.

"I'm sorry," she said. "For that. Before. I just haven't told everyone . . . everything, and I don't want them to see me differently."

Paz nodded, still looking into the flames. "I understand," she said. "I just thought you of all people would understand the danger of having secrets like that from the people you rely on."

It was a dig, and Lucha felt it. "Yeah, luckily someone was kind enough to teach me *that* lesson the hard way."

"I waited for you, you know?" Paz said, her eyes flashing, meeting Lucha's across the flames.

"I didn't ask you to."

"Yeah, well, you didn't tell me not to, either. Maybe it was stupid to feel hopeful, but I did."

Lucha sat up straighter. She hadn't retained an accurate picture of Paz's beauty, but she hadn't rightly remembered her stubbornness, either.

"It's only been a couple of months," she said. "I told you I had things to figure out. Things I needed to do."

"You did," Paz agreed, not backing down. "And I supported you in that. And I didn't expect you to come back soon. But I also didn't expect to show up here and find you had an entirely new life."

Lucha got to her feet, head spinning at the hypocrisy. "Do you hear yourself?" she asked. "You're telling me it was hard to discover that someone you trusted and believed in had a whole life you didn't know about? At least I didn't actively conceal mine from you."

"I thought we were past this," Paz said, tears glittering in her eyes as she got to her feet. "I thought you said you understood why I did it."

"I did!" Lucha said, too loudly. "I do. It's just . . . it's not easy for me, either, okay? Seeing you is . . . I just didn't expect it to feel like this."

Paz's face softened. She walked a little closer, around the fire. The darkness outside the circle was absolute. It wasn't the first time Lucha had felt she and Paz were alone in their private world.

"I wish it were easier," Paz said. "I thought about it the whole way here. What it would be like, what you would say, whether it would be like it was. I haven't forgotten what you said, but you just have this whole life now that has nothing to do with me. And I feel further away from mine than ever. The people here don't know me as myself. There's nowhere I'm really needed . . ."

Lucha didn't know what to say. She had wondered just before Paz arrived whether she'd moved on with someone else. What it would feel like to see her that way. She hadn't considered what *her* life would look like to Paz.

"It just happened like this," she said, shrugging, moving a little closer to Paz on instinct. "There were so few of us, and so much to fight against, that we had to stick together to get through it."

"And through all that you had to get the best-looking girl at camp to fall in love with you?" Paz smiled. She was closer than ever now. It took a moment for her words to penetrate.

"Wait, what?" Lucha asked blankly, trying to think of who Paz could possibly be talking about. "What girl?"

"Oh, please," Paz replied. "The one with the tattoos, always watching and whispering and teasing you. I guess I shouldn't be surprised—it took you ages to figure out I liked you too."

Lucha's mind was still an utter blank. "Cruz?" she said. "No, it's not like that at all."

"Maybe not for you. But believe me, I know what it looks like."

Paz was the one teasing now, her long eyelashes casting shadows down her cheeks that flickered with the dying fire.

"I'm telling you, there's nothing between us," Lucha said, more decisively this time. "Cruz and I just stopped wanting to kill each other. It's the farthest thing from romantic."

Paz's expression grew more solemn at this. "So, you're not seeing anyone now?" she asked.

Lucha's heart stuttered. She swallowed hard, shaking her head.

"I'm not either," Paz said.

It was hard to believe she was really here, after all Lucha's reluctant imaginings. Paz still didn't seem quite grounded in the reality of Robado, of their camp. Like she fundamentally didn't fit here now that Lucha had been to the hallowed place where she did belong.

Paz was teetering on the knife's edge. On one side were all the questions that had separated them, none of them answered. On the other side were her sparkling eyes on Lucha's and her tongue moistening her bottom lip and the space between them—so small now it seemed likely to combust . . .

The knife disappeared as Paz closed the distance. They were going to kiss, Lucha thought almost deliriously. Kiss in their first moment alone together. Kiss before they could speak of the million reasons why they shouldn't.

And they would have—if they hadn't been interrupted by a strangled yell from up the road.

17

Lucha had her knives out before the heat had fully faded.

This was not the first time she'd had to transition from almost kissing to battling some unknown enemy. Not even the second. She was well practiced at moving between these two types of heat by now.

The question was: who was shouting . . . and why?

"Stay here," she said to Paz, forgetting for a moment who she was talking to. "Or . . . do what you want," she amended. "Just . . . I have to go."

She took off at a run, heading north toward the fence. The first shouting voice had been joined by others. The unmistakable sound of conflict grew louder as Lucha approached. She did not know whether Paz had followed her or stayed put. It didn't matter. The days of Lucha believing Paz needed saving were long behind them.

It took a few minutes to reach the small crowd up ahead. Lucha followed the light of a torch, cursing herself for not grabbing one of her own from the fire. She could make out three, maybe four people. They stood in a half circle, their backs to Lucha, facing some unknown assailant up against the fence.

With Paz's words still echoing in the back of her mind, Lucha identified Cruz first. Hair pushed to one side, tattoos exposed. Her knife was drawn. By her side was Armando. Two acolytes Lucha didn't know completed the group, save for the enemy—who was visible now, in the space between Cruz's body and Armando.

It was a sabuesa, Lucha realized. But barely. Blight had overtaken its body just as it had the camp's precious calf.

As a cazadora, Lucha had dispatched her fair share of the mangy canids—with long limbs, hunched backs, small brains, and vicious teeth, they were untamable scavengers. It didn't usually take much maneuvering to be rid of them.

But this situation was different. The sabuesa's normally diminutive head had been swollen by blight to nearly twice its typical size. Like the calf, it had one clear eye and half a mouth, but the substance Lucha had last seen neutralized by salt water on the north road had enveloped its neck and shoulders.

It was grotesque, misshapen. But it was no less quick for all that.

Armando's calf had been naturally clumsy before its infection. To see it moving at high speeds under the influence of the blight had been sad, and a little sickening. But the sabuesas of Robado were already fast. Already vicious. The blight had only made this one more of both—a formidable enemy rather than a pest.

"On your left!" Lucha called as it lunged for one of the acolytes—her white robe already muddied.

She dodged just in time, and Lucha ran forward to steady her before turning to face the creature.

"Wow, it went so badly with the girl that you came looking for a fight?" Cruz asked, taunting even now. She didn't take her eyes off the monstrous creature between them, but Lucha thought she was smirking.

"Just couldn't trust you to handle it without me," Lucha said, trying not to think about what Paz had said about Cruz being in love with her. It was absurd, wasn't it? Just Paz projecting her fears. There was no way—

Before Lucha could get carried away, the sabuesa lunged for her. Its good eye was rolled back in its socket until only the yellowed white of it was showing. Toxic sludge dripped from its open mouth, hitting the ground and making holes wherever it did.

"Come over here, you twisted little bastard!" Cruz stood in a fighting stance, knife forward. Lucha remembered the spear she'd used to hold off the calf, but a quick survey of everyone present told her there wasn't anything long enough to repeat the maneuver here. The Robadans mostly had knives or short swords, and these acolytes didn't seem to have gotten their weapons training yet.

They'd have to come up with some other way to hold it still.

Snarling in fury and pain, the sabuesa ran with its strange demonic gait. Its knees bent at an angle so unnatural it turned Lucha's stomach. This time it headed right for Cruz.

"What's the plan here?" Lucha called.

Cruz didn't answer, only maintained her stance as the thing moved toward her.

"Cruz, get out of the way!" Lucha called, panic clawing up her throat. But Cruz didn't move.

At the last moment, Lucha threw herself into the path of the animal, tackling Cruz out of the way just as the creature leapt into the air, claws extended and dripping with blight, teeth bared on the side of its mouth that could still open.

It missed Cruz by a hair. Lucha by less.

They landed in a heap a few feet away, Lucha on top. She could feel the other girl's heartbeat even as her own pounded in anger and fear. "What the hell were you thinking?" she asked.

But Cruz wasn't looking at her. And from the expression on her face, Lucha knew exactly what was coming up behind her.

Lucha twisted, Cruz reached with her knife, but the thing was only inches away. There was no way they could kill it without the blight touching one of them. An image appeared unwanted in Lucha's thoughts, freezing her in place: Cruz, her face taken over by blight, only one good eye, her half mouth open in a feral smile.

"NO!" Lucha cried, too tangled up to stop it.

But just at the moment when the sabuesa would have sunk its teeth into Cruz's extended wrist, the monster's eye widened.

Its mouth went slack. Just when it would have been finishing off one of them and moving on to the next, it slumped over dead at their feet.

Lucha scrambled up, helping Cruz before stepping closer to examine the monster.

An arrow with deep green fletching protruded from its back. The blight had started to take hold of the shaft, but it became inert before it could finish the climb. Dead as the sabuesa it had taken over.

Before Lucha could bring herself to raise her eyes, Cruz uttered a low whistle, already stepping forward.

"That was a hell of a shot."

Lucha looked up just in time to watch Cruz extend her hand.

To watch Paz take it, smiling.

"Cruz Miranda," said Cruz. "I don't think we were formally introduced."

"Paz León. And you're welcome."

Paz was strapping her bow onto her back. She hadn't bothered to take out a second arrow, so sure she'd been of her shot's trajectory. It was irritating even as it caused heat to rise in Lucha's cheeks.

"Can you take them to the med tent?" Cruz asked Maria, glancing at the obviously shaken acolytes. "I don't think they were hurt, but we should make sure no one is blighted."

Maria agreed, sheathing her short sword and rounding up the girls. "Come on, come on," she said. "Welcome to Robado, you're going to have to toughen up."

"I'll get the salt water," Armando grunted when he seemed sure Cruz was safe. "Don't touch it."

"Wasn't planning on it," Cruz said.

Lucha was painfully aware that the three of them were alone. Herself, Paz, and Cruz.

"Well, I was on my way to bed," Cruz said with an exaggerated yawn.

"Wait," Lucha said, trying to ignore the awkwardness. "You need to be checked for blight."

Cruz scoffed. "You think I wouldn't know if it got me? I'm fine."

"You're a *leader* of this city. *The* leader," Lucha said, her pent-up frustration boiling over. "You don't get to play chicken with monsters anymore. People are counting on you."

"Sheesh, what buzzed into your britches?"

"Go to the med tent," Lucha forced out. "Make sure you're clear."

"I'm not hoofing it all the way back over there," Cruz argued. "You're so concerned, check yourself." She held out her arms, turning her back to them.

Lucha felt her face heat up. It would have been a normal request a few hours ago, but through the lens of Paz's accusation, it felt impossible. Especially with Paz herself standing right there, watching them.

But how could Lucha refuse without admitting the ridiculousness of it all?

Paz made the decision for her seconds later. "On that note,

I'm going to bed," she said pointedly, and she disappeared into the dark camp, leaving Lucha staring after her.

"The blight is probably spreading by now," Cruz said sarcastically, and Lucha sighed, turning to her.

Cruz wore hide pants she had made herself, tough enough to serve as light armor when hunting or fighting. Usually, she wore a jacket made of the same material, but tonight she had on only a close-fitting cloth shirt, her tattooed arms exposed where it ended at her shoulders.

The shirt looked in fine shape. Lucha lifted it slightly to make sure the gaps were covered. Cruz was pale. All lean, knotted muscle. More scars than tattoos, but not by much. Lucha had never been this close to her before. She smelled like campfire smoke and citrus.

"So, your little girlfriend left in a huff," Cruz said as Lucha checked her arms. The place where her boots met the bottoms of her pants.

"She's fine," Lucha said irritably. "It's just been a long day. And she's not my girlfriend."

"Well, she sure looked jealous enough to be one. Your turn."

Lucha had finished examining Cruz, who motioned for her to lift her arms and turn around.

"I'm fine," Lucha said.

Cruz clutched at her heart, speaking in a high-pitched voice. *"I can't believe you, the savior of all of Elegido, putting herself at unfathomable risk because she's too stubborn to—"*

"Fine!" Lucha said, holding her arms out. "Make it quick."

Cruz started at the bottom, working her way up, hands moving over Lucha's rough canvas clothes thoroughly.

Lucha, infuriatingly, felt her heart speed up. It was just the leftover nerves from her and Paz's reunion at the fire, she told herself. The heightened emotions from the fight.

"So, what was she upset about, anyway?" Cruz asked in a low voice as she reached the place where Lucha's shirt was tucked in, pulling it from her waistband.

"Being awfully thorough, aren't we?" Lucha asked. They were facing each other now, Cruz kneeling in front of her. The top of her short, shaggy hair was all Lucha could see.

"That's not an answer to my question."

Lucha sighed heavily. Cruz wasn't one to relent when she wanted information, and at least this way they could laugh about it. Get rid of the strange tension Paz's words had brought on.

"She thinks you *like* me," she said, laughing. "Which is completely ridiculous, I know. I told her we barely tolerate each other. But she's stubborn. Once she gets an idea in her head . . ."

She trailed off as Cruz got to her feet. Sliding her fingertips inside the neck of Lucha's shirt. Goose bumps spread across Lucha's skin. She hoped Cruz wouldn't notice her heart, pounding even faster now.

Knock it off, she told it. *This is* Cruz.

"I mean, she's not wrong," the other girl replied. "I do like you. Sure, you drive me up a tree most days, but I think there's a grudging respect at this point."

Lucha laughed again, huskier now. "No, I mean . . . she thinks you have *feelings* for me," she clarified. "Romantic feelings."

Cruz didn't laugh. They were very close together now as she lifted Lucha's braids, examined her hairline. "Blight-free," she declared, without reacting to Lucha's words. "Congratulations."

She took a step back, adjusting her clothes, checking her knives.

"You heard what I said, right?" Lucha pressed. "I mean, it's comical. Her thinking that."

Cruz shrugged.

"Are you saying it's not comical?"

"Is that what you want me to say?"

The torch was burning low. The corpse of the sabuesa was still stinking just feet away. It was late, and Lucha was exhausted and confused and in no mood for more of Cruz's games.

"You know, this thing you do, it's not as cute as you think it is," she snapped. "Your smirking and your teasing, nothing is ever serious to you. Everything's a joke. And that's fine. You don't have to take me seriously. But I need you to take Robado seriously, which means no more throwing yourself in front of blighted animals, got it?"

Cruz's expression was unfathomable for a moment; then the ever-present smirk returned. "I'm sorry," she said. "You're right. You and me? Not if the world were ending."

The sting landed before Lucha could register it. It was what she'd wanted to hear, of course, so why did she suddenly feel . . . like this? Like she wanted to take it all back . . .

"*Thank* you," she said instead, with almost-exaggerated relief.

"And I hear you, okay?" Cruz followed up. "I haven't ever had a reason to be careful before, but I'll try. Harder."

For Robado, Lucha wanted to clarify, but Cruz had already made her meaning plain.

"Thank you," Lucha said again. "Because I could run this place without you, but I'd miss out on too much beauty sleep."

Cruz laughed. "Get to bed," she said. "I'll wait for Armando. Can't have the *goddess's chosen champion* getting dark circles on her first day back."

"Okay," Lucha said, too tired to take the bait. "Good night, Cruz."

"Good night."

Lucha turned and made her way toward camp, but she felt eyes on her the whole way back.

18

For just a moment, when Lucha awoke the next morning, she thought it had all been a dream. Paz and the acolytes here, the sabuesa, Cruz in the moonlight.

You and me? Not if the world were ending.

A quick glance out the flaps of her new canvas tent showed her it was all real. The white tents shone in the early-morning sun. The camp was already bustling, the Robadans on their best behavior for the acolytes. The smell of food was coming from somewhere.

Lucha pulled her head back inside, standing up, stretching before dressing for the day. Río's command last night had been clear. She wanted Lucha bright and early to fulfill her end of their bargain.

Just as she was putting on her jacket, Lucha heard the voices of the Syndicate members outside. Maria, Armando, Cruz.

Not if the world were ending.

"Hey! Champ! Get out here and help, huh?"

Lucha emerged from her tent to see the three of them walking toward the cook fire.

"We're taking breakfast to the clinic," Maria said cheerfully. "We could use an extra pair of hands."

The sun was shining through the trees. The three of them looked more relaxed than Lucha had ever seen them. Everyone was moving with purpose today, with hope. Lucha knew she was supposed to be reporting to Río, but she felt the pull so strongly she almost didn't care.

"All right," she said. "I can do one trip and then—"

"Morning, everyone."

The voice came from behind her, but all Lucha had to do was look at Cruz's smirk to know who it was. As if she wouldn't have known the voice anywhere, anyway.

The Syndicate made their greetings, Maria and Armando a little shyly, Cruz without dropping her smirk.

"Horses are doing well," Armando said when a slightly awkward silence followed.

"That's wonderful," Paz replied, smiling. "Next time we'll bring the compañeras, see how you do with them."

She was joking, but the three of them looked at her blankly.

"Giant forest cats," Lucha clarified. "They're a bit intimidating."

Armando's eyes went wide with longing. "Well, that's something I'll have to see," he said, nodding to Paz, whose smile softened before she turned to Lucha.

"I thought we could walk to Río's together."

Lucha felt her face heat up. "Oh, well, I was going to help with getting breakfast to the clinic, so—"

"Don't worry about it," Cruz said, waving a hand. "We've got it under control. You have more important things to do."

The feeling of resentment that had sparked in Lucha last night kindled hotter now. She had been a leader here for weeks. Yes, she had made a deal with Río, but that didn't give this woman the right to give her orders. They were working together.

"I'm going to help," she said. "I said I would, so I'm going to. Río can wait."

Paz's face fell a little, and Lucha immediately felt mean and petty. She had only been annoyed with Río, but of course that wasn't what it looked like. Not with what Paz had said last night, and how she already felt about Lucha and Cruz.

"That's fine," Paz said quietly. "I'll go ahead and let her know you're coming."

She was gone before Lucha could back down, and she turned to the Syndicate awkwardly.

"Damn," Maria said, eyebrow raised. "What'd she do to you?"

"Nothing," Lucha said quickly. "She's—I'm—It's nothing."

"Yeah," Cruz said, slinging an arm around Lucha's shoulders. "That's how Lucha always acts when she likes someone. Didn't anyone ever tell you that's the best way to get a girl's attention?"

"Ooh," Maria said. "She is gorgeous."

"Thanks a lot," Lucha muttered under her breath to Cruz, who only smiled.

By the time the clinic patients had eaten, the sun was warming the camp and the day was in full swing. Lucha hadn't seen Paz or Río, and she made her way to the obispo's tent feeling sheepish.

"Sorry I'm late," she said, entering to find Río, Paz, and the high-level acolytes all gathered. "Had some things to take care of."

"Yes, I'm sure your camp duties are of equal importance to preventing the end of all we know and hold dear," Río snapped. "We had an agreement, and I expect you to honor it, Miss Moya. Every day. Preferably before *nightfall*."

It wasn't even midmorning, but Lucha didn't want a fight. Not with Paz looking so sad.

"My apologies, Obispo," Lucha said. "And to the rest of you, for wasting your time." She tried to catch Paz's eye, but the other girl seemed to be avoiding her gaze.

"No matter," Río said with a snap of her wrist. "Sit. We have much to discuss today."

Lucha sat, trying not to bristle at the woman's tone. Río's tent was much larger than any of the others—nearly the size of her office back at the sanctuary, and filled with real furniture, books, and scrolls.

It even had two canvas windows on either side. They were open now, and through the one on the left, the sun shone off Paz's glossy braids.

"Now," Río said, clapping her hands together. "We have

a lot to accomplish and not much time to do it. But before we can start, I need to explain what's at stake here. What we stand to lose if we don't manage to succeed."

There were four other acolytes, bringing the party to seven. Lucha recognized Juana and Francisca, Río's personal guards, and the old woman who had administered her Pensa tea ceremony in Asilo. The one where Lucha had spoken to Almudena directly. The one where she'd been encouraged to become a fugitive.

The last woman Lucha didn't recognize. She had long, light hair and eyes so pale they made Lucha nervous. The strange woman stared in rapt attention at the obispo as she began to pace the front of the room.

"In our histories," Río began, "there is little conversation surrounding the existence of this world before Almudena entered it. What little has been collected mostly serves as a cautionary tale. The stories describe a world mired in chaos. Devoid of the order of seasons. Balance. Life and death. In these tales, the cycles of life are random. Floods and fires and droughts and storms arrive unpredictably, to devastating effect."

"Sounds familiar," Lucha said under her breath, hoping to get Paz's attention.

"It shouldn't," Río replied. Her voice was the snapping of a dry twig. "What you have experienced these past weeks is barely a taste. If my theory is correct, it will worsen quickly. So quickly we will have very little time before the world as we know it is unrecognizable."

"It's the future Salvador wanted," Lucha said, thinking of the last king of Robado. His insistence that Salvador would have his revenge. "Imbalance. Ruin. The world destroyed. He'll get his wish in the end whether he lived to see it or not."

No one reacted overtly, but of course they hadn't seen what she'd seen. Salvador hadn't invaded their minds, showing them the future that was promised if she didn't join him.

Piles of bones.

The forest destroyed.

Everywhere barren and burning.

"Hopelessness is a luxury we cannot afford, Miss Moya," Río snapped. "If we die, it won't be because we were too weak to fight. It will be because the most we could do was not enough."

"I'm not hopeless," Lucha retorted. "But this isn't a story. You've never been threatened by a god. I have. You can't imagine from any passage in any book what he had planned for this world."

"Good," Río said. "Then you understand why I can't tolerate laziness and stubbornness. Why we need to work together."

Lucha was cowed by this. She nodded. Finally feeling Paz's eyes on her, she couldn't meet them.

Río resumed her lecture. "We began to comb through the histories, of course, the moment we guessed what was happening to the forest. I didn't make it far before I realized the Pensa plant was gone. That's when I made my way toward Robado."

She paused, clearly expecting some kind of interruption from Lucha, who let the moment pass.

"But the fact remains there is no Pensa. Not here, or anywhere. None of the ways we've been taught to contact our goddess, or to request guidance, are available to us. All we know at this moment is that without a divine presence in Elegido, we're very likely headed for that same devastation."

"Only worse," Lucha said, hearing the hollow tone of her own voice. "Because there are already people living here."

"What exactly will happen to them?" Paz asked. Her eyes were unfocused, like she was watching it all burn in front of her eyes. "To us," she corrected.

"Without divine order, the human race simply will not be able to support ourselves," Río explained. "Our food sources, our water, our shelter will be constantly under threat from unpredictable cycles and devastating natural events. We could potentially survive in small, nomadic groups, but it would be a brutal existence. Survival would be our only purpose. There would be no building. No learning. No planning."

It didn't sound like much of a life, Lucha thought. But it was a life.

"Even that we can only sustain for a short time, however," Río concluded in a voice heavy with regret. "Soon enough, the resources will be gone. We will die out in great numbers, then smaller ones, until there are none of us left to fix this."

As far as strategy sessions went, it wasn't the most inspiring one Lucha had ever attended. They sat in silence for a few moments; Lucha knew they were all digesting this information the best way they knew how. Steeling themselves to prevent this outcome at all costs.

"So, what's the plan?" Lucha asked when she could think no more. When the skeletons and blistered ground filling her thoughts were unbearable.

"The plan is simple," said Río, though her tone said it wouldn't be simple at all. "We will attempt to induce a trance state in you similar to the effects of Pensa. In that state, you will hopefully be able to access Almudena's guidance. To commune with her the way we once could with the aid of the plant."

It all sounded fairly ridiculous to Lucha, though she refrained from saying so.

"I promised to help you, and I will," she said instead. "However I can. But you have to understand that whatever power I had, whatever access to her, is gone now."

"Your conscious mind doesn't have access to it," said the old woman, speaking for the first time. "But the body remembers, Miss Moya. Inside you there are imprints of divine knowing that we can use, if only we can access them."

Lucha nodded as if this made sense. "I'll try," she said, thinking of the Robadans. Their full bellies. Their sense of purpose. If she had to close her eyes and let Río's followers try to put her in a trance, she would do it. "I can't make any promises, but I said I'd try, so I will."

"Good," said the old woman, getting to her feet and pulling her chair to the center of the room. "Let's get started."

"Now?" Lucha blanched. "You want to start now?"

"Do you want to wait until the food stores are gone?" Río asked. "Or perhaps until the trees in the forest all die?"

"Sorry," Lucha muttered, standing. Suddenly her palms were sweating. She felt anxious and small and wholly unprepared. "I just thought . . . well, never mind."

She sat in the chair as the other acolytes stood, circling her as if she were some kind of curiosity. Some experiment.

"Now," said the old woman. "I want you to close your eyes and let the sound of my voice guide you. Can you do that?"

Lucha, throat dry, could only nod.

"Good, then let's begin. I want you to imagine you are—"

"Wait!" Lucha said, her eyes flying open. "What's your name?"

"Excuse me?" the woman asked as Río scoffed.

"If you're going to be poking around in my head, I'd at least like to know your name."

"My name is Mariel," she said, looking puzzled. As if it hardly mattered.

"I'm Lucha," Lucha said thickly.

"I know," Mariel said gently. Lucha looked for Paz to see if she was laughing, but she wore the same expression as the rest of the acolytes. Detached curiosity.

"Can we resume?" Río asked, impatience in every syllable. "This is a matter of some urgency, you know."

"Sure," Lucha said, swallowing hard. "Uh, go ahead." She closed her eyes, feeling horribly vulnerable, resisting the urge to reach for her knives.

"I want you to imagine you're in a field."

"Sure," Lucha said again.

"No need to respond just yet," Mariel said. "Just follow the sound of my voice . . . I want you to imagine you're in a field that stretches as far as you can see. The grass is healthy and green. There are little wildflowers everywhere."

This wasn't difficult for Lucha to imagine. She had been in exactly such a field not long ago. A field surrounded by tall trees. A field that filled with the growls of compañeras as she stood in it.

Mariel paused for a long time as Lucha built the image in her mind. She was surprised to find it felt every bit as real as her Pensa vision had been—although she remained aware of her body sitting in the chair in Río's tent at the same time.

"Good," Mariel said when the details of the field were sharp and clear. "Now I want you to look around you. Is there anything moving? Anything that looks out of place?"

Immediately, Lucha was on guard again. She scanned the field for shadows, silhouettes, listened for the sounds of predators creeping in. Her heart began to beat faster, both in the vision and in the room with the acolytes.

"I don't see anything," she said. The words echoed strangely in the field around her.

"Patience," Mariel said. "Keep looking."

But there was nothing. Nothing but a beautiful meadow filled with tiny white flowers. A gentle breeze. The sun overhead. Lucha looked at the ground around her feet, feeling as though this was some kind of test she was failing. Until she saw her shadow.

Lucha had always been a knife of a girl, compact and ruthless, but this shadow didn't match her body. It was taller, for one, with broader shoulders and shorter hair. A silhouette Lucha would have known anywhere.

She gasped, opening her eyes to find the acolytes peering at her.

"What did you see?" Mariel asked urgently. "Was it the goddess?"

"No," Lucha gasped. "No, it was . . ." She trailed off, Salvador's name a bitter taste behind her lips. She swallowed it. "It wasn't the goddess. I need . . . just . . . I'm sorry."

Getting to her feet despite the protestations of Río and Mariel, Lucha made her way out of Río's tent. She needed to think. The cold, clammy fingers of Salvador's presence still felt like they were trailing across her skin.

The sunlight helped. She dragged in deep breaths, the morning heating up around her.

Lucha sat against the base of a tree and tried to order her thoughts. It had been alarming to see so clearly even without the Pensa. Proof of Río's theory, perhaps, but Lucha had expected to see Almudena, not *him*.

The last time she had confessed to a connection with Salvador, they'd locked her up. Things had changed since then, allegedly, but she still didn't think it was wise to start screaming about Almudena's son. His shadow in place of her own. With the forest so close, Lucha closed her eyes, reaching down into herself. To the place where he had once been.

If he was still connected to her, she had to know. They were looking for guidance, not punishment, and if she couldn't give them that . . .

Lucha didn't know how long she sat there silently, probing at her invisible scars. Only that she found nothing, same as she had when she reached for her power the day the calf was taken. Only that she was empty. Powerless. Alone.

19

Lucha sat beside the tree for a long time. No one came for her, but eventually she'd be called to account for what had happened in the tent. To fit it into the understanding these people all had of who she was and what she could do.

It was that idea keeping her frozen, she knew. She'd allowed Río to bring the acolytes here because she knew it was what was best for Robado. And indeed, the people were fed, the camp was more united than ever. She had succeeded in that way.

But what she had bargained with was more precious than she knew. This was the feeling she'd hated in the sanctuary. The reason she couldn't stay, even when Lis did. The reason she'd left Paz. This feeling that she'd never reconcile who she was with all that these people needed her to be.

And right now, Lucha didn't want to be that person. Their savior. The light-shrouded warrior who had defeated their greatest enemy. She just wanted to be herself.

Getting to her feet, feeling a little like a fugitive, Lucha made her way toward the center of camp. She kept a furtive eye out for Río, Paz, the other acolytes, but they must still have been shut up in that tent figuring out what to do about her.

She scanned the crowd for a member of the Syndicate. She needed to be useful. To help Maria with the patients in the clinic, or to hold something heavy while Armando hammered it. Even foraging with Marisol and Junio would have been welcome. Anything to ground her in feeling like the person she wanted to be instead of the person she'd walked away from being . . .

But she didn't see any of them. In fact, besides a few acolytes and younger Robadans, Lucha didn't see anyone.

Fear crept through her veins, heightened by her earlier vision of Salvador.

"Where is everyone?" she asked the first acolyte who passed, a young woman in a white robe. Lucha didn't know her name.

The acolyte's eyes went wide. She looked on the verge of kneeling. Lucha resisted the urge to shake her.

"No need for ceremony at the moment," she said through her teeth. "I just need to know where the Robadans are. Maria, Armando, Cruz. Have you seen any of them?"

"Th-there's a fire," the girl managed after a long moment of spluttering. "They said it was too close for comfort. They told the group to gather at the fence to head into the woods."

"Damn," Lucha said. A fire so soon after a flood? And how close was it to camp? "Thank you," she said before running off toward the compound. Now that she knew, she thought she could smell smoke on the breeze.

Lucha was furious that they hadn't retrieved her from Río's. If something this bad was happening, she deserved to know. She needed to be part of it. As it was, she didn't even know how long it had been since they left.

The gate was deserted, but Lucha could see where the group had charged into the woods. She didn't hesitate before following. Something was kindling in her, resentment heightened by fear. The need to *do* something. Something tangible. Something that connected her to the world, rather than sequestering her away from it.

She crashed through the bushes for half an hour before she heard voices on the hilltop ahead. It was the same one the other half of the Robadans had fled to during the flood, and now they were using it to scout a fire.

Lucha tried not to think about what was happening, or the solution she'd promised and walked away from, as she made her way toward the group.

Armando spotted her first. "What is it?" he asked, eyes wide with fear. "Is everything okay at camp? The horses?"

"Everyone's fine," Lucha said, pushing past him to where Cruz, Maria, and a few of the stronger Robadans were staring down into the valley. There were ten of them there, packs on their backs, bandanas tied around their necks.

"What are you doing here?" Maria asked, turning to face Lucha. "I mean, not that we can't use the help. I just thought you had special goddess champion school today."

Lucha scowled. "I'm here to help."

Maria and Armando looked to Cruz, of course. She hadn't

turned yet. Lucha stepped up beside her. Along the far side of the valley, she could see the deadly orange of the fire coming toward them.

"It's already too big," Cruz said without greeting her. "If we can't get it out fast, it'll spread to the camp by morning." There was nothing of last night's teasing in Cruz's tone now. She kept her eyes on the burning horizon.

"What's the plan?" Lucha asked.

"Most of us will head down with the supplies we have, start trying to put it out. The rest will go back for water and more supplies. Spell us in a few hours—or perhaps more."

"I'm going down there," Lucha said, feeling Salvador's shadow behind her. All the reasons she didn't want to return. "Let me help." She didn't say that she needed this more than they needed her. That she was chasing the deadly calm she always felt when doom was approaching.

Cruz looked at her at last, no smirk, just a searching gaze. Lucha hoped she had hidden it better than she thought. The plea to be allowed to do something useful instead of mulling over the worst of her memories.

For a moment, Lucha's thoughts flicked back to Paz's accusation. The sabuesa, last night. *Not if the world were ending.*

"We'll be gone until tomorrow," Cruz said. "Maybe longer. Can they spare you?"

Lucha thought of Río, of how reluctant she'd been to bring the acolytes here. Of how much she was counting on Lucha, but also of her desire to control the terms of this arrangement.

Lucha had promised to help, not surrender. What better way to teach Río that?

"They'll be fine," Lucha said, taking the pack Cruz handed her. She felt better the moment it was on her back, and then they were off.

After about a half hour of travel, when the late-morning sun was shining through the trees, the air began to turn hazy. It was spectacular, Lucha had to admit. The way the light came through the trees in columns defined by the smoke. It stung her eyes, made her throat raw. Before long, Lucha understood why most of the Robadans had bandanas around their necks.

Lucha took in the moment, feeling its significance. She'd lived in Robado all her life. There had been high water every month, of course. Salt seeping into everything. Warped wood and mud and damp and mildew.

But fire? This close to the river? They'd never even had cause to worry about it.

Those days, she accepted, were long over. The closer they got to the blaze, the worse the smoke got. Soon even the sun was a ball of red in the sky, the light filtering through air so thick with smoke it looked like a misty morning fog.

"Shit," Cruz swore, doubling back to Lucha. "There's a canteen in your pack," she said. "And take this." She tossed Lucha a bandana from her pocket. It was warm, and it smelled like her, even with the smoke filtering through it. Citrus, Lucha remembered from last night.

"Thanks," Lucha said through the fabric. "And, Cruz?"

"Yeah?"

"Don't forget what I said yesterday."

For the first time, the upper half of Cruz's face betrayed a smirk. "The part about how we'd make a terrible couple?"

Lucha rolled her eyes. "Don't put yourself in unnecessary danger."

"Right," Cruz said, the lines around her eyes smoothing. "Apparently I'm *important.*"

"Let's not get ahead of ourselves," Lucha grumbled.

There was no time for banter once they reached the burning place. Here, despite the proximity to the river, it looked as though there'd been no water for ages. The trees were nearly bare, a carpet of fallen leaves littering the ground. They crunched when Lucha stepped on them. Brittle. Long dead.

This wasn't the season for falling. They should have had months. And still, here it was. A drought zone just twenty miles from the place where a flood had recently wiped out hundreds of Robadans. Left the rest without homes.

It made no logical sense, Lucha thought as the sand sledge was pulled up as close as possible to the fire itself. And yet it did. The imbalance. The world before gods.

The world after.

Lucha shook herself. There was no room for theory or mythology here. That was why she had come, after all.

It was miserable, awful work. They lifted bags of river sand two at a time and dumped them on the edges of the fire, wetting them before advancing and doing it again to the next burning section.

The forest on fire was an entirely new animal. Even without her gift, Lucha felt it in her chest. The wrongness of burning during this season.

The entire place was cast in black and orange. The smoke choked everything, so you couldn't see two feet in front of you. The fire lit the smoke from within, making it glow red and orange. The heat was intolerable so close to the flames. Lucha was scorched and dripping sweat within twenty minutes.

But it didn't matter. This threat required every synapse. She worked like a girl possessed. Everything in her distilled down to the muscles in her arms as they hauled water and sand. The singeing heat on her face.

Hours later, they were making far less progress than they needed to be.

So close to Robado, a wayward gust of wind could easily cause devastation. They discovered that every twenty minutes or so, when they believed they had everything in an area stamped out, the wind would pick up. With that, the fire jumped.

Then they started all over again.

It was nearing dark by the time the fire was under control. Armando had gone back twice for more supplies. Where the grove had been alive with flames, there was nothing but black, soggy damp everywhere you looked.

Every part of Lucha's body screamed. She doubted she'd ever worked so hard in her life.

All she wanted was to flop down onto the newly extinguished ground and sleep for a week, but the rest of the Syndicate were still on their feet—and Lucha wouldn't be the first to drop.

"It looks good now," Cruz called out to the weary, soot-smeared, and bedraggled crowd. "But we can't let our guard down. Coals could be smoldering underneath all this, ready to catch. The wind could pick up and fan the fire back to life. I'll need a few volunteers to head back for more water and sand. The rest will stay overnight. Make sure it doesn't come back to bite us."

Armando and one of the broad-shouldered men volunteered at once, along with a woman Lucha didn't know by name who had only left the clinic a few days ago. They didn't even take the break Cruz offered them before jogging off into the trees, disappearing from view.

"Get some rest," Cruz said to everyone else. "Sleep if you can. I'll take first watch."

They didn't need to be told twice. Maria and the remaining five firefighters dropped to the ground where they stood. For some reason, Lucha stayed standing. At the sight of the demolished grove, the exhausted people fighting the flames, she felt suddenly emotional.

"They did good," Cruz said, making her way to Lucha through the soot and sand. "You did too."

"Thanks," Lucha said. They stood side by side, surrounded by the devastation they'd fought together to keep Robado safe. Lucha felt the satisfaction in her bones. *This* was where she was supposed to be. Not sitting in the midst of acolytes leafing through mythology. Here, in the blood and the soot and the sweat of it all.

Cruz sank down beside her, finally resting. Lucha took it as permission to do the same. She felt something between them, some kinship she hadn't before. Maybe this was what Paz had mistaken for romance. Lucha was just trying to figure out how to voice it when Cruz spoke up.

"You shouldn't have come."

Lucha's sentiment was doused much more quickly than the fire's embers. She didn't answer, sensing Cruz had more to say.

"You were obviously going through something, so I didn't want to turn you away, but you're being kind of a hypocrite, you know?"

"How do you figure?" Lucha asked, temper flaring even through her exhaustion.

"Well, last night you said I was too important to be risking myself in dangerous situations, right? And here you are, and you've got some key to unlocking what's happening. To actually *fixing* it instead of just putting out fires. And what are you doing? Running away to where the danger is because you're scared."

Lucha's mouth opened and closed several times. She was so mad she couldn't make the words line up right. Cruz waited, which only infuriated her more.

"I never asked to be their stupid savior," she finally managed. "This is exactly why I left the sanctuary. Because I don't want to be one of their perfect devotees. *This* is where I belong, okay? Not there. That isn't who I am."

Cruz, abruptly, looked just as angry as Lucha did. "You think that's how this works? That we have some destiny tied to who we *are* and the world just bends to it? You sound like a child. Sure, those robed people trying to make you their mascot is creepy, I agree. But are they wrong about what you can do?"

"I don't know," she said, slumping a little, the exhaustion of the day bearing down. "I don't know if I can do it. I know what they want from me, but . . ."

"But you're scared you won't do a good job," Cruz said. "You think I'm not scared of that every day? I could have run off with that brick of Olvida when you gave it to me. I could still run, anytime I want. But I don't. I stay and I do the best I can. The difference is I *can't* end this. You can. So stop being a coward."

These words cut deeper than Lucha liked to admit. She got to her feet, trying to hide the way her knees shook.

"You know, I've seen the way you are with the other Robadans. With Armando and Maria, even. You're encouraging and you're kind, you prop them up when they need it. You *lead*. And this is what I get when I'm scared? When I try to be vulnerable with you? *Stop being a coward and do it anyway.* God, I can't believe I ever let Paz convince me you had feelings for me. I must be a complete idiot."

Cruz stood as well. She faced Lucha, so close she could count her eyelashes.

Lucha felt frozen in place, outside of time somehow with the smoldering backdrop and the smoke and the exhaustion. She waited to see what Cruz would do. What *she* would do.

"You *are* an idiot," Cruz said at last, and then kissed her.

Lucha's body responded eagerly as her mind struggled to catch up. There was nothing soft about kissing Cruz. She kissed like she led, with enthusiasm and spark and plenty of encouragement.

When they broke apart, Cruz was smirking, her face covered in soot.

"What was *that?*" Lucha asked, her heart hammering against her ribs.

"Oh, that?" Cruz asked. "An experiment."

"Really," Lucha said, temper flaring again already. "And what do you conclude?"

"That there's at least one surefire way to get you to stop yelling at me."

Lucha laughed, but only because she didn't have the first clue what to do instead. Cruz laughed too, the smoldering forest around them the most absurd possible backdrop for whatever was happening here.

"So, you don't see us working if the world were ending, but you can kiss me to shut me up, is that it?"

"So far," Cruz said, laughing again. "But I'll keep you apprised."

Lucha was about to say exactly what she thought of that, but before she could, Maria approached them, out of breath. Cruz stepped smoothly away from Lucha before anything could be inferred, and was all business by the time she turned to face Maria.

"Flare-up on the other side," Maria said. "We need sand."

"On it," Cruz said, turning back to Lucha as Maria jogged away. "You need to get back. They're counting on you. We're all counting on you."

And before Lucha could do more than gape at her, Cruz had followed Maria.

20

The walk back into Robado wasn't nearly long enough for Lucha to sort out how she felt in the aftermath of the fire. Of Cruz.

She wanted to turn around and demand that the other girl explain herself. To make her stay still until they both understood what the hell that had been and what it meant.

But Cruz, even if she was completely infuriating, had been right about one thing. Lucha hiding out here was just that. Hiding. It didn't matter if Lucha's task was the one she wanted, it was one only she could do. And it wasn't fair to make everyone around her suffer just because she was afraid.

Almudena had told her there was no destiny. There were only choices. It was time to make the right one. *That* was how she could keep Robado safe.

Whatever was happening with Paz, with Cruz, would have to wait.

That much, at least, was a relief.

When Lucha stepped into the city, it was well past midnight. She desperately needed to bathe, and eat, and sleep. But she marched up to Río's tent instead. A candle was burning, and muffled voices came from inside.

"Anybody in there?" Lucha called out, ignoring her weariness. Her confusion.

It was Paz who opened the flap.

"I'm sorry," Lucha said, not altogether sure what she was apologizing for. She knew she must look wild, soot-covered and bleary-eyed, smelling of smoke.

Paz's eyes widened, but she only nodded, gesturing for Lucha to come inside.

"Good," Lucha said when she saw Río and Mariel huddled over some scrolls in the corner. "You're all here. I'm ready to try again."

If either of them thought this was strange, they didn't show it. Mariel got to her feet and showed Lucha to the chair in the middle of the tent. The one she'd vacated this morning, though it felt like a lifetime ago.

"Sit down, please," Mariel said.

Lucha sat. She closed her eyes before she was instructed to. She told herself to release everything. The resentments. The fear. The confusion. To try to be still.

"I want you to imagine you're in a field," Mariel said again.

Lucha could feel Paz's and Río's eyes on her, but she tried to ignore them. She was in a field. The same one from before. It was daylight here, the sun shining down, casting her shadow on the ground.

"What do you see?"

This time, when Lucha's shadow swelled, she told the

truth. "I see my shadow," she said. "But it's not mine. It's *his*. It's Salvador's."

The words sounded like they were coming from far away. Again, Lucha could feel her body in the chair, feel her mouth moving, but she was in the field, too. As truly as if she were really standing there.

Behind her, the shadow's cloak billowed, though she wore no cloak of her own.

She could imagine his feral smirk, turning up at the corner.

"What else do you see?" Mariel asked, but Lucha couldn't answer. The shadow was swallowing everything. The field, the little flowers, the trees in the distance. Even Lucha herself.

"I . . . I can't," she managed. "I can't see."

"Often when we see a shadow in our vision, we're confronting our own fear," came Mariel's voice, low and urgent. Closer now. "You see Almudena's son because you fear him. Because you fear that you are like him. A bringer of destruction. But you are not, Miss Moya. You know who you are. Almudena knew. That is why she chose you."

As she spoke, Lucha saw a bright hole begin to form in the center of the massive shadow. She clung to the words. *You know who you are.* She saw herself fighting for her city. Killing the kings one by one. Foraging, feeding others, doing what she could to bring Robado back to life.

"*I'm not like you,*" she said in the field as she looked at her shadow, now rippling and moving. Rebelling against her words. "*I* killed *you.*"

The bright hole widened. Lucha could hear screaming

coming from the shadow. The same grating sound Salvador had made as the mushrooms devoured him. Lucha wanted to open her eyes. Wanted to leave this horror where it was, but some instinct told her to stay.

In moments that felt like hours, the shadow was diminished, eaten from within by the light Lucha had summoned. The screaming faded, softer and softer until it was quiet again and Lucha's own shadow stood beside her at last. Sword-slim and proud.

"Is he still with you?" Mariel asked.

"No," Lucha said, both versions of her exhausted. "No, he's gone."

As she said the words, something sprouted at her feet. A silvery green stalk, growing quickly, unfurling leaves and finally blooming into a pure-white bell-shaped flower.

"What do you see now?" Mariel asked.

"I see a plant," Lucha said curiously, bending down to look at it. It was familiar, but from where? She described it as best she could, stopping when she heard Mariel let out a joyful sob.

"Oh, you brilliant girl," she said. "Come back to us."

Lucha felt hands on her shoulders, like someone was pulling her up from deep water. For a moment, she had a hard time reconciling the shadowy tent interior with the bright field she'd just come from. Paz offered her water, which she drank gratefully, settling into reality more firmly.

When she looked up at Mariel, there were tears on the old woman's face.

"What was it?" Lucha asked a little groggily. "The plant. What was it?"

"My dear, it was the Pensa plant," Mariel said, sending Lucha's stomach sinking. "The way it looked when Almudena walked the earth. The way it's supposed to look."

She handed Lucha one of the scrolls from the table, with a drawing of a plant that looked almost exactly like the one she'd seen. Lucha had never known Pensa to flower. To grow so heartily or so large.

Passing the scroll back to Mariel, Lucha felt a headache building behind her eyes. "What does it mean?" she asked. "Is Pensa going to be growing again?" She knew that the fragile community they'd managed to build in Robado couldn't withstand the return of Olvida, but Mariel looked so pleased . . .

"I don't know about all that," the old woman said, drying her eyes. "All I know is that in a vision, the Pensa plant indicates the blessing of the goddess. It's a sign that she's with you, that your channel of communication with her is open. Now we just need to figure out what to ask."

The headache was worsening. Lucha stood up, rolled her neck and shoulders.

"I mean, I imagine we'd ask how to stop all the food from dying and the forest from burning and flooding and the blight from taking over everything, right?"

Mariel had returned to the scrolls. It was Río, rising from her chair in the corner, who answered.

"We already know the answer to that question, Miss Moya," she said solemnly. "The question is, *how* can we do it?"

"Do what?" Lucha asked, feeling stupid and slow, exhaustion sucking at her heels.

"It's simple," Río said for the second time that day. "We need a divine being to replace the one you killed."

The silence that followed this statement was thick. Lucha felt it settling over all of them.

"But . . . where are we going to find a *god* lying around?" she asked blankly.

"*Finding* one is not our only option," Río said in a voice heavy with significance.

"*Create* a divine being?" Paz asked, catching up quicker than Lucha. "Is it even possible?"

"It's possible," Lucha said without thinking. She felt as though she stood once more before a tree stump in a long-dead grove. She was announcing her name. A golden vine was rearing up like a snake. A thorn pierced her through the heart. "It isn't *pleasant,*" she clarified. "But it's possible."

They were all looking at her. Lucha realized she had never told Río or Paz the details of what had happened to her in the dead grove. Paz had been tied to a tree, Río leading an unsuccessful hunt for Lucha through the woods surrounding the sanctuary . . .

"I'm sorry," Paz said, looking down as if Lucha's face were too bright to view. That reverence was back in her voice. Lucha felt it grating on her. "I should have thought."

"It's fine." Lucha waved her hand dismissively even as the memories surged back in to torment her. The long years she'd spent in Salvador's mind. The feeling of being both more and less than she'd been before when she finally dropped to the ground in a body much like her own.

"But this is the reason we need you," Río said, clearly unaware of how callous she sounded. "You have a connection with her that none of us can access without the plant. A connection through which we can commune with Almudena. To seek her guidance as we attempt to rebalance Elegido."

Her face was harshly lit by the candle before her, and her eyes danced strangely. Lucha was reminded momentarily of her own shadow in the field, expanding, cape billowing.

"The source of power that transformed me is gone," Lucha said carefully. "The tree died after it transferred its power to me."

"Then we'll have to find another source, won't we?" Río asked. "And with you connected to Almudena once more, we're closer than we've ever been."

"But first we should let Lucha rest," Paz said. "It's been an overwhelming day."

Lucha looked up at her gratefully, but Paz's eyes were fixed on Río, her expression mirroring Lucha's own troubled thoughts.

"Yes, of course," Río said, snapping out of it. "Rest. We'll begin tomorrow."

Paz walked Lucha to the door of the tent. "Are you all right?" she asked quietly when they were outside. "Where did you go today? You look exhausted."

"There was a fire," Lucha said. "It was spreading toward the camp. I had to help." She left out the part about Cruz, about the kissing. She tried to tamp down the feeling of resentment that returned then. The idea that if Paz had not made her unsolicited observation about Cruz having feelings for Lucha, none of this would have happened.

"Are you all right?" Paz asked again.

Lucha opened her mouth to say she was fine, but was suddenly light-headed, stumbling sideways. Paz caught her, and Lucha experienced a powerful déjà vu. It had only been a few months ago when she'd come out of the forest with a sombralado's scratch on her cheek. When Paz had patched her up, setting everything in motion . . .

"I'm fine," she said once she was steady on her feet again. "I just need some rest."

Paz hovered nearby. Lucha could tell she wanted to offer to walk her to her tent. But would it be because she wanted to be close? Or because she wanted to make sure nothing happened to Almudena's champion before they could make a new god?

It was the fact that she still didn't know that made Lucha walk off alone.

"Good night, Paz," she said over her shoulder.

Paz didn't answer.

The next day, the smoke from the fire created a haze over the city. The sun was a burning red eye in its center, and ash rained down on the camp. Cruz, Armando, and Maria hadn't returned, but others had—for supplies or rest—and they reported that the fire wasn't quite out but everyone was safe.

It was probably for the best that she hadn't stayed with them, Lucha thought as she made her way toward Río's tent that morning. Her body was sore in a thousand places. There were burns and scratches on every inch of skin that had been exposed yesterday. Her mind was weary from Mariel's intrusions. She certainly didn't need Cruz playing head games with her on top of all of that.

Now that the connection had been established, everyone but Lucha seemed quite energized. She arrived at Río's tent to a flurry of activity. Acolytes with scrolls moving from table to table, Mariel and Río barking orders as they scurried.

It took them a full minute to even notice Lucha had arrived.

"Miss Moya! Good!" Río said, bustling over to her. "We've been up since dawn, but Mariel thought it best to allow you some rest. Are you feeling rested?" She examined Lucha as one would an expensive instrument that might need oiling.

"I'm fine," Lucha said. "Where do you want me?"

Mariel took her back out through the tent and into the trees. Lucha was too tired to fight her, or to ask what was happening. She had donated her mind to this endeavor; all she could do was go with it.

"Sit," Mariel said, gesturing to a mossy patch on the ground. "I thought the closer we were to Almudena's domain, the easier it would be to access her."

Lucha thought sitting indoors in a chair out of the smoke might still have been preferable, but it was easier not to argue. And at least here it was just Lucha and Mariel. No acolytes to peer at her, no Río to rush her, no Paz to—

"Now," Mariel said, snapping Lucha out of her thoughts. "We were able to push through your fear and make contact yesterday. That was a great start. Today we're going to begin with a few simple questions. You'll go into your trance state, I'll ask you to hold the question in your mind, and then you'll describe the response and we'll do our best to interpret."

Lucha nodded. She wasn't feeling overly thrilled about returning to the meadow, but the distant sounds of the Robadans having breakfast motivated her—and the bloodred sun hanging overhead reminded her what was at stake.

"I'm ready," she said, sitting down on the moss and closing her eyes.

"Good," said Mariel. "Today's first question is only a check-in. To connect with our goddess and know that she is with us, that we are on the path to righting the world in her name. Hold this intention in your mind as you find your way to the field."

It took longer to reach it today. Lucha struggled to let go of the waking world. To forget the smoke, and the sun. The Syndicate out there in the forest, fighting symptoms of the imbalance. It was difficult not to feel that her own task was silly in the face of all that. Closing her eyes. Breathing. Holding questions in her mind.

But as she sat, and breathed, one by one the tethers

loosened. Lucha found herself once more in the meadow, surrounded by white flowers. The first thing she checked was her shadow, which was blessedly in its usual shape.

The sky was not smoky here. A gentle breeze stirred the trees around her.

Are you there? Lucha thought, feeling absurd. *Is this helping at all?*

Before now, Lucha's visions had often featured the goddess herself, walking and talking. Showing scenes from her history or else speaking with Lucha directly. This method of communicating was much less exact. She held the question in her mind as best she could.

"Look for anything moving," Mariel encouraged her. "Anything out of place."

For a long time, nothing happened. Lucha stared at the grass and the sky, conscious of her body seated on the ground. Of all the things she could have been doing to help if she hadn't been here.

When these thoughts had spent themselves, the tiniest of movements caught her attention. Lucha bent down to the ground to notice a trail of ants marching along the grass. Some carried small stones, others crumbs of food or bits of grass. Some carried nothing at all.

She followed the trail for a distance across the meadow until she found the hole in the ground they were heading for. There was a trail leading to the hole, and one leading away. Lucha watched them for long minutes, waiting for more, but this seemed to be it.

"When you have your answer," came Mariel's voice, "return carefully."

Lucha did so, the meadow slow to release her, the image of the ants remaining even as the rest faded. After some blinking and flexing of her hands, she was firmly back in the forest again, looking up at Mariel.

"Ants," she said. "I saw ants. Hundreds of them, carrying things into a hole."

She didn't expect this answer to go over well. Lucha didn't have much experience with visions, but she thought it would be better if she'd seen a white wolf, or a swooping, screeching owl. Something with significance.

Mariel, on the contrary, looked overcome with emotion. She dabbed at her wrinkled face, beaming. "Ants!" she said. "She is with us. She is here."

And the old woman extended her arms as if she could touch the goddess herself.

"Not to be underenthusiastic," Lucha said carefully after a long minute had passed. "But what exactly do ants mean?"

There was nothing holy about ants. They were little insects who made their way into open food containers no matter how well you sealed them.

"The ant works together with its sisters to honor their queen," Mariel said, as if this should have been obvious. "Each one has a vital task to perform that strengthens its colony's chance of survival. Don't you see? In joining together, in performing our tasks well, we are serving her will and moving toward a brighter future. She has spoken!"

"Okay," Lucha said, still not entirely convinced. "If you say so."

"It means we are on the right path," Mariel promised. "A most auspicious sign. Now let us move on to the next question."

Resisting the urge to sigh, Lucha closed her eyes again.

After three more questions, Lucha was exhausted. Her body trembled as if she'd performed some intense physical exertion rather than sitting on the ground for a few hours.

Mariel had done her best to explain that the fruiting apple tree, white hare, and gentle rain Lucha had seen were useful. But as she struggled to her feet, she couldn't help but feel it had been an utter waste of an afternoon.

"Rest," Mariel said, guiding Lucha back to Río's tent.

"But I barely did anything," Lucha said, even as she listed sideways. "We didn't even ask how to create a god. Or how much time we have left. All we know is a bunch of vague non-sense."

"It's hardly nonsense to know there is a possibility of success," Mariel chastised her. "Or that signs will be available to us if we look out for them, or that moments of rest will be necessary to restore us on our journey."

Lucha privately disagreed, but she knew better than to argue with a zealot.

21

The next three days didn't go much better.

Because Lucha's trips to the grove left her so exhausted, Mariel had insisted they journey only in the morning. The rest of the day Lucha would force herself to rest, or else read with blurry eyes out of sheer stubbornness, while the others pored over scrolls.

On the fourth day, Lucha abandoned her reading for the clinic. There had been two more attacks by blighted sabuesas, and now a bird was responsible for the first human infection.

Marco, Armando's right-hand man, bit down hard on a stick while the blight was cut away from his flesh to prevent it from spreading. Río performed the operation, with steady hands and decades of training as a healer. Lucha stood by, stomach churning, helpless as he screamed. It was Cruz who comforted him afterward, of course, sneaking him a bit of Los Ricos's liquor and whispering something bracing in his ear.

She and Lucha hadn't spoken since the kiss, and they avoided each other's eyes as they passed in the doorway.

"We need to get to work," Lucha said to Río through

gritted teeth as they headed back to their tents. "The next time, someone could die. Or get blighted and kill everyone here. I want to ask Almudena how to do it. How to make a god."

Río hushed Lucha, pulling her aside. "That's not how these things are done," she said. "Especially not without the protection Pensa provides. The forgetting effect in its mild form exists to keep your mind safe from the intrusion. To keep it in a dreamlike space so your conscious mind continues to function normally."

"That ship has sailed," Lucha said. The shadows jumped in the corners of her eyes when she looked away. "And what does it matter if my mind is safe if it gets eaten by blight tomorrow?"

"It's never been done this way before," Río said, dismissing her. "We have to take careful steps. Limit your exposure. Ease into the questions that will require more complex answers. I know it feels frustrating now, but you're conditioning. Building toward something. In the meantime, we need to do more research. To narrow the focus of our questions. You have to trust me."

Lucha only grumbled, which wasn't an express agreement to those terms. But Río, already running back to her scrolls, didn't notice the omission.

That night, late, Lucha dragged herself out to the glade alone. Armando had rounded up a group to patrol through the night because of the increased blight activity, but she slipped past them, settling into the moss.

The forest felt different at night. Already half on the border of the living world and the spirit world. Lucha could tell the meadow would come to her easily, and it did.

Without Mariel to dictate the terms of her journey, everything solidified quickly. It was night in the meadow, too. The white blossoms glowed faintly in the radiant light from a moon Lucha could not see.

This time, she could hardly feel her body in the woods. It was as if she had truly traveled to this moonlit field. She half expected to see Almudena emerge from beyond a tree. But she didn't, of course. All was silent and still, as if the night itself were waiting for her question.

Río had said they didn't know enough to ask about creating a god, that Lucha's mind couldn't handle the answer. But she had questions of her own. Questions about how to keep Robado safe.

"Where is the blight coming from?" she asked into the expectant air. "How do I get rid of it?"

Usually, Lucha had to wait awhile for an answer, but tonight the wind kicked up immediately, tossing the trees around her.

"How do I keep them safe?" she asked, more urgently. She could feel her skin prickling, here in the meadow. Her body back in the forest was all but forgotten.

The wind was howling now. The temperature dropped.

"Tell me!" Lucha called. "I've done everything you've ever asked of me! Just tell me what to do!"

This time, there was no minute movement. No tiny ant or distant hare. No drops of rain. When the answer came, it was undeniable. A massive toadstool blooming out of the field and growing. Swelling.

Mushrooms, Lucha thought, taking a step toward it. She had used mushrooms to defeat Salvador. But how could mushrooms rid them of the blight?

She moved closer still. Lucha had known mushrooms more intimately than most. Maybe there was something special about this particular one. Some answer within its flesh.

It was expanding rapidly now. Its pale flesh ravenous and reaching. Lucha, here in this place, could feel what it wanted. To digest. To destroy. These were not the mushrooms Lucha had used to consume Salvador, but without warning, she remembered exactly where she had seen them last.

A flash of memory. The cell door open before her. Her legs trembling beneath her sister's weight. Alán Marquez's voice, pleading.

Don't do something you'll regret. We can make a new deal, Lucha. Just let me go.

She hadn't, and now she could hear his screams echoing around the meadow like metal walls held them here.

"Alán," Lucha said aloud, her voice a growl. "What does he have to do with this?"

But there was a more pressing issue. The mushroom was expanding too fast. Lucha knew she had to wake up, but she didn't have Mariel's voice to follow. She had lost her connection to her body.

Wake up, she told herself, backing away from the rapid fungal growth. *You're in the forest. In the trees. Just open your eyes.*

The mushroom was reaching for her, and Lucha began to run back to the place where she'd started. The place where she'd seen the ants, and the hare. She knew instinctively not to stray too much farther outside the meadow. She would wake up, wouldn't she? She had to.

Only, time was running out. What would happen if she was consumed by the mushroom here? Lucha wondered as her heart hammered too hard in her chest. Would she wake? Would she die? Would she become some horrible blighted version of herself?

The mushroom fed on her fear. It doubled in size. There was no outrunning it now—it grew so large it blotted out the meadow. Blotted out everything with its pale, ravenous flesh.

Lucha, acting on instinct alone, threw herself to the ground.

"*HELP ME!*" she screamed, though she knew not to whom.

When she did, cold water began to tickle her face. Her outstretched hands. Raindrops falling softly, then harder. But Lucha's face was not wet. Stars were clearly visible in the field.

Lucha realized it all at once. It was raining in Robado. Raining on her real body, and she could feel it. The connection was enough. She closed her eyes and willed herself along the tunnel of sensation created by the rain, pushing herself back against considerable resistance until at last, gasping, she awoke in her body, the rain drenching her clothes.

It took her several long moments to be able to stand. At first she only grabbed fistfuls of dirt and moss, clutching them to her skin, so grateful to be back on solid ground.

When her breathing eased, she got to her feet, the panic receding.

While Almudena's messages weren't usually literal or direct, they did have significance. Lucha's mushroom had been connected to Alán, who was dead now. But there was something left of him here.

It had been a long time since Lucha visited his office full of curios in the compound. Not a soul had entered since the siege, which felt so long ago to her. But now it seemed clear as day. *That* was where the information would be on how to destroy the blight. That was what Almudena had been telling her.

Lucha, despite her exhaustion, knew she'd never get a better chance to investigate. Tomorrow it would be back to pointless exercises and poring over old books. Tomorrow they'd be watching her too closely. It had to be tonight.

On the road, torchlight flickered. One of Armando's guys making the rounds. Lucha slunk deep into the shadows of her grove and held her breath, waiting for him to pass, then pass again in the other direction.

She'd have no trouble outwitting the patrol, she knew, but seeing this one reminded her of the reason they were out here—and she was in no shape to fight a blighted anything right now. Not on her own.

Paz's tent was dark when Lucha approached it a few minutes later. She felt bad waking her, but this was important. Possibly vital. She tapped on the canvas, knowing Paz to be a light sleeper.

It hadn't been an easy decision, Paz or Cruz. Both were capable fighters who were likely to go with her. But in the end, the confusion over Cruz and the kiss and all the torturous mind games had made Paz the less complicated choice.

Perish the thought.

"Hey," Lucha whispered at the flap of Paz's tent. "You awake?"

There was a rustling from inside; then Paz appeared fully dressed, no sleep lingering in her posture or expression. "Is something wrong?"

"No. Well, sort of," Lucha said. "I need your help."

Paz stepped outside the tent. In the darkness, with no one else to judge them, Lucha let herself be overwhelmed by her presence. That scent of jasmine that always seemed to cling to her. Her eyes, dark and long-lashed and beautiful as they looked at Lucha questioningly.

Lucha shook herself mentally. This was not the time. "I saw something," she said. "A . . . vision, I guess. I know where we need to go to figure out how to stop the blight, but I know Río won't sign off and I need your help."

"A vision," Paz said, looking more keenly at Lucha. "Dammit, tell me you didn't try the trance without a guide. I know you're not that dumb."

Lucha smiled sheepishly. "I survived?"

Paz rolled her eyes. "That was incredibly dangerous," she said sternly. "If you'd been lost, or compromised, there's no telling what would have happened. The entire forest could die off without you, Lucha, don't you get that? You can't be selfish like this. Not with this much at stake."

It was so close to what Cruz had said to her that Lucha felt instantly irritated. "I wasn't being *selfish*," she said, still whispering. "I'm sick of watching people get attacked. Marco could have died today. He could have gone blight mad and killed everyone here, including me. If I'm the only one with access to Almudena, I needed to find out how to help them. And I did. So are you coming or not?"

Paz looked like she was as likely to punch Lucha as help her, but after a long minute she relented. "I'll go with you under one condition," she said.

"Can't wait to hear this," Lucha grumbled.

"No more solo journeying. If you have something you want to ask, tell Mariel, and if she won't sign off, tell me and I'll help you work on her. But you have no idea how dangerous it is to go to that place without a tether."

Lucha, remembering the mushroom, the feeling of losing her body in the glade, thought that she did know. But she wasn't about to tell Paz that.

"Fine, deal," she said. "Now let's go before someone sees us."

She turned and darted into camp, moving from shadow to shadow. Thankfully, Paz followed close behind.

They met no one between the acolytes' tents and the gate.

Lucha, for her part, fought against the exhaustion threatening to settle in her bones. After this, she could rest. Just a little farther.

"In here," Lucha said when they reached their destination. She couldn't stop the goose bumps from erupting on her arms. The weight of memory and fear from settling around her heart.

The door to Alán Marquez's office had remained locked since the sacking of Pecado. There had been those who wanted to loot it, of course, in the aftermath, but Lucha knew that whatever he had locked up in here would cause nothing but trouble. The Robadans were suspicious enough to heed her warning.

But tonight, Lucha knew it would be worth it. She had seen it. This was where she'd learn the secrets of the blight. She remembered Alán's tomes of esoteric knowledge, his jars of creepy floating specimens. Would one of them hold the key? She would just have to trust herself to know when she found it.

The door creaked open slowly, and the stench nearly knocked Lucha out. Behind her, as it spread out the door, Lucha heard Paz cough.

"Get back," Lucha said, pulling her shirt over her face. The first time she'd smelled this rancid, awful stink had been when Armando's calf was turned. There was no doubt there was blight here—and from the smell of it, a *lot* of blight.

Paz lit a torch, and together they peered inside. It was pitch-dark, and humid. Like some kind of swamp creature had taken up residence here and then died. The floor had flooded. The water—without open doors or windows—had created a layer of mildew and mold over everything touching the ground.

But so far Lucha didn't see the telltale blood red of the blight fungus, and they couldn't go back now. Not when they might be close to ending this threat for good. Giving the Robadans more time.

"Keep an eye out for blight," she whispered to Paz, shirt still over her mouth.

"I have salt water just in case," Paz replied. They stepped inside together.

"Grab anything that looks useful," Lucha said. "Books, scrolls, papers. He probably had the largest collection of forest lore outside the sanctuary. Grab now, and we'll sort later."

They moved through the room in silence—mostly because they had to keep their faces covered to keep from breathing too much of the thick, foul-smelling air. Lucha opened the drawers of Alán's desk first, remembering all the times she'd stood across it from him, awaiting his next lecherous comment or hurtful barb.

The drawers held papers and letters; most had been protected from the humidity by the metal of the desk, but a few were soggy and streaked with rust. Lucha didn't bother to read them, just shoved them in the satchel Paz had placed on top of the desk.

Lucha was peering under one last cabinet when she saw it. Something that hadn't been here in Alán's days. It appeared to be a nest of clothes. Blankets. Half-eaten food. Some of this stuff had been taken from the acolytes' provisions, Lucha realized with a shudder.

Worst of all, the whole thing was pulsing with blight. The most Lucha had ever seen in one place. There seemed to be a hole in the floor going down, a tunnel coated with the stuff.

She was peering as close as she dared when it happened. A snarling. Sudden movement. And a figure launched itself out of the hole right at Lucha.

Throwing herself backward, Lucha shouted for Paz, pushing herself along the mold-slick floor, reaching for her knives. The figure coming toward her was more monster than man, but he had certainly once been the latter. The blight had taken almost everything recognizable about him.

He was horrific, and putrid, and his one good eye rolled around in fury and agony. There would be no reasoning with him. He was here to kill them if they didn't kill him first.

Snarling, he lunged for Lucha in the small, fetid space. Paz was behind her, dragging her to her feet, but still they barely got out of his way in time.

"Don't let him out the door!" Lucha gasped, pressing herself up against the wall. He was so fast. So strong. So lethal.

Paz had drawn her bow, but the space was so small and his movements so fast that she couldn't get a clear shot. The man's face was almost all blight, a writhing, pulsating mass of fungal contagion.

She got a shot off that hit him in the arm, which momentarily pushed him back behind the desk, screaming at the pain.

But her next two arrows missed wildly as he dodged, gearing up for another lunge.

"You have the bag?" Lucha asked, something crystalizing in her mind.

"Yes, but—"

"As soon as he's still, shoot him through the good eye," she said before Paz could finish. She was seeing her vision in an all-new light now. The mushroom expanding, chasing her to the edges of her consciousness. This information wasn't going to come cheap.

"Of course," Paz said impatiently, "but when—"

In the split second before he lunged, Lucha did. She had spent every encounter with the blight trying to avoid it, but this time she didn't let it stop her. Her hands closed on the matted velvet of the man's sleeves, distended by the growth beneath him.

Velvet.

Red velvet.

"Miguel?" Lucha asked as the blight began to burn her skin. As Paz screamed:

"Lucha, no!"

Lucha looked into his good eye. The young man who had nearly died trying to retrieve Olvida from a flood. The boy who had made his way into the forest alone. So this had been his fate. The realization was almost shocking enough to numb the pain. The wrongness of the blight taking hold, suctioning to her skin, spreading . . .

If it had been anyone else but Paz, she thought deliriously, they might have tried to save Lucha first. But she knew Paz better than that.

Closing her eyes against the pain as Miguel, recognizing nothing, writhed beneath her hands with shocking strength, Lucha heard the whistle of the arrow. The thud that meant it had struck home.

The body she held went limp in her arms, and she withdrew her hands, looking down at them in horror. The vision wasn't nearly as bad as the feeling, which was beyond pain. Lucha felt the blight coursing through her sentiently, intelligently. Attaching itself to her nerves until she felt her hands move without giving them permission.

Turning, she looked at Paz as the exhaustion and the pain and the strangeness of the blight traveling through her all gathered like dark clouds at the edges of her consciousness.

"You know what you need to do," she said to Paz, and then everything went dark.

22

When Lucha awoke, there was light. Too bright. She squinted her eyes against it.

She had been fighting her way out of a tunnel, she remembered. Days and days of seeing herself healthy and whole, crawling toward her body only to be dragged away. The pain had been unbearable, inside and out, but now there was just an ache.

And the light. Pressing like knives into her eyes.

Thirst was her main concern, burning in her throat, every swallow an agony. She groaned, or at least she tried; the real sound was more of a strained whimper.

"Oh, shit," came a voice from beside her. Feet hitting the floor. A shadow passing blissfully over the light in her eyes. "Hey, killer. You awake?"

Another whispered groan. As Lucha's eyes adjusted, she saw Cruz leaning over her. She tried to point to her throat to indicate thirst but found her hands restrained. Panic began to bloom in her belly, and it must have shown on her face, because Cruz's expression turned guilty.

"Don't worry, it was just so the bandages wouldn't get

messed up. You were thrashing around pretty good and we didn't want damage. Here, I can let you out now."

More gently than Lucha would have thought possible, Cruz released her wrists.

"Go slow, okay?" she said. Then she held a cup of water to Lucha's lips.

The relief was immediate. Lucha cleared her raw throat and tried again to speak. "What happened?" she croaked, gesturing for more water.

"You mean after you held down a blighted guy with your bare hands?" Cruz asked, her tone wavering between frustration and admiration. "That sharpshooter of yours put an arrow through his eye. You blacked out, but she had salt water on her, so she was able to stop the worst of the spread. But . . . you know the rules are to remove blighted skin, so . . ."

Lucha looked at her hands at last, covered in bandages so thick she couldn't even tell they were there.

"They've been putting this special salve on it, the acolytes, but they had to take a lot of skin, and they're not sure how well it'll grow back."

"How long was I out?" Lucha asked, sitting up and scooting back without the use of her hands, which was awkward and difficult. Cruz tried to help, but Lucha waved her away. It was bad enough she had to see her like this.

"A few days," Cruz replied, worry creasing her brow. "They said it shouldn't have taken so long. That there must have been something else. They've been arguing about it in here, the priestess and the sharpshooter. They thought you might be having some kind of . . . vision?"

Lucha thought it more likely that she'd fried her synapses going to the meadow on her own, but she didn't have to admit to that now.

"It was Miguel," she said after a long moment. "The blighted . . . man in the office. He'd been living in there."

"I know," Cruz said. "I went out to help bring you in, saw the jacket."

"Maria?" Lucha asked. "Is she—"

"Pretty messed up," Cruz admitted. "They burned the body just in case, said a few words. But it was hard for her to see him like that."

Lucha closed her eyes against the emotion of it. Miguel had never been her favorite person, but did anyone deserve to go out that way?

"Did they find anything useful in the materials we got?" she asked, thinking of the backpack full of books and scrolls. The reason they'd gone. The vision that had promised Lucha a way to keep the Robadans safe.

"They don't tell me anything about that," Cruz said, shrugging. "Mostly they keep to the high priestess's tent if they're not in here. Do you want me to get one of them for you?"

Lucha shook her head. She would need to talk to them eventually, but she wasn't ready for the poking and prodding yet. The dig for significance. The censure or the praise she'd receive for doing what needed to be done.

"Good," Cruz said, sitting back down beside Lucha. "Because I have a bone to pick with you."

Feeling her face heat up, Lucha decided to save her voice. Wait for Cruz to continue.

"Why didn't you ask me to go with you? To the compound? To Marquez's office? I know you have your history with the sharpshooter, but I could have kept you safe."

Lucha remembered the moments before she'd gone to Paz that night. Weighing Cruz's talent for combat with the awkwardness she felt. She found that this close to waking, she didn't have the energy to be subtle.

"You kissed me," she said simply.

Cruz groaned, clearly frustrated. "Yeah, I kissed you," she said. "And would that have made me less useful in a potentially dangerous situation?"

"You kissed me and we never talked about what it meant," Lucha clarified, feeling childish for bringing it up.

"Not everything means something," Cruz said, her face flushing along her cheekbones. She wouldn't meet Lucha's gaze.

"So then say it didn't mean anything," Lucha replied. "That's still an answer."

"Why don't you tell me what you think it meant," Cruz countered. "I'm not the one with the complicated past with the beautiful girl in robes. I'm not the one everyone's depending on to stop the floods and the fires and the blight."

"That doesn't mean you don't get an opinion. And anyway, the onus is on the kiss*er* to define things, not the kiss*ee*. I didn't ask you to kiss me."

Cruz's eyes snapped to Lucha's then, and they sparkled a little when she asked: "Do you wish I hadn't?"

For a moment Lucha was back there, in the smoldering aftermath of the fire. The bloodred sun. The smoke hanging in the air. Burned tree trunks reaching like spears for the sky. Cruz coming closer. Lucha's heart in her throat.

"No," she said softly. "But—"

Before she could finish, the flap of the clinic tent opened and Río, Mariel, and Paz bustled in.

"Good, you're awake," Río said, as if Lucha had been taking an indulgent nap. "We have work to do."

"Yes, I'm alive, no need to be concerned," Lucha said, her head starting to ache at the temples. "Been awake a whole six minutes now, so I'll apologize for slacking off."

"You," Río said, ignoring Lucha's attitude to look at Cruz. "There are a few acolytes struggling with books and scrolls between here and camp somewhere. Can you give them a hand?"

"I live to serve," Cruz said with a sardonic half bow. Under her breath she said to Lucha, "If they try to kill you again, just holler."

The confusing heat dissipated once more as Cruz left the tent, left Lucha to Río and Mariel's devices.

"You need to tell Mariel what happened," Río said the moment Cruz was gone. "Clearly you experienced something, and we need to interpret it."

Lucha looked briefly at Paz, who shook her head infinitesimally. So she hadn't told them about Lucha's solo journey to the field. That was good; it meant they wouldn't lose any more time than they needed to.

"I had a dream," she lied, her throat still sore around the words. A dream was good. A dream wasn't intentional. "Almudena showed me a mushroom filling the field, and I knew it was telling me where there would be information about the blight."

"How did you know?" Mariel's sharp eyes said she didn't believe it was a dream. That she didn't trust Lucha's ability to interpret the symbols.

"That mushroom and I, as well as the man who used the office I went to that night, have a complicated history."

"And it never occurred to you that the mushroom might be warning you *away* from that place? A symbol filling the field of view is a warning, girl. It's not an invitation."

Lucha could hardly say she'd asked a question without giving herself away, so she only shrugged. "The people here are suffering every day. Their lives are in danger. I couldn't sit back and wait for a more opportune time to fix things."

"You should have come to one of us!" Mariel said, frustrated. "For help interpreting the vision—a skill in which you are wholly untrained."

"I think I've learned my lesson," Lucha said, growing impatient as her headache worsened. She held up her bandaged hands. They ached, though she could feel the cool healing of the sanctuary's salve doing its work as well. "Let's just move on. Have you been able to go over what we found in the office? Is there a solution to the blight?"

Río stepped forward, though Mariel showed clear signs of wanting to continue her lecture on Lucha's irresponsible symbol interpretation. "In a manner of speaking," she said.

"What does that mean?"

"It means that the blight is a symptom of a larger issue, as you very well know. And while it is currently—aside from the rapidly deteriorating food sources—the most pressing one affecting your little camp, you did promise us assistance in rebalancing the forest's ecosystem."

Lucha's temper flared. "And you promised *me* you'd help me care for and protect the Robadans as part of that deal." She raised her hands again. "I think I've held up my end of the bargain."

"Running off and nearly getting yourself killed isn't what I asked of you. What I asked of you was cooperation. The tempering of that little rebellious spirit you're so proud to flaunt." Río stepped closer, her anger more visible from this range. "Did you stop to think what would have happened to all of us had you been killed? Or your mind lost to the blight?"

It was more or less the same thing Cruz had said, and the truth was, Lucha hadn't. She hadn't thought beyond the task at hand, which was keeping the blighted Miguel from leaving Alán's office and protecting the camp from further attack.

"I didn't know he would be in there," she said, aware that it wasn't a particularly strong argument. "And chances were high we'd be infected or die anyway at that point. I had to stop him."

"Only a little faster than the imbalanced ecosystem will kill us," Río said. "You need to stop thinking like a common soldier and start thinking like a leader. Like a *savior.*"

"I never wanted to be a savior," Lucha said.

Río's mouth opened again, her eyes flashing, but Paz stepped between them. "I think your differences of opinion on this subject have been fully explored already," she said. "Let's look forward. Even if you have different reasons, we all have the same goal."

"Thank you," Lucha said.

Paz gave her a small, tight-lipped smile.

"Fine," Río said just as Cruz and the overburdened acolytes came in with a massive collection of books and scrolls. "Your healing will progress better in here, so we'll have to get used to the accommodations. Goddess knows we're used to doing things the rustic way by now."

Lucha, for Paz's sake, ignored the dig. Although after a few moments of Río's droning, she almost wished she'd picked a fight instead.

Through the throbbing headache, Lucha tried to understand Río's long ramp-up to the point. How could Lucha forget the lore of Almudena? The forest goddess who had descended to this place to nurture the life here. She had grown lonely, the only divine being in a world full of mortal seasons. She had taken things into her own hands and created a child. A divine companion among the mortals whose lives were so short compared to her own.

Lucha still got chills whenever she thought of Salvador.

The divine son. Destruction incarnate. She would never understand being so lonely you were willing to create a monster.

"In one of the tomes from your little excursion, we were able to find proof of the existence of a rumored holy site of Almudena," Río was saying now. "More central to the legends than even the sanctuary, or the grove where she battled her son."

"What is it?" Lucha asked, suddenly flooded with relief that this had not all been for nothing.

"The Forgotten Spring of Almudena," Río revealed in a hushed voice.

Lucha only looked at her, nonplussed.

Río made an impatient sound in the back of her throat, as if the kings' ban on any forest mythology that might rouse their subjects to hope was Lucha's personal fault.

"It was said to be the place where Almudena first touched down in this world when she arrived from the celestial plane," she said. "A holy place to which pilgrimages were made by the most devout in days long past. A place of potent divine energy. The signature of Almudena's arrival is said to linger in the very fabric of reality there; pilgrims experienced ecstatic visions, miraculous displays of power—even those without the gift were said to feel close to her."

"Okay," Lucha said. "It sounds great, but what does it have to do with the blight? Or the godless imbalance of it all?"

Río charged ahead without pause. "It was said the early pilgrims built a holy temple around this spring because of its special properties. A place where magic was enhanced, able to be wielded by the goddess's chosen. A place where even mortals could perform miracles. But it's never been found. Most of us assumed it was a myth, or that its power—like the sanctuary's—had faded over time."

"But this book says where it is?" Lucha asked, hope fighting its way through the headache. If they could find another source of Almudena's power, perhaps they really could stop the blight. The fires and floods. The food dying off . . .

"Not in so many words," Paz cut in. "Okay, not in any words. But we did find a clue as to why no one has ever found it."

Paz brought a book to Lucha's bedside. *A Collection of Elegido's Preindustrial Holy Sites,* opened to a page near the middle. There, Paz pointed to a passage. *Underground. Hidden entrance.*

"The spring is subterranean," she said. "Meaning you could comb the forest for a hundred years and never find it if you didn't know where it was."

"And you think if we find it, we could use the power to create a god?" Lucha asked.

"It's the best lead we've had by a mile," Paz answered. "It's not a guarantee, but it's all we have to go on right now. And it seems clear that Almudena was steering you toward this information when she appeared in your . . . dream"—Paz looked askance at her—"so that makes it even more compelling as a theory."

"So we have to find it," Lucha said. She was nearly giddy with the prospect of an actual plan after all these days of vague questions and symbols. Locating the place where the goddess had first touched the earth, a storied source of divine power. *This* felt like doing something.

"It seems like the best course of action," Río said, reaching out and taking the book.

"Okay, well, I can't go to the woods like this unless someone carries me," Lucha said, shifting forward awkwardly, still unused to her limited range of motion. "But I can do it here. Mariel, take me in, tell me what to ask."

She was about to close her eyes when she saw the old woman shaking her head. "Whatever that dream was, it did a number on your mind," she said. "You were out for days. We can't risk going back in so soon without the protection Pensa provides."

Lucha was instantly full of rebellious obstinance. "I'll be fine," she said. "I promise whatever you're worried about, I've been through worse. Let's do it."

"We're doing nothing," Mariel said flatly, in a tone that brooked no argument. "The worst that can happen is permanent madness. Total mental incapacitation. Debilitating hallucinations that will never go away. We're not playing around here, girl. You are our one chance to get this right, and we're taking no risks."

Río cut back in, her own voice just as stern as Mariel's. "The time will be useful. We have many more tomes and scrolls to sort through now that we have this new information. While you rest, we'll be refining our information as much as possible so the guidance you seek will be as useful as it can be."

"We may only get one chance," Mariel said with a significant look at Lucha. "Whatever sent you into that office the other night left you compromised. A bridge with a crack in it. It may stand for years yet . . ." She trailed off.

"But it might collapse the second you set foot on it," Lucha finished for her. "I get it."

"Then you understand the risk involved," Río said. "And the reason why any unapproved excursions could be truly disastrous for all of us."

"I understand," Lucha said, her rebellious plots fizzling out as the reality of the situation became clear. "I'll wait. Just . . . remember there's more than mythology at stake here. There are real people in Robado, and the sacrifice of their lives isn't a price I'm willing to pay."

"I remember our bargain," Río said. "See that you remember it too."

They left then, Río and Mariel. Paz lingered in the doorway, and Lucha knew she should say something, but her mind felt dangerously full, and her hands ached, and everything felt too real and not real enough all at once.

"I'm sorry," Paz said when they were alone. "I tried to get to you before they could ambush you with all that. And before that . . . If I had been faster in there, or if I had talked you out of it—"

"It's okay," Lucha said. "Not sure if you've noticed, but it's hard to stop me when my mind is set on something."

"I've noticed," Paz said, sniffing suspiciously. "But still. I could have tried harder."

"If you hadn't been there, I would have turned, or died," Lucha said bluntly. "It was stupid of me to go, and I'm sorry I dragged you along."

"So does that mean you'll be good?" Paz asked, stepping closer. "Stay out of trouble?"

Despite the bandages and the headache and the knowledge of her own impending doom, Lucha's heart skipped a beat when she looked up through her lashes.

She swallowed, hard. "I'll try," she said hoarsely.

"Good," Paz said. "Because I was kind of worried about you, you know."

Lucha just nodded. She was so tired all of a sudden that even the heat disappeared. "Thanks for being such a good shot."

"Thanks for being such a shameless martyr."

Paz turned toward the flap, and Lucha was asleep before she opened it.

23

Despite her fervent wish to be useful, Lucha slept on and off for the next several days. Dreamlessly at first, which, during one of her brief waking periods, Mariel said was a good sign.

"Your mind is still protecting itself," she said. "Once you start dreaming again, we'll know there's something to work with. But even then, we'll need to go slowly. Carefully."

Everyone told her to be careful, as if there were anything else to be. She could barely hold herself up. Her head felt like a boulder, and her thoughts were scattered and slow when she had them at all.

Outside, things were happening. She heard snippets of conversation between long periods of sleep that never seemed to restore her. The greens had finally died out, and the berries had made Marisol sick, which meant the camp's sole source of food was the preserved goods brought by the acolytes.

They'd started rationing, but it was a countdown with no end point.

Once, she heard there had been no more blighted creatures

since Miguel. That was something, she thought before sliding back into unconsciousness.

There were acolytes and priestesses in the clinic most days. They kept an eye on her, changed her bandages, fed her when she could stand it. When they weren't attending to her, they were reading the mountains of books and scrolls piled on the little tables. Talking in hushed tones.

People came in, but Lucha had a hard time remembering what they discussed. She remembered Maria, her tearstains, questions Lucha couldn't move her tongue to answer. Armando, his quiet, solid presence grounding her. Even Junio, his little hand in hers for a brief moment.

Blissfully, the first time she managed to stay awake for more than an hour, she was alone. She spent most of that time just trying to commit what she'd heard to memory, to figure out how long it had been. The bandages on her hands were much less bulky now, and they ached less, but itched more. Maybe that was a good sign.

It was dark outside the tent. An acolyte slept on the cot beside her. She'd wake if Lucha called out, but right now Lucha needed the quiet. She felt cracked open like an eggshell, exposed and vulnerable. Around her, little lights danced. An invitation.

Somewhere outside, someone was singing. Or was it within her? It was so hard to tell in these liminal hours. Lucha couldn't understand the words, but somehow she knew their meaning. *The hour approaches. The forgotten spring awaits. The hour approaches . . .*

Within her, Lucha could feel the imbalance of the forest as

if she herself were filled with trees and soil, plants and mycelia. The wrongness inside her, the scales tipping violently one way, then the other. No grounding influence. No central logic to obey. The chaos of it, not freedom but destruction.

Was this the madness Mariel had warned her of? Lucha wondered. Nothing felt truly tethered. She didn't feel like Lucha Moya, but like some small interconnected piece of something endless and enduring that had been knocked off its axis.

She thought of herself as Mariel described her. A bridge with a crack. Awaiting the footstep that would snap it.

"Even if it breaks me," she whispered out loud, "it doesn't matter. Just let me end what we started when I killed him."

The awful pressure that had been building within her ebbed a little, reminding her who she was. The limits of her body. The night seemed to sigh in acceptance, or disappointment, she couldn't tell which.

Lucha was going to call for the acolyte. To tell her to get Mariel, to tell her she was ready and it was time. But before she could, she was slipping again into the velvety darkness of sleep.

She dreamed her hands were whole. Unbandaged. She rose from her bed to find her legs strong and her head clear. She walked with purpose to the tent flap. No one stopped her.

Across the empty camp she strode, focused on her destination. Nothing was the same, and yet everything was. The trees towered. The soil beneath her feet was fertile, green sprouting from it as if things had always grown in the Scar.

The sun shone. Not too hot.

She walked until she reached a great tree. There were no familiar landmarks around it. In fact, it felt wholly separate from what Lucha knew of Robado. As if it existed within its own sphere of golden light.

At its base, Cruz was waiting for Lucha, a smile on her face. There was no hesitation in Lucha as she walked toward her. It was as if this meeting had been planned, and was not the first of its kind. She stepped into Cruz's outstretched arms, their lips barely an inch apart.

"I missed you," Cruz said.

"I'm here now," Lucha heard herself reply.

And then they were kissing. Not the kind of kiss they'd shared in the aftermath of the fire, all confusion and pent-up, unacknowledged wanting. This felt like a return to something safe. Comfortable, but no less exciting for that.

Lucha felt Cruz's hands slide into her hair, felt their bodies press closer as heat built between them. But she didn't feel afraid. Or confused. Only right.

So right that she didn't notice the shadow passing over them until almost all the light was gone.

Lucha pulled away first, Cruz's body still pressed into hers.

She looked up, and the warmth kindling in her was replaced by an icy dread.

Looming over them was the bloodred tree from the grove where Lucha had defeated Salvador, and black eyes were staring out of its trunk.

24

Lucha awoke with a scream lodged in her throat.

The tent was filled with light, and Mariel stood over her, eyes wide.

"You were dreaming," she said. It wasn't a question.

Lucha could still see the eyes from her dream boring into her. She felt clammy and cold, but she was awake in earnest now. Herself in a way that was both painful and a relief.

"I was," she said shakily. There was no point in hiding it. Especially if it meant they could move forward at last.

"Your hands are much better," Mariel said, gesturing down at them, wrapped in only a single layer of bandages now.

Lucha bent her fingers just for something to do. They were stiff, but they felt like hands again.

"Have you found more about the spring?" she asked, if only to delay the inevitable questions about her dream. Beyond the black eyes staring out from the tree trunk, she could feel that effortless warmth that had kindled between her and Cruz.

"We've been as productive as we can be given the state most of those books are in," Mariel said. "I'll let Río fill you in on all the rest." *All the rest,* Lucha could tell, was not good news.

"Tell me," she said, thinking of the Robadans. What had happened to them while she had been sleeping? "Is it the blight? Has someone else been taken?"

Mariel shook her head. "There's been no more blight since you went into that office," she said. "Small blessing, considering the river is nearly dry. The drinking water supply is very low, and there are no more forageables in the forest. Combined with the knowledge that one of their former leaders was found consumed by blight, that has made morale in the camp . . . suffer."

Lucha remembered the night Río had saved her and Cruz from the unrest of the Robadans. Their belief that Miguel was out there in the forest somewhere, a better option if things got worse. Though Lucha hoped most of them had found peace here by now, it would have been jarring to have that fantasy dispelled in such a brutal fashion.

And on top of everything else . . . Lucha felt they were lucky they didn't have a full-scale rebellion on their hands already.

"I need to be out there," she said. "Hiding all the knowledge away from the people is what made the Robadans hate the kings. If we don't tell them what we're doing, if we don't try to make them a part of it, they're going to turn on us."

"You may be right," Mariel said, her expression grave. "But you may also have a hard time convincing Río of that."

As if summoned by the sound of her name, Río made her way into the tent a moment later, with Paz attending her. "Good, you're awake," she said without looking directly at Lucha. "Did you dream?"

With Paz in the room, Lucha found herself flushing at the memory. She only nodded, praying no one would ask for details.

"Good." Río bustled over to a table in the corner, piled with papers.

"I want to sleep in my own tent tonight," Lucha said. "And I want to tell the Robadans what we're planning. If we don't, they'll have no reason to trust that we want to keep them safe. If we hoard knowledge and keep our plans secret, we might as well be in the sanctuary."

"I've been saying that all along," Río said without turning.

"This was the deal," Lucha said, sitting up, swinging her legs over the side of the bed. She felt dizzy, but it was worth it to show them she was strong. "The Robadans were supposed to be part of this. I won't let you create some hierarchy in my city."

Río did turn then, and her eyes flashed with some emotion Lucha couldn't name. "You can sleep wherever you like," she said, her tone even, though Lucha could hear the tension that kept it that way. "And *if* our next attempts at communication with Almudena are successful, we will discuss what to share with the Robadans."

Lucha knew this was the best she could do for now. "I'm ready to start," she said. "You said I'd be ready when I could dream."

Mariel looked her over. "Tomorrow," she said. "We'll try tomorrow. But slowly."

This, too, was the best Lucha could do for now.

The rest of the meeting was short. Lucha avoided Paz's eyes, the dream still lingering. She didn't dare ask where Cruz was, or if she'd visited. She was afraid her tone would give her away.

They had learned frustratingly little more about the spring during Lucha's convalescence. Mythology, yes. And history. Some potentially identifying features. But what they really needed to know—its precise location and what exactly it could do—would depend on Lucha and her half-broken mind.

When Río and Mariel left, Paz took the bandages from Lucha's hands, allowing her to see them for the first time since Alán's office. The skin was mottled, and an angry red. In places, what was once a flat plane of flesh dipped, cratered, or puckered.

These were not the hands of the girl she had once been. But in some ways it was a relief, not to look the same. There was something about scars that showed.

"They'll be a little tight for a while," Paz said, and for the briefest of moments Lucha thought she saw her eyes glisten. "But you should be able to use them. The salve does wonders for burns, and this seemed to work much the same way."

They didn't break eye contact. There was so much that was heavy between them, so much that was tender. Lucha felt herself wide open in this moment, soaking it all in.

After days in bed, Lucha needed Paz's support to walk more than she'd hoped she would. But it wasn't the first time Paz had been there to lean on. The strangeness wasn't in their closeness, but in how natural it felt after all this time.

The camp was mostly deserted—by then, many had fled for fear of the blight, monsters, or worse. All the hope and merriment that had been building had been extinguished so quickly. Lucha's heart ached that she hadn't been there when they discovered Miguel. When the last of the forageable food was corrupted. That had been the whole point of this awful arrangement—to be there for her people when they needed her.

"Don't beat yourself up," Paz said quietly, reading Lucha's thoughts, as she'd always seemed able to do. "You landed yourself in the clinic saving them from the blight. They know that."

"Do they?" Lucha asked.

"Cruz made sure of it," Paz replied. She trod almost too lightly on the other girl's name. "She visited nearly every day. Badgered us constantly about whether you'd recover. She's a good friend."

The lightness was there on the word *friend* as well, Lucha noticed. It was an invitation to confirm what she'd said before. That there was nothing romantic between her and Cruz. But Lucha thought of the night they took down the sabuesa. The feeling of Cruz's fingers running along her skin as she checked for blight. The kiss in the hazy forest.

The dream she'd had just last night.

She couldn't honestly say there was nothing between them anymore, but she also couldn't describe what *was* between them, so she stayed quiet. Focused on placing her steps carefully. On the distance to her own bed.

It took an age, but they reached her tent at last. Paz didn't speak more, but she made sure Lucha was situated before retreating to the doorway.

"Get some rest," she said. "There's a lot to do tomorrow."

"I will," Lucha replied. She could already feel exhaustion pulling at her, though she'd only woken a few hours before. "And thanks, Paz. For everything."

"It's what I do," the other girl said with a sad smile. And then she was gone.

Despite her exhaustion, Lucha found being alone with her thoughts intolerable. She returned again and again to the feeling she'd had before her dream. The imbalance at the heart of the world. And then the dream—the dark eyes staring out of Salvador's tree.

Cruz and the kiss. Paz and her tears.

Moments after she was alone, Lucha stood shakily and opened the flap to her tent, making sure she was visible to anyone walking past. She'd come back to boost morale, after all. To show the Robadans that she wouldn't retreat into some privileged council and leave them to starve.

For the next few hours, people trickled through, a few at a

time. Lucha was gratified to see the hope on their faces when they saw she'd returned. Armando came, and Maria. They told her they were glad to have her back, thanked her for what she'd done.

When Marisol and Junio came, Lucha told them they were working on something to fix the forest. To make sure the food came back, and the water was clean, and everyone was taken care of.

They walked away more cheerful than they'd entered, and Lucha, weary to her bones, felt she'd done the right thing.

Cruz didn't make an appearance all day, she noticed. But as she'd never admitted she was waiting for her, Lucha didn't let herself dwell on Cruz's absence.

Sleep came easily with the twilight. A dream had been unfolding slowly, its details still indistinct, when a tapping on Lucha's tent woke her. The darkness outside was absolute. She'd clearly been asleep for hours.

"Who's there?" she called, flexing the tight skin of her hands, feeling for her knives beneath her blanket and finding them reassuringly present.

"Can I come in?" came Paz's voice through the canvas.

"Yeah," Lucha said, her voice still rough with sleep. "Is everything all right?"

Paz didn't answer right away, but the tent flap opened to reveal her with her hair undone and her cheeks flushed. Her lips parted. Lucha felt heat bloom across her skin, the warmth of her dreams still close to the surface.

"Did something happen?" Lucha asked.

Instead of answering, Paz came inside, closing the flap firmly behind her.

Lucha got to her feet. They were close together in the small space. Paz's smell filled it, citrus and jasmine as always. Lucha's senses were still hazy with sleep. She didn't know how to respond to this closeness. To the look on Paz's face.

And still, Paz hadn't spoken. Only looked at her like Paz was drowning and the sight of Lucha was a lifeline.

"Paz, what's going on?" Lucha asked.

The other girl took a deep, shaky breath before speaking at last. "I've been trying," she began, emotion thick in her throat, "to give you the space you asked for. To respect what you need. But I've been so scared, Lucha. That night . . . I thought I would lose you before I could ever . . . before *we* could . . ." She trailed off, and Lucha's own tangled desires picked up the thread.

She remembered, in this moment, with her guard down as low as it could go, what it had felt like to love this girl. To *want* her. That feeling Lucha had carried—on fire in her chest as they crossed the forest together, fought Salvador together—hadn't gone away. She'd only been trying to convince herself it had, because the truth was so much more complicated.

"I'm starting to feel like I'm losing my mind," Paz confessed into the silence. "Like I'm the only one who remembers . . ."

"You're not," Lucha said. "I remember, Paz. I—"

She was interrupted by Paz stepping closer.

Lucha knew there were a thousand reasons to say no, but right now she couldn't remember a single one of them. She closed the distance between them, reaching up to take Paz's face in her tender hands.

Inside this moment, there was no room for doubts, or worries. There was only the friction of hands on skin, and the sliding of lips across lips, and heat building. Heat everywhere.

But right as the heat built to its boiling point, Lucha remembered Paz in the forest. Paz with her hands over her face, whispering that she was sorry before the acolytes shot them up with darts. Remembered the feeling Lucha had carried for days after. That she'd lost the only thing that mattered to her.

How could she do this again with none of the questions answered? None of the roads ahead cleared?

"No," Lucha said, pushing away from Paz, the world they'd so recently inhabited gone in an instant. "No, I can't. I'm sorry."

"Lucha?" Paz asked.

"I can't," Lucha said, stepping back, ignoring the confusion and hurt on Paz's face. "I just can't."

"Wait!" Paz said as Lucha turned toward the door, overwhelmed by the memories. The hurt. Like Paz had only just now chosen her goddess, and Lucha was alone. "You're hurt! You can't go out there in the middle of the night."

Lucha knew this was probably true, but it didn't matter. She had to get out of here.

"I'll go!" Paz said, but Lucha could barely hear her over the pounding of her own heartbeat. "Lucha, don't!"

She was already gone. Outside. The forest around her everywhere. The shadows welcoming her.

She pushed through brush and brambles until the woods became a blur and she didn't know where her feet were carrying her. She didn't stop until she was far enough away that no one would find her. Until she had space to breathe.

Her legs were trembling by the time she stopped, weak from exertion. There was a small, muddy puddle where there had once been a stream-fed pool, and in it, Lucha looked at her reflection. Her wide eyes, her flyaway hair. Cheeks flushed from running, mouth open as she breathed heavily.

It seemed impossible that the water could be gone. That the food could be disappearing and the forest burning and flooding and dying, and she was here on her knees, inside out because of a girl who had kissed her and hurt her and kissed her again.

"You need to get it together," she told herself. "Your mind is the resource they need, you can't let it be broken over—"

But before she could finish giving herself this much-needed talking-to, the reflection changed. There was someone behind Lucha. Or some*thing*. Hovering right over her shoulder.

Lucha whirled around, drawing a knife clumsily with her strange hands.

There was nothing there.

"Hello?" she called, thinking perhaps Paz had followed her, or Cruz, or some other Robadan out for a midnight stroll wondering where she was running off to in the dead of night.

No one answered. The darkness was deep, layered with shadow, but the full moon above shone bright enough for

Lucha to see in front of her. It was an all-too-familiar type of movement. The figure darted from one tree to another. A hunched, vaguely human shape that moved unnaturally. As if it were possessed . . .

The hair on Lucha's arms stood up, the back of her neck prickling with awareness. She was being watched. And not by a concerned citizen of Robado. Not by some blighted dog stalking through the trees.

This figure moved like Miguel, but more purposefully. More like a human than an animal.

"I know you're there," she said aloud. She knew that if this monster was anything close to as deadly as Miguel had been, she was a goner. Even in top form, she couldn't have beaten a blighted man alone—and she had the scars to prove it.

The shape moved again, closer now, but not close enough to be seen.

"If you'd been taken by the blight, you would have attacked me by now. You wouldn't have been able to help it. So tell me why you followed the wrong girl into the woods tonight."

The adrenaline chased away the pain in her chest. Even knowing she was too weak to fight her best, Lucha felt like herself again. *This* was what she did well.

"Come out and face me," Lucha said, taunting it, loving the power that coursed through her body. Loving the absence of everything it chased away. "The bravest beasts don't hide."

"They aren't as smart as I am." The voice that came from the trees was grating. Gurgling. Barely human. Yet it spoke.

For a wild moment Lucha pictured some fairy-tale creature, half gnome, half toad, something out of a story.

What stepped into the light was much stranger.

The creature wasn't a creature at all, but a human, with his silhouette strangely stretched. The smell of blight issued from him, caught in Lucha's nose and throat. But she refused to show that this frightened her.

"How did you keep your mind?" she asked. "When the blight took you?"

"An invasive question from someone who hasn't even asked my name," came the voice. Like oily mud bubbling. "And you were wrong, before. I'm not a beast. Or at least, I wasn't always."

"Was it recent, then?" Lucha asked. "If you've come into contact with the blight, we can help you. There's no need to stalk the woods like this, scaring unsuspecting travelers."

"I have no need of your help." His face was in shadow, though the moon lit his cloak. It looked to be made of moss. Leaves. It trailed on the ground. "The creatures you call *blighted* are mine. I turned them myself. I took your calf, and your man Miguel. All to show you my power."

Fear spread at these words. A cold and creeping feeling stealing through Lucha's veins.

"Me?" she asked. "Why me?"

"Because you're the only one who can help me. And not with your little saltwater tonic or your barbaric skin removal. But with something infinitely more difficult and important."

"Why would I help you when you've just confessed to

sending blighted creatures after my people? Following me, and watching me?" Lucha asked.

"Because you owe me," came the voice, sinister and hissing now as the figure stepped into the moonlight at last. "Don't you think?"

At first, all Lucha could do was keep the contents of her stomach where they belonged. What had happened to this man was somehow worse than being fully consumed by blight. He was an awful symbiosis of man and fungus, working together to create something unlike anything she'd ever seen before.

But his form wasn't what repulsed Lucha. Nor was his smell. It was the look in his eye, and the recognition that spread faster than the blight, activating every secret anger and hatred Lucha had managed to keep quiet since last she saw him.

Lucha knew better than most that a person's visage didn't make them good or bad. Alán wasn't a monster for anything she could see. But she knew what was underneath. In that rotten heart. In that twisted, cruel mind.

"You . . . you're dead," she stuttered as Alán Marquez stepped closer still. "I killed you. This can't be real."

"You *tried* to kill me," he corrected.

His face was too horrible to be natural. As with the creatures who had been taken by the blight, only one eye was still uninfected, one corner of his mouth, which he spoke through now. A single pale hand reached out from his cloak, but all the rest of him was covered in red fungal flesh.

The one eye Lucha could see was locked on her now as he

moved toward her. Amid the fear that threatened to strip the rest of her away, Lucha felt a tiny flicker of anger. An anger she'd been nursing for years. It was so deeply rooted, it sprouted despite the terror and revulsion coursing through her.

"You set your little mushrooms on me," he said. "And it was a pain I'd never felt. They pushed through every artifice I'd built up over the years. Ate into my flesh, choked my throat and my breath. I stayed in that cell for days. Weeks. I lost count of the time. All I could do was cling to survival. But you were stupid. You left a little of your power in them, and soon enough, I learned to make use of it."

Even with half his face obscured, Alán's smirk managed to look the same as it always had. It was this that brought Lucha back to herself. The memory of him leering at her over his desk. At her doorway, delivering the news that she and Lis would soon be homeless.

This man had brought so much misery into her life. There had been times, in the darkest periods of what came next, when the thought of him dead had been her only comfort.

"So it was revenge," she said. "The calf. The sabuesas. Miguel . . ."

"*Miguel* was only meant to keep people away from my things," Alán said. "I didn't figure you'd be stupid enough to go snooping around yourself."

"I survived," Lucha said, another spike of anger clearing away the haze of fear. "Which is more than I'll be able to say for you in a few minutes."

"You can kill me," Alán said. "Gods know you've probably

wanted to. But if you do, you'll never find what you're looking for. I wanted to give you back a little of the pain you caused me. It's only natural. Most of all, I wanted to show you I've gained some power, too. That we need each other to do what comes next."

"Quiet," Lucha snapped. "I won't let you manipulate me this time."

This man had made her feel small and unworthy for so long. Before she'd become gifted, before she'd seen anything more than this awful mud pit, he'd managed to make sure she felt like nothing. In many ways, he'd paved the road for everything that had come after.

Lucha had been stupid. She hadn't realized the power in those little spores. Hadn't known it was a goddess's gift she'd been wielding. She'd given him his power, and now she could take it away.

She stepped forward. The fear was gone. In its place was something clean, burning, and ruthless. Something that beat alongside her heart and promised her he would die tonight at her hand. That all he'd done by becoming this monster was buy himself a few months.

"I won't listen to a word you say," she said, her voice ringing and clear. "Tonight is about one thing—me keeping the promise I made to you in that cell. You've cheated death long enough."

She tightened her grip painfully around her dagger's hilt, then lunged for him before he could respond. Words had always been his best weapon. His new form was quick; he seemed to slither rather than walking on human legs, but Lucha—even wounded and winded—was fueled by pure hatred, which gave her an edge.

For a time they played cat and mouse in the grove. All he did was dodge. Deflect. Hide. He didn't even draw a weapon.

Underestimating her had always been his fatal flaw.

Within moments, despite his maneuvering, she had him up against a tree, the knife pointed right at his good eye. This time she took care not to touch the blight—although from so close, it looked different on him. Inert.

Alán smiled. The teeth he had were stained red like the fungus. "You always did know how to dance." His breath was putrid on her face. "But you shouldn't let me lead."

"You're not *leading*," Lucha spat. "You're stalling."

"Yes, but I'm also still breathing."

"Goodbye, Alán," Lucha said without sentiment. "The only thing I'm grateful for in our whole history is the chance to kill you twice."

He chuckled. At least, Lucha thought it was a chuckle. It sounded more like a bootheel being pulled from the mud.

He showed no fear. Could a man as inhuman as he had become even feel fear? Lucha wondered. "Allow me," he said, "to tell you the truth about the Forgotten Spring."

It was the one thing he could have said to stay her hand, and he must have known it. Lucha froze. She did not remove the knife from in front of his eye.

"What did you say?"

"The spring. The one you and that unimaginative bunch

of acolytes have been looking for all week. I have to say, I was impressed you made it this far—I wasn't sure the long-haired one was more than a pretty face."

Lucha hit him hard across the cheek with the butt of her knife. He spat, and the liquid that hit the ground at her feet smoked faintly, dissolving the leaves it landed on.

But Lucha didn't stab him through the eye. Even though she knew she should.

"You're close," he went on, as if she'd never struck him. "But time is running out. You might find it, but you'll never be able to use it without me."

"And why the hell would I trust you?" Lucha asked. "Why would I trust a single word you say?"

"Because I'm your only chance at clean water," he said. "At fresh food. At a life for the Robadans you inexplicably love. At one that isn't based on fear of floods or fires or blight."

"You don't care about Robado," Lucha said. "I want to know what's in it for *you*."

"The same thing I've always wanted," Alán said with an attempt at a shrug. "A chance to be a part of history. To never be forgotten."

It was such a selfish desire, Lucha thought, that she almost believed him.

"We need each other," he said when she didn't answer right away. "I can't find the spring without you, and you can't use it without me. Fate is clever, isn't it? The way it draws us back together?"

Lucha pressed the knife closer, hating the way his words

twisted in her mind, tangled all the things she'd known for sure before she came into these woods tonight.

"I don't need you," she said, more to herself than to him. "Not anymore." Just below his eyelid, a drop of blood dripped from her knifepoint down his cheek. He showed no sign of feeling it. "I'll find the spring, and I'll learn how to use it. And you'll be remembered by no one."

"And if you can't?" Alán asked, as if they were having a friendly conversation about the weather. One of them predicting rain, the other a sunny afternoon.

"If I don't, at least the world will have one less monster in it."

"Of course," Alán said. "I'm not ashamed of my monstrousness. And you haven't seen the half of what I can do."

Lucha pushed harder. A tiny river of blood trickled down.

"But what will your companions say when they find out you had the chance to learn the truth? To feed your people and save their world? And you threw it away without even consulting them?"

She didn't want to, but Lucha thought of Paz. Río. How hard they'd worked to discover the existence of the spring. Of Cruz, the leader she'd become, struggling to hold the Robadans together. *Did* Lucha have the right to make this decision on her own?

"Arrrrgh!" she screamed, slicing Alán's cheek open out of pure frustration.

"Tricky business, I know," Alán said, his croaking voice full of faux sympathy. "I'll give you a moment to mull it over."

Lucha had never wanted anything in her life as much as

she wanted to slice Alán's throat and leave him here to decompose. Not because he had been half taken by blight. Not because she didn't see him as human—but because she did. Because she knew exactly what he was capable of.

But he was right about one thing. Lucha wasn't a law unto herself. Not anymore. The Syndicate, and even the acolytes, had earned the right to weigh in on his fate.

The hatred now surging through Lucha's veins had never been more potent—at least not since she'd stood in the clearing and faced Salvador. Her hatred had clouded her judgment then, and the world had almost ended because of her selfishness. She couldn't afford to make the same mistake again.

"Let me be clear," she growled, tying up his wrists with a length of rope hanging from her belt. "I *will* be killing you. One way or another. And whatever your agenda is? I will find out. And I will make absolutely certain it never comes to fruition."

"Noted," Alán said. He stood obediently still as she tied him with her clumsy hands. Her knots were tight. He wouldn't be escaping tonight.

"Let's go," she said, and jerked the rope. He fell on his face, and she kept walking, forcing him to scramble back to his feet.

25

The camp was deserted as they reentered Robado.

"Keep quiet, or I will gag you," Lucha promised.

Telling herself it was a security issue more than anything, that Cruz was most likely to know where to put him until they could figure out what came next, Lucha walked past Río's tent and made straight for Cruz's.

"I wondered which girlfriend you'd wake first," Alán said, as if her threat before hadn't registered.

Lucha elbowed him hard in the chest, then jerked his rope again. She was satisfied to hear him let out a grunt that told her at least he was capable of feeling pain.

He didn't speak again until they reached Cruz's tent. Lucha knocked, trying not to think of what she'd been doing less than an hour before. Of Paz and her presence and the thousand complications that would keep them from understanding what was between them . . .

But none of that was important now. Now they needed a secure location for this prisoner, and a game plan for questioning him. Everything else could wait.

Cruz opened the door bleary-eyed. "Lucha," she said in a gravelly voice that made Lucha's stomach do a backflip despite the circumstances. "I'm sorry I didn't—"

Lucha stepped aside rather than interrupting, exposing the horror of Alán in full.

Cruz let out a strangled yelp, jumping backward. "What the hell is that thing?"

"It's complicated," Lucha said. "And I will explain everything. But first we need to find somewhere to lock him up. Somewhere no one will find him."

"I've told her I won't run," said Alán. Cruz jumped again at the inhuman sound of his gurgling voice. "But she insists."

Realization dawned on Cruz's face once she'd recovered from the shock. "That's not—" she began, but Lucha cut her off.

"We have to get him off the street."

Cruz closed her mouth, but her eyes suddenly burned with a hatred that surprised Lucha. Were she and Alán acquainted? Or was this venom reserved for the monster who'd been stealing from Robado and spreading blight like confetti around the city?

She would have to wait to find out.

"I have an idea," Cruz said. She was already dressed and armed. She made her way out of the door, and Lucha—pulling Alán by his rope—followed closely behind.

Lucha didn't ask where they were going. She trusted Cruz. But when the south ward housing unit came into view, Lucha found herself in awe of this girl's mind. The irony was only the first reason it was such a great place to hide him.

"No one comes out here," Cruz explained, "and if we need to make him scream, they'll think it's just the ghosts of the drowned."

"No arguments from me," Lucha said with another sharp tug at the rope. "Let's go."

This time, Lucha led. There was only one unit she wanted this monster imprisoned inside.

Alán didn't speak again until he was leashed to an exposed floor beam in the unit he'd once threatened to evict Lucha from.

"Does this satisfy you?" he asked, indicating his bonds. "I've no intention of running, as I've made clear, but this is about your comfort, after all."

"Shut up," Cruz said, then turned to Lucha. "I thought he was supposed to be dead. You said you killed him in Encadenar."

"I thought I did," Lucha said.

"But she didn't wait around to make sure they finished the job," Alán croaked. "We all make mistakes."

"I said *shut up,*" Cruz said, turning back to Alán, her knife at the same eye Lucha had pointed hers at before anyone in the room could blink. "One more word out of you and I swear . . ."

"Oh, birds of a feather, aren't you?" Alán asked. "Let her explain why she didn't kill me first, won't you? I want to hear that part."

Cruz turned reluctantly back to Lucha. "Why *didn't* you kill him?" she asked under her breath.

"It's a bit of a story," Lucha admitted.

Cruz waited. Her eyes flashed dangerously in the light of the moon through the ruined building. Lucha tried to shut out the ghosts that still lived here for her and focus on the task at hand.

"The acolytes have been working on finding the location of a sacred spring," Lucha began haltingly. "Río thinks if we find it, we could use its power to rebalance the forest. But we don't know where it is."

"And *he* does?" Cruz asked, casting a suspicious look at Alán. "How do you know he's not just saying that so you don't kill him?"

"I don't," Lucha said. "But he's been watching us. He knows much of what we know, and time is running out. If he can help us find it . . . use it . . . it could be the only chance we have to set things right before anyone else has to die."

Cruz paused, appearing to think it over, though Lucha could tell from her expression that she wasn't entirely swayed by this tenuous mythological explanation. "No one else knows you have him?" she asked after a moment.

"No," Lucha said. "I brought him straight to you."

There was a flash in Cruz's eyes at these words. Surprise—gratitude, perhaps. Lucha realized Cruz had expected Lucha to go to Paz or another one of the acolytes first. That she was happy she hadn't. There was no time to read too much into that.

"With Miguel and the blighted creatures and everything that's happened," Lucha went on, trying not to think of the dream, of the closeness and warmth between them, "I figured folks seeing us working with him wouldn't be good for morale."

"You're right about that," Cruz said. "But I still say we kill him before anyone finds out and be done with it. Whatever he knows about your spring, I'll get it out of him before the end, but we can't afford to let him live."

The edge of her knife looked terribly sharp in the moonlight. The more Lucha thought about Cruz's plan, the better it sounded.

"Okay," she said finally. She had surprised Cruz again, she could see it on the other girl's face. "I've already killed him once. And as long as we find out what he knows about the spring, there's no reason he has to be alive and a hell of a lot of reasons he shouldn't be."

"You do know I can hear you, do you not?" Alán asked, as if the fact that they were standing here discussing his torture and murder was a matter of only minor importance.

"Dead men can't hear anything," Cruz said without looking at him.

"Quite right," Alán said. "But it's a good thing *I* can, because there's a major flaw in your plan that you've yet to discover. Shall I share it with you? Save you the time and frustration?"

Cruz growled again. "You're *very sure* there's nowhere else to learn what he knows?"

"I imagine he's made sure of it," Lucha said, thinking back

to what he'd said about setting Miguel to guard his office. He'd been in the building long before Lucha and Paz had. He would have taken anything particularly damning to ensure his usefulness when he finally approached Lucha.

"I know the two of you are acquainted with my humble powers," he said. "You've seen the way the blight obeys me. The way it gnaws at the minds of its victims and turns them into monsters."

"There are long-range weapons," Cruz said. "Who says we have to get near you?"

"True, but not my point," Alán said. "How do you think I came by those powers? Hmm? You both knew me when I was a mortal man much different in bearing, did you not?"

"You were the same monster then," Lucha growled. "Your visage makes no difference to us."

"Yes, but *how?*" he pressed.

"It was the mushrooms," Lucha said. "The power I left in them. Get to the point."

"Quite so," Alán agreed. "But you know fungus, don't you, Lucha? Rather intimately? Do you think the mushrooms you left were content to confer their power on me without a battle of immense wills?"

Lucha didn't answer. Instead, she remembered the way he'd screamed.

"Now you're getting it," he said, presumably responding to the look on her face. "The torture, the agony, the absolute horror I endured in that cell were unlike anything you could possibly imagine. My very bones were digested. Slowly. My brain breached and penetrated and devoured in places. I should have died a hundred times. Surrendered my consciousness, at the very least. And believe me, I wanted to. But within that pain was power, and I wanted *that* more than I wanted the end of my agony."

Lucha and Cruz stood horrified, transfixed as a strange light danced in his features. This was the true change, Lucha thought. Not his body. This man was nothing like the boy Lucha had known, or even the man he had later become.

"You could peel every inch of skin from my flesh. It wouldn't come close to equaling the horrors I've endured," he said. "You're welcome to try. But it will only delay the inevitable."

"The inevitable, I imagine, being the burning, drowning, starvation, or revolt of everyone in Robado," Cruz said flatly.

"You've come a long way, Miss Miranda," Alán said. How he could still condescend even in that croaking gargle was a mystery to Lucha.

"Why should we trust you?" Cruz snapped. "I know you, you worm, and you'd let the world burn a hundred times before you did something that didn't benefit you. The only way I don't put a knife though whatever part of you looks most human and damn the consequences is if you tell us the whole truth."

"I plan on it," Alán said without hesitating. "But I don't want to repeat myself. Bring the rest, Lucha. I'll tell you together or not at all."

Cruz looked at Lucha questioningly, but Lucha understood.

He knew she'd never make a decision like this without consulting Paz and Río—no matter how much she professed to disagree with the former and distrust the latter on principle. Whatever Alán told them, it would be the acolytes, not Lucha, who would have the context to decide whether the information was worth his life.

"We do need Río's input on this," Lucha said, turning her back on Alán and lowering her voice. "I don't know enough about the mythology to know if what he's saying is true, or valuable."

"This *thing* is a slimeball," Cruz said emphatically, not bothering to keep her own whisper quiet enough that he couldn't hear. "He'll turn on us the first chance he gets. We can't trust him. Not even for a moment."

Lucha shook her head. "I have more reason than anyone to hate and distrust him," she said, feeling like a traitor even though she knew she was doing the right thing. "But we *are* running out of time to save the forest. The next flood, the next fire could wipe us out if the food doesn't run out first. And people are already starting to get antsy. We can't lose them."

Cruz let out a frustrated grunt. "Bring them, then. But if we're keeping him alive, I want Armando and Maria here too. We deserve to be represented in this."

Lucha nodded. "I'll get them all. You're right. Río shouldn't have the chance to overpower us. This is about Robado, too."

At this, Cruz stuck out her hand, and Lucha took it with the tender new skin of her own. Cruz didn't flinch. For a moment Lucha was back in the shadow of the tree, kissing her like she'd done it a million times before.

"Stay with him," she said, pulling away. "I'll run and fetch them quickly."

"If he tries to escape, he's dead," Cruz said with a disgusted look at Alán, who was watching their back-and-forth like it was some sort of game played for his entertainment.

"You have my blessing to kill him if he tries anything at all," Lucha said, looking at him instead of Cruz. Making sure he understood just how little his life was worth to her.

"Hurry back, or I might start carving off bits," Cruz said, her knife glinting menacingly in the moonlight.

Lucha took off at a run.

26

She went for Armando and Maria first, knowing that Río would do her best to keep the presence of the Syndicate to a minimum. When Armando's tent was empty, she found them both in Maria's.

"Not a word," Maria said in a low voice after Lucha had explained the situation. "He's been comforting me."

"I wouldn't dream of it," Lucha said, but she smirked, and Maria groaned. "For what it's worth, I think you make a cute couple."

"Do you *want* me to kill you?" Maria asked. She stalked off before another word could be spoken.

Paz's tent was also empty, and for a moment Lucha was visited by a strange idea. That when Lucha had run off, Paz had sought some comfort of her own. It was an odd vision. One that didn't quite settle. But Lucha had no right to judge. Not when her own head was filled so often with thoughts of someone else.

She went to Río's tent instead, and though she would never

admit it, she was relieved to find a candle burning. To hear Paz's voice drifting out into the night.

Less thrilling, however, were the words she heard when she got closer:

"*—seems unfocused. Reckless. I'm worried about what might happen if we push too hard.*"

"*It's a valid concern, Miss León, but an irrelevant one. If we don't make contact soon, there will be nothing we can do to stop what's coming.*"

Lucha opened the tent flap without bothering to announce herself. "Hope I'm not interrupting," she said.

Paz flushed prettily, but Río looked at her without emotion. "What can we do for you, Miss Moya?"

"Something's happened," Lucha said, trying to forget what she'd heard in favor of the matter at hand. "I've found the source of the blight. He's sentient, and claims to have information about the spring."

Both pairs of eyes went wide.

"He was once someone I was familiar with," Lucha went on after a moment of silence. "It wasn't a pleasant relationship, and I don't trust myself to be objective in deciding his fate, even if he has the information he claims."

"Who was it?" Paz asked.

Lucha took a deep breath. "Alán Marquez. I thought I'd killed him when I escaped prison, as you both know, but I used Almudena's gift to do it. The mushrooms. And it seems they didn't kill him so much as *transform* him."

"What have you done with him?" Río asked sharply.

"I nearly killed him," Lucha admitted. "But with time running out, I feel we have no choice but to listen to what he has to say. See if it's worthwhile. Currently he's imprisoned in a south ward housing unit, being guarded by the Syndicate."

Paz's expression shifted, and Lucha thought she was realizing the truth beneath the facts of the situation. That Lucha had gone to Cruz and the Robadans first.

"You should have come to us right away," Río said, getting to her feet. "This situation is much too delicate to be handled by your *Syndicate*. We need to get there immediately."

Lucha saw it again in that moment. The flash of hunger in Río's eyes she'd seen when they were discussing the spring. Suddenly, Lucha wasn't at all sure she was doing the right thing. But it was too late to turn back. Río was already pushing her way out into the night.

"We'd better go," Lucha said just as Paz asked, "Are you all right?"

"I'm fine," Lucha said, her cheeks burning a little when she thought of the way she'd run out earlier. The things they'd been doing when she had. "Are you?"

"I just need to know," Paz said. "Did you run straight to her after we . . ."

"No," Lucha said vehemently. "I went to the woods. Alán was there. It was a security issue." She could tell from the look on Paz's face that she didn't really believe her.

"Right," Paz said, then walked toward the door, her head held high as always. "As you said, we'd better get going."

Thankfully, no one stopped them on the way to the housing unit. Paz and Lucha caught up with Río, walking quietly as the camp slept. Cruz hadn't lit a lamp inside—which had been wise, of course. It was best not to draw attention until they understood Alán's agenda. The fewer people who knew about this—about him—the better.

"I should warn you before we go in," Lucha said, the other two stopping to listen. "This man is the best liar I have ever known. He's a master manipulator, and if you let him, he will take advantage of you. So everyone, please keep your wits about you and take everything he says with a pile of salt until we can corroborate it with facts."

Río nodded once, clearly in a hurry to get inside. Paz didn't reply, but then again, Lucha thought she might be the least susceptible to manipulation of anyone Lucha had ever met. Her faith made her nearly impervious to it.

"Okay," Lucha said, taking a deep breath. "Let's go, then."

Paz choked a bit when they opened the door, and Río's eyes began to water. Lucha was almost surprised to find Alán alive. Armando and Maria stood on either side of Cruz, their heads bent in conversation.

"Welcome back," Cruz said when they made their way through the door. "I was just introducing the others to Alán Marquez of Robado, the slipperiest, slimiest man this city has ever had the displeasure of birthing. He should be dead. I'm sure you'll all get along just famously."

Armando and Maria had weapons drawn. It was clear Cruz had filled them in on more than just this during the time it had taken them all to get here.

Río didn't bother to acknowledge the Syndicate members at all. She craned to see Alán, who for now was quiet at the back of the room. The Syndicate formed a barrier between him and Río, and Lucha, not caring how it would look for once, moved to join them.

"I brought him back because he says he has information about the spring. I brought you all here," she said to the acolytes, "because you understand the lore well enough to know if he's telling us something valuable."

"My strong recommendation," Cruz cut in, "is that we kill him as soon as possible."

Paz had been quiet so far, staring at Alán from Río's side of the room—but not with judgment for his body or his motives. She looked at him like she looked at everything. As if even the transformation he'd undergone held some proof of divinity in the world.

"You used your gift on him?" she asked Lucha without looking away from Alán.

"In Encadenar," Lucha replied, trying not to sound testy. "He had taken my sister into his club, injected her with lethal doses of Olvida, and probably done worse. He'd left me in a cell to starve, told the entire city I was a dangerous murderer and worse. That he'd killed me. I was angry. I set the mushrooms on him." If that wasn't enough of an explanation for anyone who wanted to blame her, Lucha could do little about it.

"But they didn't kill him," Paz said.

"That's right," Alán said.

Paz started at the sound of his voice. Río's eyes snapped to him, though her expression remained tightly controlled.

"They would have," he went on. "If I were a lesser man. But I had been looking for evidence of divine power in the forest all my life, and Lucha's display was my first taste of it. Once she flipped it on me, once I felt the unnatural movement of the fungus in my body, obeying her will, I knew this was my only chance to turn things around."

"Quiet," Cruz snarled, charging toward him with her knife drawn. "You don't speak unless you're invited."

When silence fell again, Paz cleared her throat. "The mushrooms killed Almudena's son," she said, still seeming to look inward. Lucha remembered this expression from their travels together. The feeling that Paz occasionally disappeared from her body and went somewhere much more important. "But they left him alive."

"What's your point?" Cruz asked.

"My point," said Paz, returning to the room to fix her eyes on Cruz, "is that Almudena clearly has some use for him. The power—even wielded by an inexperienced person—would have been plenty to kill him. The question is: why didn't it? I believe it's because Almudena needed him alive. Perhaps to give us the very information he's ready to tell us now."

Lucha wasn't sure she believed Almudena had as big a hand in this as Paz thought. Or any at all. If the goddess had been able to intervene directly, why not simply show up and end the imbalance herself? Why not leave them a sign clearer than this?

Paradoxically, Paz's support for the plan nearly made Lucha lose faith in it. What if they were making a huge mistake, letting Alán state his case? Unfortunately, she also understood that the clock was winding down. And Alán might be the only chance they had to get the information they needed.

"We have to hear him out," she said, though she couldn't quite meet Cruz's eyes when she said it.

This was all the encouragement Río needed. She stepped forward to face Alán with the impressive, straight-backed bearing that had so intimidated Lucha on their first meeting.

"I am Obispo Río of the Asilo sanctuary," she said. "High priestess of Almudena's temple. I demand you tell me everything you know of the Forgotten Spring."

Alán laughed. It sounded like bubbling mud. "All you people have done with the massive power entrusted to you is squander it. Create endless bureaucracy that cuts the folks most in need of power off from its source. If it were you and I alone in this room, I'd die before I shared this information with you. Know that, *Obispo*."

"Your motivations aren't relevant here," Lucha said when she was certain Río's expression could pucker no more. "You're not in a position to look down on anyone in this room. We're here to decide if your information is true, and if so, valuable enough to warrant the continued beating of your heart. I wouldn't take that lightly if I were you."

Alán sat still. Lucha wondered idly if he'd refuse to talk now. But when the silence had stretched a moment longer than anyone could bear, he spoke again.

"I've been studying the ancient lore of the forest since I was a child," Alán began. "I collected every scroll and volume I could get my hands on. Most of them"—his eye darted to Río like he couldn't resist riling her—"contraband from the sanctuary that didn't trust the information in the hands of the people. I discovered the myth of the spring years ago. I did my due diligence. It exists. There's proof across centuries. The only question is: where is it hiding?"

"*Get to the point,*" Lucha growled, stepping close to Alán despite the stench. "We already know it exists, and that it's hidden. I didn't lug you back from the forest to hear this."

"The important thing to know about the spring," he said, unbothered by the interruption, "isn't its location, but its function. That's what I've spent all these years trying to discover. And once I entered this form, the matter only became more urgent."

"What is its purpose?" Río was asking now, as if she were speaking to some scholarly acolyte over the sanctuary's breakfast table and not a half-dead horror worse than anything a storybook had ever conjured.

"It acts as a conduit," Alán said. There was a gravity in his tone that said he'd been holding on to this revelation for some time. "Between our world and the celestial plane, the origin place of the gods. There, anyone with divinity in them may wield power as the gods do, unfettered by the limitations of our world and its natural laws."

For a moment, Lucha forgot who was speaking. What was at stake. As the only person in the room who had ever wielded the power of the divine, she could hardly imagine it being *increased*. Couldn't imagine it ever even needing to be. She had drawn light from the sky, called animals to her aid, created abundant growth from the barest of life.

What task couldn't be accomplished with all that at your disposal?

"She created *him* there," Río said in a breathy voice. Lucha snapped back to the present, surprised. She'd never seen Río quite so undone. The greed, the longing on her face were plain as day as she stared at Alán. "Her son."

"Indeed," Alán replied. "Divine edict rendered the creation of gods impossible in this world—and probably all of the others. That power is reserved for them alone. Even divine beings are bound to honor that decree once they set foot in this world."

"Except at the spring," Lucha finished for him. It all made sense. Almudena had been sent to this world to protect and guide the trajectory of all life here. She had been sent alone. Based on her own laws, she had been expected to remain alone. Only, she hadn't. She'd reached for more power than even the nearly infinite well she'd had to draw from.

She'd stolen Salvador from the celestial plane, and her own kind had punished her for it.

However, she hadn't been the only one to pay for her selfishness.

Lucha thought of the kings. Of Robado, mired in addiction and misery for generations. Of the sanctuary, created to support and spread the will of the guardian. Abandoned. Left with scarcely any power after their goddess used hers for her own selfish purposes and fled. Left them unprotected.

Lucha had had cause to question Almudena's methods before, but with this information she felt a new revulsion for the goddess half the people in this room had given their lives in service of.

She'd created a son, against the laws of the gods. When he'd emerged a monster, a punishment for her hubris, she'd had a duty. To kill him. To right the wrong she'd done. To pay for her greed. But she'd refused.

Almudena hadn't kept her son alive out of mercy, Lucha realized with horror. She'd known what would happen if there was no divine power in Elegido. She'd known the imbalance would come. That she had to stay or doom humanity. So she'd plugged him in, run him like an engine while he went mad at the center of the world in his amber prison.

And when it had become clear he couldn't be contained, she'd come to Lucha in a vision and sent her to be transformed. To make *her* responsible for the fate of humanity so she could continue to hide from what she'd done.

Blood was pounding in Lucha's ears. Almudena had never

cared for the son she made. Never cared for the people she was supposed to protect and guide. She'd been as selfish as any mortal, and now they were all going to die because of that selfishness.

Lucha came back to herself when Alán began to speak once more, and she was shocked to find that not everyone seemed to have reacted to this news the same way she had. In fact, they were all watching him, waiting for what came next, like he hadn't already dropped an explosive into the room and watched it detonate.

"If we can find the spring," Alán said, "I believe we can repeat her experiment—but with a much higher chance of success. I believe we can—"

"Create a god of our own," Río finished for him in that voice that made the hair stand up on Lucha's arms. "Ensure Elegido's safety for generations to come."

"Precisely. Only, we won't be so careless with our attempt. Almudena's mistake was to create a deity from nothing. To trust the whims of celestial power for his creation. We've seen now how terribly wrong that can go. We have another option. One I didn't realize was possible until I heard whispers of Lucha's transformation spreading through the forest. We can choose a champion. Give them the power of a god. Save the world."

A hush fell over them at the thought. Lucha, to whom this idea was horrifying, was surprised to see the awe on Paz's features. The surety. Río's face said she was ravenous for this outcome. A potential future where she could control the destiny of the world.

But did she mean to choose a divine guardian for Robado? Lucha wondered. Or to become one?

"How?" Río asked, getting closer to Alán than Lucha would have dared under the circumstances. "How can it be done?"

At this, Alán leered again. "*That* information I'll keep to myself until we've found it," he said.

Cruz's weapon was out before he could even finish the sentence. Armando and Maria flanked her. Río turned as if to defend him.

"Wait," Lucha said, holding up her hands. "We need to think before we do anything. We need a way to know for certain." She looked at Paz. "Can you wake Mariel? I have an idea."

Mariel arrived at a tense standoff in the stench-filled housing unit. Lucha was glad the acolytes were outnumbered.

Río made no secret of her disdain for the Syndicate, who did not drop their defensive postures during the long half hour it took Paz to return.

"What is it?" Mariel asked.

Lucha explained as quickly and succinctly as she could. "We need to divine whether his information is true," she concluded. "And whether his life is worth sparing, given what he has left to tell us about the spring. As far as I know, there's only one way to do that."

"It's too dangerous," Mariel said flatly. "We must save the

final attempt to divine the location of the spring. And you must be at your strongest when we do."

"I understand that," Lucha said. "But we have no choice, so we just have to hope I'm strong enough."

Mariel seemed determined to stand against it, but Río approached then, saying something in a low voice that no one but Mariel could hear.

Still extremely wary, the old woman held out her hand for Lucha's. "We will try," she said. "But we'll try something different. Less accurate, perhaps, but also less prone to crack your conscious mind like an egg."

Lucha understood that this was the closest thing to a compromise she would get.

"You need a good night's sleep," Mariel said. "We'll do it first thing in the morning."

No one—least of all Lucha—was pleased by the delay. Cruz insisted on being the one to guard Alán, but Río insisted equally forcefully that an acolyte be there to prevent her from doing anything rash.

Lucha, despite her assertion to Mariel that she was fine, had never felt so tired in all her life. Alán had gambled, and at least for tonight, he'd won.

27

Lucha woke early and made her way quickly back toward the housing unit. Things seemed bleak in the camp this morning. Everyone was listless. Knots of Robadans sat together and muttered.

The cook fire was out, and meager rations had already been consumed. Lucha hadn't taken hers. She would suffer rather than let one of the Robadans go hungry. It was her faulty mind that was dragging this out, after all.

Before long, they'd need to find something to energize the people. Something like the overthrow of Los Ricos or the building of the camp. Idle like this, with no control over the outcome of their lives, it was no wonder they weren't happy.

Her body was sore and tired from the events of yesterday, and her hands were cracked and bleeding from overuse. She'd have to remember to ask one of the acolytes for more salve. Couldn't be unprepared if the occasion to stab Alán arose today.

When Lucha arrived at the housing unit, Río and Mariel were already there, speaking in hushed tones, while Cruz was scowling at Alán from the doorway. Lucha approached her first, pretending not to notice the way the conversation fell silent.

"Morning," Cruz said. She looked wan, bags under her eyes.

"Did you stay here all night?" Lucha asked, concern flaring.

"It's fine," Cruz replied, waving a hand. "Armando and Maria slept. They can spell me for a while this afternoon."

Lucha nodded. It wasn't like she could really lecture anyone on the benefits of self-care. Still, she wanted to say something encouraging. Something that reminded Cruz of the resilience that had helped them defeat the kings.

Before she could, Mariel and Río made their way over, determination on their faces.

"Are you ready?" Río asked. "Today could be a big day."

"I still don't think it's such a good idea, given Lucha's condition," Mariel muttered. But on the subject of Lucha's safety, it seemed she'd been outranked.

"I'm ready," Lucha said. She wasn't sure if it was true, but even if it wasn't, it needed to be. "Best-case scenario, I get to kill him the second it's over."

Against the wall, still leashed to the beam, Alán laughed his horrible laugh.

Lucha ignored him while Río looked at her, scandalized.

"The best-case scenario is that he's telling the truth, and we're one step closer to finding the spring," she said sternly. "Don't let pettiness sway your judgment here, Miss Moya. We're counting on you."

But that wasn't strictly true, Lucha thought as she followed

Mariel outside. As usual, it wasn't her *judgment* that was needed, just her strange mind with its faulty conduit to the divine.

Cruz patted Lucha on the shoulder as she passed. "Hang in there," she said.

The swooping feeling in her stomach brought Lucha's dream back to mind momentarily. It was so strange. Like a memory only one of them had. But even without the memory, Cruz's eyes lingered on Lucha.

If she was lucky, she'd live long enough to figure out what this all meant.

Outside, away from Alán's stench and Cruz's befuddling influence, Lucha took a deep breath of forest air and tried to steel herself for what was to come. Mariel found a flat stone some way from the housing unit and gestured for Lucha to sit on the ground before it. In her hands she held what appeared to be a set of dice.

"These are symbols of Almudena," she explained when Lucha was settled. "A crude method of communication used by the devotees of old. They've been out of fashion for decades, as they require a relationship with the goddess to be used accurately. As you know, that's been uncommon for some time without the assistance of Pensa."

Lucha nodded. Her head ached. She wanted to get this over with. To have the issue of Alán settled, at least for the moment.

Mariel handed the dice to Lucha. There were four of them, and they were satisfyingly heavy in her hands. Each had six sides, and each side had a different symbol carved on it.

"In order to use them, you must enter a state of demi-consciousness. Not the full immersion required for your trip into the meadow. Sort of like having your eyes half closed, but in this case it's your inner eye. When you've achieved that state, you ask Almudena for her guidance and cast the dice before you. Afterward, we will work together to interpret the result."

"And this is supposed to be safer than the other thing?" Lucha asked, a little skeptical.

"The demiconsciousness is much easier on the mind than full meditative immersion," Mariel explained. "And much easier to return from, as well."

"So why don't we just ask these things about the spring?" Lucha asked, rolling one around on her palm. On its sides were a triangle, a leaf, a cloud, a sun, a fang, and a snake eating its tail.

"They are imprecise at best," Mariel said. "The limitation of the fixed symbols and the potential for interference when one is not fully immersed make the results nonspecific. For something like this, they may give us an answer we can work with. For something like the spring, the creation of a god, there would be far too much room for error."

"Okay," Lucha said, still not fully understanding, but imagining that Mariel's many years of study eclipsed what she could comprehend in a few minutes. In any case, she wasn't over-eager to return to the meadow where the mushroom had nearly devoured her—even if she did desperately want to know what Alán was up to.

"So. Close your eyes halfway. Reach your consciousness toward your image of Almudena, feel it meld with the state of communion."

As ridiculous as this sounded, it made sense to Lucha. There was a particular feeling she got when the channel of communication was open. A sort of liminal feeling that was much like going underwater and opening your eyes.

Lucha took care to keep her actual eyes half open, feeling immediately that to close them would be to topple headfirst into the meadow. She could almost feel it there, like a physical place, beckoning her.

"When you have achieved demiconsciousness," Mariel said in a low, soothing voice, "you may cast the dice onto the stone. As you do, ask for the truth of the information imparted by our guest. Ask for the information we need to interpret his motives and move in the direction of justice."

Lucha did as she was told.

She thought of Alán first. His tales of the spring and its powers. In her mind, she asked the goddess to shed the light of truth on his words. To tell her whether they might be believed enough to take a step forward, or whether his trickery meant he should be discounted. Punished.

The thought of punishment sent her teetering perilously close to the edge of her consciousness. In the haze before her, a vision began to take shape. Alán, his half mouth open in a scream, Lucha—

"Focus," Mariel snapped. "Remember your body. Remember the objects in your hands."

It was enough to bring Lucha back, though she pulled away only reluctantly. Refocusing on the question at hand, she cast the dice at last, opening her eyes once the clattering of bone on rock had ceased.

Mariel was already peering over her shoulder.

The first face showed a tiny sword. The second, a triangle, point up with a line across the top. The third was the cloud Lucha had seen earlier, and the last appeared to be a fox.

"What do they mean?" Lucha asked, trying to shake the feeling of that other place pulling at her. She thought she could feel it even now, with her eyes fully open and the sun on her face.

"His information is good," Mariel said after a long moment. "See? The sword indicates truth, and the triangle is the symbol for air. Together they mean truth was communicated."

"What about these?" Lucha asked, pointing to the remaining two.

"They complicate things," Mariel said, a wrinkle between her brows. "The cloud obscures the truth, and on the other side is the fox. Resourceful and cunning. Deceptive."

"So he's lying," Lucha said. Anger made the pull feel stronger. She tried to breathe.

"No," Mariel replied decisively. "He is telling the truth, but not the whole truth. We may trust what he has told us but must be on the lookout for what is being concealed, and why."

Lucha's head was spinning. She felt nauseous, and still only half present.

"You did well," Mariel was saying, but Lucha was hearing

her voice as if from the end of a long tunnel. "With this information, we know we can pursue the avenues that have opened before us. With . . ."

Mariel was still speaking, Lucha was sure of it. Only, she couldn't hear her anymore. The trees around her began to look indistinct. Lucha tried to remember her body. The very real consequences that could occur if she didn't remain in it.

Madness. Permanent hallucinations.

It didn't matter. The pull was inexorable. Opening the channel even a little had allowed the flood, and now Lucha was awash in it. The housing unit was gone. Mariel, gone. The ground beneath her, even. Lucha was hurtling through her own mind toward something dazzlingly bright, and there was nothing to do but surrender.

28

Lucha expected to land in the meadow, but she didn't. In fact, there was no landing at all. Eventually, the bright light faded and cast the scene into darkness. Lucha watched, powerless to do anything else.

It was dark here, but there were pinpricks of light, like holes punched in a box with the sun shining in. As it clarified, there were swirls of color, too. Then the subtlety of the darkness made itself known. Not an infinite blackness, but shades that encompassed everything.

She streaked through this strange landscape as if hurtling down from some great height. Under normal circumstances she would have been terrified, but within her there seemed the capacity for a wild joy she had never felt in her human form.

Just as understanding began to dawn, a blue-and-green sphere came into view. First small, then larger, then larger still. The colors and the subtle play of darknesses retreated, bringing this sphere into focus.

Soon she was so close that the sphere was no longer round.

Just the rim of a circle, dotted with tangled trees, massive blue bodies of water. The otherworldly joy within her, which wasn't truly hers, bubbled up as she descended more quickly now, feeling the gravity of this place take hold of her. Claim her.

The last thing Lucha saw before she plummeted into the earth was the curve of a massive river. Wide and wild. Serpentine and lovely. Then she made impact.

With the speed she'd been traveling at, the ground didn't immediately stop her. She rocketed through the brown soil of this place with her unyielding flesh, digging down so deep that the surface almost disappeared above her.

She reached out with hands that were not burned. Not even human. So ethereal and shining, they began to move large quantities of the dirt out of the way, clearing space to see where she had landed. Sparks from her fingers released into the soil, but only when she struck water was she satisfied.

Lucha, with a goddess's lips, drank of the groundwater. She let it run over her and through her. By so doing, she spread the divine matter of her being for the first time into this new world.

The water bubbled up in response, and she felt it join with the river outside.

This would be the place, she thought, the joy settling into something that felt permanent. This would always be the first place she'd arrived at her new home . . .

Lucha gasped for breath. The air tore at her throat as she sucked it in, as it filled her lungs. The painful reality of this body was a disappointment after what she had left. Tears spilled down her cheeks at the loss.

Once again, there were bodies gathered around her. She was slow to focus on them. This all felt so horribly familiar that she reached mentally for her arms to make sure they were unrestrained.

"Lucha?"

"Lucha, can you hear me?"

Yes, she tried to say, but it came out as the language of a streaking comet. Unintelligible. She couldn't remember where she ended and the vision began. Who was she? What was this?

"Lucha, I need you to focus on me, can you do that?"

This voice, Lucha knew. This beloved voice with music bubbling just beneath it. She knew the face that belonged to it, and she focused on it now, bringing it to life before her.

"Paz." This time her tongue obeyed.

"Okay," Paz said. "Can you try to sit up?"

She found she could, and so she did. "What happened?" she asked. There were trees around her. Sun on her skin. People all around.

"You went too far, I think," Paz said. "One of your fatal flaws, I'm afraid."

Lucha laughed, a low rumble that ached a little in her chest.

"She's awake? Good. Miss Moya, I need you to tell us everything you saw immediately. Where were you? Did the goddess speak to you?"

The goddess. Lucha was streaking through the sky again at the mention. Drinking of the water in the ground.

"Obispo." Paz's voice again. "We need to give her a moment."

"We don't *have* a moment! This accursed hovel is going to combust at the first opportunity. We need answers and we need them now!"

"Enough." This one was Cruz, Lucha thought, and her voice brooked no argument. "Give her a moment."

"I won't be ordered around by some feral brat. *Get out of my way.*"

There was a flurry of movement, and then Río's hands were on Lucha's shoulders. Her grip was hard and unyielding. She pressed her face close to Lucha's. Her skin smelled of metal.

"Where is the spring, Miss Moya. *Where is it?*"

She shook Lucha as she spoke. The ache in her skull sharpened.

Then, as suddenly as she had descended, Río was gone. She'd been shoved off by Cruz, who stood between them as the priestess spluttered, color rising in her face.

Lucha, the pain in her head ebbing, was profoundly grateful, even though this probably meant nothing good for the unity of the two groups in their tinderbox camp.

"I'm all right," she said, not knowing if it was true. "I didn't mean to do it, it just sort of happened."

"It was a risky proposition at best, my dear," Mariel said, kneeling beside Lucha now. She said it loudly enough for Río to hear plainly, and Lucha noticed she had not come to her superior's defense. "How are you feeling?"

"I'm all right," Lucha said again, sitting up straighter. "Everything's still a little . . . off. Is that normal?" It was the trees, Lucha thought, reaching too high, dancing a little as if they were half mirage. The sky, too, felt too bright, and there was a rushing in Lucha's ears like a windstorm or a river, though everything was still.

"We left normal behind weeks ago," Mariel said with a chuckle. "You're here and you're talking and you've got control of your faculties, so we'll call that good enough for now. Just try to keep awareness in your body as much as you can. Feel the heaviness. Feel the weight and the sensations on your skin."

Lucha nodded. Mariel, Río, Paz, and Cruz were all still close by. Farther off, Armando and Maria stood guard in front of the housing unit door.

When she spoke, it was more because the words inside her needed to be purged than anything else. Río tried to step closer, but Cruz stayed firmly in her path.

"I was in the sky, I think." Lucha tried to stay firmly rooted in her body as Mariel had told her, even though the words brought a longing to return to that stunning free fall. "Plummeting toward the ground. I saw Elegido, the whole world, from far off. The water and the trees. It was beautiful . . ."

She trailed off, taking a few deep breaths. Feeling her backside planted on the ground. Digging her fingers into the soil as if she could cling to this world.

"When I got closer, I saw a river—huge, the biggest one in

the world by far. It had all these bends and curves, and I hit the ground near it, but I was going so fast the ground didn't stop me."

"You fell as the goddess did, from the celestial plane." Río's words were awestruck, filled with desperate longing.

"I don't know," Lucha said, still clinging to the earth with her bleeding hands. "I think so. Down beneath the ground, I could barely see the sky. And there was water. I drank it and I . . . changed it. Put some power in it to spread it through the ground."

"The spring," Río said, the desperation more pronounced now. It formed a harsh edge on her words, and she pushed closer, only to encounter Cruz again. "She showed you the spring, just as I predicted."

"There was no spring," Lucha said. "But there was water, and if it's supposed to be the place she first touched the earth, then it's possible." The trees were stretching for the sky again, everything shimmering and strange.

"It's more than possible, it's— *Oh, will you let me by!*"

"Not until you get yourself under control," Cruz said in a tone that had probably never been used on the obispo before. Superior, condescending. A wall she wouldn't get past.

Again, Lucha was flooded with gratitude.

Paz knelt beside Lucha. "You saw Elegido from above," she said gently. Her words didn't hurt like Río's did; they lapped at the frayed edges of Lucha's consciousness like cool water. "On a map, could you point to what you saw?"

"I could try," Lucha said.

"Good thinking, my dear," Mariel said to Paz. Then, to Lucha: "Let's get you somewhere more comfortable. That was quite an ordeal you went through."

It was Mariel's coddling, more than anything, that told Lucha there was more risk than she knew. But still she got to her feet shakily, allowing herself to be led back toward camp.

"Wait," she said, turning back toward the unit. "Alán. He told the truth, but he's hiding something."

"Don't worry, killer," Cruz said with a smile that looked almost sad. "He's not getting out on our watch. You just take care of yourself, okay?"

"Thank you," Lucha said. It was too dangerous now to think of dreams. But she felt the warmth between them anyway, and she wondered if Cruz felt it too.

Back in Río's tent, Lucha sat while Mariel summoned an acolyte to reapply the salve to her hands and give her a drink that smelled strongly of earth and herbs.

"Remember your body," Mariel said as she and Paz dug through scrolls and books, looking for the oldest map they could find. One that might show the landscape of the world as it had looked in the time when Almudena had arrived. Or at least as close as they could get to it.

Río, for her part, stood apart from the others. Uncharacteristically, she didn't offer guidance or suggestions or demand to do the research herself. In fact, she didn't say anything. That desperation Lucha had seen on her face back at the south ward had not faded—if anything, it had sharpened. Focused.

"Here," said Paz, holding up a leather-bound tome. "This might work."

Lucha watched the obispo's face change. Smooth into something impassive and poised. Either that, or Lucha had only imagined it—the effects of her journey still playing with her perception. But if that was the case, did it make what she'd seen less true? Or more?

Paz brought the map to Lucha, set the heavy book in her lap. It was beautiful. Spread across two pages, lovingly rendered and painted in color, which was rare for the time it had been made.

In this map, unlike the modern ones Lucha had seen, the forest wasn't a blot of ink. It was still largely unknown, its borders indistinct. But a few locations were marked. Lucha, however, wasn't interested in those.

She stared at the map for a long minute, trying to match it with her memory of what she'd seen in the vision. At first, nothing looked familiar, but then she picked it up. Rotated it. And then it was so clear.

The curves of the wide river were there, just as she'd seen them—not only in her vision, but every day of her life. It was the cursed river. The salt river. Lucha hadn't recognized it because the water had been fresh, but of course the change to salt water could have come later. Some remnant of Salvador's destruction.

It was long, far longer than she knew, and the shape of it had changed so much it was impossible to pinpoint where she had landed. But there was no mistaking it.

"I can't say exactly," Lucha said finally, tracing the river with her finger. "But this is the river. The salt river. The spring is somewhere along it."

The book disappeared from her hands in a flash. Río clapped, a satisfying sound.

"Yes," she said. "This is good. This is perfect. We have a direction, we have a guide. We are going to find that spring, we are going to create a god, and we are going to save the forest."

Lucha, who had been worried that her vision wasn't specific enough, felt relief wash over her. She had done her job. All she wanted to do now was sleep, but she could still feel that yawning void. Its pull had lessened, but it hadn't disappeared, and somehow Lucha knew that to sleep before she had mastered it would be to risk another vision. Her mind couldn't take it. It felt fragile enough as it was.

Lucha watched throughout the day as the tent filled and emptied and filled again. Río was back to herself, ordering and delegating as the acolytes and the Syndicate discussed plans for scouring hundreds—possibly thousands—of miles of riverbank.

"We'll form two parties with this camp as the rendezvous point," Río said once they had gathered. "One will be led by Miss León, the other, if she will consent to assist, by Miss Miranda."

Lucha, who had not left her chair for hours, looked to Cruz with surprise. She had assumed she would be allowed to lead the second party.

"It's just Cruz," Cruz replied, but she didn't turn down the request.

"Good," Río said with a decisive nod. "You may each pick the team to best assist you. I will remain here to receive you when you return. Miss Moya will represent your Syndicate in the leadership of the city in your absence."

"What?" Lucha asked. Her first words in a long time. "What do you mean, I'm staying here? You need me out there." The idea of staying here, alone, the claustrophobia of purposelessness, the yawning void beckoning her without distraction—it was unbearable.

Río shook her head. "I'm afraid we simply cannot risk your safety unless it's absolutely necessary."

Lucha felt a familiar fire heating her chest and cheeks. "If you think I'm going to stay here and sit on my hands after everything—"

"She's right." Paz. Her words cut deep. Stopped Lucha in her tracks. "We're doing all this for the barest chance of fixing what's happening here. We don't know what will happen when we get there, but we do know you're the only one with a connection to Almudena. We may need it to operate the power source, and if we do and something happens to you on the trip, we've done it all for nothing."

She didn't look at Lucha as she spoke, but straight ahead. Lucha thought of the night Paz had appeared in her tent, all acquiescence and desperation. Lucha had run from her—was this Paz's way of punishing her for it?

"So I'm to be excluded *in case* I'm needed later?" Lucha asked. She looked right at Paz, who must have felt the blistering gaze even though she would not meet it. "If it weren't for me, you wouldn't even know where to look."

"She should be allowed to come," Cruz cut in. "I'd never let anything happen to her. I'll—" She stopped, her cheeks coloring a little.

Lucha felt her own response, despite the tension in the room.

"Just saying I'm pretty vicious with a weapon and I've protected her before," Cruz finished quickly. "If that makes any difference."

Río's face said exactly how much difference it made to her.

Paz's expression was impassive, but Lucha recognized it. This was Paz, priestess of Almudena. Paz, who thought of the greater good.

"She stays," Río said in a tone of authority Lucha hadn't yet learned to counter. "It's too big a risk to take."

Cruz looked mutinous. Lucha knew her well enough to know she'd stand here arguing all day if she thought she was doing what was right.

"Lucha, no one is doubting you could handle yourself," Paz said. Finally, her eyes found Lucha's across the room. "But there are things you can do that the rest of us can't. Please understand."

The trouble was, Lucha did understand. All too well. She

thought back to another vision she'd had, what felt like a lifetime ago. Sitting on a throne in Asilo, held back by delicate chains. It seemed that that future had found her after all—no matter how she'd tried to outrun it.

"Now that that's settled," Río said, putting her hands together, "we plan."

Lucha got up as Río began to discuss routes, supplies, and timelines. She walked toward the door, half expecting someone to stop her. No one did.

She walked out into the camp, the feeling only intensifying of being behind some veil that hung between her and the real world she'd always wanted so much to be a part of. She knew these people, knew their faces and their names and their stories and how many days of rations they had left, but what did any of that matter if she couldn't save them?

Lucha understood now why morale had been so low. When all you could do was wait for the end, for other people to solve things, nothing seemed to matter very much.

She walked without direction. Turning at random and doubling back. Walking into the woods for solitude, only to find she preferred the listless company of her fellow Robadans.

Río's tent stayed busy all day. Caught up in their planning. No one came to find her. The most indispensable person in the city, she thought bitterly, and the loneliest.

When the sun began to sink, Lucha made her way back toward her own tent. Dark clouds gathered ominously above the river, drawing her eye. There hadn't been rain for weeks.

She didn't dare hope for it now. But if there was lightning, the whole place was a tinderbox.

She knew she ought to tell someone. One of the acolytes or the other Syndicate members. But she couldn't bring herself to face any of them now. They could see the clouds as well as she could. What did they need her for?

She walked inside her tent alone. Lay down in her bed. The tugging of the beyond was gentler now—maybe there was enough of it inside her. If she could sleep, maybe tomorrow would be easier.

But of course, now she couldn't. Instead, she thought about what would happen if the search was successful. If Alán's knowledge about how to operate the spring proved true. She thought of Río's desperate, covetous expression today.

About creating a god.

It made Lucha sick to think about it. All-knowing Almudena from the celestial plane had tried the same thing in all her infinite wisdom and had still ended up with Salvador. What chance did they have of achieving something better?

This was the last thought she had before sleep took her.

29

Lucha awoke on her back. Her chest was on fire. Something was rising up her throat, pushing her lips apart.

She leaned over without deciding to, coughing up copious amounts of water until there was nothing left, but the coughing went on and on. Something had happened. Someone had been in danger. But who? And what was she doing here?

It took a few minutes to recognize the Lost House across the water from her. It was destroyed, walls collapsed, the whole place a ruin as the river rose dangerously again. . . .

Lucha tried to get to her feet, knowing there was urgency even if she couldn't remember who needed saving. But there was something there, pushing her back down.

"Don't get up. Not yet. Take a minute."

Paz, Lucha realized as she came slowly back to herself. It had been a dream. A vision. Something . . . She remembered her mother swimming in the rising river, drowning. Paz begging her not to go. Lucha's mind felt so muddled, she could no longer remember what was real and what was a dream.

"I have to go back," she said. Her voice was a rasping thing, jagged against the tender, salt-ravaged walls of her throat. She coughed again. "I have to go back. My mother was there. In the water. I have to save her."

More memory returned to her, strangely shimmering again between dream and waking. Lucha was wet and cold, her knee scraped and bleeding. The Lost House was there, across the bank. That meant she had gotten up, walked there, gone into the water. But did it mean she had really seen her mother?

"You're not going anywhere until you hear what I have to say," Paz said.

"Paz, I don't have time—" Lucha argued, but Paz cut her off.

"What on earth were you thinking?" she asked. All the awe and breathiness of her tone was gone. There was no sign, in her face or voice, that she was normally a pious girl who found beauty in everything around her. Including, occasionally, Lucha.

"I saw my mother . . . ," Lucha said. "I saw her . . . or Almudena showed her to me. I wanted to save her. What happened to the house?"

Paz huffed in frustration. "It was a metaphor, Lucha. And you're surrounded by acolytes who could have told you that, even if you didn't want to ask me. But of course, you're *Lucha Moya,* so you had to charge off on some harebrained mission and nearly get yourself killed in the process. The house collapsed with you inside. I barely got you out."

Lucha felt empty inside. Cold. This made sense. But she didn't know how to explain to Paz that she barely remembered rising from her bed. That she was having trouble telling the difference between sleep and waking. That her thoughts, her memories, and her dreams were all bleeding into one.

It seemed clear to her now, however, that she had not been truly dreaming. That she had in fact charged toward the Lost House in a storm in an attempt to rescue her mother. That the rain was coming down. That the water was rising. She sifted the details as best she could.

"A metaphor," she said instead. If she confessed the extent of the damage to Paz, she would never be allowed to help anyone again. She would never be left alone again. "Right. It just . . . it felt so real."

Paz didn't soften at this. Lucha could feel the anger coming off her in waves. "Real or not, you could have *died,*" she said, her voice harsh with emotion. "You very nearly did. If I hadn't gotten you out of there in time, this all would have been for nothing. Everything we've done. The whole world could have ended before we ever had a chance to find out what Almudena was truly asking of us."

And then, abruptly, Lucha was furious. The anger felt good, like an old friend, burning away the cold and the emptiness. She struggled to her feet.

"So that's why you're really upset, is it?" she fired off, the anger spilling over.

They had been tiptoeing around each other ever since Paz arrived. Pretending Cruz was the problem, when the problem was here, plain as day.

They were so inextricably tied together, the goddess and

the girl Lucha loved. She stared Paz down as the clouds above them rumbled, the rain threatening to fall again any moment.

"I want to know why you cared that I was in danger," she said. Clear. Precise. She had refused to shine a light on this subject for so long because she was afraid of the answer—but now she was more afraid of not knowing.

She took a deep breath. Paz waited.

"Was it because you could have lost your connection to Almudena? The chance to find the spring? I need you to answer me honestly, just this once."

A few raindrops spattered the ground between them. The sky threatened to break wide open, but for the moment it held.

Paz seemed stalled. Across her face played a mix of warring emotions. Lucha couldn't read them all. Didn't want to.

"This isn't the time to talk about it," she finally said. "There's so much to do, and—"

"We've spent this whole time talking *around* it, Paz, but this is it, for me. The end of the line. Tell me that the first thought you had when you thought I was going to drown was of Almudena. Of the opportunity you'd miss. Of the suffering it would cause the world. Tell me you didn't think of *me*, the girl you came to find in the tent the other night. I'll accept it. I'll let you go be what you need to be. But I need to know, once and for all. What came first?"

"It's not that simple!" Paz cried. "Of *course* I thought of you. I thought of never kissing you again. Never watching you fight with those graceful movements. Never hearing the way you laugh when you're surprised. I thought of how a life without you in it wouldn't be worth living, Lucha, before I thought of everyone in the world *dying*. I was *selfish*. Is that what you want to hear?"

"YES!" Lucha shouted as the rain began to fall in earnest. "Of course that's what I want to hear! Didn't you ever wonder why I really walked away from the sanctuary months ago? Why I didn't want to take you with me? Why I couldn't stay?"

"Every single day!" Paz shouted over the next clap of thunder. "And a hundred times more since I got here. So why don't you just put me out of my misery!"

"It's *her*!" Lucha said. "That damn goddess of yours. The one you've dedicated your whole life to. I want to know whether you love me because of who I am, or because of what I represent in your world. I want to know if you *want* me, if you think of me outside that devotional lens you see the world through."

She took a deep, rasping breath, pushing on even though every word was a knife in her throat.

"I want to know if you feel like a feral animal around me, Paz! Because I feel mad when I look at you. Like there's nothing else in the world that makes sense and I never want there to be. And if you don't feel the same—"

"I *do*," Paz said, stepping closer, her eyes dancing with something violent and terrible and true. "I do want you. I do feel like an animal. I feel like I don't care if the whole world burns and me along with it as long as I can have you, and it's *ruining my life*, Lucha. Can't you see that?"

More thunder. The rain letting loose at last, the eye of the storm moving past them. Lucha, stunned by the true answer to the question she'd been asking all these months, stayed quiet. Waiting.

"I've spent my whole life trying to be a perfect vessel for the goddess's will," Paz explained, not looking at Lucha. Her gaze pointed up into the rain, which fell into her eyes, streaking down her face like tears. "To empty my mind of desires, selfishness, and attachments so that I might serve her without conflict. I was *good,* Lucha. I was *perfect.* She came to me in visions when she wouldn't even appear to the priestesses. They whispered about me. I moved up so quickly they'd already planned my life out by the time I came here for my mission."

"Then why bother with me at all?" Lucha asked. "Why not keep your distance?"

"You think it was my *choice?*" Paz asked, coming closer still, until Lucha could see every line of her through her sodden clothing, every lash casting a moonlit shadow on her cheek. "You think I *wanted* to feel this way? I saw you, Lucha, and my body came alive for the first time. I finally knew what it was like to want someone. To need them . . ."

These words hit Lucha right in the heart. The heat of them spread through her own body, an answer to Paz's desperate confession.

"It's agony, wanting you," Paz said, so close now that Lucha could feel her breath on her face. "It makes me selfish, and weak. It takes me away from her. From that flawless, pure light I always felt before. That purpose I thought would never leave me. Wanting you, loving you, it takes up all the space inside me. I'm not a vessel anymore, I'm just a girl and I'm on fire for you."

That fire kindled in Lucha, too. Hotter than ever before. More punishing and more urgent and more consuming than it had ever been.

"But I love her, too," Paz whispered. "I can't help it. When I'm close to you, I feel so far from her, and when I'm close to her, I feel far from you, and it's tearing me to pieces and I don't know how to stop it because I can't stop loving either of you!"

Paz collapsed in on herself then, her shoulders hunching to protect the precious heart at her center, her body shaking with sobs.

"*I'm sorry,*" she said over and over again, and this time, Lucha found it didn't matter whether it was her or the goddess Paz was speaking to.

For the first time, Lucha understood what it had cost Paz to want her. Why it had always felt so tangled. So terrible.

"Everyone leaves," Lucha said, causing Paz to peer up in wonder. "Everyone who was ever supposed to love me left, whether it was by choice or by force. My dad died. My mom could never love me as much as she loved Olvida. My sister is incredible, but she's always chosen herself first. It's right for her, but it just leaves me . . ."

Lucha gestured helplessly, her hands at her sides, her eyes trained on this beautiful girl she had just begun to understand.

"And then I met you, and you . . . you sewed up my face. You waited for me the whole time I was in prison, and even though there were all these reasons for you to reject me, to never speak to me again, these rumors around town that made me look like a monster . . . you stayed. You helped me when no one else would. You helped me heal Lis and you taught me about the forest and you looked at me like I was someone worth loving. You chose me."

Paz was no longer crying; her eyes were fixed wide open, and she listened as if this rainstorm were the end of the world. As if they'd never have another chance.

"So when I found out you'd been *sent* here—that you had only helped me to further some other goal—it wasn't just a girl I'd known for a few weeks turning out to be something I hadn't bargained for. It was the *only* person who'd ever chosen me, ever stayed, turning out to be a liar. And maybe I could have gotten past that, Paz. I wanted to. I still do."

Lucha pulled at her hair, droplets scattering from the ends of her braids, blending with the water still cascading from the sky in vengeful torrents.

"But I *know* you love her. And if I were just some other kind of girl, some normal girl, I could share. I would do it in a heartbeat, but I'm so tied up with her. Every moment will be a choice, and I can't spend my life afraid you won't choose me because she's always between us."

Paz laughed. It was hollow, ironic, yet somehow still warm. "We're quite a pair, aren't we?" she asked.

"Of people fated to bring out each other's worst insecurities?" Lucha asked, aware again of how close they were. "Maybe we are."

"I don't know how to be good for you," Paz admitted. "I understand what you're saying, about not feeling chosen, about wishing you could be someone else. I wish the same thing. But we're not anyone else."

"We're not," Lucha agreed.

"Only, that doesn't stop me from wanting you." Paz's tongue darted out, sweeping subconsciously over her lips. The heat between them, the anger and the desire and the horrible frustration they'd each been carrying wordlessly since they met, seemed to mellow. To focus.

"It doesn't stop me from wanting you, either," Lucha said, her voice lower and rougher than normal after shouting for so long over the rain.

"So what do we do?" Paz asked. Her expression was desperate, yearning in every line. Her eyes, though. Her eyes were two calm, still ponds in the center of it all. Never moving, always fixing somewhere on the distant horizon Lucha couldn't see.

"Maybe we pretend the world has already ended. Just for tonight," Lucha said, her breath catching in her throat as she finished, a little hiccup punctuating this undeniable yet horribly bittersweet idea.

"We wouldn't have to pretend much," Paz said, glancing up at the rain, looking back at Lucha with water clinging to every eyelash.

"Is it enough that I want you this much?" Lucha asked. She didn't say the rest of the sentence. The part that was currently in the process of tattooing itself on her heart. *Enough to make you forget her, just for the night.*

"It's everything," Paz said. And it was such a beautiful lie that for the moment Lucha gave herself to it fully.

"I'm going to kiss you now," she said. "Unless you stop me."

Paz didn't smile. Her eyes were still. She leaned forward and did it herself.

The kiss was nothing like the ones Lucha had shared with Paz months ago. Those kisses had been like exploring. These were like learning a new language. A language only the two of them could speak.

Mouths overlapped, hands gripped sodden clothing, tongues and teeth and lips danced like they had practiced this a hundred times. Like it was written on the pages of some dusty old scroll yet to be discovered. They kissed like they were proving a law of nature. Divine beings with all their power and influence had nothing on what they created, Lucha thought deliriously.

In the dead of night, as lightning forked through the sky and the water grew deeper and deeper at their feet, Lucha and Paz chose each other. Each kiss, each touch. The whispered questions, the enthusiastic answers. The clothing discarded, the mud ignored, two girls detached from their mythos for one night, finding each other and holding on tight.

Lucha didn't have to wonder what was real and what was divine. With Paz, it was always both. Behind them, as it had in Lucha's dream, the river reared up. Wave after wave of salt punishing the shore.

30

When it was done, they lay together, eyes turned up to the sky, which had, at some point during their interlude, ceased its weeping in a way that felt permanent.

The storm had passed. The tension leached slowly out of the air, leaving something sultry and humid in its wake. The breeze caressed their skin like breath.

When Lucha looked at Paz out of the corner of her eye—the rise and fall of her chest, the gentle slopes of her curves—she felt as though she was discovering something precious all over again. Something that looked nothing like she'd imagined, but was somehow better for that.

The wind changed, and Paz turned to face her. She did not appear embarrassed, or regretful, but her eyes were distant stars. Stars Lucha knew she could never reach. Not with all the portals in all the world to the celestial plane.

The night seemed divided. There was the during, and the after, and they were firmly in the after now. Paz shifted. Air filled the space she'd left. Lucha registered it as a loss, but one she'd expected. One she'd somehow steeled herself for even as she was surrendering at last to the pain.

"You found it, didn't you?" Paz asked. "The spring?"

The question illuminated a part of the vision Lucha had forgotten. Or had this part been real? It didn't matter much. She remembered the closet of the Lost House. Always locked. The light that had glowed from beneath its stone floor and the power she'd felt as it bathed her.

Lucha nodded. For once she didn't feel the need to qualify. To second-guess. Perhaps this was what Río had meant by her experience being invaluable. There was some understanding deep within her; the *yes* resonated like there had never been any doubt.

"It's in the Lost House," she said, hearing her words on the air. Knowing she could never take them back. "Beneath it. The stone floor in the closet." She remembered the stone giving way for her. The light illuminating everything. The way open.

"Of course," Paz breathed, and Lucha knew she was feeling the irony as it knit the story together. The Lost House. The place of forgetting. The place of Olvida. Proof that no matter how hard Salvador had tried, the poison he made still shared a core with his mother's gift.

"What are we going to do?"

They sat up, facing each other. Paz handed Lucha her shirt, wringing it out first. It settled, a little clammy, on her skin.

After, she thought as Paz did her best to dry her robe, sliding it over herself and erasing those curves from view.

After.

"I don't trust them," Lucha said simply. This transition would be pored over later, its meaning dissected, but for now it felt natural to speak of it. "I thought we'd have more time."

Paz nodded. She pushed her sodden hair off her face. The color was beginning to fade from her cheeks.

After.

"We *need* more time," Lucha said, for emphasis.

"But we don't have it," Paz replied.

That was true too.

"Let's dig it out ourselves first," Lucha said, the idea occurring to her only seconds before she spoke it aloud. "Without Río. We'll see what's there, and then we'll decide what to tell them."

Paz seemed to turn an idea over in her mind carefully before setting it face up between them. "We should ask Cruz, too," she said at last. Her eyes found Lucha's. They shone in a way that said this meant more than the sum of the words she spoke. "We can trust her."

"We can," Lucha agreed. This should have been strange, in the moments after what had transpired between them. To speak of Cruz, casually. To discuss the future without hinting at what it might mean for the new thread connecting them.

But it wasn't. It was as easy as breathing.

"I'll go check on the Robadans, make sure Cruz has them under control."

Paz nodded. "I should go to the clinic. Check on the patients."

Lucha tested her weight on the sore knee, grateful to find

that it held. Paz began to walk down the road. She was so beautiful, Lucha thought, like the moon hanging over the woods, so bright without the torchlight of the city to compete.

So distant. So lovely.

She caught up easily. Paz's hand was there, she could have taken it. But she didn't. And when they reached the clinic, they said goodbye like their separation would merely be a temporary thing. A bird alighting with the promise of future flight . . .

In the marketplace, Cruz was organizing everyone as the rain continued to fall, as the river rose as it had twice before. The storm had subsided, but there was still much to be done.

Cruz looked relieved as Lucha approached. "I couldn't find you," she said desperately. "I thought . . . the river . . ."

"I'm okay," Lucha replied. "But I need to talk to you."

Cruz took inventory in that sharp, incisive way of hers. Lucha noticed that almost everyone was cleared out of the marketplace now. The only people left were the volunteers.

"We found places for everyone to sleep," Cruz said, noticing Lucha's curiosity. "It wasn't fair to keep them out in the rain. Especially not the kids."

"You're awfully good at running a city," Lucha said, finding herself a little in awe.

Cruz left the marketplace in Armando's capable hands, and she and Lucha walked up the road together toward the compound. "It's going to take time to rebuild again," Cruz said, clearly scattered. "I don't know exactly how that's going to happen with so many of us going off to search for the spring."

"What I have to tell you is . . . about that," Lucha began. She didn't continue. Not yet. She couldn't quite find the words for the dream she hadn't known was a vision. The metaphor of her mother. The closet and the stone floor and the light column rising through the water.

"I'm listening," Cruz said. Not pointedly. Just a reminder.

"I went to the Lost House tonight," Lucha said finally.

Cruz whistled. If she thought it was strange that Lucha had brought her all the way out here to tell her about a dream, she didn't show it.

"When I was sleeping, I dreamed my mother was drowning. I went to find her." Even to Cruz, Lucha wouldn't confess the extent of her confusion. The tangle of dream and waking and vision. "The Lost House was flooding, but I went inside and saw this . . . light, coming from the closet door that's always locked."

"I wondered what was in there," Cruz said, as unashamed of her past as ever.

"I did too," Lucha said. "Today, the house was flooding, and the door was open. There was all this light pouring out from a crack in the floor."

Cruz just listened, waiting. They had stopped walking. They stood in the mushroom forest—a place the new Robadans mostly avoided for superstitious reasons.

"I passed out then," she admitted. "Nearly drowned."

"Let me guess," Cruz said with a wry smile. "The sharpshooter pulled you out."

"She has an annoying habit of saving my life," Lucha admitted.

There was a pause. A flicker of something in Cruz's eyes. Then she gestured for Lucha to continue.

"A huge portion of the house collapsed. The rubble buried the place the light was coming from. I don't know if it was the light that did it or just the water, but either way, we figure it'll take days to unearth it."

"That place is a graveyard," Cruz said, her expression a little haunted. "We should leave it as it is."

"The thing is," Lucha replied, "I think . . . no, I *know* it's inside. The spring. The place where we can make a god. End all of this."

Cruz's eyes grew very wide. She held them there for a moment, taking in everything Lucha had said. All its implications.

"So you think we're better off digging it out than searching the riverbank."

Lucha took a moment to remember the feeling of existing in a beam of divine light. She no longer had her gift, but based on Río's mythology, she wouldn't have needed it. Río had said the spring granted power even to the most mundane. What else could have affected Lucha that way?

"I do," Lucha said finally. "But Paz and I agreed we don't

trust anyone besides you. We'll have to do it in secret, or try, anyway."

Another long, low whistle. Cruz's expression was faraway for a moment. Lucha waited patiently for her to return.

"Not even the High Priestess of Self-Righteousness?" she asked.

"Especially not her," Lucha said. "I might trust her the least out of all of them. She wants the power too much. If we can excavate the spring ourselves, we'll have the upper hand. I don't think we can hide it from her forever, but if we can get to it first, figure out what it really is, what it does, I think we'll have a better chance of doing the right thing."

"Of course I'll help you," Cruz said without hesitating. "But how are we gonna break it to Río? Tell her we're not taking her to the spring?"

Lucha hadn't thought that far ahead, and honestly she didn't feel capable of it now. She swayed on her feet. Cruz stepped closer.

"Are you all right?" Cruz asked. "I know you're tough, but that must have been a lot, even for you."

Cruz, Lucha realized as she looked at her, was probably the one person who truly understood how Lucha felt. Having left something behind so long ago that you thought you'd forgotten it, only to find you'd been fooling yourself.

"I'm fine," she said, shaking her head. "Nothing a good night's sleep can't fix."

Cruz looked skeptical, but she didn't press the issue.

"I'll figure something out for Río," Lucha said dismissively. She was sure tomorrow's version of her wouldn't be thrilled she'd put this off, but her head was throbbing, her chest aching. She needed to get to bed. "It means a lot, though." She looked up at Cruz, the moon lighting the angles of her face. "That you're willing to help us."

"I told you before," Cruz said. "There's nothing I wouldn't do, Lucha."

Her expression was mellow. Sweeter than usual.

"Thank you," Lucha said, because she did not know how else to express what it meant. "Thank you."

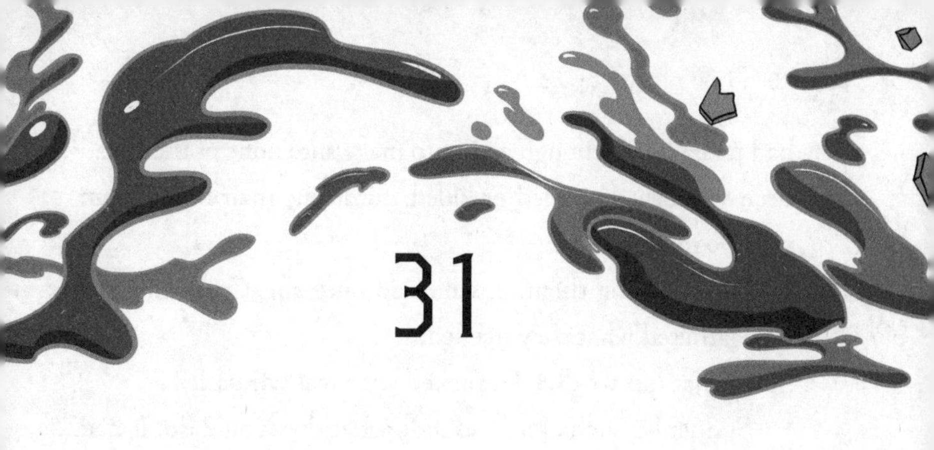

31

It was Cruz, of course, who came up with the plan that solved the Río problem.

She told Río they couldn't look for the spring, or spare anyone else to do it, until they found somewhere stable to put the Robadans who needed to stay behind. There was a place, but it would take work to dig it out and fortify it. A few days, at least.

Reluctantly, Río agreed, but only once she'd been reminded rather forcefully of her agreement with Lucha. They were granted three days, during which time Río would be in her reconstructed tent with Mariel and the acolytes, going over the texts in an attempt to find any more information about the spring that would help them in their search.

The camp had been almost entirely destroyed. Worse still, most of the provisions had been damaged or ruined. There was less food than ever, and Lucha felt her stomach growling as they gathered what resources they could to take to the Lost House.

Around them, the Robadans looked utterly hopeless. Cruz

had taken quick enough action to make sure none of them had been seriously wounded or killed, but losing their home again was too much to bear.

"We're losing them," Lucha said once she, Cruz, and Paz had gathered what they needed.

"What can we do?" Paz asked with real sympathy.

Suddenly, Lucha knew exactly what they could do. It had been just the other day that she'd been walking around hopeless, purposeless . . .

"They can help us," she said. "We don't have to tell them exactly what's happening, just that we're hoping to find something that might help and not to tell any of the acolytes."

Paz looked as if she wanted to protest, but Cruz was already smiling.

"It's brilliant," she said. "I'll spread the word."

By midday, a small crowd gathered at the Lost House. They looked gaunt. Exhausted. But they wanted to help. Lucha's heart swelled.

"I know these aren't ideal conditions," she said, trying to sound not like a leader addressing constituents, but like a friend. "And I wish I could say more about what we're hoping to find here. But please know we wouldn't be asking for your help if we didn't think this had a real chance of turning the tide for all of us."

It was enough. There weren't many shovels, but there were

branches blown down by the storm. People used their hands, trading tools when nails cracked and bled.

As they dug out mud and shifted boards out of the way and made slow but steady progress over the course of the day, something occurred to Lucha that should have been obvious but wasn't. Until now.

If Alán's information was correct—which Lucha had done her best to confirm—they would have the chance to choose a new deity for Elegido as soon as the spring was uncovered. Lucha had been so focused on getting here, on keeping Río from knowing, that she hadn't stopped to think of who it might be.

As she shifted silt and mud and the remains of a place she'd once hoped to destroy, Lucha couldn't help imagining it for herself. Her body, shining again, wreathed with divine power. She had worn it well, hadn't she? Even if she'd been at war the whole time she had it. What would it have been like to have an immortal life ahead of her with nothing but balance to achieve?

She would grow things. She would improve them. She would bring order and fairness and justice to this dying place. And this time, with everything she had learned about the world, she wouldn't leave the most vulnerable out.

Lucha thought of the way she'd felt, promising to rebuild Robado. Doing her best by the people of the city. She had loved it. So much more than she'd ever expected to. Wouldn't being a goddess be that same thing on a much larger scale? Hadn't she proved she could handle it?

"Lucha?" came a voice into her reverie. It was Paz, and from the look on her face, she'd said Lucha's name several times.

"Sorry," Lucha said, shaking her head to clear the thoughts there. "I was just thinking . . ."

"It looked like it," Paz said. "We're gonna take a break. Join us?"

Lucha shook her head. The only thing she cared about was doing away with this rubble.

"I'll save you something," Paz said, that concerned crease between her brows again. "Don't work too hard, okay?"

But Lucha was already shoveling again.

It was dark before Lucha unclenched her fingers from around the metal handle. Her body ached and burned in a thousand places. She was exhausted, but still some unnatural fire burned within her, driving her on. They were so close. They would be in within a matter of hours. A day, tops. She wanted to suggest they work through the night, but Paz and Cruz were already hiding their equipment, getting ready to head back into town.

"Where is everyone?" Lucha asked, bewildered at the empty site.

"We sent them back to rest an hour ago," Cruz said. Her brow furrowed like Paz's had. Concern. Lucha tried to think of the last time she'd eaten a whole meal. It had to have been about a day ago . . . the last time she saw Alán, if not longer. Around her, the trees were stretching again. The haze shimmering, like a layer between her and the world. "You okay, killer?"

"I'm . . . I'm okay," Lucha said, though something felt strange.

Out of the corner of her eye, a dark spot bloomed in the mud and spread. Viscous. Seething. Lucha's blood went cold as a wave of realization crashed over her.

"Lucha, you don't look well," Paz said, stepping forward.

"Don't!" Lucha said, holding out a hand. "It's the blight! Everyone stop."

It was everywhere now, spreading across the road, filling in the cracks in the flooring they'd broken, pooling in the holes they'd dug. There was no way they could escape it.

Cruz and Paz were both moving toward her, uncertain. Afraid.

"Stop!" she shouted as the blight crept between them. "If you touch me, you'll be turned. You have to run!"

"Lucha?" Paz said, reaching out a hand toward her. She was about to step right into a seething puddle of the stuff.

Without thinking, Lucha leapt forward, tackling Paz out of the way, into the only section of ground that was clear of the blight—so far.

"What the hell!" Cruz exclaimed, drawing her weapon and running toward them.

"Alán," Lucha said, breathless. She rolled off Paz and back to her feet. "He must have gotten free somehow. We have to run. Be careful where you step."

Paz struggled to stand, but neither she nor Cruz moved from their spot. They stared at Lucha like she'd grown another head.

"Lucha, are you seeing blight?" Paz asked, cheeks flushed, mud clinging to her hair.

"What are you talking about?" Lucha asked, impatient and frustrated. "It's everywhere! It's . . ." But when she looked again, there was nothing there but mud.

"Did you see it?" Paz asked, stepping toward Lucha, her voice urgent. "Here, where we've been digging?"

Gradually, it dawned on Lucha that there had never been any blight. That the door between this world and the one she had visited in her visions was cracked, and things were getting through, just like they had the night she dreamed of her mother drowning. With the barrier between the physical and spirit worlds punctured, Lucha was scrambling to tell the difference. She feared she was going as mad as Mariel warned her she would.

Cruz was still pointing her spear in Lucha's direction, looking confused and worried in equal measure.

"It was just here . . . ," Lucha said. "I saw it."

"A warning," Paz said, more to herself than to Lucha. "She's sending a warning." She spun to face Cruz. "Who's guarding him? The prisoner?"

Cruz, still looking at Lucha, hesitated.

"I am," came a voice through the trees, and from between them stepped Obispo Río and a group of acolytes. From Río's hand dangled a chain Lucha recognized—delicate, silver, impossibly strong. On the end of it walked Alán, his half smile gleeful.

The blight, Lucha thought, mind racing to catch up. It had been a warning.

"What the hell is this?" Cruz asked. "Why is he out?"

"I thought it only fair after he was so helpful to me today," Río said. Her expression was like nothing Lucha had ever seen on her face. Triumph, some twisted joy, but also furious, burning anger.

"Helpful with what?" Lucha managed, her voice seeming to come from somewhere far away. Paz and Cruz pushed closer to her on either side. A united front—but against what enemy?

"Imagine my surprise when one of your little mud rats came up to me this morning wanting to trade extra rations for information," Río said, as if she were giving an informative lecture and not advancing on them. "I'm never one to turn down a suffering soul in need—but what he shared with me was more than worth a few extra bowls of grain."

Her eyes glinted. Lucha thought back to this morning. Asking the Robadans to join them. One of them had run to Río, but who? It hardly mattered now. But still, Lucha's eyes darted sideways to Paz out of instinct. It wasn't the first time they'd been surrounded by devotees of the goddess just when they thought they were making headway.

But Lucha could see—with a relief she felt all the way through her body—that Paz had had no prior knowledge of this ambush. She was as shocked and angry as Lucha was, if not more.

"This charming man told me of your little entreaty this morning. I knew if you were lying to me, there could be only one reason. You thought you could keep the location of the spring a secret from me." Her eyes were intense, like flames burned in the heart of each. "Use some feeble excuse to claim all the glory for yourselves. Selfish children. We could have shared it all, and now you'll hand it over or die trying to keep it."

"But what's *he* doing here?" Lucha asked, still staring at the monstrosity that was Alán on the end of his chain.

"I didn't have enough acolytes to ensure victory on my own," Río explained, as if this were obvious. "I didn't choose my attendants with betrayal in mind, you see. And Mr. Marquez here was very persuasive."

This time, Lucha could tell from the widening of Cruz's eyes, the little gasp from Paz, that she wasn't seeing things. Pools of blight swelled into existence around them as Alán held out his hands, his eye rolled back in his head.

"Together, we can make quick work of your camp," Río said as the blight spread, then contracted and disappeared. "We will have the spring whether you cooperate or not, so consider your next move carefully."

"She never should have trusted you," Alán gurgled. "So selfish, Lucha. You always have been."

"This is *not* what Almudena would counsel," Paz said, straight-backed and righteous in the face of this ambush. "Consorting with the likes of him? Turning against innocents? What could possibly be worth betraying her tenets this badly?"

Río's eyes were cold on Paz. Her prized protégée. The girl poised to take over the temple. The most natural vessel for Almudena's will who had ever set foot there. "There is more at stake here than any of you can imagine. I couldn't risk that power falling into the wrong hands. Almudena will understand—she, too, has taken extreme measures when the situation demanded them."

Lucha knew it then—there was nothing but a blank buzzing in her ears where there had once been hope. Río and Alán would have the spring, and Lucha had led them right to it. Had instructed her people to dig into the earth for the selfish plans of someone else. There was no way to prevent it.

Paz shook her head sadly. "You'll pay for this," she said. "Just as our goddess paid for her own hubris."

"I'm going to *be* a goddess," Río said. Her eyes weren't cold now; they danced with some inhuman fire. "In a hundred years, no one will remember *what* I did to save the forest. Only that I did it."

It happened all at once. Lucha and Cruz, without looking at each other, lunged forward, ready to kill Alán and Río and anyone else who believed this madness. Paz shouted "Don't!"—stopping neither of them—and from the edges of the circle they'd formed in the trees, three of the acolytes of the Asilo sanctuary loosed their all-too-familiar weapons.

The bite in Lucha's neck felt like a mosquito. She ripped it out instinctively, barely understanding. She saw the point, the feathers in the fletching. She heard Cruz's body hit the mud first, squelching, settling. And then her knees gave way and the darkness took her.

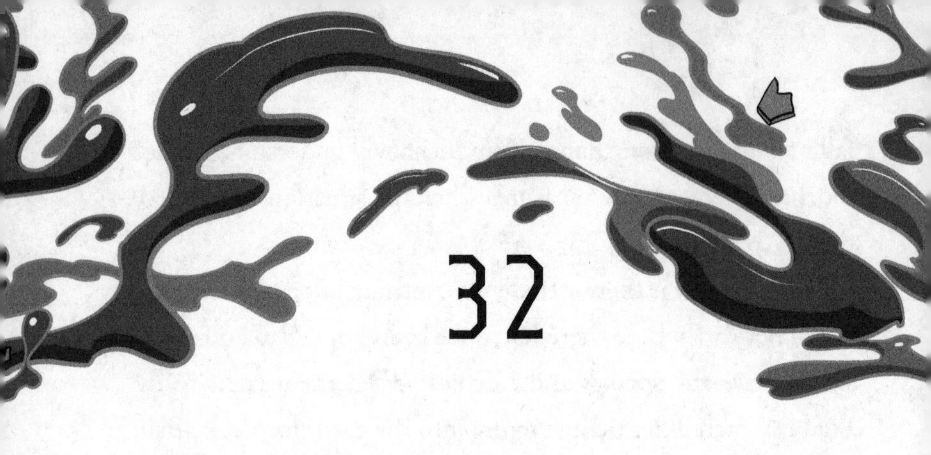

32

Lucha awoke with a dry mouth and a splitting headache. Her nose itched. When she reached up to try to scratch it, she found her hands were tied.

Everything around her was hazy, slow to focus. She felt the growling in her stomach, and the accompanying pang of terror. She was back in her cell in Encadenar. She would die here. No one would ever find her . . .

Only, her cell in Encadenar had been made of metal. The ground beneath her now was stone. Ancient stone grown over with moss. Veined with green. There was a humming sound somewhere nearby. It brought to mind a memory of Almudena's grove. The stump. The golden vine.

Her heart racing, the haze cleared from her vision at last and she could see. She could see everything.

The stone room was perfectly circular. At its center was a massive fountain hewn of white marble. Water flowed continuously from it, pooling, flashing, glittering. From where Lucha was tied, she could see little silver fish flashing in the torchlight. The hum she heard came from the walls. The floor. Some primal power Lucha had never felt so strongly.

She was tied to a pillar, one of twelve evenly spaced around the perimeter of the circle. On one side, Paz was bound and unconscious, her green robe torn and muddy. On the other, there were only untied ropes, abandoned on the ground.

"Hold still," came a voice before Lucha could wonder who had freed themselves. Cruz, breathing in Lucha's ear, barely audible. Lucha felt deft fingers on the ropes at her wrist. Then she heard other voices, and the hands stilled. The breath shallowed, quieted.

"—be awake soon, and then we'll force her to do what must be done. When she sees the leverage we have, she won't be able to refuse."

"We've underestimated her before."

"Not this time."

Lucha could barely turn her head, but she waited. Her patience was rewarded when she saw Río—dressed now in a silver robe that gleamed in the light—leading two acolytes through the room toward the fountain. A third followed, holding Alán's terrible chain.

"Pretend you're still out." Cruz's voice again. Just behind her. Lucha did as she was told, letting her head loll to the side as Paz's was, letting her eyes very nearly close. Through lash-framed slits, she watched Río approach the spring.

"Wake her!" Río barked to the acolytes on either side of her.

"Wait for my signal," breathed the voice behind her. Lucha

felt the ties around her wrists loosen, but not fall. She could be free when she wanted to be.

She would wait for the moment when it would make the greatest impact.

Lucha watched as Río's acolytes approached. She saw what was coming a second before it happened. The struggle was to remain inert as the acolyte threw a bucket of cold water over her.

Spluttering, Lucha did her best to look as though she'd been shocked out of a drug-induced sleep. "Wh—what's happening?" she asked. "Where am I?"

"Don't play dumb with me, girl," Río said, stepping past the acolyte to stand in front of Lucha, that strange expression on her face again. "You discovered the location before any of us. It's under my control now, and you'll find things go easiest when you do as I ask."

"And what's that?" Lucha asked, trying to remain expressionless though every cell in her body screamed that she should lunge now. Dash this traitorous, power-hungry woman's head on the stones and damn the consequences.

"We know the secret of the spring and its forge, as you surely must have all this time. It requires a divine being to operate it. To activate the connection with the celestial plane. And since you still inhabit the body Almudena made you when you transformed, you will give the order. When the spring obeys, you will use it to make me the goddess I was destined to be."

"There is no destiny," Lucha snorted. "If your precious

goddess had ever deigned to speak with you, it would have been the first thing she said."

Río stepped forward in one long stride and slapped Lucha across the face. This time, Lucha didn't have to feign shock.

"You ignorant little mud brat. Do you have any idea what I've sacrificed? What I've *earned*? You think your gift makes you special? That Almudena's blessing sets you above the rest of us? What have you ever done to gain her favor? What have you ever *lost*? I've put up with your self-importance long enough. Get up. Activate the forge."

"Or what?" Lucha asked, careful to keep an eye out for Cruz's signal. Their best bet was to keep Río talking until Cruz could complete whatever she was preparing.

"You'll talk down to me?" Lucha continued. "Bark orders at me? Torture me and attempt to subjugate my will like Salvador did? He would be impressed, you know. You took this page right out of his book."

"Do not blaspheme to me," the obispo hissed. "You want to know the lengths I'll go to, Lucha Moya? Fine. I won't be judged by the likes of you." She turned to the acolyte on her left. "Fetch her."

The acolyte went straight for Paz—still unconscious against the pillar she was tied to. Cruz hadn't loosened her bonds, Lucha noticed as the white-robed girl untied her with trembling hands. Unconscious, head lolling, Paz—as great a warrior as she had always been—could do nothing to defend herself.

"You won't do it for me, but will you do it to save her?" Río asked. She took Paz's limp body from the acolyte's arms and held a short knife to her throat.

Wait for my signal, Cruz had said, but Lucha was done waiting. She was going to destroy the obispo for threatening the girl she loved. For attempting to manipulate her the same way every other power-hungry monster in her life had done. This ended—

"*NOW!*" came Cruz's shout from the shadows behind the fountain. Lucha, who had been tensed for motion, leapt up from her bonds and reached for the knives they had been stupid or arrogant enough to leave strapped to her sides. She lunged for Río. Gone were the moments they'd shared, the times she'd believed they were on the same side.

In her eyes, Río had declared herself an enemy. So Lucha would treat her as one.

Cruz charged forward, her own spear out, and she wasn't alone. Lucha's heart swelled when she saw Armando, Maria, Marisol, even Junio pouring in from the door. Every loyal Robadan Lucha had been so proud to call her community was here. They were ready to fight.

With this unexpected twist searing in her chest, Lucha was faster, stronger than she'd ever been. Unfortunately, the acolytes of Asilo were more than robe-wearing, tea-drinking devotees. They were trained as warriors from the moment they set foot in the sanctuary.

The acolyte who had handed Paz to Río came at Lucha first, wielding a silver dagger identical to the one Lucha held in her nondominant hand. Lucha growled in frustration, engaging her instead of the target she truly wanted. The girl was short and slim, and she moved quickly. Lucha, with the dart's drug still in her system, could barely keep up.

She thrust with her dagger, going on the offensive immediately. The girl parried gracefully. Her fighting style reminded Lucha of Paz's. That fluidity, almost like a dance. But Paz had always had a weakness—one Lucha had never shared. She believed she was being guided by a goddess, that she fought according to someone else's will. Lucha's urgency drove her every step, every turn, every parry and thrust, and soon she had the girl on her heels with willpower and wild fury alone.

"You'll have to kill me," she said, backed up against the stone column on the far side of the door. Lucha had been aiming for nonlethal areas, hoping to stun or immobilize, not to kill. This was nothing like fighting a sombralado, or a sabuesa. Not like fighting Los Ricos and their guards. Not even like fighting a god. This was a girl, with a story. A girl like Paz, who had only wanted to—

Lucha's charitable train of thought was cut off by a dagger. Its blade emerged from the center of the girl's throat. She spluttered, clutching at it, but it was already too late.

When her body collapsed, Paz rose from the ground and pulled the knife back. Wiped it on her robes. It seemed she, too, had been feigning unconsciousness. Her eyes were lined, slightly puffy from her long drug-induced sleep, but otherwise she appeared perfectly in control. Her expression held not a trace of pity.

"She betrayed her goddess," Paz said evenly. She turned the acolyte over with a boot to make sure she was dead. "She knew the consequences."

Before Lucha could react, Paz took the bow off the girl's back into her own hand.

Once, Lucha had ached at the idea of asking this girl to face off against her sisters, but she had been wrong to question Paz's devotion. She saw that now.

The moment this acolyte had chosen Río's side over Almudena's, she had exited Paz's world. And now she was gone from the rest of theirs too.

This was the thing that had held Lucha at arm's length for so long, she thought, looking at this beautiful, ruthless warrior as she lined up her first shot with the dead girl's bow. Paz saw things in harsh contrast. There was wrong and there was right. No in-between.

"Are you—?" Lucha began, but she was engaged from behind before she could finish. From the ruin of the Lost House above, more acolytes were entering the room that held the spring.

"Behind you!" Paz called, but Lucha had already turned. She clashed daggers with another girl—this one rather taller and broader of shoulder—and all thoughts of Paz fled her mind as the urgency of battle took over, driving everything.

33

This warrior wasn't quite as fast as the first, but she was strong.

She only took two steps for every five of Lucha's, struck only half as often, but the blows each packed a terrifying force. She fought not with the traditional bows and knives of the acolytes, but with a wide sword, longer than average, which she wielded with one hand when it had clearly been forged for two.

In another life, Lucha thought as a vicious blow glanced off her dagger, sending her rolling across the ground and lithely back to her feet, she would have asked this girl to teach her what she knew. In this one, she would have to kill her, or be killed herself.

The sword went up again, faster than it should have been able to rise, given its weight. Lucha had been lunging, not thinking the girl could heft it in time. Now she was in trouble. Paz was across the room, looking down the length of an arrow in the opposite direction. The blade was coming down and Lucha was overextended, she couldn't recover in time to dodge . . .

The split second before the sword would have cleaved her in two at the shoulder, it was parried, glancing harmlessly aside. Lucha rolled instinctively to safety, not seeing who had come to her rescue beyond the telltale silver of their acolyte's dagger until she had righted herself and turned back toward the battle.

Lucha was shocked to see Obispo Río, knife in hand, standing over the acolyte.

For a disorienting moment, Lucha wondered whether the sight of Lucha nearly dying had stirred some human instinct in Río at last. If she was ready to give up this foolish desire to become a goddess and cooperate.

"Stupid girl," Río hissed at the acolyte, who looked appropriately chastened. "I told you we need her alive! At least until she's transferred the power to me. After that, I've promised someone else the honor of ending her miserable life."

So Río *hadn't* come to her senses. Lucha could work with this, too. Lucha got back to her feet, preparing to fight to the death.

"Must I do everything myself?" Río was asking now, turning to face Lucha. "The goal is to incapacitate, not to kill. End this little rebellion by subduing its leaders."

She spoke more to Lucha than to the other girl now, her eyes dancing in the light coming from the splashing fountain.

"Kill the others," she said without a trace of remorse. "They won't be needed for what comes next."

Lucha couldn't help it. She knew that it would be a devastating mistake to take her eyes off Río, but she glanced around for her friends anyway. Cruz was locked in battle with Alán, who flung his blight toward her, slithering across the ground. Armando and Maria fought together against a girl with a bow, struggling to stay at long range.

But Paz, Lucha thought, scanning more desperately. Where was Paz?

The room was much fuller now than it had been when the fight started. More acolytes, more Robadans. Perhaps Paz was only lost in the crowd.

Instinctively, Lucha knew that wasn't the case. If Paz was here, she would know. She would feel it.

It was this sinking feeling in her stomach, the realization that Paz was nowhere to be seen, that allowed her to deliver her first real strike since the battle had begun.

Río swiped low, slicing through something vital at the back of Lucha's ankle. She cried out, pivoting, the pain nearly blotting out her vision. For a moment, there was a rushing in her ears, and then she was back, spinning, leaving a trail of blood behind her as Río followed.

"You never had to learn how useless these attachments are," Río said in a thoughtful, sinister voice. "I almost envy you. Being allowed to think a single life matters. What matters, Miss Moya, is the collective."

Río struck again, quick as a viper and just as deadly. Another hit to the same leg, which buckled uselessly under Lucha as she backed toward the edge of the fountain.

Río moved like water. Like smoke. Impossible to dodge, impossible to surprise.

Lucha did her best, running forward as fast as her wounded leg would allow. But the fire that had given her an advantage over the other acolytes was useless against Río, who had as much determination and urgency as Lucha herself—or more.

Lucha's drive was cut short by an expert parry from Río, who hadn't taken a single hit, it seemed. Even her hair was still in place, her breathing steady as she spoke.

"There's no point in trying to stop it," Río said in a low, hypnotic voice that must have been very effective against the pilgrims at the sanctuary but merely made Lucha's hair stand on end. "The arc of the universe bends toward power. There are those who have it foisted upon them, and then there are those—like me—who have earned it. Who have paid dearly for it."

Another swipe, this time to the arm Lucha held her bone knife in. When Río decided to move, she almost seemed to disappear and reappear instantly at her destination. Lucha needed more time, but there was none. Río was relentless. The backs of Lucha's knees were against the fountain. Her arm and leg were both bleeding freely, red pooling on the stone.

Her breaths were coming heavier now. It was almost too tempting to just give up. Fall back into the water. Sink to the bottom. She could not beat Río. The last few minutes had shown her she was desperately outmatched.

She remembered the feeling she'd had in the beam of light as she swam through the Lost House above. The vibrating in her body that made her think her power had not gone. Not truly.

But there was none of that magic here. And Lucha was alone. Alone with Río advancing like some terrible predatory feline.

Río wouldn't let Lucha die until she'd done what she wanted. She would make her stand here and operate the forge. Design the second-worst catastrophe to ever befall humanity.

Then Lucha would die anyway. Río had said as much herself.

Wouldn't it be easier, cleaner, Lucha thought, to just take matters into her own hands? Blunt the sharp edge of the tool Río so desperately needed before she could do anything worse?

Lucha held the bone knife loosely in her right hand. The blood made its way to her wrist, then down her fingers, staining the white of the blade pure red.

Río watched with a predatory smirk on her face, as if Lucha's unraveling was the best entertainment she'd found in all her sixty years of life. She didn't need to continue to attack her, Lucha thought. She only had to wait.

Just fall back, she told herself, the water suddenly louder in her ears, as if drawing her attention to it again. *Just let go, you've done your part . . .*

Perhaps Cruz and Paz and the Robadans would find a way to go on. To operate the forge. To save the forest and the city. Or perhaps the world had reached its natural end, and the release—for all of them—would be a blessing.

Either way, Lucha had fought, and she had lost. It was time to admit that, no matter what came after.

From the tip of the bone blade, a drop of Lucha's blood dripped into the fountain. It bloomed like a crimson flower at the edge of her vision, reminding her of the moment when she and Paz had faced off in the sanctuary—an arrow to her throat, Paz's narrowed eyes above it.

Beautiful, she remembered now. She could admit it, couldn't she? At the end?

The crimson flower that had fallen from the sky. Paz had believed it was a sign from Almudena, sent to urge her to help Lucha even as her heart broke.

Paz hadn't hesitated, Lucha remembered. She'd picked up the flower, and just like that she'd changed her mind. A life-time of training out the window. The new path open to her, which she took without hesitation.

Then, Lucha had called it lunacy—if only in her mind. Now, with time softening the edges, she remembered it as faith, and she envied it.

The blood continued to spread, to grow petals and a stem, stamens, and pistils. Could anyone else see it? Lucha wondered. Or was it a sign for her alone?

The ground began to shake. At first, Lucha thought the vibrations were happening in her mind, a result of exhaustion or delirium, or else the aftereffects of the dart's drug.

But Río's eyes widened slightly. Surprise. She could feel it too.

As Lucha looked around the room, she noticed everyone widening their stances, bracing themselves as the rumbling grew more intense beneath their feet.

"What have you done?" Río asked.

Lucha hadn't done anything, but she didn't have to tell Río that. She laughed. A forced bark of a thing that sounded nothing like her true laugh, but how could this woman who had never bothered to know her tell the difference?

"You really believed I had nothing up my sleeve?" Lucha asked, knowing how ridiculous she'd look if whatever was happening now favored Río and the acolytes. She only wanted to keep Río off-balance. To stop her from taking advantage of the quickly spreading chaos.

"We can come to some kind of arrangement, surely," the high priestess said. "There's no reason to destroy the spring just to stop me from taking power. It's a childish response. One I'd hoped you had grown out of."

"If I'd grown out of it," Lucha said, her voice barely audible above the din the vibration was causing, "I'd be aligned with Salvador right now, and the whole world would be a pile of ash and bone."

Río lurched sideways. Lucha knew this was the only chance she'd get. She lunged on legs made steadier by her resolve, making for the obispo, who was tangled in her robe.

Lucha's knife was ready; she stretched it out, reaching for Río's chest. It was time to end this before Río could find a way to seize power. To destroy the world. Lucha knew she was the only one who could do it, even if it felt awful. Even if she could never flip the switch in her mind between ally and enemy as cleanly as Paz could.

But just as Lucha's knife was about to do the job she'd assigned it, two things happened at once:

First, a shadow fell over Río's face; then it swallowed her whole in a darkness as dense as a storm-tossed night's.

Second, a body launched into Lucha, tackling her away from Río and out of the spreading shadow's range.

"What the hell?" Lucha shouted when she could breathe again. "I had her!"

It was Cruz, disheveled beside her. She didn't answer, only gaped at the place where Lucha had been moments ago.

When Lucha turned, she could see why. Her own jaw fell open. Where she'd just been standing was an enormous foot. Scaled, hoofed, the ankle supporting it at least as big around as Lucha's waist.

"You were saying?" Cruz shouted back.

"What the hell is that thing?" Lucha asked, afraid to take her eyes off it. Unable to, as it turned out.

The creature made sense of the size and scope of the room. It was three times as tall as Lucha—some bizarre cross between a deer and a reptile. Its long, scaled tail was tipped with deadly-looking spikes. Its crown of antlers was overgrown with moss. From its back—what Lucha could see of it, at least—grew foliage of various kinds. It had been down here long enough that the fauna of the spring had begun to consume it.

The creature's tail whipped around, sending anyone within

range sprawling to the ground. The spikes caught an acolyte in the chest. The blood dragged behind the tail, leaving a gruesome train in its wake.

Lucha had barely been outside its range.

"What do we do?" she asked Cruz. "We can't ask the Robadans to fight this with us."

"We can't tell them not to, either," Cruz countered. "This is their city too."

With an earsplitting cracking and groaning, the creature stretched up to its full height, interrupting Cruz as she took Lucha's hand and ran flat out for the wall surrounding the spring.

"Junio," Lucha panted. "The kid who helped with the foraging. He's in here somewhere. Would you—?"

"I'll find him," Cruz promised. "I'll get him out of here." The expression in her eyes said she would have agreed to anything.

"Thank you," Lucha said. "Again."

"I dreamed about you, you know?" Cruz said as chaos reigned all around them.

Lucha's own dream came back into her mind then, as true as a red flower falling.

"Me too," she said.

The creature made an unearthly sound. One that filled the chamber and reverberated until Lucha clapped her hands over her ears.

Cruz, covering her own, took off into the fray without so much as a goodbye. Lucha turned her sights back to the beast.

Of course it wouldn't be as easy as a vision. Lucha should have known there would be some other trick.

Some of the acolytes had already begun to fight. Lucha scanned once more for Paz or the Syndicate. Mariel. All she found was Río.

The obispo hadn't moved from the place where she'd gotten tangled in her robe. She knelt down, staring out in front of her as if too stunned to get back up.

Lucha couldn't imagine Río losing control, but that was the least of her worries now. She had to get rid of this beast, keep her friends and the Robadans safe, and not lose sight of the lines drawn between them and Río's acolytes. If they could survive the awakening of this ancient monster, there would still be a power-hungry priestess to deal with.

And a god to make.

34

Knives in hand, Lucha stalked through bodies and blood and water splashed from the fountain. The stones were slick, her boots sliding when she stepped wrong. The monster was in the center of the room, two feet still in the fountain, the other two on the stone floor. It was surrounded by acolytes and Robadans, who were doing their best to keep it at bay, but it was so large. So strong.

Lucha thought about fighting the sombralados in the forest. The way she'd had to climb and leap to reach their hearts. She hoped she could do the same here . . .

With the beast engaged, Lucha ran for the edge of the fountain, throwing herself into the water, bleeding freely, a trail of crimson blooms following her footsteps. She planned to get around to the beast's back. See if she could climb on top of it, incapacitate it, get to its vital areas without moving in reach of the head or tail.

What she didn't expect was to see that the ceaseless splashing of the fountain had stopped.

To see that within that waterfall's endless propulsion was a chamber that hadn't been visible before. Split in two. On one side was a pale stone disk in the base, faintly glowing. In the other was a golden handle coming up like a branch from the stone.

Was this it? Lucha wondered, everything else falling away. Was this the divine forge Río had demanded Lucha use?

Something in Lucha's chest caught at the sight of it. It felt like when she'd first met Paz, first seen the sanctuary. Like this was something she'd known before. Like the gravity of this place had been impressed on her heart before her earliest memory, and she'd been carrying it around with her ever since.

She stepped toward it with wonder, awe. The sounds of the battle were far away now.

Lucha Moya had never believed in fate—least of all when she'd been told it didn't exist by a goddess—but at this moment, with her skin tingling and her heart strangely full, she thought this was the closest she'd been to believing.

Before she could get near enough to touch the delicate instrument, to examine the shining disk, something caught her hard in the chest and swept her away.

The spell was broken. Lucha cursed herself for allowing the distraction.

It was the beast's tail that had caught her, and she'd been lucky to miss the spikes twice. If the look on the creature's face was any indication, she wouldn't be as lucky next time.

The beast looked straight at Lucha. A cold plume of fear

spread through her. It knew she was trying to reach the chamber, she realized, not knowing how she knew but positive she was right. For one wild moment, she felt a glimmer of recognition from within its eyes . . . an intelligence that said it understood. That perhaps this didn't need to be a fight to the death . . .

Before she could expound on this theory, one of the acolytes shot an arrow directly into the creature's neck. It reared up, its antlers nearly brushing the ceiling Lucha could barely see from the ground.

When its hooves landed again on the ground, they cracked the stone in two. And then it charged.

The next endless minutes were nothing but a desperate bid to survive. Lucha had lost the silver knife as she struggled out of the fountain. She fought with the bone knife, as she had always done, doing her best to dodge the beast's frequent charges, its surprisingly lithe, reptilian movements as it caused havoc in the chamber.

Before long, the ground was littered with the wounded and dead. The fountain was murky with blood. Lucha had lost track of anyone she recognized. As she had when she'd looked at the chamber in the center of the room, she felt she was alone with the beast. A battle of wills.

Unfortunately, it bested her in size, strength, and speed. She'd barely managed to wound it, let alone take it down. There was no way she was going to be able to operate the forge with it in here. She thought perhaps she could run inside unnoticed, transfer the power to herself before anyone was the wiser. With a goddess's power, Lucha would be able to take care of the creature without a problem.

Only, it seemed to know this. It kept its body between Lucha and the glowing disk at all times. Perhaps that was why it took Lucha so long to notice Río, making her way through the muddied water on the other side.

"No!" Lucha called out. Even from here she could see the greedy look on the obispo's face.

Río clearly intended to use the monster's distraction to take the power for herself. But could she succeed? Was Lucha's blood in the water enough? Río couldn't be allowed to find out. Even if it meant that every one of them died here and now.

"What are you doing?" Lucha screamed at the beast, losing her head entirely as Río reached the chamber. The monster had been so determined to keep *her* out that it had allowed Río to waltz in without a second thought.

Lucha felt sick to her stomach. For a moment, though she was not experiencing a divine vision, she thought she could see the vines parting. The future peeking through.

Río, atop a throne of precious metals, ruling her sanctuary with an iron fist and all the power it took to make sure her authority was never questioned. Those she favored were safe, but Robado, the cities across the river, the areas of forest too secluded or shadowed to be worthy of her notice?

They would remain neglected and uncared for. All the resources in Elegido would nurture the places Río cared for most. Even the distance and perspective of divinity wouldn't stop her from doing as she'd always done. Salvador had been the perfect example of that.

And then Lucha came to another realization—a much more troubling one. One that left her strangely purposeless, with the fate of the world on the line.

Río had proved her selfishness. She had already been given power—much more than most people would have in a lifetime—and she had squandered it. Keeping those most like her comfortable and safe without a care for the rest of the world. She was unworthy, yes.

But by that measure, divine gift or not, so was Lucha.

She thought back on her life. Her hatred of the kings and Olvida. Her fierce love for her sister, which had driven her to extremes. Lucha had come back to Robado willing to level the whole place because of her prejudice against the olvidados.

Her anger toward her mother for abandoning her. For always choosing forgetting over the daughters who needed her.

Lucha had been surprised to find Cruz a worthwhile friend and companion, had fought hard against the innate fear that told her not to trust a person with a ladder of scars up their arm.

Even now, as she defended the city she had grown to love, Lucha knew that that love was selfish. She had given the Robadans who stayed her blessing, because of their willingness to put aside their old lives and commit to a collective that benefited them all. Because they had aligned themselves more closely with what Lucha herself believed was right.

But could she use her divine power to protect those whose views were different from her own? Would she use it fairly to protect those who strayed outside the circle of her moral compass?

What of the Robadans who had left to seek intoxication in other forms? Would she ever have enough empathy for them?

Could Lucha care for those who chose that life, those who chose *any* life, with the same fervor she felt for Lis? For Paz and Cruz?

Unlike Río, Lucha had already experienced the expansion of time that came with immortality. With power that could shape worlds, balance them, destroy them. She knew in her heart of hearts that who she was wouldn't change. She *hadn't* changed. She had nearly destroyed the world because of her personal hatred for Salvador. For Olvida.

Lucha wasn't worthy. She knew it now as surely as she knew water had soaked her boots. She had never wanted to be a goddess, and for good reason. The only reason she'd come close to changing her mind was because of the lure of the gift. The hunger to feel divine again.

The same hunger that had led generations of Robadans to the drug that destroyed them.

Lucha was no goddess. No fair and balanced source of inspiration, guidance, and protection.

She was a girl, and she was flawed, and she would not doom the world just to feel the rush of divinity once more.

It had only been a few seconds, but Lucha felt as though

she'd just landed here from another world. Since she woke up tied to the pillar, she'd had one goal in mind: to get herself into the forge. To take the power. To stop Río and save Robado. The forest. The world. Now? She had nothing. And Río was nearly inside the chamber, and the beast cried its horrible cry, and Lucha felt the loss of her power a final time.

"LUCHA!"

Cruz. Lucha snapped out of her reverie to look around for her. Cruz's eyes were panicked when Lucha found them—they said she had seen Río climbing into the chamber and that she knew exactly what it meant.

At that moment, Lucha cut off the musing on the future and the helpless spiral her thoughts had taken. She would do what she did best before it was too late. When it was quiet, when the forge was theirs, they could decide what to do. For now, it was just fight the monster in front of her. And that was what she had always done best.

Lucha took off running at the same time as Cruz did. They leapt simultaneously over the wall around the fountain, boots splashing in the water, which was now miraculously clean and sparkling again.

They weren't going to make it. Lucha knew it before she was halfway there. Because Río, with manic joy lighting her features, had entered the chamber. She stood on the glowing disk. She reached out for the golden handle.

From behind them, the beast called its awful, lowing call once more. Lucha saw several acolytes and Robadans drop their swords and cover their ears as the creature charged—not toward Río, who was seconds away from being a goddess, but toward Lucha, who had gotten too close to the chamber herself.

Unworthy, Lucha heard in some hissing, terrible voice she took a moment to register as Salvador's. As her mother's. As Alán's. As every villain her story had ever held. As her own, looking into the mirror, seeing a scrawny sixteen-year-old with a knife and the burden of an entire family on her shoulders.

The room seemed to hold its breath. Lucha did not know if the rest of their eyes were on the chamber, where Río had just taken hold of the handle, but soon the glow of the disk was growing brighter, drawing every eye to the stage upon which this last of Río's delusions of grandeur was about to play out.

There was nothing else to look at in the room. In the world. The priestess in her silver robe—torn and soaked with water and blood from the fight—held tight to the golden handle, an expression of ecstasy on her features as they were lit by the brilliant beam inside the chamber.

Lucha's chest ached as she watched. She had bathed in that very light. She could almost feel the warmth, the purpose, the *power* that must be coursing through Río at this moment. She envied it so much, she craved it so much, she thought she might lose her mind from wanting it . . .

Río's cropped gray hair lengthened into strands of gold. The wrinkles on her skin smoothed out, giving her an appearance of eternal youth and beauty. Even the robe she wore turned white, clean, and brilliant as an acolyte's on their very first day at the sanctuary. Their old life behind them, the new one beckoning . . .

They were too late, Lucha thought with despair. It would be Río's world now, a world of privilege and poverty. A world of harsh divides . . .

Any moment the light would go out, and Río's feet would touch the ground, and she would step toward them with all the power she had been craving for a lifetime. All the power she had been denied.

But Río's feet didn't touch the ground. The light continued to grow brighter. The ecstasy that had lit her features transformed into something more . . . panic.

A scream rent the air. One far too human to be coming from a divine being. A scream of pure terror, of relentless pain.

The light grew brighter still. Brutal. It stung Lucha's eyes even from a distance, and now she could feel the heat of it. Smell the burning. The chamber of Río's transformation had become her pyre, and she was burning.

It took only seconds. There was no blood. No body. No bones. The chamber stood empty, the light went out. It was as though no one had ever stepped into it at all.

Except that Río was gone.

35

Everything in Lucha felt scrambled. A quail's egg on a hot pan. She could barely remember her name. All she could think of was the cost of power. The one no one ever thought of before they reached for it. The one that had just claimed Río as payment past due.

Lucha wanted to fall to her knees in this fountain. Better yet, to lie down and let the water take her. Drown out the sounds of people fighting, and dying, and for what? To find the perfect person to take over this world? To be its guardian? When all evidence pointed to the fact that no such person existed?

There was no time to process, Lucha thought, dragging herself with effort up from the depths of her weary, spiraling mind. She was standing in the middle of a massacre. The monster had barely paused as it witnessed Río's demise, and it seemed emboldened now. It fed off the fear and uncertainty now coursing through the crowd. Who would venture into the chamber now? Was anyone worthy of this?

Lucha took two steps forward, her knees threatening to

give way. All around her, the factions had abandoned their infighting. Acolytes and Robadans stood together, facing the monster. Had Río's death done this? Lucha wondered as she moved to join them. Had she been the only thing standing between them?

Cruz had dived back in, Lucha saw, leading the charge though she bled freely from a wound in her side. Maria and Armando were in the fray again, faces scratched as they made attempt after attempt to get close enough to the creature now crying its strange cry through the room.

They were beautiful in their certainty, Lucha thought, feeling once again as if she walked through a dream. As though she were not truly part of her surroundings. The air in front of her seemed to shimmer, an invitation to pull back some unseen curtain, to peer behind it at a truth she had not acknowledged.

If you don't fight this monster, you will die, she told herself. *Cruz will die. No one will take up the mantle. The world will perish in flood and fire and chaos, and you will be to blame.*

It didn't work.

Lucha felt hollow and slow. A step behind, after all she had seen, and she had lost so much blood. Still, she made her way to the fighting force holding off the monster. Still, she held her knife. But only because she knew no other way to fight. No one had ever taught her a better way.

As she joined them, Cruz and the twenty or more Robadans and acolytes remaining in the chamber seemed to take heart. She was a symbol to them, Lucha thought, in different ways across different mythologies. To the Robadans, she was the girl who had escaped Pecado and Encadenar, who had returned with magic to help them reclaim their city.

To the acolytes, she was the savior of the battle with Salvador. The girl who had delivered them from the threat they'd spent centuries hiding from behind their walls.

But she hadn't done any of that alone. And Paz was still nowhere to be seen.

Was she alive? Lucha wondered, walking through them, bloody and wounded. Would any of this matter if she wasn't?

Lucha had tried so hard to hide from these truths, but she saw them now the way they were intended to be seen. As something she could offer the people around her. As hope. As life. Even if she had never felt more like a broken, empty husk, she could stand tall. She could let them pin these hopes on her. She could fight alongside them.

Once the beast was gone, they could decide. They could take their time.

And there it was again, shimmering before her, the answer that would not reveal itself. The vines that would not part. Lucha shied away from them, turning to the knife instead. She had the sense that she wasn't ready. Not yet.

She raised her knife in the air almost without her own permission. Some force moved through her. Something more than the sum of its parts. She roared, a battle cry that rivaled the beast's own. She couldn't secure their future, but she could do this thing. This one thing in front of her.

Lucha felt barely human as she launched herself into the

fray. She swiped and stabbed at the creature's legs, letting her instincts take over, her wild impulse to survive at all costs.

The beast whipped its tail; she hopped over it neatly, not turning when she heard someone fall. This was her chance. She darted in, not minding the clawed hooves or the unnatural speed. The look in its eyes that sized her up even from its great height.

Around them, the rest of the spring fell away. Lucha and the beast locked eyes. They danced.

First, the creature's tail nearly took off her knife arm. Next she plunged the bone of her blade up into the tender place where its front leg met its body. It howled again. Blood unlike anything Lucha had seen flowed from the wound. It was clear, tinged with blue, like the water in the spring. It fell, cool as rain, onto Lucha's body.

This time, the flash in the beast's eye looked like admiration. But a second later, it was attacking again. Lucha was parrying. The dance reached a fevered new pitch.

Swipe, parry. The clash of spike on bone. Another plunge, near the heart. Was anyone else here? Lucha wondered. She hoped they had gotten free. Either way, she found it didn't matter. She had entered some other dimension as this fight wore on. Some ecstatic, embodied moment she would have been glad to stay inside forever.

Testing, breaching, retreating. She took a gash to the thigh she barely felt. She delivered a third blow, this time leaping high to attack the creature's neck. The strange, clear blood dripped down again, rejuvenating her where it touched her skin.

But the moment she was still, it launched its deadliest

attack yet—antlers and teeth and clawed hooves and spiked tail all converging to some final horrible end. An end Lucha almost welcomed . . .

Just before it came, a voice rang out. A clear drop of water hitting a still pond, ripples fanning out in every direction.

"Enough."

Lucha obeyed without even knowing she did. Her body stilling by instinct.

The strange thing was that the beast did also. They stood together, reacting to the same primal pull deep within them.

Later, Lucha would deny it, but when she turned in that moment, she expected the goddess from her dreams. The white-robed, weeping woman who had set her on this course before she had ever understood the reason why.

But it wasn't Almudena descending the stairs into the holy spring.

It wasn't a goddess at all.

It was Paz.

Unarmed, she walked toward Lucha and the beast with her hands open in front of her, palms up.

Lucha wanted to shout at her to be careful. To leap in front of her, to protect her. But the beast was still, and the words stuck in Lucha's throat.

Paz wore the same torn, soaked, and bloodied robe she had when Lucha had seen her calmly stab into an acolyte's neck at the beginning of the fight. Her hair was unraveling from its dark braid. Nothing in her outward appearance had changed—and yet everything had.

It was the way she carried herself, Lucha thought. The quiet, radiating confidence. The bearing of her shoulders. The complete and utter peace on her features despite the circumstances. Together, it made Lucha want to kneel. To weep.

Before her, for the third time, that truth shimmered just out of sight. This time, Lucha thought she could see the shape of it through the veil, and every part of her heart rebelled. She wasn't ready.

But she would have to be.

Paz approached the beast with her hands out, and somehow Lucha knew before she reached it that it would not fight her. When it sank to its knees, she understood the reason.

No, she thought with increasing desperation. *She doesn't belong here. She belongs with me, hunting rabbits in the forest and roasting them over a spit. Kissing in a devastating rainstorm and coming apart beneath my fingers and my lips . . .*

Every word her heart offered up, Paz's posture denied. It said Lucha had stolen these moments. That *this* was who Paz had always been.

And that Lucha, too, was meant for something different.

When Paz laid her hands on the creature's face, it no longer looked like a monster. The buds twisted into its antlers bloomed.

Around them, half the robed acolytes sank to their knees.

"You've done well," Paz murmured to the creature. "You may rest now."

An eternal, elemental sigh seemed to emanate from the creature. It lay in the pool of the spring, the wounds Lucha had inflicted on it weeping that same cool water. Before their eyes, it began to fade bit by bit from sight. Not disappearing, merely becoming what it had been when they arrived. The water of life. The spring itself.

The guardian, Lucha thought, of the place where the earth met the stars.

Within seconds, the last of it had faded—leaving only a single pale pink blossom behind. An offering at Paz's feet.

She lifted it carefully, placing it in her hair before turning to Lucha.

Her eyes had already taken on the distance of the divine. In fact, Lucha thought, as tears streamed down her face, it hadn't begun today. She had seen it first when they arose from the mud. After the storm. She just hadn't been ready to understand it.

"You weren't ready," Paz said, answering her thoughts, a small—and still very human—smile twisting one corner of her mouth. "And neither was I."

"But you're ready now," Lucha choked out around the tears in her throat. It wasn't a question, and Paz didn't answer. The fact of her standing there was answer enough.

"I told you once that you were the greatest test I'd ever been given," Paz said, and now her own eyes—those beautiful, distant stars—were sparkling with tears of their own. "Without that, without you, I wouldn't be here now. Tell me you don't hate me for it."

"How could I ever?" Lucha asked.

Paz crossed the distance between them, taking Lucha's

hands in hers. The tears that had been gathering in her eyes finally spilled over.

"Have you always known it would be you?" Lucha asked, needing to put off the final moment as long as she could, needing to understand. The things Paz explained to her now would be the structure on which she could build what came after.

A life without Paz.

"It wouldn't have been, without you," Paz said, shaking her head, letting go of one of Lucha's hands and holding firmly to the other. Around them, acolytes and Robadans together began to tend to the wounded, to take the dead aboveground. Cruz, along with Maria and Armando, stood some distance away, conversing quietly. Giving them time.

"What do you mean?" Lucha asked.

"I told you, I was the perfect acolyte. That place would have turned me into another Río if I hadn't met you. Obsessed with the lore, immune to the urgency of human life. I didn't understand it. I couldn't have, I was too distanced from it. And then you . . ."

Lucha remembered the moment they'd first laid eyes on each other. She had charged in through the door of the night greenhouse to find Paz being harassed by two olvidados. She had saved her, and all the time she'd wondered why Paz hadn't been afraid.

The sparks when Paz had touched her cheek. Those stitches had dissolved, but the mark they left on Lucha's heart had never faded.

"It was the first time I'd ever wanted to be in *this* world. I was so content to sit above it before. To believe I was better. To heal the sick and tend to the poor with my eyes on the sky and the divine. But I crash-landed on the ground, for you. I would have followed you anywhere . . . I loved you so fiercely, so urgently that I forgot everything divine. I only wanted to be imperfect and human. To give myself over to the flesh and the heart and the choice I had always known I had but never used . . ."

It was torture, Lucha thought, to hear this now, knowing it would all have to end so soon, but she couldn't help seeing her own experience reflected in Paz's words. The way she'd had to leave Robado, to gain divine power and lose it to truly understand the tenacity of the people she'd been born among.

"I had never seen anyone that way before," Lucha admitted. They sat side by side on the edge of the fountain. Like any other day. Except this one would be the last. "You woke up parts of me I didn't even know existed. You changed me."

"The only reason I can hope to be worthy of this now is because I've loved you. Because I've felt what it's like to be truly human. I couldn't have been worthy of the position if I hadn't."

Lucha saw the sense in this even as it tore her apart. The pain was just emerging, like a sprout from fertile ground. She knew it would hurt for a long time. Perhaps it would never stop.

"I don't want you to change," Lucha admitted. The words were torn from her. Selfish. The very reason she could never have taken the mantle herself. "I would rather put anyone else in that chamber. I can't imagine you different. But I suppose I'll have to get used to it."

For the first time since awareness had dawned, hope took root in the deepest recess of Lucha's heartbreak.

"Maybe it won't be the end . . . ," she said, remembering. "When I had Almudena's power, I still wanted you. You were still different to me. Maybe, if it's the same, we can still . . ."

The smile that lit Paz's features was beautiful, and desperately sad. It stopped Lucha in her tracks, the bud of hope withering as quickly as it had grown.

"I was knocked unconscious in the fight," Paz said, forestalling the inevitable even as Lucha braced herself for it. "One of the acolytes came up from behind and hit me with the butt of her knife. She dragged me upstairs to get me out of the way, but she couldn't kill me . . ."

Lucha waited. The pool was still behind them, but not for long. She pictured Paz, her eyes steady on the acolyte Lucha had been fighting. She hadn't hesitated before taking her life. Perhaps you needed both the detachment and the love to be worthy of something like this.

"Almudena came to me while I was unconscious. It was the first time I'd seen her since I left for Robado at the end of my acolyte training." Another smile. This one full of love and faith and pride. It twisted in Lucha's heart like a knife. "She showed me what must be done. All of it. I finally understand what all of this was for."

There was nothing to say. Nothing to do to stop it. Almudena had been pulling the strings since the beginning. It was the very thing that had made Lucha walk away, the not knowing. But the knowing was somehow worse.

"Río wasn't right because she had no sympathy for the oppressed. Felt no obligation to love or protect them. You weren't right because you had too much love for them. You could never hold it all in balance."

"But you have both," Lucha said, trying not to be bitter.

"Because of you," Paz said again. "Together—"

"Don't say it," Lucha interrupted. She got to her feet. "Don't tell me that's all it was for. You and me and everything we felt for each other. Everything we *did* together. Don't tell me it was just some stepping stone to her perfect will."

Paz didn't have to tell her. The truth was written all over her face.

"Just because it's not the ending you want, that doesn't mean it's the wrong one," Paz said gently, standing up, taking Lucha's hand again.

"So it's you on the disk and me at the handle, is it?" Lucha asked. "That's how it ends?"

"That's how it begins," Paz said.

For a moment, Lucha remembered her hope. "And after . . . ?" she began. "Once it's done, we can find a way to make it work."

But Paz was already shaking her head. "She showed me that future," she said before Lucha could protest. "But it can't be. Because of how I feel about you, I could never be impartial.

I would let the world go out of balance before I let anything happen to you. I couldn't be fair . . ."

"Oh, because *she* was so fair?" Lucha asked, heated again. "She literally created the god of destruction because she couldn't give up what she wanted. And you're expected to give up everything?"

"Exactly," Paz said. "She wants me to learn from her mistakes. To be better than she was . . ."

"Well, you could hardly be worse," Lucha retorted. She wanted to refuse to do her part. This wasn't right, to string two people along like this, to play with their hearts and their will and their love, only to shunt them into the boxes you'd made.

"I'll be in a new form," Paz said, as if it were nothing to give up her body. Her life.

"A new form?" Lucha asked. "So I won't even be able to speak to you?" Lucha wanted Paz to fight. To rail against this injustice. To deny her fate and promise they'd always be together. That she'd never let anyone tear them apart.

But there was no such thing as fate, of course. She'd learned that from Almudena herself. There were only choices. And if she really thought about it, Paz had never wavered. Not when it came to her faith.

"Try to understand," Paz said gently. "We have to do things in a new way. Ask yourself what you would do if you were the one who had to choose."

"I'd tell that goddess to go to hell," Lucha said.

"Easy for you to say," Paz said with a little smirk. "You've never been overly fond of her. But what if it were Robado you had to give up? Your city. Your chance to make a better world for the people in it?"

At this, Lucha paused. The anger left her. She was thinking of it as if she and Paz were the same person. That had always been her mistake. The truth was, they had *both* chosen what they believed in over each other.

Just because it's not the ending you want, that doesn't mean it's the wrong one.

And just because you weren't right for the person you once thought you wanted, that didn't mean either of you was at fault.

"I couldn't leave them," she admitted, knowing Paz needed to hear it. To be absolved one last time before they stepped into the chamber.

"You won't have to," Paz said. "I'll be listening, Lucha. I'll be protecting the people, the trees, the creatures of the forest. Holding them all in balance. And Robado will no longer be a place of exploitation and sin, it'll be the gateway city to the forest. The place where the goddess's temple stands. Someone will need to make sure it's worthy of the title."

Almost without her own permission, Lucha pictured it. A beautiful city where once there'd been a muddy shantytown. And Lucha at the helm of it all, making it safe, filling it with abundance and joy.

"You see it, don't you?" Paz asked.

Lucha nodded. Perhaps it *had* always been heading this way. But not because of a goddess pulling the strings. Because she and Paz had always been truly, unapologetically who they were. That was what had drawn them together, and that was what would separate them.

The tears were back, matching tracks on both sets of cheeks. They gripped their hands so tightly together, Lucha felt her fingertips start to tingle.

"I'll never, ever forget you."

"As if I'd let you," Paz said with a tearful laugh. "I'll be listening in every tree. Every leaf. Every change of every season."

Drawn by some unopposable force, they began to walk slowly to the center of the fountain. To the chamber that would tear them asunder at last. But of course, it wasn't a force, Lucha thought as the water soaked into her boots, cool and refreshing. At least, not an external one.

Paz stepped into the right side, placing her feet on the glowing disk. Lucha's hands hovered over the golden handle. They faced each other this way, waiting for some signal. Waiting for their lives to begin.

Between them, in the still, clear water of the spring, a crimson flower bloomed. The same flower that had fallen at Paz's feet as she held an arrow to Lucha's throat. The same one Lucha's blood had made in this very fountain earlier.

It was time.

36

There would never be a painting or a poem or a stained-glass window depicting what happened next. To all who saw it, it would remain the most sacred event they'd ever witnessed. No art could have done it justice.

Lucha reached out for the handle, feeling the power coursing from it like a hum in her bloodstream. It beckoned her for one last dance, but this time she wasn't afraid to use it. Not for this. The greatest thing she'd ever do.

The handle began to heat beneath her hands, the floor to vibrate once more. She didn't think of Río. Of the light that had incinerated her. Paz could never have met that fate. Lucha had scarcely been certain about anything in her life, but that much she knew.

Around the circular room, the acolytes, the Robadans, Cruz, Maria, and Armando turned to face them. They watched as the light swallowed Paz whole. Listened as her screams began, high and clear and piercing. The price of transformation.

For Lucha, it was a giving over. The last vestiges of borrowed divinity lingering in her body flowing forth in a golden river, magnified by the portal open to the celestial plane.

Before she could feel the flooding of power, it was over. The screams stopped. The light went out. The handle beneath Lucha's palms was cool, and she felt dizzy, exhausted, as if the last of her life force had been drained from her.

The entire gathered crowd held their breath until at last, from a heap on the ground, Paz rose.

Lucha exited the chamber, joining the mortals to gaze on their new goddess.

She wasn't so different, Lucha thought. Not in any of the usual ways. There was still that long hair and those high cheekbones, the full lips and the deep brown eyes. But in every other way, she was unrecognizable.

Comparing the old Paz to this vision rising naked from the pool would have been as useless as comparing a single jacara seed to a towering, ancient tree. A single tree to the entire, sprawling forest with all its secrets and hollows and meadows.

Lucha felt her heart twist again as she returned her gaze to Paz's eyes. That distance she'd sometimes seen there, even during Paz's most mortal moments, had evolved into the wise, steady stare of an immortal being. Any hope Lucha had had that things would stay the same between them died in its eternal light.

But the most upsetting part was that Lucha's feelings had changed too. The lust she'd once felt for this girl, the desire and the urgency and the overpowering need, were gone—even in the face of Paz's nakedness. It was as if Lucha's fragile mind couldn't comprehend the body before her enough to desire it.

She had thought she'd have her own feelings, lingering on as proof of what they'd once meant to each other. But even those were gone.

The people they had once been to each other were of the past now. The grieving would be different for that, Lucha thought. Not a separation, but a death. A rebirth.

Around her, everyone fell to their knees. Even Robadans raised without goddess lore could not mistake the holiness of the being before them.

Lucha dropped to her knees too, feeling the stone bite into them, wondering how long it would take the cracked and torn pieces of her to truly heal.

"Thank you all." Paz's voice rang through the room, clear as the bell of her transformation cries. "I'm so honored that you're here to witness this moment. Honored by your devotion. I'd like to show my gratitude."

One of the acolytes rushed forward with her own cloak, and Paz wrapped herself in it without shame.

The ruins of the Lost House were still scattered in the mud as they made their way up through the cracked stone, but the air felt different as Lucha took her first lungful. She hadn't been aware of the imbalance feeling any particular way in the world around her, but there was no question now that it was healing. The scales making their way back to equilibrium now that a divine being was in the world once more.

Robadans and acolytes gathered around the entrance, waiting for Paz. When she arrived, they walked some distance away, to the tree line. The ghostly grove where Lucha had once screamed after the loss of her mother. It was a strange backdrop for a goddess's first show of power, but it seemed fitting, somehow.

"False authority has driven a rift through our community," Paz began into the hushed silence once everyone was still. "The kings of Robado, created by Salvador. The high priestess of Asilo, unable to see her own greed. But you are the people of the Bosque de la Noche. The acolytes. The Robadans. One group of you protects the heart of the forest, the other its gateway. From now on, we must work together."

Without Río there to create false enmity, with a goddess in their midst, Lucha sensed the peace stealing in like a fog. It was a new world. They would all live in it according to her decree.

"Please, join me," Paz said, and she beckoned Lucha and the Syndicate.

Lucha wasn't sure she could approach her, she didn't even know how, but her boots moved her forward until they stood together.

"I may be new to divinity, but I am not new to the needs of these places. The city of Robado has long been plagued by the memory of Almudena's son. It was the place of Olvida. The home of the immortal kings he created to oppress the mortals who wandered into his trap. No more."

Paz turned to Lucha and Cruz.

"The two of you don't need my blessing to lead this place," she said with a smile. "So instead, I offer an invitation."

Lucha looked somewhere to the left of Paz's face. She found she could not take all of her in, nor process what that meant to her.

"This city will soon be known as a holy site the world over. I invite you to create a city worthy of the honor. To open its borders and welcome all who would settle here. I've never known two people more worthy of a challenge in all my life."

Cruz inclined her head first. Lucha knew she didn't have the stomach for too much pageantry, but Paz's newfound divinity seemed to affect even her in its own way.

"We accept," said Cruz, and Lucha nodded her agreement, not trusting her voice.

"Good," Paz said with a smile both familiar and, heartbreakingly, foreign to the one Lucha had grown so used to these past months. "I will do everything in my power to make this world a safe and abundant one for all of you. Thank you for trusting. For believing."

As Cruz returned to the crowd, Paz reached out a hand to Lucha.

"Will you walk with me?"

Lucha took Paz's hand. It felt the same. Cool, smooth. A hand that had healed Lis and clung to Lucha's and wielded a bow to defend them all. Together they walked back to the ruin in silence.

At the entryway, Paz turned to face her one last time.

There was no pull left in either of them to make promises. To kiss. To pledge their love. The words had all been said at the last threshold. This was only goodbye—and they'd said it so many times by now.

"Thank you," Paz said.

"You'll be perfect," Lucha replied.

"So will you," Paz said.

The moment Paz León made her final transformation would become the stuff of legend. Her mortal name would be forgotten, but the form she took would be shared—held up as the holiest creature of this generation and beyond.

The knife of nostalgia twisted in Lucha's breast before the moment had even passed. The human form shrank, sprouted pure-white tufts of fur, the ears elongating, whiskers sprouting.

In moments, it was done. Paz was no more, and in her place was a glorious, shining white hare. Lucha laughed as she cried, reaching down, extending her fingers. The hare twitched its nose, and suddenly Lucha was back in the forest, Paz at her side, teary-eyed at the sight of Almudena's favored symbol.

She recalled what Paz had said at the spring. That she would take a new form. That she would listen to the whispers of prayers from the people of Asilo, from the wind, from the water and the trees and the grasses, the fish and the prowling cats and the wolves. The birds.

The ears looked equal to the task, and with a joyful bound, the hare disappeared into the dense forest. With that, Paz León was gone.

Lucha did not wail, did not cry, but as the forest swallowed the first love of her life, she felt a part of herself bound away as well. Free because of love. Because of loss. Because of choice.

She had turned to walk away, feeling more lost and weary than she'd ever felt in her life, when the ground at her feet began once more to shake.

The acolytes and Robadans looked up in alarm. Cruz raced to Lucha's side.

At their feet, from the mud, a single shoot sprouted, vivid green against the brown. Before Lucha could point it out, it had grown to knee height.

"What the—!" Cruz shouted, jumping out of the way.

Lucha followed as the tree—for it was certainly a tree—continued to grow at astonishing speeds. Soon it was the tallest tree in the forest, by far, reaching a hundred feet into the sky, its roots rising like giants' fingers out of the ground at their feet. The first thing to grow in the Scar in five hundred years. The curse broken at last.

As Lucha watched, it burst into full leaf, and then into bloom. Crimson blooms that drifted down out of the sky, delighting the gathered crowd.

But the magic didn't stop there.

From the roots of the tree, green began to spread, racing across the mud—moss and grass and plants and flowers growing over the ruined house and shooting toward the city. Before the eyes of everyone gathered, the first miracle of Elegido came to pass.

Within minutes, the Scar was healed. The curse broken. The world as they knew it reborn.

Standing with the Syndicate, Lucha surveyed this new place, feeling the scar on her own heart blooming too. There would be time to grieve. Time to understand. But there would also be time to build. To celebrate. To *live*.

"It's a miracle," Cruz said in an awestruck voice.

"It's Paz," Lucha replied, and together, they walked back toward their new city.

After all, there was work to be done.

Epilogue

It was a beautiful day in Robado. It was always beautiful now. Even when it rained.

Sometimes, Lucha thought as she gathered a bundle of roasted tubers and spring onions, it was hard to reconcile all this beauty with the grief she felt. But that, too, was getting lighter with time.

It had been a month since Paz had become a white hare and disappeared into the wood. Since the Guardian Tree—as the Robadans had taken to calling it—had grown a hundred feet in a matter of minutes. Already the city was full of tourists. Pilgrims. People from throughout Elegido who had heard the tale and come to see for themselves.

Lucha left her little house and walked toward the river alone. Soon she would join the rest of the town in the square to bid farewell to the acolytes heading back to the temple. But there was something she had to do first.

In the city center, Cruz and a team of Robadans had started the process of paving the north road, but out here it was still dirt. Little houses had sprung up like mushrooms between the marketplace and the old housing units. In front of them, gardens had taken root and started to sprout.

The days of hunger were done, as were the days of desperation. That was the gift Paz had left them. The Scar was no more, and the people crossing the river to see the forest for the first time would never know Robado for the cursed, miserable place it had once been.

Lucha reached the river just as the sun began to peek out from behind the clouds. The morning's light rainstorm had left a twinkling brightness on every surface, every leaf. A breeze chattered through the leaves, lifting Lucha's hair off the back of her neck.

I'll be listening in every tree, she could almost hear Paz saying. *Every leaf. Every change of every season.*

Sometimes, when Lucha felt alone, she imagined this white hare of a goddess with Paz's sparkling eyes. Listening to the world through the forest's rhythms. Answering the prayers of humans and nonhumans alike. It helped her feel that the world was all truly connected. One community, bound by a creature with an ear to the ground.

The one dark cloud on their clear horizon was the disappearance of Alán Marquez, who had vanished sometime during the fight. Saving his skin. Betraying his allies. Lucha imagined him sometimes too. Lurking out there, biding his time.

But the city and the sanctuary were united on this. They

knew the signs of his coming. They would find him. And when they did, there would be no mercy.

Along the river, plants Lucha had never seen before were reaching out of the mud. The water was clear—you could see all the way to the bottom. The salt was gone from it too. Another product of Paz's miracle. The serpentine curves babbled merrily as Lucha walked alongside it. It behaved itself now. No more tantrums.

Cruz had made Lucha promise they would make the crossing one day soon. Alert the leaders of the cities across the river to the republic they planned to build here. Establish trade, and tourism, and other things that would benefit the people who settled here.

Lucha loved the idea, in theory. But she'd put Cruz off by insisting on a little more infrastructure first. The truth was, she was only just starting to feel like Robado was really theirs. Change would come, it always did, but she wanted to keep it to themselves just a while longer.

Up ahead, the Guardian Tree towered over even the tallest sentinels surrounding it. It was already the stuff of myth. The story had changed and warped and stretched, as all stories do, before the last of the acolytes had even left the site of the miracle.

Lucha didn't bother to correct the Robadans or the acolytes when they embellished. In this Robado, all stories that promised safety and hope would be allowed. Encouraged. Told over generations. She got a contented feeling in her chest when she thought about it.

The base of Paz's tree was no longer recognizable as the place where the Lost House of Robado had once stood. The new growth of the Scar had pulled all remnants of it belowground to use as fertilizer. Without the salt mud and the dangerous rocks, the walk was no longer treacherous. Lucha made the trip once a week.

At the base of the tree, she laid the tubers and onions. She always felt a little strange, leaving offerings to a divine being who had once kissed her on this very bank. But she supposed that was what one did when praying to a goddess.

"Hey, Paz," she said to the wind. The leaves. The changing season, beckoning fall. "You really outdid yourself on the weather today. This place barely looks real. Tone it down, will you? Or every pilgrim will want to stay forever."

The wind blew again, that chattering in the leaves. Crimson blossoms drifted down all around Lucha. She closed her eyes and sighed contentedly.

Beside the tree, in the shade of its beautiful canopy, there was a small wooden cross hammered into the ground. *Lydia,* it read, in Lucha's untidy carved letters.

"I hope you'd both be proud of me," she said quietly.

Lucha would likely never know what had truly become of her mother during the horrors of a post-Salvador Robado. In all likelihood, she was gone. But sometimes, when the wind was right and the sun sparkled on the river's surface, Lucha liked to imagine her free. Roaming one of the cities of the golden planes, or the ports. Happy. Or at least at peace, as Lucha was in Robado. As Lis was at the sanctuary.

In the beginning, Lucha had sat here for hours, talking to them both, telling them the ins and outs of the town and the work they were doing to make a city worthy of the guardian title.

Lately, though, she'd preferred to sit in silence. To listen. To dream.

"Looks like we had the same idea." Cruz's heavy boots were surprisingly light-footed as she made her way toward Lucha's hiding place. She carried a bundle much like the one Lucha had left at the tree's base, which she settled among the roots before sitting down next to Lucha. Resting her back on the vast trunk of the tree.

"Wouldn't be the first time," Lucha said with a lazy smile as the wind played across her face.

They sat in comfortable silence for a while, just listening. Finally, Cruz spoke.

"Maria came back with a foraging party today," she said. Her voice was careful, a little worried. It made Lucha sit up and take notice.

"What is it?" she asked.

Cruz didn't answer, just took a small, three-leafed plant with spindly roots and dropped it in Lucha's lap.

Even stunted as this one was, there was no mistaking it. Pensa. Lucha felt the shock like a spear through the stomach.

"Where?" she asked hoarsely.

"Two miles or so from here," Cruz answered. "She says no one else saw, and she didn't find any more, but . . ."

"It's only a matter of time," Lucha finished for her.

Another silence, this one thoughtful. The pain caused by the sight of the plant eased slightly. She should have known it would be back, she supposed, now that a goddess resided in Elegido once again. The question was, what did they do about it?

The question she asked was different, though. More personal.

"Are you tempted?"

Cruz met her eyes, steady, unashamed. "Not by that," she said.

Heat spread through Lucha's cheeks. Cruz had been very respectful, but Lucha could see it sometimes, lurking beneath the surface. That smoldering that had been so much less complicated before.

She'd felt guilty about it at first, of course, but it was more natural these days. Like the wind through the branches of this new tree. Like the sound the river made now that it was no longer tainted with salt.

"So what should we do?" she asked.

Cruz shrugged, letting her gaze drift up into the trees. "The warehouses are destroyed. No one living knows the full process of manufacturing Olvida. Maybe we just . . . let it be. Trust people to choose wisely."

There was a time when Lucha would have demanded every plant be ripped up by the stalk. Burned in a fire. When she would have made absolutely sure no one ever got near it.

But she hadn't gone through everything she had just to come out the same. The trouble had never been the drug itself.

It had never been the people who looked to it for comfort or escape. The problem had been a world that needed to be escaped from.

"We build a better world," she said, laying the plant with the other offerings at the base of the tree. "We make sure people have resources and care and support, no matter what their choices are. That's all we really can do."

Cruz reached out and squeezed Lucha's hand. They looked up at the tree together. Between them, something kindled, like soup keeping warm in a big pot over a fire. In no hurry.

"You ready to head home?" Cruz asked after a while.

Lucha let Cruz pull her up to her feet. *Home,* she thought. And for the first time, she thought she really understood what it meant.

About the Author

TEHLOR KAY MEJIA is the author of the fast-paced fantasy *Lucha of the Night Forest,* book one in a duology. They are also the critically acclaimed author of the young adult fantasy duology *We Set the Dark on Fire* and *We Unleash the Merciless Storm.* Their debut middle-grade series, Paola Santiago and the River of Tears, is in development at Disney as a television series to be produced by Eva Longoria. Tehlor lives with their child, wife, and two small dogs in Oregon, where they grow heirloom corn and continue their quest to perfect the vegan tamale.

tehlorkaymejia.com